SHE'LL BE KILLING 'ROUND THE MOUNTAIN

SHE'LL BE KILLING 'ROUND THE MOUNTAIN

BRYAN E. ROBINSON

Advance Praise for She'll Be KILLING 'Round the Mountain

"Fabulous—Einstein Pope is terrific."—**Lee Child**, *New York Times* best-selling author of the electrifying Jack Reacher series

"Deliciously dark, devious and gripping, Robinson writes with real verve!"—**Peter James,** UK # 1 bestselling author of *Absolute Proof*, best known for writing thriller novels, and the creator of the much-loved Detective Superintendent Roy Grace

"With adrenaline on every page, *She'll Be KILLING 'Round the Mountain* delivers gripping suspense with a riveting glimpse into the macabre world of doomsday survivalists."—**Steve Berry**, *New York Times international* bestselling author of *The Malta Exchange*

"The most unique character to hit the shelves in years, Einstein Brad Pope—think Ghandi meets Jack Reacher—battles a groundswell of survivalists nestled in the Blue Ridge mountains. Robinson offers powerful psychological insights, an authentic voice, and a healthy dash of humor in his realistic tale set in spectacular Asheville. A rare talent."—**K.J. Howe**, international bestselling author of *The Freedom Broker* and *Skyjack*

"Bryan Robinson has written a unique and fascinating thriller which pits Brad Ein Pope—a brilliant, tough psychologist against gun-toting survivalists murdering people to prepare for the end of the world as he thinks and fights his way out of deadly danger time and again. I highly recommend this book!"—**R.G. Belsky**, award-winning author of the Clare Carlson mystery series

"Colorful, quirky, and full of heart. When Einstein Bradley Pope confronts gun-wielding extremists in the Blue Ridge Mountains, it's the end of days or new beginnings—depending on who survives. Bryan Robinson delivers again with a deft hand and a twisty plot."—**James L'Etoile**, award-winning author of the Nathan Parker series & the Emily Hunter series

"Bryan Robinson has done it again, blending action, humor, and heartache in this nonstop thriller. Packed with memorable characters and danger at every turn, She'll Be KILLING 'Round the Mountain is one engrossing tale."—**Bruce Robert Coffin**, international bestselling coauthor of The Turner and Mosley Files

"End of days, survivalist militias, drag queens, and murder—Robinson whips up a high-octane stew of southern trouble. Hatchets, bullets, and deadly intentions fly fast and furious. A compelling and frequently hilarious read. Not to be missed."—**Barry Lancet**, award-winning author of *Japantown* and *the Spy Across the Table*

"In *She'll Be KILLING 'Round the Mountain*, Bryan Robinson delivers a fresh look at the psychological thriller with his original choice of characters, setting and theme. The introduction of the outspoken Dr. Ein Pope and his wedding crew had me hooked from the start. Add a bunch of violence, a ton of guns and enough doomsday extremists to wreak havoc on America and I'm down for a good time. Anytime."—**Linda Sands**, Georgia author of the year and author of *3 Women Walk Into a Bar*

"Love this thriller! Great pacing, likable characters and excellent writing make it a compelling read!"—**Susan Crawford**, author of *The Pocket Wife* and *The Other Widow*

"What a great story and timely topic! Anti-gun proponents, survivalists, and those caught between them in an effort to do the right thing to protect everyone. Bryan Robinson paints a picture of Asheville, North Carolina, that will not be easy to forget."—**Rick Reed,** author of the Jack Murphy Thriller Series

"When the Chariot Comes" *

O, who will drive the chariot when she comes?
O, who will drive the chariot when she comes?
O, who will drive the chariot, O who will drive the chariot,
O, who will drive the chariot when she comes?

O, King Jesus, he'll be driver when she comes, when she comes,
O, King Jesus, he'll be driver when she comes, when she comes,
O King Jesus, he'll be driver, O, King Jesus he'll be driver,
O, King Jesus he'll be driver when she comes.

She'll be loaded with bright Angels when she comes…
She will neither rock nor totter, when she comes…
She will run so level and steady, when she comes…
She will take us to the portals, when she comes…

*Sung to the melody of "She'll Be Coming 'Round the Mountain When She Comes," this old slave song from the late 1800s refers to the Second Coming and the destruction of all humankind. During the nineteenth century, the song spread through Appalachia, where the lyrics were changed into their current form.

Prologue

Something unholy flickered in the shadows of the autumn dusk. The bleached blonde stood outside Mission Hospital, the entrance—hard-edged and stark—glowed bright against the fading gray daylight, as if she were seeing it for the first time. She tugged at her stringy hair, her face twitching with the sharp, private thrill of what she was about to do.

She pulled her handbag tighter to her chest, and the twelve-inch slicing knife inside jabbed a hateful poke just above her heart. At that moment, the automatic doors slammed open, swallowing her, then slammed shut behind her with a hard bang.

She loved to toy with danger, but her heart battering her ribcage told her to play it cool this time around. She approached the graying, pot-bellied security officer—laughing with a younger, attractive female sidekick—and he reached out his arm. "Hold on, Ma'am. "Your security badge?"

A bead of sweat slid beneath her blue scrubs. She swallowed hard and flashed the fake ID. When she started forward, he stopped her again.

"Just a minute," slipped through one side of the officer's mouth.

His cold fingers clinched around her arm. She jerked back, thought about closing her eyes for a second to hold down the rumble of bile in her stomach, but then she would be unprepared for what happened next. He lifted his gaze from the photo to her face, taking her in head to toe.

Finally, the officer nodded and handed her ID back.

She feigned a smile, quickened her stride, and winced at the loud squeak of her rubber-soled nurse's shoes. She noticed her bleary reflection off the polished floor and let out a long breath she didn't know she'd been holding.

In the empty stairwell, she climbed toward the fourth-floor ICU, pausing halfway to brace a hand on the metal banister and adjust the squeaking shoes.

Goddamned shoes!

At the heavy wooden ICU door, she pulled blue latex gloves over freshly manicured fingers. She was close now—within reach of the government zombie who'd tried to confiscate her guns. The one she'd poisoned days ago.

Nothing would stop her.

The knife handle nudged her again, reminding her of its tag: *Granton Edge Blade, stamped from cold-rolled steel.*

She pressed her back to the wall to stay out of the security camera's prying eye, slipped the carving knife from her handbag, and tucked it into the pouch of her uniform. Then she held her badge to the scanner, waited for the familiar click, and pushed through the heavy door.

The blonde stopped in the doorway, wide eyes roving the empty corridor, listening for footsteps of staff. At the far end, a uniformed officer stood outside a room, face set straight ahead with military precision. She fast-walked down to the end of the long hallway as if she belonged.

Room E-368. This was it.

She wrapped her hand around the slick, metal handle and glanced at the young officer with bushy brows. He flashed his emerald-green eyes to meet her gaze. "Nurse."

"Officer." She tilted her head toward the door. And he gave a small, imperceptible nod before returning to face forward.

I knew I could count on him.

Once inside the room, she heard the toilet flush and ducked back into the hallway, glancing at the officer, who raised his palms and shrugged. A plump gray-haired woman, the patient's wife, maybe, emerged from the bathroom and caught sight of her retreat.

"Oh, nurse." The woman hitched her black purse into the crook of her elbow and stepped forward. "I can't get him to eat a bite. I brought his favorite barbecue from *12 Bones.* He still says he thinks he has food poisoning."

The blonde knew *12 Bones* was Senator Clarence Plemmons' favorite.

After watching *Breaking Bad*—Walter White poisoning a child—she'd figured she could do worse by upping the dose of epoxy resin in his Memphis-style beef brisket. That guesstimation landed him in the hospital for a few days, but not enough to finish the job.

Having studied the rotation list, she also knew it was only minutes before the real nurse came on duty. She checked the empty hallway, then pasted on a smile. "I'll see what I can do."

"Would you? I have to go." The older woman squeezed past, then hesitated at the threshold and stared hard. "Are you new? I haven't seen you before."

"I work part-time."

"Humph." The woman's eyes dropped to the handbag for a long second. "Do you always carry your pocketbook on duty?"

"Oh…well…I'm just getting in."

Eager to leave and ready to accept any excuse, the woman nodded. "Okay, I hope you can get some food into him. I'll be back in the morning."

The blonde's wide gaze followed the heavy-set woman down the hallway. Halfway to the nurse's station, the woman turned and gave her another once-over, then sidled up to the nurse's station. She gestured to one of the staff and pointed toward her husband's room.

The blonde rushed back into E-368 to the guttural sounds of struggled breath and the oxygen tube running up the senator's nostrils. She set her handbag on the industrial plastic armchair beside the bed, barely registered the huge window—a majestic view of the Blue Ridge Mountains silhouetted against a magenta Asheville sunset.

For months since the Charlotte mass shooting, Plemmons had made gun control his crusade, pushing stricter policy, pressing hard against the National Firearm Association.

The NFA's president, Wayne Herman, came under widespread scrutiny for not only his opposition to the bill, but the speculation of his relationship to The Real U.S.A., a.k.a., the United Survivalist Army. Wayne Herman—the NFA president—was under fire for opposing the bill, and for the rumors tying him to the United Survivalist Army.

In retribution, the blonde had tried to poison Plemmons and failed.

Now, the woman crouched over the sleeping senator's bed, the cross around her neck dangling above his chest, and ripped the oxygen tubing free. His eyes snapped open, and his gasps came in ugly staccato bursts.

She fumbled into the pouch of her scrubs and froze at the sound of approaching voices. She darted to the door, peeked through the crack, and saw two nurses enter the room next door. Behind her, Plemmons tried to call out, releasing a welling-up urge to scream through a weak mumble. She moved back to the bed, pulled the knife free and drove it into his throat.

Hard.

Here you go, you government zombie—some cold-rolled steel. The blade punched in and out of the meaty neck beneath his jaw. Blood surged. Heat. Brightness. She dodged the spray as it sheeted over the white linens.

A childhood image escaped. The crimson flow unearthed images of her mother jabbing an old-timey icebox with an ice pick—followed by images of cubes spinning in her mother's raspberry lemonade, lifting the corners of her mouth from a grimace to a grin, making her chest thump with delight. In her head, she recited from Proverbs 6:20: *And do not forsake the teachings of your mother.*

One last slit—ear to ear—then she rammed the blade into the ruined center of his neck, leaving the blade protruding like a flag from the cavernous hole. His mouth gaped in a rictus of startled alarm. She dodged the spurting blood that spilled over a wiggling Adam's apple, staining the crisp white sheets. She backhanded the drooping yellow tresses in her eyes and shivered with pleasure at the lovely vermillion.

The loud wail of the Hewlett-Packard monitor alarm set her heart beating wildly.

She peeled off the gloves, stuffed them into her scrubs, shouldered her handbag, and edged out the door.

The officer was gone.

Just as planned.

She ducked into the empty room across the hall, braced her back to the wall, and listened—breathing so fast she could hear her heart hammering her chest.

Thunderous footfalls echoed down the hall. She grabbed an abandoned supply cart, hid her handbag on the lower shelf, and rolled the cart out of the room, sidestepping the tide of doctors and nurses forging up the hallway. She inched toward the stairwell, wincing at the squeak of her rubber soles.

Fucking shoes!

She tugged at the door, shielded her face from the security cameras with her handbag, and hurried down the stairs, her stomach growling.

Dinnertime.

In the parking garage, she noticed dark specks on her security badge.

Blood.

She ditched it into a trash can, swung onto her Harley, and stared at the eagle-winged fuel tank, reflecting the overhead lights. Her hands clamped the handlebars. Her foot jammed the peg.

The revved engine barked—*vroom, vroom*—echoing off the concrete walls.

Hmm. Steak sounds good.

The bike coughed and sputtered for a few seconds, then coughed another *vroom, vroom.*

As she roared into the night, a pensive smile formed on her lips at the thought that rose, clean and clear, in her mind.

Rare.

Chapter One

Mama's headstone was subtle. A small white stone with slender black letters, just her name and the years she spent on this earth. Grandma Gigi didn't have the money for anything more. Always said she'd write the rest the way she talked about her.

Every time I see *ADA LEA POPE* stretched across the top, it rattles me. It took a long time to muster the courage to stand here again. *How could she not still be here?* Even now, years later, it feels unreal. After everything that happened that summer, I found myself standing in front of her grave, reading Mama's letter again—the one she'd entrusted to Sally Cutter, known around town as Voodoo Sally.

Brad, I hope we can be together again soon. When you read this letter, if it was not meant to be, I may be nothing more than a faint memory. If that is the case, I want you to always remember how much I love you. And even though I cannot hold you in my arms in this moment, I will hold you close in my heart forever.

The words seared through my heart like a bullet, knowing that was it. I pictured Mama on Gigi's dock, stretched out in her favorite lounge chair, watching the sun descend into the water and the tune she hummed until I fell asleep in the warm cradle of her arms. And I realized there would be no more of that.

Ever.

My daddy—Johnny Devillers—started the fire that set my life ablaze. After my baby sister died in the inferno, Mama sent me up to Asheville the first chance she got, draining her bank account to pay for the boarding school—anything to keep me out of that madman's reach.

Three days later, Johnny came back looking for me. When Mama refused to give him what he wanted, the bastard took her life.

Over the years, I put to rest the notion that I could wind back the clock and see her again. Despite my own psychologist's advice, I found it nearly impossible to apply to myself.

Nothing on God's earth would mean more to me than seeing her face again—her blue eyes, soft smile, warm embrace. The way she wound herself up like a child's toy when she laughed, only to let loose until she wheezed with tears. The way she hollered my name when it was time to wash up for dinner. The way she tucked me in at night, resting her cheek against my forehead as she whispered prayers over me. The way she wiped blood from her broken nose, smearing red across her cheek without noticing. The way she pulled herself up off of the floor after Johnny had one too many. The way her face looked when she sent me away—sunken, hopeless, like she knew she'd never see me again.

Goddammit, Ein.

I found it damn near impossible to separate the good from the bad, as if they were fused together in my mind—a sick tango of love and violence, memory and loss.

Beside Mama's headstone lay my baby sister, *LYDIA POPE*. Even flashes of Lydia came weighted with grief, the same fire blazing through my memory. I couldn't stop imagining what she must have felt—the terror, the confusion, the pain. The firefighters said her body was too badly burned to recover. I hadn't been there for either burial, and that absence left a restlessness in me I could never quiet.

Wishing, hoping, dreaming they were still out there somewhere.

The only clear memory of all three of us belongs to the banks of the Suwannee River. We'd spread a blanket in a patch of grass in a clearing. Mama brought sandwiches and sweet tea and packed a couple of board games and coloring books for us to play with as we waited for the manatees to surface.

Without Johnny there to bark orders and shove us around, we felt like a family. Lydia and I played all afternoon—something forbidden when he was present. He told me not to play with dolls, not to crawl around "like a bitch, like her." Said I was too soft, that playing with my baby sister would turn me into a "gay-ass little pussy boy."

I'd love to see his face now, knowing he couldn't stop what was coming.

But *that* day, we played for hours. Mama chased us, laughed freely. We never saw the manatees, but it didn't matter. It was as pure a day as I can remember.

"Brad?"

The scratchy voice pulled me from my memories.

I turned, adjusted my black-rimmed glasses, and saw Gigi—my boyhood failure at pronouncing "grandma" had stuck—winding toward me through the headstones of the cemetery. At seventy-three, she was trim and spry and moved with an ease of a woman half her age. High cheekbones, chiseled nose, full lips—time had been kind to her.

I pitched her a smile. "You spent all that time trying to call me Einstein, and now you're back to Brad?"

She shrugged, grinning. "Old habits…. You okay?"

She wrapped her arms around me. I nuzzled my head into her shoulder, soaking in her scent of lavender, sure she could feel the quiver in my gut.

"What's wrong, Ein?"

"Today was, uh…it just got to me. I needed to come see her—both of them."

"What happened?"

I pulled away and faced Mama's grave. "I came back home. You and I, we picked up where we left off. I found a piece of myself I thought was gone." My throat tightened. "And I'm getting married. I just wish she were here to see it."

Gigi nodded and fished Mama's ring from beneath my shirt. "Don't you know she's watching?"

"I look over my shoulder for a hawk every now and then," I said softly, looking down into Gigi's azure eyes. I told her about the day Mama put me on the bus to Asheville—the suitcase in one hand, Lydia's stuffed manatee in the other. How, just as she cupped my face, a majestic Cooper's hawk swooped down and landed next to us. We looked at its bluish-black feathers and red eyes, and it looked at us…then it spread its wings, flew off, and shot through the treetops.

"That's how I'll come back," Mama had said. I'll land close to you, make sure you're okay, and then fly off to be with Lydia."

I swiped at the tears streaming freely now. "For years, every time I saw a hawk, I felt nothing but anger. When I came back to Whitecross, I thought that would change. But it didn't. Not until Sally gave me that letter. You tried to tell me what was in it, and I tried to remember. But I felt like I was just filling in the gaps, like I was making it up. And then when I finally read it…."

"The truth is…I was so mad about being sent away. I knew she was protecting me, and that Daddy was out of his fucking mind. But when I heard she had died, anger gripped me so hard I started heaving and gasping for breath through the grief. I had to find a way to make it stop."

Gigi, through tears of her own, comforted me with her signature back rub. "Son…I…."

"You know how you see a duck on the water, and everything's calm up top but underneath its feet are churning? Most of my life, I felt like God and the devil were waging war inside of me. Everyone sees this calm psychologist facade, but underneath—"

Gigi interjected, knowing where I was headed, "Mayhem."

I nodded. "But after I read the letter, everything went still."

She held my face. "You're not alone, son. You hear me?"

I shrugged, forced a quick smile.

"Your mama, just like Gladys, did the hardest thing anybody has to do. There ain't nothing but pain that comes with giving up your child. But if it wasn't for those women, Rufus…and you my Tug-a-love…neither of you would be here because evil men wouldn't have allowed it. I know your chaos, son. I felt it, too. Just know, if my daughter was alive, she'd be mighty proud of her son. Same as me."

I looked down at her through a bleary gaze and gave her a hard squeeze.

She hugged me with such force, I felt the muscles across my back constrict.

I welcomed the comfort when she looped arms with me. "Now, what do you say we get on with it. Smiley's probably burnin' my twice-baked potatoes four or five times to a crisp."

I chuckled as we ambled toward the parking lot. "And Ein," she added, "She's watching. You can bet your sweet ass on it. She'll find you when the time is right."

Chapter Two

The next morning my Pathfinder squeaked to a spot at the Hatchbend fishing hole next to Bobby-Cy's Dodge King Cab truck. My newfound half-brother already had a line in the water, bare feet dangling off the dock. He looked over his shoulder at me, removed the cigar clenched in his mouth, and threw his hand up. "Brother Boy."

"Brother Boy," I returned the jovial greeting. What had once been a taunt now served as our genuine call to each other.

Bobby-Cy and I had spent the last couple months getting to know each other. Every Sunday morning, we'd sit out on the dock, him sipping his signature sweet tea and me nursing a beer or two, catching up until the drinks or bait ran out, whichever came first.

He told me about almost moving to Texas with an old girlfriend to work her daddy's ranch and how he got cold feet when his mama got sick. I couldn't picture anything more fitting than Bobby-Cy roping a steer on the Texas prairie. After his mama passed, he studied to become a lawyer.

When he failed the Bar exam twice, he knew he was in over his head and didn't want to waste another drop of whiskey—or his grandparents' money—when his heart wasn't in it. He sobered up in Alcoholics Anonymous, found his calling in law enforcement, and came back to Whitecross, where he settled in as deputy under Uncle Ronny Devillers, Whitecross's infamous former sheriff.

"Tea?" He asked, in the midst of pouring a glass.

"Brought some brew."

I cracked a beer, baited my pole, and gazed out at the Suwannee River. Its glassy surface hid the limestone caverns that snaked below. I took a swig of beer and crooned Thomas Rhett's "Half of Me Wants a Cold Beer."

Bobby-Cy hooked eyes with me and, with a crooked smile, sang back, "And the other half does, too."

We laughed before a long, comfortable silence fell over us, as it often did. Those quiet moments always brought me back to the letter Voodoo Sally had given me before she was murdered.

The limestone yields as the Suwannee encompasses it and becomes one with the rushing water. The Suwannee carves the limestone into shapes and images, and it becomes a feature of the river. In time, the limestone becomes a smooth, well-polished cavern. And the strength of its true character is revealed. That's limestone gumption.

Townspeople dubbed her Voodoo Sally because her brand of wisdom and compassion scared them. The name never bothered her. "What's in a name," she'd say, "if you know yourself?" When I applied that to my own life, *Einstein Bradley Pope* meant both everything and nothing.

The name was a blueprint of my boyhood. Mama called me *Brad* out of love. Daddy called me *Einstein* out of rage, wielding it like a blowtorch to bend and shape me like sheet metal in his image. I never knew if *Einstein* was some sick joke or his way of using me to make up for his failures. I resisted that name my whole life—until Sally showed me resistance only fueled the war inside.

Yielding, she said, reveals strength—like limestone surrendering to the Suwannee. The same truth therapists live by—what we resist, persists.

I took *Einstein* back, disarming anyone who tried to use it against me the way Johnny and my schoolmates ridiculed me. I was finally uncovering my true character here in Whitecross. I accepted a part of myself I'd fought for too long—and gained more than I ever lost.

I glanced at my brother, "Caught anything yet?"

"Bucket's empty, ain't it?"

"You're not tryin' hard enough."

He laughed at the absurdity of trying harder to fish. "Shit, I put my pants on today. That's effort enough for an off-day." He took a swig of tea. "So, where'd we leave off?"

"Uncle Ronny."

"Oh, yeah, that prick."

"You'd just been made deputy."

"You know, Ein, it's funny. Ronny never knew I was his blood kin. Never guessed I was Johnny's bastard. A few times, I'd catch him lingerin' on me too long. Like, maybe he was startin' to figure it out, but he never wised up. He'd tell me all kinds of stories about Johnny. 'My brother this, my brother that.' One time, he told me about when him and Johnny got piss drunk and took a shit right on the bar top at Britches."

I shook my head. "They really got away with everything."

"From shittin' on bars to murder. Especially after Ronny made Sheriff, he'd get into all sorts of underhanded things."

"You mean illegal shit?"

"Oh hell, I remember him tellin' me…sometime right before your mama passed…but they were out on some farm outside Whitecross. Bunch of good-old-boy types had a couple women out there with 'em, Preacher Abrams, too. They had this crazy idea, thinkin' the world was gonna end soon."

"Yep. Johnny used to tell me those stories when I was a boy. About the end of time, when the shit hits the fan, and zombies wandering the streets in Whitecross. Scared the dickens out of me."

"Well, Ronny got his hands on some dynamite. Not no quarter sticks either. I'm talkin' the real deal, twelve-inch candles. And they were doin'… what'd he call it…perimeter defense testing—basically, they lit *all* the fuckin' dynamite at one time."

Something clicked. "I remember that."

"They blew a crater so big you'd think an asteroid hit."

"We felt the shock all the way on the other side of town."

"Everybody felt the damn shock. They knocked loose a huge chunk of limestone in the caves, which is all protected land."

"Fuck, man," I said, swiping at a swarm of no-see-ums. "Let me guess, not a single one of them had to pay for it?"

"A hundred percent. Ronny swept it under the rug, paid folks off, handed out a few get-out-of-jail-free cards. Preacher Abrams prayed over the rocks to heal, whatever the fuck that meant."

"Ever find out who else was with them?"

"Nope. Ronny and Johnny stuck together like glue till our daddy disappeared."

"You mean till Gigi took a shotgun to him."

We clinked our drinks, cheering the act of revenge we always wanted.

"You know, even when I joined the force," Bobby-Cy added, "Ronny swore Johnny was still alive—hidin' out, waitin' on the apocalypse and zombies."

"We had one fucked-up daddy."

"Amen, Brother Boy."

We chugged the rest of our drinks, he refilled his glass, and I popped another beer.

"So, what's the real story on Ronny? Why'd he quit?"

"He was forced out. Finally, all that yahooin' caught up with him. A couple years back, there was a big cocaine bust outside of town. They were using a little shed to cook out in the swamps and dumping the excess into the Suwannee. A certain women's environmental group…you may or may not be aware of…tipped Ronny off to what was happenin'. He said he would look into it. Of course, he never did."

"Are you shitin' me? My grandma and her Women's Preservation Club brought down Ronny Devillers?"

"Gigi in particular. You see, once Ronny refused to do anything, Gigi went to Smiley, who got in the ear of the other mayors surroundin' Whitecross. The sting turned into a coordinated effort, and the shed got busted. Ronny caught wind, hightailed it."

Tangled in my own delight, I chugged my beer, fizz pouring down my chin. The picture became clearer. Gigi and her sisterfriends—The W.P.C.—Whitecross's geriatric avengers.

I wiped the sweat streaming down my cheek. "Ever hear what happened to Ronny?"

"Heard he shot himself. Heard he overdosed. Heard he made like a bandit down to Mexico. I don't know. I just know he ain't here. And good riddance."

***

After the booze and iced tea ran dry and the bait failed, we packed up. As we headed to our trucks, an idling pickup caught my eye.

Big Jake Nunn's pickup.

A bearded scowl and dark eyes underneath a red cap tracked us from the driver's seat. I squinted for a split second to make sure my mind wasn't playing tricks on me.

"You see that?" I muttered out of the side of my mouth.

"A hundred percent," Bobby-Cy said. "Big Jake's brother."

"He's still pissed, spreading the lie that I killed Big Jake all over town."

GAWKERS blazed in bold white letters across the front of Eldred Nunn's hat. He spat in our direction, revved the engine, and peeled off slinging gravel in a cloud of dust.

I side-eyed Bobby-Cy, "Still lookin' into them?"

"They've been layin' low lately. Even put Giard and DeLoach on them for a week when Eldred got back to town. Nothing."

"It's been a couple months. You think cooler heads have prevailed?"

He smirked, "I think they're smarter than they look."

"Any connection between Eldred and the Gawkers?"

"You just saw the hat. Other than that, nothing concrete to follow, except I suspect cocaine's involved." Bobby-Cy extended his arms towards me. "You let me know if they start barkin' again."

I wrapped my arms around him for some good old fashioned brotherly love. "Bet your ass I will." Sliding my arm off his shoulder, I added, "You sure you can't come to the wedding?"

"Oh, hell, Ein, I wish I could. But until Mayor Bishop ups my budget, I'm stuck here. If I left this town in the hands of Deputy Charles and the rest of that bunch, I reckon Whitecross would be ash upon my return."

"It's just a couple days."

"Almost four states away."

"Alright, you're off the hook. But we're celebrating when we get back."

"You got it, Brother Boy."

* * *

On the drive home, unease clung to me. Eldred's cold, steely eyes sizing me up through the windshield snarling back at me. I half expected him to pull a gun and shoot me dead on the spot.

I told myself he could be reasoned with, but it sounded like wishful thinking, even to my ear.

I wasn't a Big Jake fan, but I didn't kill the bastard.

Eldred and the rest of the Gawkers vanished after the shoot-out with Swayze Badger. Bobby-Cy kept me updated on their activity. To our collective surprise, they had remained quiet over the last three months. No noise around town. No threats aimed in my direction…only the occasional truck engine rev with piercing eyes gawking at me.

Fitting, really.

I shook it off. The next week belonged to Chris and me—eight hours north to Asheville to get married. I had every intention of putting my life on hold, lazily sitting out back of our rental cabin overlooking the Appalachian Mountains—wine by day, entwined by night. Nothing mattered more than tying that knot tight.

I hope you're watching, Mama.

Chapter Three

The next morning, a pothole juddered my Pathfinder, and a car horn blared as I cut a swift left off Main Street onto Duval, stealing the gap in front of oncoming traffic. My tires crunched into my usual parking space. Shadows stretched across the pavement in front of the old Victorian house I bought for my psychotherapy office. I checked my watch and trudged up the creaky front steps.

Fifteen minutes until my session with the Nelsons.

I paused to survey the wear the years had done to the building—the yellow paint peeling in patches, shutters hanging sideways, roof shingles weather-beaten. But the years had been good to the structure. And the house still held its charm: wraparound porch, gingerbread trim, a weathervane, that high-arched roof that made the whole thing feel like it had stories to tell.

The heavy oak door groaned in protest as I pushed it open. My shoes echoed on the hundred-year-old heart-of-pine floors, the sound rising into thirteen-foot ceilings. Daylight filtered through stained glass windows, speckling the Persian rug in the airy waiting room with dots of yellow and green. I clicked on the two floor lamps I'd bought to chase light into the dark corners, straightened the magazines on the coffee table, then crossed the foyer to my office.

A thunderous roar stopped me cold as I passed through the doorway.

I shrugged out of my backpack, sliding it onto the file cabinet, then adjusted my glasses and glanced out the window. Two motorcycles tilted in the space beside my Pathfinder.

A squeak of wood on the front porch. Sounds of heavy footsteps.

Odd to see choppers here. Maybe they belonged to the new couple—his and hers.

Then came a loud *bam-bam* on the front door. I'd told the Nelsons to come straight into the waiting room. I swung the wide oak door open anyway.

A broad-shouldered man who had to be six-nine filled the doorway. Behind him stood a stringy-haired blonde with tattoos crawling up her arms, a nose ring glinting. The red-bearded behemoth's forearms bulged like coiled rope. His T-shirt sleeve folded over a half-hidden pack of Marlboros— just like Big Jake used to carry—and a handgun swung from the holster on his hip. The woman stayed quiet, but her Bette Davis eyes bulged with menace.

"Open yet?" the man asked, fiddling with the American flag do-rag tied at the nape of his neck.

"Are you the Nelsons?" I asked, noting his black eye and the twitch that did a nasty dance across his face.

"Nope." He squared his shoulders and tugged at his gun holster. "We're the Mallory's. Don't need no appointment."

"And what can I do for the Mallorys?" I kept my voice level.

"Name's Frank." He thumbed toward the blonde. "This here's Tonya. We got a message for you." Before I could stop him, he brushed by me into the foyer, Tonya trailing behind. "Nice digs." Frank lit a cigarette, blew out a cloud of smoke, and sauntered into my office like he owned it.

Despite his size, I didn't back down. I followed them across the threshold. "This is a non-smoking facility. And if you're not the Nelsons, you need to leave."

"Yes, sir, mighty nice," Frank said, taking another drag on his cigarette and flicking ashes onto the carpet. "Looks like you're shittin' in high cotton."

"I'm afraid I must ask you to leave."

"You *afraid* to ask me to leave?" Frank stepped close, pressed his nose into my face, and blew another cloud of smoke.

I stepped back, waved it away, and took off my glasses. "You heard me. Out."

He studied me. "Look at you—slicked-back hair, black-rimmed glasses, designer clothes I betcha. Big city smell on you, Dr. Einstein." His mouth twisted. "Ain't that your name?"

"My name is Dr. Einstein Pope, like the sign out front says." I thumbed toward the window.

"Einstein?" He glanced back at Tonya and laughed. "You some kind of weird genius or somethin'?"

A ball of tightness squeezed my chest. I caught the patch on his vest—a bearded skeleton gripping an AR-15 in one hand and a knock-off American flag emblazoned with *THE REAL U.S.A.* in the other. The sight of it pricked nerves, but I wasn't about to let this strange ragtag trigger my Achilles' heel. Schooled by the best, Johnny Devillers, I had learned to handle roughnecks a long time ago—from being bullied as a child to my training as a psychologist.

I raised an eyebrow. "Anything else you need to know before you leave?"

"I done my homework on you, Einstein. A high-falutin' genius with a *Ph.D.* after your name. Fancy name, fancy clothes, fancy house." His voice sharpened. "I know a lot of people who want to kick your ass, and I'm one of them. You stuck your nose where it don't belong. Pissed off the wrong people. And we don't take kindly to it."

"I don't even know you."

"Oh, yeah, you do." He leaned in. "Jake Nunn. Ring a bell?"

Tonya poked her head around him. "Yeah, you killed him, you son of a—"

"Shut up, Tonya." Frank furrowed his brow and elbowed her back. Then he jabbed a finger into my chest. "Tell you something, Doc. 'The Gawkers don't forget zombies like you."

Tonya shoved around Frank again. "When the end of days comes, zombies like you gonna roam the streets, tryin' to take our food and guns, but you ain't gonna loot ours. You done fucked up, takin' one of our own—"

Frank raised his palm and swatted her back. "Jesus Goddamn Christ. Will you shut the fuck up?"

The puzzle pieces started to fit together. "You're here because Big Jake's brother, Eldred, sent you."

Frank scoffed. "Look at you—puttin' that Ph.D. to good use."

"I didn't kill Jake."

Frank leaned close, voice dropping. "The Real U.S.A. knows you got arrested for it. And your asshole brother covered it up. I also heard your name's on that bullshit book about takin' our guns."

"Real U.S.A., huh? So that's who the Gawkers answer to?"

"That's who everybody's gonna answer to. We spreadin' countrywide."

I saw the intent in his eyes. His hands curled into fists, then he lunged.

I dodged his swing, but he shoved me hard, knocking me backward over my desk, the green lamp crashing onto the floor. Frank crowded in, his breath hot and sour. "You seen the damage we done in Raleigh. The massacre? We took out fifty-eight zombies at that rally, winged nearly four hundred. The Alabama pipeline explosion—" He sneered. "We takin' this country back, boy."

Tonya cut in like a yapping dog. "And we takin' out every one of you zom—"

Frank whirled and slapped her back again, his temper boiling as she kept stepping into his moment. "I got this. Shut. The fuck. Up."

That half-second was all I needed.

I reached for his holster, yanked the Smith & Wesson free, and drove the muzzle into the soft hollow beneath his jaw. Frank froze, the color draining from his face.

"Now," I said steadily, "who's got this?"

Tonya drew her own handgun and aimed it at me. "Hold it, motherfucker!"

I kneed Frank's leg, shocking the meat above his kneecap, bringing him down to my size. I grabbed a handful of his ginger-colored beard, wrapped it around my fist, and hauled his massive body in front of me, using him as a shield.

"Hey!" Tonya shouted, sidestepping for an angle.

I jerked Frank by the chin, blocking her line of fire again.

"Easy, goddammit!" Frank winced, eyes wide, knowing there wasn't much he could do without accepting a bullet to the base of his brain.

Tonya barked, "Let him go, or you're dead meat!"

Frank snapped, "Shut up, bitch!"

"I got him, baby," she cooed, jockeying for the right angle, her gun pointed at Frank's back. "Don't you worry."

"You idiot," he growled. "You're gonna shoot me in the back of my fuckin' head."

"Tonya," I said. "Put the gun down."

"Fuck you."

I thumbed the hammer on the semiautomatic, the click widening the big man's eyes. There was no tremble in my trigger finger. "Tell her, Frank."

"Dammit," he rasped. "Do what he says."

Tonya dropped her pistol. The thud on the wood floor sizzled irritation across Frank's face. "You don't just drop the fuckin' thing," he muttered. "It's expensive."

She cowered behind him, "Sorry, baby."

I tightened my grip on his beard, "Don't worry about the gun, you're not getting it back." I hiked my attention at Tonya. "Kick it under my desk."

She hesitated, saw I meant business, then booted it across the floor, slamming it into the wall beneath my desk.

Frank rolled his eyes. "Goddammit."

I stared him down, pulled tighter on his beard. "Eldred, right?"

Frank nodded, jaw clenched.

"Like I said, I didn't kill Jake Nunn."

"Like I said," he whispered, "it don't fuckin' matter noways. You marked, no matter what."

"Meaning?"

"We gunnin' for you, boy. And if anything happens to me, they'll track your ass down and do what the Romans did to keep out the marauders. Cut your goddamn head off and stick it up to warm the other zombies."

"What *is* the Real U.S.A.?"

"The apostles of the apocalypse."

"*Apocalypse?*" I couldn't stop the scoff, escaping from my mouth.

Frank's yellow-stained teeth flashed through the mustache hairs hiding his mouth as he laughed. "When the shit hits the fan."

The words hit me like a brick through glass. My forehead curled above my brow. Beads of sweat prickled down my back. Hearing that phrase again—especially from an extremist's mouth—shattered something old and ugly inside me.

Frank seemed to enjoy my reaction. "You got guts, Doc. But there's a whole world you don't know shit about."

"Then let's take our time and figure it out." I released the grip on his beard and reached into my pocket for my phone. "Maybe the sheriff can help you with that."

"You wastin' your time." He smirked. "Your brother won't be joinin' us today."

I double blinked. "And why's that?"

"If Bobby-Cy walks out of his office while we're here," Frank said softly, "he's got a personalized bullet with his name on it waitin' for him."

Alarm shot through me. I loosened the phone back in my pocket. It was too risky. If these two clowns were bold enough to show up on my doorstep, they might be brazen enough to follow through on the threat.

I leaned close to Frank's ear. "You've got ten seconds to get your ass out of here before I shoot you both."

"Fair trade," he said through a shit-eating grin.

He eased away, grabbed Tonya by the arm, and hauled her to the doorway, where he paused and sneered. "This ain't over, Doc. You can get that tattooed." He nodded for Tonya to trail him and turned on his heel. I heard the oak door squeak open then bang shut before pushing myself off of the desk and dropping to one knee, letting out a long, slow breath I didn't know I had been holding then stood.

I fumbled for my cell phone and called Bobby-Cy to make sure he was okay.

No answer.

Outside, engines revved—*vroom, vroom*—drawing me to the window. Frank and Tonya mounted their bikes. Frank looked up, shook his fist, mouthing something, and flipping me off. Tonya rode close behind, angling her bulging eyes at me, her plump lips opening wider and wider, but I couldn't hear a word. Red flags emblazoned with a coiled snake and *The Gawkers* flapped behind each of them as they roared off in a howl of rage.

Shaken, I sank into my armchair and removed my glasses. The Nelsons would arrive any minute. I had to pull myself together. I forced my attention to my breath—slow, deliberate—inhaling the present moment, clearing my mind, and lowering my heart rate the way I taught clients to meditate.

When I opened my eyes, the weight in my palm startled me.

Frank's gun.

Heavy thoughts stampeded through me. I would've shot Swayze Badger if my brother hadn't nailed him first. And when I'd jammed a semiautomatic under Frank's jaw, something had risen in me—cold, instinctive, effortless. Not thought. Reaction. Had my forced childhood love affair with guns put more Johnny in me than I wanted to admit? Sure, I was a psychologist, but sometimes it's easier to figure out someone else's issues than your own. I wondered if I was capable of being like my daddy, and if "when the shit hits the fan" was a coincidence?

A beeping horn outside my window brought me back to the moment.

The Nelsons.

I slid open the desk drawer, shoved Frank's handgun into the back of it, and slammed it shut.

The front door creaked. "Dr. Pope, we're here." Mr. Nelson called from the waiting room.

I grimaced. New clients never remembered the protocol. I scooted my chair back, its wheel bumping Tonya's dropped pistol. I lunged, snatched it up, and tossed it into the drawer just as the Nelsons stepped into my office.

They froze in the doorway, wide-eyed.

"You okay, Dr. Pope?" Mr. Nelson asked, concern lifting his voice.

* * *

After the session, I tore across town to the Sheriff's office. I burst through Bobby-Cy's doorway. He sprang up, hand hovering over the pistol at his hip. Obviously taken aback, he gave me a hard, fixed stare until he recognized me. I explained my run-in with the Mallory's—the Mallorys. The threat. The gun at Frank's throat. The "personalized bullet." Everything Frank had told me.

"The lyin' fuckers." Bobby-Cy muttered. "I been goin' in and out of my office all mornin'. Went to Glenda's Diner for breakfast. No bullet found me yet."

"Thank goodness." I exhaled, plopped into a chair. "I tried to keep my game face on with the Nelsons, but I fidgeted through the whole session."

Bobby-Cy paced back and forth, his thumb dragging along his chin. I'll put an APB out on Frank and Tonya and bring in Eldred."

"They've probably hightailed it out of town by now. But I can handle them."

"What?" He looked me up and down.

"They're not the brightest bulbs in the bunch, if you catch my drift."

He stopped pacing. "I can smell their kind a mile away. They didn't come to your office for common ground, Brother Boy. They came for blood. And Eldred wants it too."

"I can handle them," I said again. "Can you convince Eldred I didn't kill Jake?"

Bobby-Cy's mouth tightened. "That's a tall order."

"Maybe while I'm out of town it'll blow over."

He shook his head, propped against the edge of his desk. "Never gonna happen."

"If you showed Eldred the report—if he saw the evidence pointed away from me, and that Sally Cutter wrote that letter taking responsibility— maybe he'd come to reason and call off the dogs."

He kept shaking his head. "I've talked to Eldred till I was blue in the face. He's convinced you killed Big Jake, and I covered it up because we're brothers. You can't stop something that has no logic, Ein. When emotion takes over, it's like a runaway train." He paused, looked over at me, and saw something in my face, perhaps, that changed his mind. "Tell you what, I'll try one last time, if it'll satisfy you. Just don't get your hopes up."

"Much obliged." I stood and sighed, but my fingers trembled at my sides.

Bobby-Cy noticed. He eased off the desk and stepped closer—six-foot-two meeting six-foot-two—and patted my back. "Got you shook up real good, huh?"

"Yeah," I admitted. "But it's more than you think. When I shoved that semiautomatic into Frank's neck, something rose up in me, shut off my mind. Instinct kicked in. I wasn't thinking, just reacting."

I am not Johnny Devillers.

"I tried to keep my wits about me. I did the breathing, meditated…but it came up a lot easier than I thought it would."

I am not Johnny Devillers.

Bobby-Cy hooked his thumbs in the belt loops of his uniform, face solemn. "You got a killer in you, Brother Boy…." Deep concern plastered across his face, he exchanged a look that said I had unearthed a dormant truth.

My chest caved.

Then he erupted into laughter. "Yep. My older brother. *The killer.* Till he steps on a nail and falls face-first in the mud."

I rolled my eyes and let out a laugh, too.

"And then I gotta save your ass while you makin' snow angels in the mud," he said, mocking, *"Bobby-Cy, save me!"*

"Oh, fuck you," I said, grinning. "I did the hard part, distracting Swayze Badger. All you did was shoot the asshole in the back. Anybody could've done that."

The ribbing—one of the new joys of having a brother—helped. It loosened something in me. Calmed the adrenaline.

Still, I didn't say the truth out loud: Bobby-Cy was right. My psychologist mind had a habit of hunting for the best in people, for a conversation with Eldred and his gang of Gawkers that could fix what violence had broken.

But logic and emotion were enemies more often than friends. My clinical training had taught me that the eighteen inches between head and heart was the longest journey anyone ever took.

And I was fixing to put that theory to the test.

Chapter Four

Blood drizzled from my eyebrow. The bloody beast stood at the foot of my bed, raw flesh dangling from bony arms like drooping sleeves off a choir robe.

Sharp claws lunged at me.

Twisted teeth taunted me.

Daddy's face housed soulless black eyes, set deep beneath his brow. His head stitched back together, large gashes of scar tissue and mangled flesh painted over his once handsome features.

He ripped me from the bed

Mama begged him to stop.

Johnny consoled her. "Prepare to survive...or die."

My eyes flew open, sweeping the perimeter of the room.

Ain't it so, boy. It's just you and me. Ain't it so, boy?

I bolted upright, peeling free of the sweat-soaked sheets, a deep gnawing lodged in my chest.

It was just a dream.

The PTSD Johnny Devillers left me was doing its job far from beyond the grave. After the traumatic run-in with Frank and Tonya, Bloody Bones had visited again—right on schedule, like he always did after stress.

Drenched, I sat on the edge of the bed, practiced deep abdominal breaths to regulate my rapid heartbeat until it began to settle. I wiped beads of moisture from my brow and dragged my clammy hands across the sheets hanging off the mattress.

The psychologist in me knew there was more work to do. I still hadn't made peace with the bastard's dark side or what that meant for me.

Was I capable of being like him?

I looked down at the beauty beside me, eased back under the covers. I draped my arm across Chris's body, pulling him close, pressed skin to skin. He welcomed my embrace, curling his hand around my wrist and smiling in his sleep. I kissed his shoulder and eyed the engagement ring on his finger. Nothing flashy or gaudy, just a simple gold band looped around a lean, soft finger.

After the shootout with Swayze Badger, the dust had settled around Whitecross. And once my name was officially cleared of Big Jake Nunn's murder, I knew I had to marry this man. Chris stood by me through one of the most trying periods of my life. Arrested for murder, threatened, forced to prove my innocence by helping my brother catch the real killer.

Chris had every reason to walk away, but instead drew closer, grounding me. He was there for Gigi when she learned Voodoo Sally—her longtime friend—had been murdered while I sat in jail. Chris did everything a good man could do. And for once, that good man was my best friend.

And now, my fiancé.

For a brief moment, I considered telling him about the attack in my office. After I hid the Swayze Badger mess months earlier, Chris had been upset that I kept him in the dark, but the words wouldn't come—not until I could see it clearly myself. Besides, this was his week. The planning, the energy, the care he'd poured into our wedding. I wasn't about to ruin it with more Whitecross bullshit.

I was determined to leave it all behind for our wedding weekend.

Chris turned toward me, searching my eyes. "Ein, what's wrong?"

I shook it off. "Nothing. Just lost in thought."

"What thought?" He felt my chest. "You're all wet."

"Another dream."

"You mean another nightmare. You were yelling in the night."

"Daddy again. They're always about Johnny Devillers."

"Mumm," he teased. Daddy issues. Hot!"

I squeezed his ribs. "I love you."

"I love you, too, sweaty boy."

I threw off the covers and rolled out of bed.

"Where're you going?"

"I'm drenched. Gonna hop in the shower."

"Put on the coffee first?"

I smiled and leaned back over him, planted a kiss on his cheek. "Anything for you, my love. Speaking of, Gigi found a house in Asheville big enough for all of us. A wedding present. Says it's a show-stopper."

"One week," Chris reminded me, rolling onto his side, fumbling for the remote, and clicking on CNN.

"Oh, yeah? One week till what?"

"Husbands!"

Laughing, I scooped up a handful of coffee beans and started grinding.

"The Alabama Pipeline that runs up the eastern seaboard is under investigation," Chris called over the noise.

I dumped the coffee into the stovetop coffee maker, set the heat to medium, and glanced at the screen. An explosion leveled an entire facility just outside of Helena. Debate of whether or not it was an accident spread across MSNBC and FOX News. Headlines scrolled across the bottoms of TV screens, *"Was this a tragic accident claiming the lives of 13 people or an act of terrorism?"*

"Gas prices on the East Coast are gonna spike," Chris said. "Did you fill up?"

"Yep. We'll keep it full," I said before hopping in the shower.

The hot water poured over me, spiking the crown of my head, massaging it before cascading down my body, but the dream lingered. So did the whisper:

Sticks and stones and Bloody Bones...will bind your wrists and bend and twist... and cave your chest to steal your breath... now split your lips and give him a kiss.

In recent months, the waking apparitions had faded, but the nightmares had grown more intense. Almost every night, the monster came.

Daddy issues.

During the shootout with Swayze Badger, right before Bobby-Cy stepped in, I'd come to grips with pulling the trigger. And the truth unsettled me: it scared me less than I expected. After the adrenaline drained and the nail came out of my foot, the hospital recovery gave me time to examine what lived beneath the surface.

I'd never killed another human being. As a therapist, my job was to heal, not kill. But I'd touched something in myself that wanted Swayze dead for the hurt he'd inflicted on others. He didn't look like Johnny Devillers—but his cruelty was the same animal.

I shook off the dark thoughts and exited the bathroom in a fresh pair of pajama pants. I knocked out a few pushups while Chris sat up in bed, watching me, sipping coffee from my *I Love Lucy* "Vitameatavegamin" mug, with the iconic image of Lucille Ball wincing as she drank the syrup.

"That's right. Work those muscles," Chris ogled. "You've gotta carry me over the threshold."

"We're still doing that?"

"Yes, and do you know why?"

I slid beside him, gulping my own coffee. "Why?"

"Did you know…it's a symbol that the groom is protecting his love interest from the evil spirits below."

"Seriously?"

"Yep." Doughy-eyed, Chris leaned against my shoulder. "So, you have to protect me."

"Since when do you need my protection? You're the most independent person I know."

"Everybody wants to be protected." Chris gazed into my eyes, combing back my wet hair with his fingers. "Feel better?"

"I'm looking at you, aren't I?"

"Oh, you're a charmer. It's nice to see you."

I traced the ring on his finger and thought about the day we met—when he stepped behind me in the Harris Teeter checkout line. I'd put about twenty dollars' worth of groceries in my cart, then unloaded them onto the conveyor belt.

"That'll be one-hundred twenty-five dollars and thirty-five cents," the clerk said.

"What?" I was shocked.

I'd been busy making eyes with the gorgeous Asian man behind me. I'd forgotten to place the plastic divider between our groceries, and the clerk rang them up as one.

I would later claim the mishap was divine intervention—proof we were meant to be together. Our groceries were carbon copies: Tillamook vanilla ice cream. Brown rice. Organic nonfat milk. Chalk Hill Chardonnay. The same brands of lettuce, broccoli, and cabbage. Even Duke's Mayo.

Chris and I looked at each other, laughed, and introduced ourselves. After the bill was sorted, Chris asked, "Wanna grab a Starbucks?"

We talked for hours. Chris was a flight attendant for American Airlines, based in Charlotte. I had a private practice on East Boulevard. By the time we finally said goodbye, the ice cream had melted, and the milk had soured in the backs of our cars.

He told me the loss was worth the gain of getting to know me. I felt the same way.

As time passed, we finished each other's sentences and shared the same values. We were so deeply in love that being separate felt unnatural. He became the only person I trusted with my past. Chris agreed to leave American Airlines, and we settled down in Whitecross.

Two weeks later, we ran a corn maze together. At the exit stood a lattice wall woven with roses and sunflowers—his favorite flower. Chris gasped. When he turned around, I was already on one knee.

I barely managed, "Will you mar—" before he shouted, "Yes!"

Chris searched my face with those dark almond eyes, pulling me back from my trip down memory lane. "You're a million miles away," he said.

"Just thinking."

"Oh, yeah? What?"

"About us standing at the altar exchanging vows."

"Yes, but before that, we've got eight hours of driving ahead of us."

"Then let's go," I said. "You take the first driving shift."

Chris always anchored me. The thought of the long drive—music, laughter, hours alone—steadied something in my chest.

And still, beneath the calm, a warning whispered. "When you let your guard down as things finally settle, that's when something wicked comes for you to take you down."

Chapter Five

The drive from Whitecross to Asheville passed in a blur of fast-food restaurants, gas stations, and motels. By the time we made it through Georgia into South Carolina, hours were reduced to minutes. I had spent the first half of the trip caught in my web of cautionary loop, replaying Frank's threats a dozen times in my head.

This ain't over, Einstein.

Bobby-Cy was right. Frank and Tonya didn't come to my office to smoke a peace pipe. But who was at the top of the chain pulling their strings? Who or what was the Real U.S.A.? And why me? How far were they willing to go? Chris was clueless about my run-in with the Mallorys because I didn't want anything to spoil our marriage, although I couldn't help but feel maybe that process had already begun.

I yawned and took a long gulp from the Starbucks from our last gas stop near Beaufort, South Carolina, where we'd switched drivers off I-95. While waiting for the tank to fill, I'd had the gnawing sense I spotted Eldred.

Sunlight had slashed through the trees, and for a split second, I was sure I saw a man with the same bushy beard, tattooed arms, and robust frame. I couldn't get a good look at him before he disappeared into the Gas Mart. Slurping coffee, though I tried to stay focused on the road, I couldn't help but wonder if it really was Eldred or imagination fatigue. Or simply an unpleasant coincidence.

The closer we got to Asheville, the more I realized we were one of only a handful of traveling vehicles on Interstate 26 West ahead of the morning bustle. The city was a progressive island in a conservative sea—a breathtaking oasis of southern liberalism, but its outskirts were home to doomsday militants—people just like Frank and Tonya. And I was driving straight into their territory to get married.

Headlong.

We already had two strikes against us. Plenty of mountain folk wouldn't approve of our union, and they didn't care much for Floridians either. *Southern Yankees*, they called us—outsiders who bought up their land, developed it, and ruined the landscape.

Under the circumstances, the beach might've been a better choice, but it was Chris's idea to marry in the mountains. He wanted to come back to where it all began for us, the first time we used the "L-word" and said we loved each other.

"Isn't that right, Ein?"

Chris's voice and a pothole along I-26 jolted my thoughts back into the present. I slid my sunglasses down and rubbed the sleep from my eyes, trying to refocus my attention. "What's that?"

"We've covered everything. Right?"

"Oh, the wedding? As far as I know." Even now, the way his brow furrowed, he could tell I was absent. I smiled to myself. He was always showing his love through the details—rings, hors d'oeuvres, or centerpieces. Minutiae were not my forte. I hadn't been as invested in the finer points of wedding planning. Still, it was important that I showed I *was* invested in marrying him.

He leaned in my direction and checked the tilt of the gas needle. "Ein, what're we gonna do? Gas lines in Columbia snaked around the corner, and now every service station we passed was totally out."

"We still have a quarter of a tank. Enough to make Asheville."

Chris plucked his cell phone from the console and checked the news. "Pipeline explosion. It says the interruption will be felt by millions in states up and down the Eastern Seaboard. They're leaning toward calling it an act of terrorism now," he said.

My grip tightened on the wheel. Frank's words echoed—The Real U.S.A. was probably responsible. Information he probably thought at the time I would take to my grave.

Chris continued, "Says they found militia paraphernalia."

"What militia?" The blood drained from my face.

"Apóstoles del Apocalipsis."

My heart sank, knowing how it sounded, "Apostles of the Apocalypse."

Chris smiled. "Look at you, speaking Spanish with the best of them."

My chest tightened. The Apostles of the Apocalypse, talks of zombies pouring from Tonya's mouth, *"When the end of days comes, you zombies will roam the streets tryin' to take our food and guns, but you ain't gonna loot ours."*

Straight out of the Johnny Devillers playbook.

Chris playfully elbowed me in the arm, "You *are* a genius, Einstein."

A forced chuckle was my best effort to engage with his lightheartedness, but a motorcycle in the review mirror stole my attention. The biker pulled behind me and hugged my bumper. He leaned low over the handlebars, squinting and nearly ramming his bike into the trunk of the car. Then he dropped back slightly, only to zoom past us. It's never a good sign when the only vehicle on the highway is you and a motorcycle on your tail.

Imagination fatigue?

Maybe.

Maybe not.

As the rider sped by, Chris snapped a photo of the license plate. "What the hell was that all about?"

"I don't know. Did you get the plate?"

He frowned. "They're blurry."

"We're almost there," I said, pointing toward the county line.

WELCOME TO BUNCOMBE COUNTY

The autumn sun sheared through a lifting fog, revealing the looming mountain peaks and a leafy haze of pink sky cascading around their pointed tops. Chris started singing off-key, "She'll Be Coming 'Round the Mountain," before getting a ping on his phone and abruptly jabbing me in the ribs. "Oh, my god, they're ready."

"What?" I slid my sunglasses down my nose and peeked over the frames, yawning hard and stretching my back. The long drive was catching up with me.

"I got an email from Jewels That Dance."

"Who?"

"The Asheville jeweler. Remember? They said our rings will be ready after we get in."

"Oh yeah…." I took Chris's hand in mine, then caught movement in the rearview mirror. The motorcycle came back into view, slinging a cloud of dust as it sped back onto the highway. "I'm excited to see them…."

As we rocketed toward the Asheville city limits, the bike rode our bumper again. I couldn't clearly see the driver's features through the open-face helmet. The body frame and mouth, twisted in a raging wail, could've been Tonya's but were too small to be Frank's.

Digging my fingers into the wheel, I tried to calm the shiver that seized me and roiled my insides. I glanced over at Chris, trailing off, wrapped up in his cell phone.

"That chopper's tailgating us again," I said.

Hiking his attention from his phone, Chris looked over his shoulder. "The same one?"

I changed lanes. The biker darted behind me, glued to my bumper, and revved his engine. I swerved back into the left lane, and the biker cut behind me again, riding my tail. The sunlight glinted off the chrome of the handlebars.

"Did you cut him off or something?" Chris asked.

"No." I tapped the brakes lightly.

"Well, he's pissed about something. Why doesn't he go around?" Chris waved the biker to go around us.

I felt a line of sweat slither its way under my T-shirt. I switched into the right lane again, adjusted the mirror, and tried to sound calm. "That's not a *him*. That's a *her*. Don't you see the long blond hair flying underneath the helmet?"

"You can't tell a biker's gender from hair length. Just about everybody in Asheville wears a ponytail."

The chopper's engine amplified into a growl as it continued to trail us.

I grew more alarmed and lightly tapped the brake again. The motorcycle screeched, and the wheels began to skid, causing the bike to swerve.

As I focused on the road ahead, I heard a sharp buzz by my ears. At first, I swatted at what I thought was a bee. Then I heard the sound of a bullet nearly graze my head before it shattered the windshield just to the left of the rearview mirror. The fracture lines spread outward from the bullet hole in concentric circles like a spider web.

Chris looked back and screamed. "She's got a gun!"

"Holy shit! Get down!" I had the sudden realization we were about to die—either from the gunfire or from careening off the side of the mountain. Clutching the steering wheel, I slumped in the seat and peered gingerly over the dashboard at the white lines in the middle of the highway zipping by. The roar of pursuit swelled in my ears. I flicked my eyes to the rearview mirror, saw the outlaw rider, grasping the handlebars with only a right hand, firing a pistol with the left.

Terror fluttered in Chris's black eyes. He ducked just before another bullet penetrated the passenger side headrest, then shouted. "What the fuck?"

Blood splashed from somewhere.

I yelled, "You okay?"

"I'm bleeding."

I floored the gas pedal, tried to shake the biker as more bullets riddled the car.

A jagged fear knifed my chest, too, but my shoulders were stiff and unyielding.

Treacherous mountain curves came at me fast. The car swung perilously close to the edge, and tires screamed as I swerved to stay on the road. Blood trickled onto the floorboard, pooling at Chris's feet. He had one hand braced against the glove compartment, the other bloody hand clamped to the bottom of the seat.

I had nothing to lose, so I floored harder on the gas pedal, making the car zigzag. As the speedometer rose to eighty, the throbbing of the chopper behind us rose to a holler that matched my speed.

Another bullet whizzed overhead.

I overtook a big rig in the far-right lane as it crept snail-like up the winding curves. Two cars chugging beside it clotted the other two lanes. The Pathfinder shook as I spied a clear path and managed a tight squeeze between the two slow-moving cars. I was vaguely aware of high-pitched squeals and sounds of angry, blaring horns.

I made a jerky maneuver around the truck and found a straight line of road for a long second before the highway curved again, the car straining against the sideways momentum. In close pursuit, the motorcycle vibrated in deafening, irregular spasms, and the car lost traction as it made an unsteady sway left, then right.

As I crested another rise in the road, my eyes sharpened on the steepest curves on I-26, the Green River Gorge. It's strange how the mind works just before you're about to die. A stunning clarity grabbed hold of me, and I realized I wouldn't make the curve around the next ravine at this speed. There was a chance the car would careen off the side of the mountain into the river below. Such a deep plunge would surely kill us.

On the other side of the hill, the Green River widened before me.

"Brace yourself." I stiffened against the sharp curves.

The vehicle bounced and shimmied. I locked a swift gaze with Chris. Our eyes lit with an unspoken understanding before his head collapsed into a pool of blood in the passenger seat.

Upon entering the impossible curve, I hit the brakes. With a screech of motorcycle tires, the rider peeled around my back bumper into the passing lane and thundered up beside me. I took in the Harley's eagle-wing fuel tank emblem, the rider's blond hair, and the pistol aimed directly at my head.

And I got a clear shot of the biker's features.

The familiar face seared a bolt of horror through my chest.

Bee-stung lips. Blue eyes. Perfectly sculpted nose. Wide cheekbones. A smile that left me breathless.

Mama?

My dead mother's face, staring back at me, twisted from a smile into a snarl.

I jerked my head from the trajectory of the bullet, just as she pulled the trigger and fired.

Chapter Six

Shattered glass littered the front seats. A lifeless Chris slumped beside me, unmoving.

Was he dead?

I jammed the gas pedal to the floorboard, jerked the car onto the shoulder, and slammed on the brakes. The vehicle skidded to a halt. I grabbed him, shaking hard. "Chris!"

Blood soaked through his shirt, flowed over the seats, and now it smeared me as I fought to wake him.

I groped for his phone, but it slipped through my blood-soaked fingers and wedged beneath the seat and console.

I jammed my fingers into the narrow space, scraping knuckles, coming up empty.

"Goddammit!"

When I looked up, the biker skidded to a full stop and wobbled the motorcycle into a nearby scenic overlook. The blonde glanced back over her shoulder, as if inspecting her handiwork.

Sirens wailed in the distance.

The biker revved her motor and sped off, her tires squealing in a trail of smoke.

An eerie ringing silence followed—loud enough to hear my own heart slamming against my ribcage.

"Baby, stay with me!" I yelled, placing my hand on him and inching the car into the rest area a few yards ahead, just inside the city limits. Adrenaline pulsed through me so fast, it took a long second to register the flashing blue lights behind us. When I opened the door to flag for help, a booming voice crackled through a patrol car's loudspeaker.

"Stay in the vehicle!"

I blew a bolt of air between my lips, banged my head against the steering wheel.

How could I put the one I love in danger?

An officer stepped from the cruiser. His spotlight surveyed the bullet holes and shattered glass, lighting the interior of the vehicle like a crime-scene exhibit. I squinted against the glare as he approached, gun drawn.

"Step out. Hands on your head."

I obeyed, raising blood-smeared hands and dropping to my knees.

"Please—call an ambulance!"

"You been up to no good?" He said in a thick drawl. "Got blood all over you."

I explained what had happened, words tumbling out, and he got on the horn with dispatch immediately.

He identified himself as Officer Wiggins and helped me put pressure on Chris's wound while I gave more details. Within minutes, medics arrived and rushed Chris away in an ambulance.

While Officer Wiggins ran my ID, I sat on a nearby picnic table, wiping away blood from my hands and tears of regret from my cheeks. A North Carolina highway trooper walked up beside the car, firing questions, shoving a handkerchief toward me more out of duty than genuine concern.

"So, you're sayin' the assailant was a left-handed blond woman on a Harley, riding your bumper at eighty miles an hour and firing at you?" The state trooper lifted his hat and scratched his bald head.

"Yes, sir. I sped up, and that's when Officer Wiggins pulled in behind me."

"Did you agitate the biker? Cut her off?" The patrolman knitted his brow. "That happens all the time."

I gritted my teeth. My fists clenched.

Nearby, a tall Asheville city cop leaned against my Pathfinder. A sergeant—judging by the triple chevrons. She raised her palm to shield her eyes from the glow of the headlights and studied me in silence. Something about her scrutiny raised the hairs on the back of my neck.

"No, I didn't agitate anybody. The chopper came out of the blue and was on my tail. I swerved back and forth to dodge the shots, but Chris took a bullet before I could lose her."

"Maybe she had you mixed up with somebody else," the trooper said.

I shrugged, hung my head.

I knew I should mention Frank and Tonya, or Eldred, at the gas station. But I wasn't sure it *was* Eldred, nor was I sure Tonya was the biker who shot at us.

My thoughts were only half present, the rush of adrenaline leaving my body. My mother's face lingering behind my eyelids. The swish of four-lane traffic on the nearby interstate sounded far off. A whining semi belched a cloud of black smoke in front of the rest area, struggling against the interstate's sharp incline. Cars squealed to a stop in front of a stone building that housed restrooms and vending machines. Heads rubbernecked to inspect the commotion.

"How do you know it was a woman?" the trooper asked.

"She pulled right alongside me."

"So, you saw her face?"

The city cop raised herself off the Pathfinder, and I stood to meet her six-foot height. "Good question, Jack." She smoothed a drooping lock of auburn hair over one ear to tighten her ponytail, revealing a faint scar on her left cheek. Then she turned to me. "How is that possible? Surely, she wore a helmet and faceguard?" A skeptical eyebrow arched, and she tilted her head to one side.

"The shooter wore an open-face helmet. Everything happened so fast."

"What made you think she was a female?"

"She had…blue eyes. Plump lips."

"Plump lips?"

"Like Angelina Jolie." *Like my mother.*

"Your mother? She let out a cynical laugh, clamped her hands against the hips of her blue uniform pants.

"I know that sounds weird, Officer, but please try to understand why I'm not laughing." I rubbed the back of my neck, trying to decide if I should mention Tonya.

"Asheville prides itself on weird. You'll fit right in."

The female cop gave the trooper a few hard pats on the arm. "Jack, I'll take over from here since we're in the city limits, if you'll keep the media hounds at bay."

She nodded toward a WLOS-TV Eyewitness News van that had set up equipment. A newscaster, microphone in hand, was broadcasting about the attack. A swarm of reporters clambered up the sidewalk of the rest area and shoved microphones in the surprised faces of travelers coming out of the restrooms.

"You got it, Sarge."

"Get a shot of the vehicle," one reporter yelled to her cameraman, his bulky camera balanced on his shoulder as he pushed through the crowd in our direction.

Several newspaper and radio reporters milled around in the distance, probably waiting to pounce after the sergeant finished with me.

The state patrolman headed back to his cruiser, his palms motioning back curiosity seekers. The media hounds groaned and slapped their notepads against their hips.

The female officer turned toward me. The headlights caught her gold metal badge and glinted small flashes in my face like a searchlight. "Sergeant Mary Phillips," she said, offering her hand.

"Einstein Pope," I said, her handshake almost too firm for comfort.

"It's pretty unusual to drive a Harley one-handed and fire a gun with the other, topping speeds of...how fast did you say? Eighty miles an hour?"

"That's what happened, officer." A defensive edge crept into my voice.

"You'd have to be a daredevil to do that."

"Well, I—"

"Most bikes have manual transmissions. You need your right hand for the throttle and front brake, and your left hand for the clutch. I suppose if you're cruising in gear at high speed and don't have to break, turn, or change gears...that takes skill. Not impossible, but unlikely."

"You seem to know a lot about motorcycles," I said.

"Ridden a few." She cleared her throat. "Anything else stand out about the shooter...besides her lips?"

I thought for a second before shaking my head no.

"From everything you're telling me, you're lucky both of you aren't dead." She absent-mindedly rubbed the scar on her face, which didn't indicate whether she was glad about that or not. "Okay, let's start from the beginning. What brings you to Asheville?"

"I'm getting married. My grandma and her friends are coming up for the wedding later. This was supposed to be an easy week."

"So, where's the lucky girl?"

"*He* is on his way to Mission Hospital with a bullet wound."

Beneath two arched brows, her eyes widened with understanding. "Got it. My apologies."

"No apology necessary. We thought Asheville would be the perfect place to get married."

"Yep. Got it."

I checked my watch. "Is there any word on my fiancé?"

"I'll call in for an update." Impatience rode on her stern expression. Her right foot eased forward, and her hands moved into position above the gun on her hip. "What do you do for a living?"

"Really, Sergeant Phillips, this has been traumatic." Hungry, exhausted, and tired of being pelted with personal questions, I sighed, having thought I made myself clear, "I'm a psychologist."

"A shrink, huh?" She examined my face and cracked a slight smile, unable perhaps to resist asking, "Anybody ever say you look like Clark Kent, the man of steel?

"Nerd glasses," I said weakly. The response escaped with a nervous chuckle.

She moved to the side of the Pathfinder, swiped fingertips over the rear until her forefinger found a bullet hole, and entered it. She smacked the dust off her hands and banged an absentminded fist on the door. "Well, *Doc,* you're gonna have a helluva time explaining these bullet holes to your insurance company."

I shrugged and followed her to her police cruiser, while she continued talking over her shoulder. "No worries, though. I'll make sure they get a full report."

She slid under the steering wheel, gazed down at her computer, and clicked her fingers across the keyboard.

I rested my arm across the top of the open car door. "Thank you, I appreciate—"

"Once we know *exactly* what happened."

A long silence pushed up between us while her eyes scanned the computer. When she finally looked up, she shot me a strange look. As she stood, a palm went up to tent her face from the light, and she emphasized her next question with the full force of her penetrating eyes. "Tell me, Dr. Pope, do you have any enemies?"

"I'm a therapist. Probably hundreds."

Stone-faced, her eyes narrowed on me. Obviously, she wasn't amused.

I straightened. "I don't know anybody in the area, and I strongly doubt anybody knows me. I went to private school here when I was a boy, but that was a long time ago. I live in Whitecross, Florida now."

"School? Where?"

"Asheville School for Boys."

She nodded in appraisal.

"Just a few business trips here to the VA Medical Center in the last few years."

She nodded again. "We'll need to take you downtown to test the car for drugs. You know, bullet holes?"

My mouth fell open.

"Procedure."

"Officer, I was trying to get away from somebody pumping bullets into our car. You think I did this?"

She slanted her head at me. "That's *your* version of the story."

"It's the only *version*." Something she found on the Internet must have poisoned her attitude. "There is no other *version*, Officer."

"It's Sergeant. And we'll straighten it out downtown." Her left hand clutched my bicep. "Based on your history, you've got some explaining to do. Now, if you'll come with me."

"Let go of me." I jerked my arm from her grip, blood rushing to my face. "I want to speak to your supervisor and an attorney. We nearly died, and you want to *arrest* me?"

"I'm not arresting you, Doctor, just taking you in for further questioning. I'll see to it that your fiancé is taken care of. And you can speak with my supervisor and call your lawyer at the precinct."

"Unbelievable," I said. I shook my head and let out a long, slow breath. She took my elbow, guided me toward her squad car. "Un-fucking believable."

"Whoa, easy there, soldier," she said with a frown.

I could hear the pistol holster slapping against her hip. I looked down at the butt of her gun. Wooden. Just like my insides.

Although I didn't like guns, I wondered if hers was window dressing or if she was as tough as she came across. "Ever shot anybody?"

"Lots," she replied. "Ever been arrested?"

I blinked and looked at her.

She tightened her grip at my elbow. "Of course, you have. You were arrested on a murder charge."

A hot scar shot through me. *She knows.*

She swept me over to her cruiser, pushed firmly but gently down on my head. I arched my body into the grungy, worn backseat. The hard slam of the door corralled me in an eerie quiet except for the pounding in my head.

I can't believe this is happening. I scrubbed my unshaven face, felt the roughness of an early beard.

My eyes landed on a fruit stand on the other side of the road. Boxes of red apples and globes of bright orange pumpkins scattered on the ground flanked the shack. In the foreground of the red and orange orbs, a sign read *Happy Halloween.* A figure, draped in a black witch's costume, clutched a broom with her claw-like hands and waved customers into the parking lot before turning to me.

Sergeant Phillips grunted as she slid behind the steering wheel. As the patrol car pulled away, I angled my head back at the Pathfinder, now reduced to evidence in a crime scene.

Feels like the end of an era.

Across the highway, the fruit stand's old crone continued to beckon. The Indian summer breeze caught her hair and whipped the long black strands across her face into her eyes. She brushed the strands aside and gaped in my direction. Her long, dark shadow did a convulsive dance on the ground behind her, and she shook the broom at me like a madwoman, as if to reprimand me for something. Then suddenly her evil snarl morphed into rotted, jagged teeth. The long sleeves of her costume slipped open to reveal mangled, dangling flesh, falling off her arms.

Here we go again. Bloody Bones.

He stalked me in my sleep, sometimes haunting me when I'm awake. The shiver that followed made the grown man in me feel shame. But the clinician part of me—my rational mind—was consoling, reminding me that PTSD turns stressful situations into bigger threats than they really are.

I shook out the gruesome thoughts and looked back at the witch. Her hooked nose, piercing eyes, and ghoulish smile, as she waved customers over, reminded me that there was more on my plate than just PTSD. Now, it was as if she was warning that something unholy was closing in on me, and it had the sour taste and one-two-stomach punch of stark, cold reality.

Questions outweighed answers.

Who was the shooter firing at me? And how could it be my dead mother?

Chapter Seven

The drive to the downtown precinct was the longest twenty minutes of my life. I knew the route by heart, having taken it hundreds of times when I lived in Asheville, but never in the back of a police cruiser, never with a driver who said zip.

I tried to focus on the looming mountains ahead of us, but jagged edges of rough images from long ago stalked me. I stared at the back of my eyelids, tried to shake off the motorcycle, the gunfire, Chris slumped beside me. But Bloody Bones hijacked the space behind my eyelids like he owned it, awakening past traumas.

Alcohol convinced Johnny Devillers that the world was coming to an end. To "save me," he set fire to the house and yanked me out of bed in the middle of the night, breath hot with whiskey.

"The shit's about to hit the fan, boy," he growled, dragging me by the arm. "And your mama's sided with the zombies. Your sister and her, they lost causes. It's just you and me, boy. Ain't it so?"

I jerked my arm back from his grasp, and he turned on me, too, dead eyes glaring, "I'm gonna make a man out of you if it's the last thing I do."

He seized an old lantern, a prize I found in an abandoned house, and hurled it at me. The metal edge cut a deep gash above my left brow, warm blood spilling into my eye. Then he ripped the telephone from the wall, marched into the living room, and flung it into the roaring fireplace, like he was tossing a bone to hell.

I ran behind him, clutching my head, gushing blood. As the phone melted, I felt the heat against my face, smoke filling my lungs, and water welling in my eyes. He grabbed a handful of Mama's hair and dragged her across the floor, just before

I blacked out.

When I came to, Mama was nestling me in her arms, outside staring at the flames exploding through the roof of the house, spraying the night air with splintered wood and jagged glass. Johnny fled. Lydia died in the fire. And Mama was in shambles.

That memory slept inside me for years until therapy unearthed it in full color. Johnny Devillers killed at least two people: first, my sister, then my mother. I spent most of my boyhood thinking of ways to kill him. Even though I'd never get my chance at redemption, I felt the burden of hate lift the night Gigi told me how he died.

Yet, somehow, he still rented space in my head.

Damn you, Johnny Devillers. Damn you, Bloody Bones.

Johnny taught me early that I couldn't rely on anyone, that I had to carry my own weight and the mother lode of everybody else's. No wonder I became a therapist. Johnny taught me to stand up for myself and a lot more, but the most important lesson he taught me was not to be like him.

Ain't it so, boy? Ain't it so?

"Isn't that so, Dr. Pope?"

I opened my eyes. Sergeant Phillips had broken the uncomfortable quiet, and I spoke to the back of her auburn hair. "What's that?"

She was on the phone. "You wanted to speak with my supervisor when we get to the station. Right?"

"That's correct."

One of the sights I focused on to bring me back into the present was a billboard on the side of the road that read: *Prepare to Survive Expo. Buncombe County Agricultural Center. Join Us for an Action-Packed Weekend and Learn How to Prepare Today and Survive Tomorrow. October 26-27.*

"Prepare to Survive Expo?" I muttered.

She glanced at the sign. "Humph," was her only response, and the heavy silence returned.

"My father...used to...believe in that philosophy."

No response.

I tore my gaze away and searched the silhouetted vistas that encircled the city and the hazy clouds that hung over several jagged-jawed mountain ranges. The pungent smell of burnt wood slipped through a crack in the window, and I broke the silence again. "Is the smoke coming from wildfires?"

"Yep, no rain since March. Forests burning in north Georgia and western Buncombe County."

As we cruised into the city, it was like stepping into a memory yet seeing it for the first time. I loved the Art Deco, Gothic Revival, and Arts and Crafts buildings that called to mind the city skyline during the heyday of the 1920s. I savored the sight of outdoor restaurants that overflowed with diners, a cop on a Segway, and trolleys carrying sightseers that created a unique village feel. A bedraggled, dark-headed woman wore a faded bandanna and scruffy overcoat as she shuffled along the street, a shopping bag at her side and a burning cigarette hanging from her lips.

Another couple of stoplights and one tattoo parlor later, we arrived at the city's court plaza. I looked up at one of the old familiar buildings that rose from its marble foundation, capped by an octagonal roof tiled in bright red terra-cotta like a postcard from the 1920s.

Sergeant Phillips pulled into the parking lot marked *Asheville City Police Only*. As we climbed the steps to the Buncombe County Courthouse, I glanced at the hardened scar on her face. It looked old and clean, like it had healed too neatly. She kept her eyes set forward, jaw locked.

Strictly business.

Just you and me, boy. Ain't it so, boy? Ain't it so?

The words timed to my footsteps like a drumbeat, and I wondered what more misfortunes, in a life filled with them, awaited me.

* * *

A plaque by the entrance to the lobby read: *Completed in 1928*. On the inside, a marble staircase swept upward beneath a coffered ceiling with ornate plasterwork and a mosaic tile floor that reflected the ceiling's tones like still water.

I emptied my pockets into a plastic tray. A bored officer waved me through the scanner, and I gathered my belongings on the other side where Phillips waited. As we strolled down the hallway, the thudding of her boots echoed on the hard tile. A faint whiff of floor wax reminded me of Bobby-Cy's office back in Whitecross. I was more at ease in those halls.

A bank of vending machines and two newspaper stands—the *Asheville Citizen-Times* and *The Mountain Xpress*—lined the barren walls. The elevator doors opened with a slow, metallic sigh, and Phillips directed me inside to the third floor.

While Officer Wiggins took my statement, the sergeant disappeared for a half hour, then returned and escorted me to her office, indicating a seat in front of her desk.

"Officer Wiggins is impounding your Pathfinder," she said. "We're arranging for a rental."

"Thank you."

"No problem. Least we can do, seeing we're inconveniencing you. Still on your dime, though."

I nodded.

She tapped a pencil against a stack of papers on her desk then looked up. "We did a background check. I spoke to the Whitecross Police Department. Wanted to know why you were accused of murder there a few months ago."

I drew my head back. "And?"

"Sheriff Abbot said you're more a nerd than a killer," she said. "Never been in trouble, aside from that one...shall we say...blemish of a false accusation, Dr. Pope?"

I adjusted my glasses, blood rushing from my chest into my face. "Call me Ein, if you don't mind."

She leaned forward over her desk, dropped her voice. "Why didn't you tell me your brother was a sheriff?"

"Didn't think it mattered."

"Of course, it matters." Her stare remained steady. "Your brother's part of the family in blue." She sighed. "Listen, Ein, I know you're tired, and I know you're angry. But I'm trying to figure out why I have a high-speed shootout in my city. You work with me. I'll work with you."

Leaning in, cutting through the nice-cop routine, I asked, "How's Chris?"

"Stable. Blood loss was the worst of it. He'll be there overnight, probably discharged in the morning."

A long sigh of relief hit me so hard my eyes stung. "I want to see him."

"After you answer a few questions."

I leaned back. If talking would get me out of here, I was game. "Okay, shoot."

The pun made her head jerk ever so slightly, her tight lips curling into an imperceptible smile. "For a peaceful-loving nerd whose profession is helping others, you sure make a shitload of enemies."

"That's not a question."

"Who's Eldred Nunn?"

"A local back in Whitecross."

"Why does he think you murdered his brother?"

"You got more out of Bobby-Cy than I expected."

"He's worried about you."

Her tone softened, her walls were crashing, enough for me to loosen my guard, too. "Eldred's convinced I killed his brother. I don't know why he won't let it go," I said. "Grief needs a target. Sometimes it picks the wrong one. I've kept my contact with him…limited."

"Your brother says he hasn't had any luck locating this Eldred character. Do you know where he is?"

I kept my poker face on, catching my eyes before they widened. "If I knew, my brother would know."

Phillips studied me. "What do you know about the Gawkers?"

"Biker gang, maybe pushing drugs."

"Maybe worse."

I stiffened, met her stare. "Sounds like *you* know them. Care to share?"

She grimaced, her jaw tightening. Maybe I was hitting too close to home.

"I ask the questions." She pushed back from her desk, leaned back in her chair, increasing the distance between us.

I pressed anyway. She was playing her cards close to her chest, so I tried to pull at the loose tooth. "Nothing to say, Sergeant? The Gawkers. The Real

U.S.A. Domestic Jihadists. Homegrown versions of Al-Qaeda, preparing for what they call 'the end of times.' Know anything about that?"

Her eyes sprang open—a flash of something real. Then she masked it. "Domestic terrorism?" She slid her chin into the V of her thumb and forefinger, lifting her eyebrows. "You're jumping to conclusions. Asheville prides itself on diversity, welcomes all kinds of people. But when you welcome everyone, you attract creatives along with the crackpots. You can't have one without the other. And you don't get to label every survivalist a terrorist. Mountain people just want to be left alone. They have a tradition of stockpiling food and resisting outsiders. They raise their own food and stockpile supplies because of bad winters. You can call them survivalists, but that doesn't make them domestic terrorists."

"A hundred percent, as my brother would say." I wondered why she felt the need for this diatribe. "I'm not labeling mountain folks. I'm labeling the people that shot at me."

She combed loose strands of silky hair over her left ear, revealing her scar. "I've kicked a few beehives in my day, but that's my job. I get paid for it."

"You mean...?"

"What I mean is you don't want to get stung."

Mama's face on that bike flashed through my mind like lightning striking a tree—blue eyes, plump lips—snarling. I absentmindedly thumbed Mama's ring dangling out of my shirt.

Phillips noticed my distracted tick, "Is that the ring your fiancé gave you?"

Realizing what I was doing, I replied, "No. I put a ring on his finger. This was my mother's."

"You were close with her?"

"I was," I said. "She passed away when I was nine."

Phillips's gaze went distant. "My mom died when I was young, too. Shoeing a horse. Something spooked it, and he shot his leg straight into her temple. Killed her instantly."

A long minute of silence stretched between us. Her vacant stare made it seem like she wanted me to share more, but I kept my mouth shut.

The sergeant clicked the shuffled papers against her desk into a neat stack, then aimed a pencil at me again. "Here's what I can tell you. We don't have terrorists running around Buncombe County. This area has one of the lowest crime rates in the country. That's why I moved here with my fiancé."

"Ah, so you're engaged, too?"

She nodded. "We wanted out of the big city."

"Can't say I blame you," I said, as the family-in-blue effect continued to open her up.

Before female cops could carry heat, I had a desk job with the D.C. Police Department. When my boyfriend came to Asheville for a job interview, I tagged along, and it was love at first sight. The firm hired him, and I landed a position with the Buncombe County Sheriff's Department. We bought a fifty-acre alpaca farm in Leicester outside the city limits."

"Alpacas?"

"My father raised alpacas. When I was a little girl, I would help him shear their fleece, spin the fiber, and weave the felt to make scarves, gloves, purses, socks—you know, whatever we could sell at local craft fairs."

Out of the corner of my eye, I saw a figure lean into the doorway. "Knock, knock." A tall, handsome man rapped on the doorframe, exchanged glances with the sergeant.

"Speak of the devil," she said, motioning toward the man. "Ein, this is my fiancé, Jim Warren. Jim, Dr. Pope."

"Pleased to meet you, Dr. Pope." Jim extended his hand.

"Name's Ein. Likewise."

"I was telling Ein about the farm."

Jim shot me a crooked smile. "Oh man, we love it down here. I've been a self-sustainability geek since I was a teenager. I used to read *Mother Earth News* cover-to-cover, dreaming of the day I could grow my own crops and live off the land. And Mary's dream was to raise alpacas."

"Well, I wouldn't call it a dream," Phillips said, downplaying his enthusiasm.

Now that I was apparently "family," I went for it, "Say, either of you ever run across a big red-headed dude named Frank? Has a blond girlfriend named Tonya, stringy hair, wears a nose ring?"

Jim shifted on his feet, ran awkward fingers down his scrawny tie. "We don't rub shoulders with extremists, if that's what you mean."

Phillips cut in quickly. "Honey…." She angled her head at me. "It's a touchy subject."

"Oh, I didn't mean to imply—"

Jim spoke over me. "We're prepared for mudslides, road washouts, and long winter snowstorms. That's mountain living, not extremism."

The temperature in the room dropped. Asking about the ragtag duo obviously touched a nerve. Phillips swapped glances with Jim before looking back at me. "I thought you said you didn't know anybody in these parts."

"Didn't know they were from around here."

Jim crossed his arms and rolled his eyes up and to the right, then back down to examine my face. "The names don't ring a bell. Why do you ask?"

"Oh, just wondered," I said, recalling my psychological training. When someone looks up and to the right when they're answering a question, they're usually lying. And after the corrupt department Ronny ran in Whitecross, I knew it wasn't unusual for cops to cover up crimes their cronies committed.

A tense silence pushed up between us, the sergeant's eyes flitting back and forth between Jim and me. She folded her arms across her chest in a defensive gesture. The shutters in Jim's face closed, too.

I could take the hint and took the opportunity. "Right. Well, I'd like to get on up to Mission Hospital if we're done here."

Phillips nodded. "Of course." She hesitated. "But what about speaking to my supervisor? The attorney?"

"Forget it." I waved it away with my hand. "You know, the family of blue. You were just doing your job."

The tension hung like a dark cloud over the three of us anyway.

Officer Wiggins poked his head inside the door, dangling a key fob to the rental. "Got you squared away, Dr. Pope."

Phillips' eyes stayed on mine. "Watch where you step, Ein."

A warning or a threat? Phillips was a tough read, so it was hard to tell. She had her battle scars but wore a pretty good poker face. Still, my psychologist's trump card told me she was hiding something behind the cards she held close to her chest.

When I hoisted myself out of the chair to gather my belongings, my gaze dropped to her cleared desktop. Beneath the neatly stacked paperwork, I spied the corner of the magazine.

Survival Today, the doomsayer flagship magazine.

My teeth clenched, keenly aware from their sideways glances and coolly kept distance vibes that something was off.

I made hurried strides through the station, shoving the door open and stepping into the haze of the sidewalk lights. The October air hit unseasonably warm against my face. I descended the courthouse steps, noticed how the building squatted in the middle of a circle of mountains, the western rump visible where the forest fires smoldered.

Rogue thoughts stirred.

The strange vibes from Phillips and Jim Warren made me question if I'd stepped too close to their secrets. Or was I spinning trauma into conspiracy? Who reads survival magazines unless they're part of the doomsday survivalist ring—the enemies within.

It wasn't all that far-fetched. It'd been widely reported that ex-military, firefighters, police officers, even high-level government officials were members of white nationalist groups. From everything I could surmise, the same sentiment would fit with the Real U.S.A., which meant Phillips and Jim would report my arrival in Asheville.

No question they were hiding something, but what? Why weren't they more forthcoming about who was trying to kill me? Frank and Tonya, Jim and Mary, it began to feel incestual. And the most important question of all was, where did Mama's face fit into all of this?

You warn your patients not to jump to conclusions, I reminded myself. *And here you are, sprinting toward them.*

Head-spinning suspicions are a natural consequence of trauma to ease the tension. Though my therapist mind staggered, I still knew enough to trust it. Something was off. Too many glances. Too many closed doors. Too much practiced neutrality.

I slid into the Toyota RAV4 rental and plugged in my dead phone.

There had to be a logical explanation.

But how many stones would I have to turn over to find it?

And how many more gun barrels would I have to look down before I got answers?

Chapter Eight

I spent the fifteen-minute drive to the hospital on the phone.

The first call was Bobby-Cy. I knew he would be blunt, no fluff, no comfort wrapped in ribbon. He asked about Chris and me, then urged us to come back to Whitecross.

"There's no calling off the wedding," I said. "Too many people are on their way, plus Chris put his heart and soul into this. Clipped wing and all, he's walking down that aisle, and I'll be standing there, ready to receive him."

Bobby-Cy groaned, the sound of a man swallowing a dose of panic and irritation at the same time. I told him coming home wouldn't fix things anyway. Whoever was after me knew where I lived back home, and now they knew where I was.

"That's your stubbornness talking," he said.

"It's genetic," I told him, and chuckled even though it came out thin.

He said Sergeant Phillips had promised to keep an eye on us. Then, like he couldn't help himself, he asked why I was always getting tangled up with the wrong people.

I wanted to add, *Johnny Devillers beat it into me to never walk away from a David and Goliath fight*, but instead I shrugged and said, "Just can't help it if I keep winding up on the wrong side of a gun."

The next call wasn't so brief.

Bobby-Cy had already told Grandma Gigi that I was being detained and that Chris had been shot. Part of me laughed when he admitted calling her—like he knew exactly what was coming my way. Like he was sticking it to his big brother on purpose.

True to form, Gigi covered her alarm with humor, saying, "Now, don't you two go careening off the mountain *Thelma and Louise style.*"

Then the barrage of questions—rapid-fire, sharp-edged, and full of concern she refused to call love. She wanted to know everything. Who was the blonde? What did she look like? What did she say? Who had I talked to? Did I eat? What did I eat? When was the last time I slept? Did I have my sweater? Did Chris have his?

I gave her what I could without falling apart. Told her I was exhausted and almost at the hospital.

"I'm packin' casseroles," she declared. "And I'm bringin' a cooler. And another hoecake."

Grandmas never change. The sky could be falling, and she'd still ask you if you had enough to eat before you got crushed.

Inside Mission, the air hit me cold and sterile. I shut off my phone at the entrance, walked through the scanner, and asked the front desk for Chris Cross. A brunette nurse peered at me through oversized glasses, kindly pointing me toward the elevators.

On the way up to the third floor, I passed a vending machine. My stomach growled at the thought of casseroles and hoecake, but hunger was hunger. I grabbed a bag of Lay's cheddar-and-sour-cream chips and a Little Debbie Swiss cake roll.

That'll have to do.

Chris was asleep when I entered his room. His left arm was wrapped, hooked to an IV, and he was tethered to a heart monitor whose steady beeping instantly narrowed my world to a dull, metronomic rhythm. Those machines would keep me awake, but Chris could sleep through a tornado. The painkillers had him floating—face slack, mouth slightly open, like a man who'd finally been allowed to let go.

My eyes fixed on the bandage around his elbow and bicep—white gauze, a small red bloom soaked into the center. I imagined the moment the bullet tore through him, the searing pain he must have felt.

I closed my eyes and tried to shut it out.

But all I saw was blood.

Mama's face on that bike.

The pistol pointed at my head.

"Hey there, Mr. Charming…."

Chris's groggy voice yanked me back. I blinked hard and smiled at him. "Husband."

He lifted his wrapped arm like a trophy. "Husbands," he corrected, then winced and lowered it.

"Careful." I crossed the room and eased my hand onto his shoulder. "How are you feeling?"

His dark eyes rolled up to meet mine. "High as a fuckin' kite."

I chuckled at his childlike slurred speech—relief and guilt braided together—and gave him a smooch on the lips.

His gaze, through heavy eyelids, drifted to the chips and cake roll in my hand. "Those for me?"

"Can you have them?"

Chris shrugged, "I dunno. I want 'em though."

"Let's hold off till morning."

He stared at me like I'd insulted his ancestors. "Babe. I got shot."

"I know." My voice thinned. The guilt pulled my chin down.

"That sucked."

"Yep. What did they say?"

"Went straight through." He blinked slowly. "I got two holes…"

"Okay."

I grinned despite myself, because of course, he would reduce a near-death experience to geometry. I leaned down and kissed his forehead. "You can tell me the rest in the morning."

His eyes fluttered shut again, a sleepy smile plastered across his face.

I sat in the chair beside him, propped my feet on the edge of the mattress, unwrapped the Swiss cake roll with careful, quiet fingers, and took a bite. I barely swallowed before exhaustion dragged me under, too—beeping machines or not.

* * *

Early the next morning, after checking Chris out, we stopped at Ingles for groceries. Then we wound the RAV4 up Town Mountain Road.

New leather smells of the car, clean mountain air, and the hard, unreal light of morning. Asheville spread below us like a painted map. Chris and I were still shaken—dog-tired, raw—yet Tina Turner roared from the speakers, *Better Be Good to Me*, as if the universe had a sense of humor.

Even with the music, unease rode shotgun with Chris.

In my head, I replayed Phillips and Jim's exchanged look. The way their friendliness had edges. The way their silences felt… curated. Where was the line between "live off the land" and "prepare for the apocalypse"? Between alpaca-utopia and something darker?

The higher we climbed, the tighter the road became. Orange maples flared along the shoulder. One sharp right sent us even higher, onto Clampton Street—a narrow, one-lane dead-end, terminating in a cul-de-sac.

I kept my eyes on the navigation screen. The rental house was only a few yards away.

Then I felt pressure against my ankle. I assumed my laptop had slipped between the seat and the console. When I tried to edge it back into place with my heel, something wiggled against my shoe. My foot gave it an absentminded nudge, and I kept driving.

Through an open gate, I caught sight of the cabin, just as I felt the sensation of something slithering up my calf.

"Holy shit!"

A woozy Chris looked over at my outburst, "What?"

This wasn't PTSD. Something was moving up my pants leg inside my jeans. I slammed the brakes, threw the car into park, and yanked the door handle several times.

Locked.

My hands trembled.

Panicking, I jerked the door handle in rapid repetition.

Nothing.

Chris looked dumbly at me.

Then it hit me—the child safety lock. I fumbled it off, yanked the handle again, and wrenched the door open. I hopped onto the empty street and did a jig backwards, kicking with all my might.

An unsteady Chris staggered out of the passenger seat, bracing himself against the car, and rounding the back of the SUV, dazed at me awkwardly dancing my way across the street. "Ein! What the hell—"

A coiled snake plopped from my pant leg onto the blacktop.

It uncurled, raised its head, its forked tongue flicking the air to taste my fear. It hissed, slid toward me, and struck lightning fast at my calf.

"Jesus!" A wide-eyed Chris stumbled backwards, bracing his arm, "Where the hell did that come from?"

As I leapt out of striking distance, I recognized the markings. A Copperhead—one of the most venomous snakes in the North Carolina mountains. Its skin shimmered in the sunlight as it slithered into the bushes on the side of the road.

Then I felt it—eyes looking down on me—the sensation of being watched. I looked up at the sprawling house perched on the ridge above us. I thought I saw curtains part, then fall back into place. Whoever it was probably thought I'd lost my mind, doing a Saint Vitus dance in the middle of the street.

I took a deep breath and collapsed onto a stone wall by the roadside. Chris plunked down beside me. The only sounds were the hum of bugs in the bushes and the rasp of my breath. Adrenaline, hunger, and exhaustion mixed into a lethal cocktail. The long trip—and everything that came with it—was catching up to me.

But Chris was the one with the bullet wound. I had to be the anchor. I examined his face to make sure he was okay. His meds were doing the trick.

"That was…that was fucking interesting," he said, his eyelids drooping.

"That was fucking terrifying." Having a venomous snake that close to my…." I snickered nervously. "Could've ruined our honeymoon."

As we climbed back into the rental, I shook my head side to side. How did a Copperhead get in the car? And who put it there? Names flooded my brain for answers. Frank? Tonya? Some other "Eldred puppet?" Jim? Phillips? Officer Wiggins?

What game were they playing? Somebody was trying to kill me, but they wanted to terrorize me first.

Calculated violence.

Maybe they thought I was an easy target, expecting me to fold at the snap of a finger.

A cold day in hell.

Little did they know, Johnny Devillers got to me long before they ever would.

As we inched toward the driveway, the majestic peaks rose before us, and my mind switched gears. I thought of what the poet John Muir once wrote, *I'm in the mountains, and the mountains are in me.* I closed my eyes, imbibed that image and the cool mountain air, and let calm wash through me, as we continued to the end of the street and passed through the gate.

When I pulled into the circular driveway, a huge black bear paraded her three cubs along the wooded slope above us. Chris clutched my arm, marveling at the ebony family. Being that close to nature loosened the tension inside me.

When we stepped out, clouds of my breath bloomed in the cool air.

I slung my backpack over my shoulder and lugged a suitcase and a bag of groceries from the car. A wooden artisan handrail of dark locust wood guided us down the stone stairway to the massive round house. Chris admired the ornate Arts and Crafts footplate on the door before turning the handle and swinging it open.

Inside, the expansiveness of the main living area took my breath away. The circular living area rose into a peaked ceiling so high I felt the stress lift instantly. Walls of glass windows ran across the back of the house, offering an unimpeded view of the Blue Ridge Mountains wrapping back toward the stone stairway in front.

"Gigi's friend was right," I said. "This place is awesome."

I stepped onto the screened deck overlooking the city. The view stretched forever, hazy in the distance. "The Great Smoky Mountains are earning their name."

Chris slid his good arm around me, leaning in. "Isn't this sweet?" I could feel the tenseness settling in his body, too.

"Just what we needed." I inhaled deeply. "Back in the old days, people with tuberculosis came up here for the fresh air. That's why the old Victorian homes in the Montford area still have breathing porches."

"Breathing porches?" He tilted his head. "How'd you know that?" As the history buff in the family, he was surprised that I had a random factoid about Asheville's history.

"Just one of those things I learned growing up here."

"I read that Zelda Fitzgerald, F. Scott's wife, died in a hospital fire here, too. We should take a tour of the historic district."

"That's a given," I said with a wink.

I plunged into the cushion of a lounge chair and leaned back, letting the cushion squeak beneath me, trying to erase the image of the Copperhead striking. Frank's red beard wrapped around my fingers. Mama's piercing blue eyes. All of it.

I stretched like a lazy mutt, breathed in the fresh pine-scented air, and let out a long exhale. Chris dropped beside me. I eyed his hard-toned stomach and gave his backside a firm squeeze. "Swear to god. Those skinny jeans are torture."

"Well, Babe, we all have our crosses to bear."

"Yep, Chris Cross is *my* cross." I teased.

He laughed, his clear mind coming back online. Nursing his left arm close to his chest, he pulled out his cell phone. "I got snapshots of the Harley. Think we should turn them over to the cops?" he asked. "I was so out of it when they questioned me at the hospital, it didn't cross my mind. Look at these pictures of the license plate."

He offered the photos, frowning. "Dammit. Too grainy."

I scooted closer, squinting. "Looks like six letters and four numbers. I can make out…there's an M and…let's see…does that look like a seven and nine to you?"

Chris sat upright, one elbow resting on the knee of his ripped jeans. His lips pressed tight as he studied the pictures. "I see the M, but I'm not sure about the numbers."

I waved the photos away. "I think if they're blown up, we might be able to read the whole plate."

"Should we turn them over to…what's her name?"

"Phillips?"

"Yeah. She could get them analyzed."

I reached into my shirt pocket, pulled out her card, and handed it to Chris. "Yeah, she gave me this. Said she needs a proper statement from you, too, actually."

"I'll call tomorrow." He slid the card along with his cell into his jeans pocket.

"On second thought, maybe—"

"*Maybe what?*" He side-eyed me with a puzzled look.

"Maybe we should…hold off with the photos."

"Why?"

"I just—I think we should do our due diligence first before handing something like that over."

Chris stood and snapped back at me, "What in the *hell* is that supposed to mean, Ein? We're talking about the police here. They can solve the problem."

"Can they?"

Befuddled by my response, Chris stood over me, looking down, hooking my eyes.

"All I'm saying is maybe there's more to consider."

"What do we need to consider?" Chris shook his head in confusion, but he knew me too well to not see through my hesitation. "What are you *not* telling me?"

I sighed. *Fuck. Here we go.* "The day before we left…I had visitors."

"You mean new patients."

"No."

"Just *fucking* tell me." His soft face wrinkled into annoyance.

"Two strangers, Frank and Tonya, showed up on motorcycles before my appointment and basically…tried to rough me up for lack of a better term."

"Jesus Christ. *Motorcycles.*" His hands landed on his hips, the disappointment radiating off of him. He was pissed for good reason.

"I was going to tell you, but I didn't want to ruin the trip—"

"Well, that worked out, didn't it? I got a bullet through the arm because you wanted to keep secrets from me. Is that what you mean, *Einstein?*"

"Chris, don't." I raised my palms. "I didn't mean for you to get hurt. I didn't think it was that serious a threat—"

"Which? Too serious to ruin our wedding, but not serious enough to just tell me."

I hung my head; he had me dead to rights. My protection of him had become a curse, instead of a blessing, and I had to stop shielding him from curve balls.

"Fuckin' idiot!" Chris threw his good arm up and turned his back on me. "We could've died."

I cringed, feeling the same measure of shame and embarrassment I did when I was three, falling off the bed. My daddy stabbing me with those words: *"Fuckin' idiot."* I felt small. I cowered into myself, like I did as a boy.

"Getting shot hurts…but…finding out you still don't trust me enough to tell me things hurts worse."

"I'm sorry. I didn't mean to deceive you. I was bearing the weight of the burden to protect you *and* me." I looked into his eyes. "I learned a long time ago that my best course of action is to say nothing about what you're thinking or feeling so you don't get your head knocked off. I want you to know that's not an excuse; it's an explanation. I made a wrong choice, and that's not fair to you."

A long silence impaled our conversation. Seconds stretched into minutes. The only sound was the frenzied chirping of birds in the bushes. In the distance, the sun hung low, casting an orange glow across looming mountaintops. Below us, city lights winked on in the windows of boutiques, private condos, and public buildings. From our perch, I could make out City Hall, where I'd met with Phillips.

I lifted my eyes in Chris's direction. "I deserve everything you said."

"No, you don't." He turned toward me, his good arm wiping away tears, and started backtracking. "Not the name-calling. I just want you to tell me the truth. I'm a grown man, not a child. When you hide things from me, I can't trust you. I'm always playing catch-up with you, and I don't like the feeling of being in the dark about what's going on."

I nodded and cleared my throat.

Chris closed the distance between us and took my hand in his. "For a psychologist named after a genius, you sure make for a clumsy shyster sometimes."

I wrapped my hand around his. "Let's not let anything else derail our wedding."

Chris released my hand and let out a bolt of air. "In the spirit of transparency and not keeping secrets, I have something to confess, too."

"What's that?"

"I had a conversation with Dean Krystek."

"My agent?"

"He's always encouraging you to arrange more events. So…since we were going to be in Asheville anyway, I scheduled a reading at Malaprops a few weeks ago."

"The bookstore/café downtown?" I looked at him in disbelief. "When?"

"Tomorrow. I know how much your new book means to you. And I know you're getting back to your roots, but I want a very large house and several acres of fenced-in yard for the countless number of dogs that will roam it. And book money is better than shrink money."

I always found his mock whiny housewife tone amusing. Credit to him, he was better at cutting through tension than I was. I threw my arms around him. "You're incredible."

"Ouch, still sore." He pulled away, sheltering his arm. "Clumsy shyster moment number twenty-seven."

I leaned in and kissed him, long and good, smiling as our lips touched.

Twigs snapped in the woods below, breaking the spell.

I froze, peered into the trees.

A body half-hidden behind a tree. I double-blinked.

A face stared back at me.

Mama's face.

I jolted, stumbling over the lounge chairs.

"What is it?" Chris asked.

"I thought I saw—"

A figure bolted up the side of the mountain. I yelled into the shadows where the sun had lifted above the oak and maple trees. "What do you want from me?"

No answer.

A haunting stillness.

"Something or someone?" Chris asked.

"I'm not sure." I stepped toward the banister and focused on the trees. Nothing was there. Just the sounds of crunching leaves and snapping twigs underfoot. My fingers settled at my throat, and through the slight struggle of my anguished breath, I felt an unholy presence–a vengeful reach from someone, from somewhere far beyond this place.

Then a loud *bam-bam* pounding on the front door.

Heart racing, I tried to rationalize my mind playing tricks on me again, but the insistent banging continued.

I crossed the deck in loud steps that clicked on the wooden floor, then softened once I rounded the corner and stepped on the Persian carpet in the living room. I grabbed a hand-carved lamp of a bear from one of the side tables and crept to the front door. Chris trailed behind, sharing my concern but looking more confused than alarmed.

"Ein, what are you doing?"

A flash of white through the strip of glass lining the front door.

I swung the door open to Gigi, her head protruding forward, top-heavy with urgency. "Ein, hurry the hell up. I've had to pee since the interstate."

Looks like they came early.

A caravan of guests meandered down the stone steps behind her. I placed the lamp back, pretending to alter the *feng shui* design of the cabin. Gigi brushed by, wrapped brief arms around Chris, whispering, "Poor baby," and scurried to the bathroom.

I threw my arms open. "Welcome to Ashevegas!" Mayor Smiley Bishop, Gigi's new husband handed me a slip of paper. "This was on the doorknob."

With his signature billboard smile, he slung his duffle bag into the entranceway. Four of Gig's sisterfriends from the Women's Preservation Club streamed behind him, toting suitcases and zip-up dress bags, probably gowns for the wedding.

Smiley beamed at me through rosy, plump cheeks. "This city's a lively place, Ein. We went shopping to get a few things. Downtown was crawling with people in Halloween costumes, singing and dancing in the streets until it started to rain."

I chuckled. "Oh yeah, just remember what happens in Ashvegas stays in Ashvegas."

"Would you get a look at this place?" Jackie squealed, weaving her way towards the view.

"They got a back patio lookin' down on the city," Wilma-May said, meeting Jackie at the sliding doors.

"Where's Betty-Jewel?" I asked.

Gigi came out of the bathroom, frowning, and kissed me on the cheek. "She's out of the hospital but still on bedrest, recovering from Swayze Badger's attack. She sent her love."

The other sisterfriends—Jackie, Gladys, Wilma-May, and Shirley— crowded Chris, inquiring about his injury. "Gigi's been giving us the low-down on your adventures," Gladys said. "Or should I say misadventures?"

I took a moment to step outside alone. I peered up the stone steps, across the driveway, to the side of the mountain where the mama bear and her cubs had climbed earlier. No sign of anything. No long-dead mother haunting her son. The cool breeze flapped the bumper sticker in my hand.

Prepare to Survive or Die.

Those words, Daddy's words, sucked the color from my face. The bitter taste of bile rising in my throat told me they had followed me.

They were here.

Watching me squirm.

Waiting for the right moment.

They didn't want me dead just yet—not until they were done toying with me.

I could tell the difference between projections of my trauma and what's real.

And I knew—without question—that Mama's face in the woods had been real.

Ain't it so, boy? Ain't it so?

Chapter Nine

When I reentered the cabin, shock hung on Chris's face. He stood in the doorway, staring, reading me the way he always did—squinted eyes, fists balled, shoulders tight, muscles coiled. As he stared back at me in the doorway, inventorying my squinted eyes, balled up fists, muscles coiled like a Copperhead ready to strike. My skin had gone bloodless, too. The concern rumbling around in his eyes said everything without a word.

I knew I was to speak first.

"I'll tell you later."

"Why can't you tell me now?"

"Let's get everybody settled in, and then I promise I will tell you everything I know. Deal?"

A stark hesitation hung between us. I could read his face like he could read mine. He was trying to decide if he could trust me. "Deal." He walked back into the house.

I followed, nerves buzzing under my skin.

Jackie made pasta in the kitchen, helping herself to the pots and pans and boxes of rigatoni Chris and I had purchased on our way home from the hospital.

"Y'all want some? I'm making my special recipe, but sauce, salt, and cheese is all you got."

"I'm okay," Chris retorted quietly as he put away groceries.

"We should eat," I said.

Chris looked up, reluctant, then nodded.

"I'm makin' plenty," Jackie called over her shoulder as she dumped the rigatoni into boiling water.

I jumped in, unpacking groceries alongside him, "We'll take a couple bowls."

I was still spooked but didn't mention the prowler to the ladies. The last thing we needed was more drama, especially with this crew. One whiff of danger and the barrage of questions would come like a swarm. Better to ease the burden where I could.

Wilma-May gushed, "I'm gonna win that Powerball!"

"She bought lottery tickets," Gladys announced.

"And here I thought gambling was a sin," Gigi said, drying her hands on her jeans.

A gleam in her eye, Wilma-May flashed the tickets. "It's not a sin because I bought three. One for the Father, one for the Son, and one for the Holy Ghost."

Jackie yelled from the kitchen, "It's only sinnin' if you ain't winnin'!"

Shirley folded her arms and sniffed.

Gigi shook her head, "Jackie, we brought casseroles in the cooler."

"I know. The girls and I wanted Italian, though."

Shirley narrowed her eyes, "I didn't say nothin' about Italian."

Wilma-May added, "Me neither."

Jackie tapped her chest, "These girls."

Chris fought the urge to laugh. We shared a quick smile, a necessary moment of relief.

Gigi slapped her hands together and lowered herself onto the arm of the couch in the center of the living room. "So, 'bout time we got into the mess that you two got yourselves into, huh?"

Back to reality.

Chris went on the defensive. "Not *my* mess."

Smiley interjected, "What did happen?"

I brought them up to speed on every detail. The chase. The crash. The hospital. Even Chris listened like he was hearing parts of the story for the first time. Blood loss and his passing out had erased whole stretches of his memory.

The only missing detail was the part about Mama's face. I didn't know how to explain it, and thought Gigi couldn't handle.

Gladys piped up. "What are the police sayin'?"

"Not much." I shrugged. "It's an active investigation. They're looking into it."

Gigi squirmed, anger winding her up. "That bastard, Eldred, is out of his damn mind. I feel sorry for his mama. Two sons gone bad. Such a good woman." Gigi waved a hand, remembering. "I ran into her after Big Jake's funeral at the Piggly Wiggly, offered her my condolences. And thanks to her, we have this beautiful house to enjoy."

I blinked, cocked my head. "What do you mean?"

"I told her about the wedding—how I wanted to rent a place in Asheville as a wedding gift, big enough for all of us. She said a family friend owned the perfect place."

I leaned against the kitchen island, crossing my arms. "What *family friend?*"

Gladys must've noticed the edge in my voice. She started handing out bowls of pasta to change the subject. "Smiley, can't you do anything about Eldred? He's a roughneck like Big was—two peas in a pod."

"You can say that again," Wilma-May replied. "The cheese slid off Eldred's cracker a long time ago."

Smiley shoveled noodles into his mouth, red sauce drizzling at the corners. "Well, now, I'm sure Bobby-Cy's doin' everything he can to remedy the situation. But from the sound of it, you ain't even sure Eldred had anything to do with that motorcycle woman attacking ya'll."

Gigi slapped a paper towel at her man, "Fix your face, Smiley."

"Yes, ma'am," he replied, wiping his mouth.

"Gigi," I pressed. "What family friend did you rent this house from?"

"I told you—Eldred's mama tipped me off." She frowned, trying to remember. "I booked it through a management company on Airbnb." She drummed her fingers against her temple. "Mountain Capes or Mountain Cabins—somethin' like that. Why?"

I exhaled slowly. "So, Eldred's mom recommended this place...through a family friend." My fingers went to my glasses, shoving them up my nose. I shook my head and hiked my gaze at Chris, rolling his eyes, as if to say, *of course.*

Chris stepped in. "There's no hard evidence Eldred's behind anything. But he *did* send Frank and Tonya to warn Ein at his office—and they *are* linked to a domestic terrorist group."

I chimed in, kept my tone casual, not wanting to alarm the group. "Yeah, and if Eldred's mom helped land us here, it doesn't take a rocket scientist to connect the dots." I left it at that. Chris knew what I meant: Frank and Tonya probably knew our location.

Gigi stood abruptly. "Why didn't you tell me any of this was goin' on, son? I could've been more...discretionary."

Chris leaned toward her. "Communication isn't his strong suit."

"Okay, okay." I straightened, lifted my hands, and voice. "I messed up. I thought logic and reason would make this go away, but it didn't." I scanned the room. "Gigi, I'm sorry I didn't say anything. Chris, I'm sorry I put you in harm's way. And I'm sorry if I put any of you in harm's way."

Nods all around.

"The last three months—being accused of a murder I didn't commit—have been a whirlwind." Lines of creases rose on my forehead. "I think we can all agree on that."

Quiet nods all around.

I continued my peace offering. "All I wanted on this trip was to escape the dramas in Whitecross," I said, glancing at Chris, "and meet that handsome face at the end of an aisle. So far, it's been...not ideal. I get that. But the police are handling it. The wedding is still on. You're all here. Can we please—please—try to right this ship?"

Smiley swallowed and asked, "What about that bumper sticker I handed you? 'Prepare to Survive or Die'?"

I shrugged it off. "Just an advertisement. Survivalist expo outside of town."

Gigi stared at me, skepticism stamped across her face. "I'll find the receipt."

I pushed pasta around my plate before shoving it away. "I'm gonna take a shower."

In the bedroom, I tossed the bumper sticker onto the side table and, rubbing my eyes, hopped in the shower. The water spattered my face, my thoughts wouldn't stop tugging at me.

This wasn't going away. Who was in the woods?

Had Eldred gotten wind of our location from his mother and leaked it to the U.S.A.?

When I stepped out of the bathroom, Chris was sitting on the bed, waiting in calculated silence so deliberate it felt like a trap.

No running from it.

I threw on an old shirt and a pair of worn jeans, while he stared at the wall.

I sat beside him.

He didn't look at me. "What did you see?"

My first impulse was to deflect—to soften it, downplay the psychological aspects, make it manageable. But I'd promised. No secrets.

So, I told him. Both times. Mama's face. The way it didn't feel like imagination. The way it felt like *presence.* I tried to rationalize it as I spoke.

Chris said nothing.

A strange look, one I'd never seen before, shrouded his face. He tilted his head with an expression I couldn't name—skepticism, alarm, hopelessness maybe. But after what we'd already gone through, I didn't push for an answer. I'd kept my word. That had to be enough.

Finally, he stood, unsettled, and turned to me. "I don't know what to make of it. But I don't think you're lying."

I rose to meet him. "It's freaking me out. Believe me or not—Gigi can't know. It would destroy her."

He nodded, still mulling it over in his head. "Help me get this shirt off. I need a shower, too."

* * *

After a night of gossip—who was sleeping with who back in Whitecross,

WPC projects, Town Planner meetings from the mayor, what Preacher Black and wife Edna were up to for Christmas at Free-Will Baptist Church—one by one, we went off to our separate bedrooms.

I slid in beside a snoring Chris and tried to sleep. I tossed and turned for an hour or so, jagged images from another time rolling over me.

I was five again, on the floor behind the couch, playing with the puppets Grandma Gigi bought me for Christmas. They'd quickly become my favorite toys, but somehow, even in my young age, I knew to hide them from Daddy.

He appeared out of nowhere, squatting beside me, reeking of Ancient Age, slurring his words. "Look at you, playin' dolls like a sissy. I'm gonna make a man outa you."

He head-butted me in the face, sending my five-year-old frame backward onto the floor.

"They're just puppets!" I cried.

Swaying side to side, he chuckled cruelly. "They're just puppets," he mocked. "Stand your little girl ass back up and fight me, goddammit!"

I stood, wobbling. He punched me in the stomach, tackled me to the floor, and pinned me down until I cried uncle. I cried, cried for Mama—who stepped in like she always did, yelling and clawing at his shirt collar, trying to pull him off me.

"Johnny, you're hurting him," she screamed.

"Hell no, I'm not. We're just playing, ain't we, son?" His drunken eyes warned I'd better agree.

I looked at Mama. I wanted to be a man. I wanted Daddy to be proud of me. I wanted Mama safe. I wanted the pain and terror to stop.

"I said ain't it so?"

"I guess so," I squeezed out a reluctant reply.

He tackled me again. My eyes gazed up at Mama for help as my head banged the floor. She bit her bottom lip, knowing if she interfered, he would sock her too, and make things even worse for me. Then we'd both end up bloody on the floor.

It was my earliest memory of my father, but variations of it replayed in our house over the years.

Eventually, I stopped crying and started fighting back. My childish fists pummeled him with all the hate that had built up inside me. His belligerent fists taught me to defend myself, but they also taught me how to despise him.

As I grew older still, I realized he wanted me weak and vulnerable. Hate hardened me. I refused to show fear. It emboldened me. His fists still did their damage, but in my own way, I became the victor.

I woke drenched in sweat, realized I was too wired to sleep. I left Chris snoring away, crept into the kitchen for a glass of Chardonnay. The house felt eerily quiet—too exposed to whoever might be watching without our knowledge.

Moonbeams, streaming through the glass windows, cast shiny fingers of light across the table and my face. I flopped onto a chair, leaned back, and stared at the full moon, letting the wine rinse the edge off my nerves. I thought of the abuse survivors I'd worked with—mostly women—preyed upon and violated. For the first time, I understood the particular horror of being watched without your consent.

The locals called it a harvest moon. It hung low over the mountaintops. I stared up at the man in the moon. As the wine took hold, he seemed to stare back, the crevices of his face illuminated in the bright orange globe.

The day's events had uprooted my boyhood fears—the bitter memories that were never far away. The lyrics of "Bad Moon Rising" swirled in my head. I sang softly under my breath, "I see trouble on the way."

"Can't sleep either?" A soft voice startled me.

I turned to see Gladys walking toward me. "Care for some company?"

"Absolutely. Grab a glass."

I supplied Gladys with a generous pour you'd receive on your birthday as she eased down next to me. "What's got you up?"

"Oh, I was just thinkin' 'bout Rufus. Maybe I should've brought him up with us. This is the first time I've left him alone since gettin' him back in the house."

Over the last three months—since Jake's death—Gladys and I had become quite close. She divulged that it was Sally who helped to relocate Rufus right before his fourteenth birthday.

No surprises there.

Gladys told me when she first met Rufus again, right before his fourteenth birthday. She was at the Piggly Wiggly while Jake was diving. As she rolled her cart to her car, she saw a skinny shirtless boy picking through the trash cans out back, gnawing on fried chicken scraps. When she neared him, he spooked and took off.

She said she thought it harmless enough till she spotted a dark circle on the boy's back, just above his left hip. A birthmark. Her son's birthmark. She tried to chase him but couldn't keep up and lost him in the woods.

For a week, she hung outside the Piggly Wiggly for hours. Big Jake, of course, accused her of carrying on with some other man, but that didn't deter her. Every day for eight days straight, she'd buy a Lunchables pizza kit, a six-pack of juice boxes, and a chocolate bar. And on the eighth day, the boy finally came back.

Gladys said she offered him the food like you'd offer a wild animal. He was just about mute, mostly grunting at her, but he took the food and headed off into the woods. She'd come to find out that he was in and out of foster homes over the years. Most of his caretakers would get impatient with his disabilities and either send him to another home or turn him loose.

It wasn't until he turned fifteen that Preacher Black and Edna gave him the gravedigging job at Bowen's and put him up in the shack out back of the funeral home.

Eventually, the boy warmed to Gladys and would even come home with her from time to time when she knew Jake wasn't going to be there. She'd feed and shower him. Offer him some of Jake's old clothes.

Gladys said she didn't know he was hers for the first few months, but she had hoped. She said it didn't matter to her either way. As far as she was concerned, the boy was her long-lost son, and she was going to do what she could to help him, whether her abusive husband approved or not.

Soon after Rufus turned sixteen, Gladys took him to Doc Roger's office and paid good money for a paternity test. She said when Doc Rogers confirmed Rufus was hers, she'd never cried so hard in all her life. Even more than when she had to give him up. It was a second chance.

Gigi was the only other soul who knew, Gladys, having no one else to confide in. And Gigi kept her lips sealed until that wild evening during

Founder's Day.

"How's the adjustment been going?" I asked.

"Some good days, some bad. Took some convincing to get him to keep a pair of drawers on…the amount of times I've seen that boy's balls, Brad."

I chuckled as she hurried to correct herself.

"Ein. Sorry."

"Nah, *you* can call me Brad," I said with a wink. "How are you handling the change?"

Gladys's voice softened. "Wish it came sooner."

I nodded. *What do you say to someone's regret?*

"I still think…how could I have done all that to him? What kind of person was I? Why didn't I just leave that man and live my life? Instead, I spent all that time being a shell—and he spent all that time alone. It ain't right."

I nodded, careful with my words. "Seems we're always at war with time. When things are bad, we want to fast-forward. When they're good, we want them to slow down. When we lose something, we want to go backward. Rarely are we content with the time we've got in this moment."

As she continued reminiscing, it hit me that Rufus and I had walked similar paths. Our fathers *destroyed*. Our mothers *sacrificed*. Both of us exiled from our homes and then finding a way back. Only difference between Rufus and me—I didn't get to come home to my mom. I didn't get a second chance.

"Every day, Gladys, every day, I wish for one more hour with her. When Gigi told me she had died…all I could think to do was figure out a way to go backwards, bring her back. But you can't. That's not how life is."

I reached at my chest, my fingers poking through my shirt, and fumbled with the ring dangling from the thin chain around my neck. Chris had fashioned Mama's ring into a necklace and surprised me with it after my proposal at the sunflower maze. Seems we both had jewelry to exchange with each other that day.

"All you can do is try to find what contentment you can in the time you have now. Thinking about what you could've got back leads nowhere. You *are* his mother, Gladys. That's all you have to be."

Gladys leaned in and kissed my cheek. "I wish your mom could see you now. She'd be proud." She stood to go back to bed, her words lingering in me like an ache.

"I wish your mom could see you now."

The wine was working its magic. I stood and stretched, clumsily knocking a copy of the *Asheville Citizen-Times* off the coffee table, scattering sections across the carpet.

"Shit."

The headline caught my eye.

Senator Brutally Murdered at Mission Hospital.

I reached for the paper, snatched it up. Clarence Plemmons—an eighteen-year senator—murdered while recovering from food poisoning. He'd been spearheading a "Winds of Change" push for gun reform after the Raleigh mass shooting months earlier.

I flipped the page and felt my pulse spike.

Mass Shooter Manifesto Emerges, *"The real U.S.A. must rise..."*

On August 16th, disgruntled gunman, Ronald Thompson, 46, opened fire on a gun regulation rally in Raleigh, slaughtering 58 marchers and injuring 396. From the roof of the Bank of America building, Thompson, a self-proclaimed survivalist expert, fired more than 1,100 rounds before turning the gun on himself.

Today, Thompson's manifesto leaked across Tumblr and Reddit forums, quickly spreading his words, "It's time. The real U.S.A. must rise and take back our God-given freedoms. The world is coming to an end, and the zombies are coming to steal your families, your shelter, your food, your lives."

At least a dozen assault rifles and other military-grade weapons, 23 boxes of ammunition, and a handgun were found in the hotel suite where Thompson's body was found, according to federal authorities.

The paper slipped from my hands. I rubbed my temples.

The Real U.S.A.

I grabbed my backpack off the floor, pulled out my laptop and opened it on the dining room table. Phillips told me she'd tangled with the local survivalists before. I wondered what she meant. I opened the search engine and Googled *"Asheville Citizen-Times*, Sergeant Mary Phillips."

Three hits. Not bad.

Her photo popped up along with a November 10th headline, *Local Deputy Hospitalized After Deadly Showdown with Local Landowner.*

I read fast, my heart racing.

Chet Clement, local survivalist, had refused to pay Buncombe County Taxes for over ten years, claiming the government was trying to unlawfully take his land. Local residents had complained that the Vietnam War veteran sponsored military drills on his farm, with excessive gunfire resulting in a disturbance of the peace charge.

When Deputy Sheriff Mary Phillips tried to serve a warrant, the landowner's son shot at her. Phillips returned gunfire, leading to the death of Clement's son, thirty-six-year-old Vernon Clement of Barnardsville. Deputy Phillips was injured in the dispute and admitted to Mission Hospital in critical condition.

I took a deep breath, shut the laptop, and sank back. These were the doomsday terrorists Phillips had tangled with. I hesitated before opening the laptop, thinking that Chris might wake at any minute. I scanned the empty hallway. I didn't see or hear anything except for the sound of freight train snoring, probably from Smiley.

I opened the laptop again and searched for Chet Clement's contact information. It only took a few minutes to find a phone number and address in rural Buncombe County. I tiptoed into the bedroom and fished my cell phone from my jeans pocket. On the way back to the computer, I saved Chet's number and address in my contacts.

Then I went digging for local survivalist websites. I scrolled through over thirty results until I landed on something called SHTF.

My jaw dropped.

Amongst themselves, doomsayers spoke of the coded plan, SHTF—"Shit Hits The Fan"—the zombie apocalypse when all hell breaks loose and modern civilization ends.

For years, I heard the term. *"When the shit hits the fan...."* I felt nauseous.

"When the shit hits the fan...prepare to survive...or die."

All that nonsense about zombies was founded in some twisted, backwoods ideology.

I nervously fiddled with Mama's ring as I clicked on the SHTF link. The chilling website described the end as not a matter of *if* but *when* a solar storm or cyberattack knocked out the U.S. electrical grid, destroying the country's infrastructure.

Once that happened, in a matter of three days, there would be no refrigeration, no food. People would fight for resources. But preppers, who'd spent years amassing what they'd need, would enjoy abundance. Not only would they survive, they'd be ready to fight off hordes of so-called zombies—the unprepared scavengers would feed on the survivalists' preparation after the apocalypse, plundering their supplies and stealing their carefully stored food.

I searched for Chet's name. It popped up in a local *Survivalist Newsletter* boasting 5,983 prepper cells nationwide, many of them traveling to Asheville to train with Clement.

One trainee recalled Clement helping him prepare for mass shootings and unrest in the streets as it becomes more commonplace: "We go to Clement Farm out in nowhere land, help the old man with repairs. The women and kids get together in the house. Then, out come the guns, and everybody wants to give it a go with the M4-style rifles, ARs, 9mm revolvers. I was dying to shoot my friend's Henry Lever .22. It was a nice little rimfire. When the cell networks go down, my ass is ready. Chet told us to wear these on our clothing to identify friends from foes so we don't get hoodwinked by the zombies."

I drew closer to the screen, squinting at a photo of the patch, but the design was too small to make out. Then I remembered Phillips and her fiancé had bought a farm on the outskirts of Asheville. I pulled up the Buncombe County Register of Deeds and clicked on the online document search to view public real estate records. I typed "MARY PHILLIPS" and up popped the date of purchase and a description of the property.

Fenced 50-acre compound. Main house 2,560 Sq.Ft. with two water wells and spring-fed water reserve. Additional 1,780 Sq. Ft. Bunker with a 3,566 Sq. Ft. Metal Building on top. 2 RV stations with water, sewage, and electricity.

From down the hall, I heard rumblings and Chris coughing. Time to head back to bed. I closed the laptop and meandered back down the hall to a stirring fiancé. I curled up next to him, trying to focus on falling asleep, but couldn't stop thinking.

Johnny Devillers was a doomsday prepper. A man fooled by belief, one of these so-called survivalists.

The Real U.S.A.

Instead of counting sheep, my mind jumped from thought to thought.

Eldred Nunn. Frank and Tonya. Alabama pipeline explosion. Mass shooting in Raleigh. Mama's face. Clement's farm, training doomsday terrorists.

The realization thundered in my head.

The threats directed at me were part of a larger, national conspiracy.

Chapter Ten

That evening, we arrived at Malaprop's Bookstore and Café—an Asheville hive where locals and tourists browse books, sip lattes, and hunch over their computers, tapping out what they hope would be the next bestseller.

Gigi, her sisterfriends, and Smiley flanked me as we approached the entrance. When I saw a line already curling around the corner, a small twitch of excitement lit in my chest. I wiped my damp palms on my jeans and tugged my black sport coat into place. Posters for my new release—*Take Our Guns, NOT Our Lives*—leaned against the mammoth glass windows on Haywood Street.

Through the glass, copies of my books towered on a table and were stacked by the register at the checkout counter, waiting to be sold and graced with my John Hancock.

Chris said, "Let me get a picture of you in front of your book in the window."

Smiley snagged the phone from him. "You jump in next to him. Gigi, you get in there, too."

Though writing was my first love, I didn't crave the spotlight that came with it. Gigi and Chris knew I didn't like folks making a fuss over me. Still, I knew they enjoyed feeling proud, so I posed with them in front of the book display and tried not to look like I wanted to melt into the sidewalk.

After the photo session, Chris herded the sisterfriends inside. "Go, go," he said, shooing them through the swinging doors, flapping his good hand behind them.

I shuffled inside behind them, tantalized by the pungent smells of fresh-ground coffee, commingled with a new-ink sharpness and the musty aroma of stories growing old—thrillers, mysteries, memoirs, histories, broken secrets, and sage advice on life—enticing us from every bookshelf with seductive calls. I'd never been able to resist the magnetic pull of a bookstore.

I picked up a copy of my newly published hardback and ran my fingers over the slick cover, enjoying the feel of the raised letters: *Take Our Guns, NOT Our Lives*. A feeling of completion and satisfaction came over me. I flipped to the dedication page.

To my mother, Ada Lea Pope, my magic potion.

I was in my element.

I jerked my head to the clank of several bookstore clerks, slamming rows of fold-up chairs into upright positions, arranging the space into a theater. A lectern with a microphone was stationed up front. As customers meandered to their seats, a strong hand clamped down on my shoulder. I turned around to find a beaming Sergeant Phillips.

"What a surprise," I said over the *clink-clink* of coffee cups in the café and low hum of the swelling crowd. "What're you doing here?"

"Wanted to see the famous doctor in action," she said, shaking my hand. "Congrats on your new book."

It caught me off guard that she would show up at all to attend. Maybe she was vetting me. Or maybe she was stalking me. Or maybe she was simply keeping her promise to my brother.

"Thanks," I said. "I'm honored you took the time."

Out of uniform, she looked different—more feminine, softer. Her black knee-length skirt, leather jacket, and pair of vintage over-the-knee leather boots made her look elegant. A white blouse lay open at the collar, baring the long line of her throat. A handmade metal necklace rested against her ivory chest. Her auburn hair was gathered at the nape, exposing the scar on her left cheek. Despite it—or maybe because of it—she was striking.

"I look forward to a signed copy," she said.

"My signature will cost extra."

At first, she startled, then smiled when she realized I was joking.

I nodded toward an empty corner in the bookstore and, pulling her aside, muttered, "Do you mind?"

"What's up?"

I swallowed. "Sergeant, I—"

"Call me Phillips."

"Thanks. And I prefer Ein." I drew a breath. "Phillips, someone was prowling around our place last night."

"A prowler?" She gave me that police officer's look—slanted skepticism sharpened by training. "There are a lot of wild animals up that way. Bears. Deer—"

"I'm positive I saw somebody in the woods, watching us. The same face as the motorcyclist. She left a bumper sticker on the doorknob that read, *Prepare to Survive or Die.* I took that as a threat."

Phillips tipped her head back, exhaled, then leveled her eyes on mine. "I don't want you to think I'm dismissing you, but how would anyone know where you're staying? You couldn't have been followed. You're in a different vehicle with a North Carolina plate."

"I've been telling myself the same thing," I said. "But my grandmother rented our house from a friend—"

Before I could finish, Emöke—Malaprop's founder—walked up and rested her hand on my shoulder. "Dr. Pope, we're ready to begin your introduction."

"Okay, thanks."

Phillips straightened. "If anything else happens—anything out of the ordinary—give me a shout. My cell's on the back of my card."

It dawned on me that I'd given her card to Chris. "Actually...do you have another one?"

She dug in her purse and produced a business card. "Here you go. Call or text if you have trouble. Let's touch base tomorrow afternoon."

"Will do." I slid the card back and forth between my fingers. "Thanks, Phillips."

"No problem." She gave my arm a firm, friendly knock and said, "Break a leg...Ein."

As she sauntered across the room, my eyes were drawn to her. She glanced back over her shoulder and smiled, then disappeared into a seat among the crowd.

"Ahem." Chris appeared beside, doing his best Chris Farley impression. "It's show time."

"Yeah," I said. "I'm coming."

I stepped toward the lectern feeling confident—excited even. Fatigue nipped at my heels from the lack of sleep, but it wasn't exhaustion that had me wired.

It was the anticipation of a showdown with Frank and his pale-faced girlfriend—if they were going to show, this would be the place.

Emöke welcomed the room, explained the book signing after my talk, then introduced me. I stepped in front of the microphone, my eyes sweeping the crowd. A few browsers huddled in the aisles, leafing through books. I didn't see any openly hostile faces.

And two faces in particular were missing.

Chris nodded and smiled from the front row.

I opened with a line to warm up the crowd. "It's pretty hard to relax on vacation when someone's trying to kill you."

The audience cracked up and, true to form, the jitters drained away.

"Let me tell you what happened on my way into Asheville," I said. "Maybe it'll help you understand why I wrote this book in the first place."

The audience hung on every word as I described our harrowing arrival on I-26—coming around the mountain, bullets buzzing past my head like a swarm of bees. Phillips leaned back, arms crossed, her expression unimpressed, as if my account were less anecdotal and more evidence.

I used the near-death example to illustrate the need for gun control and pivoted into what my book offered: resilience and recovery after gun trauma. "The old belief that you can't teach old dogs new tricks isn't credible anymore. MRI studies show the brain is malleable. We can build new neural pathways. The science is clear: meditation changes the brain and modulates stress. People who meditate regularly show greater resilience. Brain scans show more gray matter density, less shrinkage, less overall cognitive decline."

A ripple of impressed murmurs stirred through the crowd. Still no signs of hecklers.

Half an hour in, I opened the floor for questions. Hands shot up.

"Yes?" I nodded to a man in the front row, mid-twenties maybe—bushy eyebrows, eyes wide and earnest. He wore a beret and full-dress blues, his lapel decorated with medals: Bronze Star, Purple Heart, and more.

"I'm back from deployment," he said, "and I've tried meditation, but I can't stick with it. Does your book give other techniques to deal with PTSD?"

"What's your name and branch of service?" I asked.

"Major Rudy Norris, Special Forces, U.S. Army, sir."

"First of all," I said, as the room turned toward him, "thank you for your service, Rudy."

A thunderous applause.

"Great question. For anyone who doesn't know, PTSD stands for Post-Traumatic Stress Disorder. And you're right—meditation isn't easy for everyone. One of the simplest techniques in the book is called Grounding. We use it with returning vets."

Rudy's voice thickened. "People don't understand what it's like. Everybody expects you to just pick up the pieces and go on with your life. But the stupidest shit sets me off. I'm angry all the time. I can't get past wanting to shoot somebody."

Gasps and mumbles peppered the room. Heads craned in Rudy's direction.

"That's a common feeling after combat," I said evenly. "It's unresolved grief with nowhere safe to go. Sometimes it comes out as tears. Sometimes it comes out as rage."

"Exactly," Rudy said. "It's like you lose yourself. The hardest part is you don't recognize who you are anymore. What you feel and how you act is so different from who you used to be, so different from who you want to be. I hear the same story from my vet buddies. We did everything for our country, but it did nothing for us when we got back. Of course, we're angry. Our government screwed us big time."

"You didn't get into this condition on your own," I said, "and you won't get out of it on your own."

I heard the urgency behind his words—how easily that kind of pain could be hijacked if he got mixed up with the wrong crowd.

"The resiliency tools can help," I added. "See me after. I'll give you a complimentary copy of my book and connect you with someone at the VA."

Rudy nodded. "Thank you, sir."

"Any other questions?" I asked.

My eyes scrolled the sea of faces and zeroed in on one person in the far back whose glaring eyes gave me pause. Long strands of blonde hair poked through a black turban that wrapped her head and brushed the collar of her black dress. When she raised her left hand, her palm looked unusually broad, her forearm muscular. Metal bracelets jingled when she rotated her wrist.

I pointed. "Yes, in the black dress."

She spoke in a husky, Lauren Bacall drawl. "You said it was a woman chasing you, firing a gun. Right?"

"That's correct."

"Well, you sounded surprised." Her red nail clicked against her cheek. "Were you shocked a woman could ride like that? Or that she'd be capable of violence? I bet you thought she'd give up. Women are weak. No way she has the resilience of a man. Isn't that right, Doc?"

A few groans, punctuated by nervous cackles, rippled through the crowd.

In the dim light, her lips looked plump and overpainted—ruby and smug, curling at the corners like a Harley wing.

My jaw tightened, and I struggled to keep my train of thought. Left-handed. Blond hair. The bracelets. Bee-stung lips. The painted Geisha half-smile.

Chris fidgeted in his seat. Phillips scooted to the edge of her chair. Gigi's face soured. The sisterfriends looked stunned.

A long pause stretched into a tense silence.

Then, something clicked inside me. The heckler wanted to battle with words—a weapon I was quite adept at wielding. She wanted to fight, and that was my home turf, so I returned her fire.

"Implicit bias leads most people to assign a masculine label when we don't know someone's gender." I lectured. "Especially around motorcycles and gun violence. I'll admit—when I realized the rider was a woman, I was surprised. But I wasn't surprised she didn't quit. Resilience is a survival skill most women have in spades." I let a small smile in. "After all, you need it to put up with us men."

A handful of chuckles echoed throughout.

The woman in black stood again, more agitated. "This isn't a fucking joke."

The room hissed to a silence.

She glowered at me, fiddled with her turban, mumbling something unintelligible. "Are you saying when women find their resilient zone, it's like finding the G-spot?" Her hands settled on her hips, like she was proud she'd just fired the final shot, then blown across the barrel of a gun to emphasize her victory.

Laughter erupted—unrestrained and loud.

Phillips lifted an anticipatory eyebrow. Chris craned his neck to check out the stranger, then did a double-take—panic stampeding across his face.

I let out a controlled chuckle—just enough to keep the room in my hand.

"You could say that," I said. "I call it your C-Spot—when you feel confident, courageous, calm. On top of the world. Your best self."

I paused for dramatic effect and raised my forefinger for emphasis.

"In fact, your analogy of one's sexual self—in this case a woman's G-spot— and the psychological C-Spot is spot on...if you'll pardon the pun. Both zones do have the capacity to put one on top of the world."

Laughter ricocheted off the bookshelves, and the audience broke out in applause, popping like firecrackers.

Except for Chris, whose body language spelled warning.

My eyes fell on the woman, and I fired one last shot. "I hope that clarifies the concept of the resilient zone, Ms...?"

Clearly rattled and unwilling to offer her name, she shook her head before slinking back into the chair.

"Another question?" I said, as hands went up again. "The man in the corner."

A nondescript, middle-aged man rose. "I'd like to ask about the—"

"—This is a crock of shit!" the woman in black bleated, drowning out the man's question. She sprang up again, flipping a white scarf around her neck.

She stumbled through the row over the knees and feet, threading a path to the door and jabbing her finger in a diatribe.

"People need to know what resilience really is—survival—the right to bear arms and protect ourselves against corruption in D.C."

My eyebrows shot up. A survivalist heckler after all.

"When we shut down the government, cities will be paralyzed," she shouted. "Millions displaced—dead—running for their lives. I advise all of you to prepare to survive or die!" She clutched her purse to her chest like an NFL fullback running a football and barreled for the exit.

"Just wait. You'll see. The United Survivalist Army—the real U.S.A.—ain't putting up with this shit about takin' our guns. We'll take back this country. We'll seize army bases if we have to!"

She shoved through the swinging doors, her white scarf flashing behind. Snatches of her angry voice filtered from the doorway. I was pretty sure I heard a faint refrain of "crock of shit!" as she retreated.

She's after the five thousand dollars Survival Today offered to the next spectator who would heckle me in public, I thought to myself.

Chris shot up, ran to Phillips, and whispered in her ear. Phillips bounced to her feet and rushed out, Chris on her heels. Through the plate glass window, I saw Phillips plant her palm on Chris's chest to stay back before tearing off down the sidewalk.

Major Rudy Norris scrambled to his feet, too, likely to lend his military weight.

At first, you could hear the proverbial pin drop.

Then the crowd began to murmur, a low anxious swell.

That left me with crowd control—smiling, steady, while lingering questions spun in my head.

Who was she?
Why was she here?
And what, exactly, had she come to set in motion?

Chapter Eleven

The crowd mingled before funneling toward the autograph line in the *Personal Growth* section at the back of the bookstore. I chatted briefly with a few readers at the lectern, my eyes scouring the room for any sign of Phillips or Chris. I did my best to stay present, to be gracious, but my focus kept slipping. I needed to know Chris was safe.

A tap landed between my shoulder blades. I turned to find Gigi, concern etched across her face as she nudged me with her middle finger. "What's going on?"

"Walk next door to Zambra," I said quietly. "Chris and I will meet you there in a few."

A bearded bookseller hooked my elbow. "We've got a long line, Dr. Pope."

"I'm sorry for the delay," I said. "If you'll excuse me for one second." I broke away and dashed out of the bookstore. I scanned up and down Haywood Street as I dialed Chris.

"The heckler got away," he said, breathless. "I wanted to talk to her—find out who sent her."

"Where's Phillips?"

"She chased after her. Told me to stay back."

"I'll handle things here," I said. "You stay with Gigi and the sisterfriends at Zambra."

I went back inside, apologized to the bespectacled bookseller, who guided me to my seat at the autograph table. A long line of customers waited patiently to get their books inscribed, copies tucked under their arms. Gratitude welled up—but it carried an edge. I was living one of my dreams, yet instead of savoring it, I was pushing away the image of the woman in black—those thick, painted bee-stung lips, the glare in her eyes.

Could she be the shooter?

I smiled and greeted fans, signing and thanking them, keeping my game face intact.

Another fifteen minutes before a text buzzed in from Phillips. She hadn't found a trace of the woman in black.

The line thinned. I downed a final glass of Chardonnay, chatted with the director of the local mental health center, and fielded a few questions from longtime readers, dealing with various kinds of stress. When they drifted off, I massaged my aching wrist and shuffled toward the front window.

Through the glass, amid street musicians, mimes, and throngs of bodies crowding Haywood Street, I spotted Phillips. She fitted a helmet over her head, slipped on a leather jacket, and mounted a motorcycle.

Curiosity tugged me closer. I watched her hitch her short skirt beneath her, jam her trendy leather boots on the peg, and rev the engine. The Harley shot down Haywood, leaving a flash of white blouse beneath the jacket and a lingering puff of smoke.

"MOTOR-M-6279." The bookseller spoke from behind.

"What?" I stammered and looked at the white-headed, bespectacled man, hands on his hips, peering out the window. He could probably tell I was somewhere else.

"Motorcycle Mary. She's in here all the time. You never see her without that bike."

"Motorcycle Mary, huh?"

"Yep. She's a paradox, all right."

"Paradox?"

"She doesn't take any crap. If you're on her good side, she'll risk her life to protect you."

"And if you're not?"

He shrugged. "If you rub her the wrong way, she'd just as soon shoot you as look at you."

I frowned. "What do you mean?"

"Couple years back she had a shoot-out with a survivalist fanatic. Rumor on the street was that Motorcycle Mary carried a grudge against the Clement clan—they wouldn't let women drill with their army. She wouldn't take no for an answer."

"I read about that online."

"The Clements claimed the government was trying to steal their land because they refused to pay Buncombe County property taxes. That gave her the excuse she was looking for. When she went to serve papers, Chet Clement's son opened fire, told her to get off the property." He paused. "She shot him dead. Right between the eyes. Made the front page of the *Citizen-Times*."

The phrase "Right between the eyes" hit me harder, hearing it spoken aloud.

"I've got to start closing up, man," he said.

"Yeah, sure," I replied. I glanced at the café bar, the clink of cups alerting me to how late it had gotten. "Thanks for hosting me tonight."

"No problem."

My attention returned to the window. "Motorcycle Mary," I murmured.

It didn't escape me that her license plate contained the same letter *M*—and the same numbers, seven and nine—that Chris and I had teased from those blurry photographs.

Chapter Twelve

A whistle of smoky air squeezed into the bookstore as I shoved through the swinging doors, heading to meet Chris at Zambra. I stepped into the dimly lit street, struck by how chilly it was, and realized that my lightweight sports coat wouldn't withstand the blustery wind. I ducked cross Walnut Street to the parking garage to grab my ski jacket from the car.

As I rounded the corner, the smells from Zambra snaked up my nostrils—aromas of garlic, something baked, and what I believed to be sautéed eggplant in wine. My mouth watered. I pictured tapas from past business trips: an arugula salad with roasted Chioggia beets, pomegranate-braised pork spring rolls, and prosciutto-wrapped medjool dates.

"Yum!" I mumbled into the late-night air, rubbing my hands together.

Inside the parking garage, the air shifted—from culinary seduction to something damp and earthy. Motor oil darkened the asphalt in uneven stains on the parking garage floor. Water dripped from a leaky ceiling, pooling in shallow puddles that reflected the sickly yellow glow of overhead lights.

Hurrying to my car, I felt something snag my shoe. I instinctively kicked free, then stopped. Looked down. I bent over and picked up a large piece of soft black fabric. I squinted in the yellowish glow of dim light, and my stomach dropped.

A black turban, just like the woman in the bookstore wore.

I stood frozen in the stillness of the empty garage, glancing at the parked cars and across the street. The yellow letters on Zambra's neon sign blinked back at me. Reverberating down a lonely Walnut Street, an eerie soundtrack drifted through the darkness—the rhythmic slap of a belly dancer's tambourine, the thud of drums, the syncopated clapping of patrons caught up in Mediterranean revelry.

Streetlamps shot slender threads of buttery light through the parking deck, shimmying across the concrete floor. Shadows swallowed the stairwell leading down to the second level where I'd parked. Above me, several garage lights were busted-out, leaving pockets of darkness overhead.

I grabbed the handrail, and I started down. At the bottom of the steps, my foot tripped over something so sizable that it hurled me hard onto the pavement, skinning the side of my head and blasting the breath from my lungs. A moment of white-hot pain blinded me.

Jerking my head up from the oily concrete, I swiped at a line of wetness streaking over my left eye.

Blood.

After a moment, I caught my breath, only to lose it again when I spotted two lifeless eyes, frozen open, locked with mine.

I was lying next to a corpse.

A sound tore from my throat as I took in the gash of geisha-red lips, plump and curled into a grotesque grin. My body lurched violently backward. I bobbed up onto my knees, squealing like a schoolgirl.

A blood-drenched blonde wig lay half on, half off the corpse's bald head. I noted his tired eyes, an Adam's apple disguised underneath a white scarf, deep lines dipping across his forehead, and traces of a five o'clock shadow beneath thick makeup.

The woman in black was a man.

Dumbfounded, I reached in my jacket for my phone but came up empty. It must've slipped out of my pocket when I fell. Still on my knees, I slumped forward as far as possible and fished in the shadows around the body. My fingers hooked my phone near the corpse's head. Scraping the device toward me, I saw a deep crack in the skull and pieces of brain, pink as chunks of freshly boiled shrimp.

I felt dizzy.

I staggered upright, backward against a cement column, and puked.

My right hand braced my hunched frame and wobbly knees. My other hand wiped the sweat from my forehead, the vomit from my mouth.

"What in god's name?" I uttered into the shadows, cloaking me in silence, except for the far-off pounding of Middle Eastern drums beneath a *plink-plink* of a tambourine. My shaky hand dialed 9-1-1.

"9-1-1, what's your emergency?"

"I—I just tripped over a dead body," I stammered. "I'm in the parking garage at Walnut and Rankin."

"Are you safe?"

"Yes…no…I mean, yes."

"Are you in immediate danger, sir?"

"I'm fine. I'm safe. Just shaken."

"We have a unit on the way. Do you want me to stay on the line with you until they arrive?"

"No. I'm okay, thank you."

"Alright. Call us back if anything changes."

I hung up and texted Chris. I dropped the hand holding the phone limply to my side. With the other, I dabbed a trickle of blood oozing down my cheek. I pressed my back against the concrete column to steady myself.

No matter how hard I tried, I couldn't keep my eyes off the corpse. My eyes traced the length of the body—tall, muscular, the bloody, hairless head wrapped in a woman's black dress like a burial shroud. Red-painted toenails protruded from shiny black pumps, each straining to house an enormous foot.

I stared so long I could've sworn the body moved.

Then the truth came crashing down on me.

I remembered the first time I'd laid eyes on the plump lips, not from the motorcycle shooting, but in a photograph over a year ago, back in Whitecross.

With that realization came a far-off wailing of sirens, growing steadily louder, shattering the unnatural stillness.

This time, the staccato rhythmic beat wasn't coming from drums or tambourines.

It was the wild hammering *thump-thump, thump-thump* of my own beating heart.

Chapter Thirteen

In the distance, I heard giggles of giddy restaurant patrons emerging from Zambra. By the time Chris and the sisterfriends arrived, the media hyenas had already descended. WLOS-TV Eyewitness News and various newspaper jockeys milled around a fifty-foot circle of bright yellow crime-scene tape warning *DO NOT CROSS*.

Late-night curiosity vultures drifted in from nearby restaurants, night-clubs, and stage shows, drawn to the pulsing blue lights of the Asheville City Police cruisers. A special forensics van idled nearby, its cargo of gloved detectives combing the cordoned-off murder scene.

When the flashing lights and somber mood finally registered, Chris asked, "What's going on?" He cupped my chin, tilting my face toward him. "What happened?" Did you get mugged?"

I raised my hands to fend off the barrage of questions. "I texted you before you saw all of this—to tell you I was okay. Where's Gigi and the sisterfriends? Smiley?"

"They're inside, gossiping over the food." Chris said, glancing at his phone—though his attention never really left my face. He pulled a handkerchief from his pocket, pressed it to my bloody forehead, and tried to brush grime smudging my black jacket.

"I'm fine. Can't say the same for the *woman* in black—the troublemaker at my signing. *He* wasn't so lucky."

"He?" Chris asked, blinking.

"The woman who attacked us on the interstate and heckled me at the bookstore turned out to be a man. I tripped over him at the bottom of the garage steps—split skull, deader than a doornail."

Chris gave me a sideways look. "A drag queen?"

"When I saw the blonde wig and bald head, it clicked. I'd seen that Geisha smile before. In one of our therapy sessions, Gladys Nunn showed me a photo of her nephew dressed as Cher—those blown-up lips."

"Plump lips like your mother's," Chris said, exhaling a bolt of air. "Wow. That explains why you thought you saw your mother's face on the motorcycle. And in the woods. He's been stalking us."

"Hold on—"

"We don't have to worry about somebody trying to kill us anymore." Chris spun in a tight circle. "Now, the authorities can handle it."

"Was he trying to kill us?" I dabbed my forehead and cheek. "I'm not so sure. What I want to know is who killed *him*. And why."

"Hatchet to the head," Officer Wiggins announced, ducking under the crime-scene tape. He delivered the verdict in a strong guttural voice. "Somebody wanted him dead in the worst way."

"How do you know it was a hatchet?" I asked.

"Forensics found a blood-stained one in that trash can." He pointed toward the corner of the parking deck. "We'll confirm it, but it had strands of what looked like matted blonde wig hair." Then he eyed back at me. "Dr. Pope, reporters want a word."

"No way." I raised my palm like a stop sign. "I'm done for the night."

"Don't blame you one bit." He rolled his tongue against his teeth, as if savoring a meal. "I'll handle them. But could I speak with you privately?"

I nodded.

We stepped into a darker pocket of the parking garage, backlit by spills of streetlight, silhouetting the officer's dark face and short frame. He scratched his head, studying me with a hard look. "What kind of shit are you mixed up in?"

"What do you mean?"

"This is the second call involving you in two days."

"Officer, the victim was a doomsayer. He heckled me at Malaprops. I tripped over his body on my way to the car. That's it."

"Not quite." His jaw tightened. "We found a semiautomatic pistol in his purse. He could've been waiting for you."

I tried to ignore the chill that lifted the hair on the back of my neck. "That crossed my mind. But now I'm not so sure. I *do* know where I recognized him from, though."

"Where?"

"His Aunt Gladys showed me a photo of him in drag, performing as Cher in a Charlotte nightclub. It was the swollen, ghoulish lips that stuck in my memory."

"Yup, background check says his name's Bucky Clement. Worked at Babette's Feast—a drag bar west of town. Family's got a hundred-acre farm a few miles north of town."

The name instantly struck a chord. "The Clement family? Chet Clement's son?"

"Yup, whole bunch of whack jobs, if you ask me. Doomsdayers. Sergeant Phillips tangled with them more than once."

Tangled? Shooting somebody seemed like more than tangling. "Any idea why he was after us—or who killed him?"

"No telling. He's had plenty of run-ins with the law."

"Speaking of the sergeant. Why isn't she here?" I removed the blood-splotched handkerchief from my brow.

"Beats me." Officer Wiggins flashed a jagged-toothed smile. "I guarantee you one thing, though, she'll be all over this tomorrow like stink on skunk. Meantime, we know where to reach you if we need you, but you'll need to come down to the station Monday to give us an official statement."

"This is getting old, but I'll be happy to, sir."

We parted ways. Wiggins bent under the barricade of yellow tape and vanished into the swarm of officers.

The exit gate was permanently raised at that time of night, making our departure easy. I turned left onto Rankin Street to collect the others at Zambra.

Across the street from the parking deck, shadows lengthened. A half-silhouetted figure stood in a doorway beneath a lamppost, smoking, the smell of cannabis drifting into the night air. He wore dress blues, medals dangling from his chest.

Major Rudy Norris, the vet from the book signing.

His bushy eyebrows lifted into a lazy gaze, briefly meeting mine through an exhale of smoke. I thought of the woman in black's shouted rants about the government. Bucky and Rudy—both disgruntled with the government and military. And Rudy's despair echoed in my head, *The stupidest shit sets me off...can't seem to get past wanting to shoot somebody.*

A question seared through my mind.

Was Bucky Clement connected to Rudy Norris?

Or worse—*Did Rudy Norris kill him?*

And if so...why?

Chapter Fourteen

A woman's high-pitched scream shattered my sleep.

I bolted upright. Was it real? Or had it been my own ragged warble—Bloody Bones trapped inside a dream?

I flopped back into the pillows, arms pinned at my side, body heavy and stiff like a corpse. Holding my breath, I listened. A soft hum answered—steady, mechanical. I squinted up at the swirling ceiling fan. Morning light seeped through the windows, casting leaf-dappled shadows across the bedspread and carpet. I checked the digital clock on the nightstand. It blinked 10:17 a.m.

Damn, I slept like I was drugged.

I tried to push the phantom scream from my foggy mind, but then two more blood-curdling shrieks tore through the woods. Panicked, I rolled out of bed and fought my way upright. Though my sore legs felt like concrete, my feet found the floor. Still in socks and pajamas, I padded into the main living area and slid on my glasses. Everyone sat calmly around the wide-screen TV.

"Two recent earthquakes, the massive devastation of Hurricane Helene that tore Asheville to shreds, and wildfires raging across the South have U.S. survivalists convinced the end of the world is nigh," the newscaster announced. "They're clearing store shelves to stock bunkers for what they believe is Earth's final chapter. Sales of freeze-dried food, gas masks, and survival gear have spiked in recent weeks as so-called 'preppers' pack their bug-out bags to ride out what they say is an impending disaster."

Talking over the newscast, Jackie held court. "Those Brussels sprouts from last night gave me gas." She burped cheerfully into her coffee.

Shirley fanned the air around her. "Take it outside, Jackie."

"What were those screams?" I asked, yawning and chuckling at the same time, rubbing sleep from my bleary eyes.

"We were just talking about that," Gigi replied through sips of coffee. Her legs were slung over the arm of a stuffed chair, bare feet dangling off the side. "That was a fox."

Gigi knew everything there was to know about nature.

"Sounded like a woman screaming," I said, running my fingers through disheveled hair and moving into the kitchen to pour a cup of coffee.

"The high-pitched yelp of a fox does sound like a woman screaming," Chris said, reclining into the sofa cushions, cradling his wounded arm.

"They're out during the daytime?" I asked.

"It happens," said Gigi.

From the beginning, Chris and Gigi had bonded over nature. After growing up in the Asheville boarding school, then college, I'd gone back home to settle old debts with my long-lost daddy and reclaim what family I had left. I reconnected with my crusty grandma and introduced her to Chris. They'd hit it off instantly over southern cooking, the outdoors, and why I'd gone by Brad instead of Einstein most of my life.

"You two are at it again." I stirred my coffee with a splash of half-and-half, then grabbed a Danish from the crumb-littered plate. "Showing off your knowledge of wildlife."

"How's your head?" Chris asked.

"Hard as ever," Gigi teased.

"Just a scratch. I'm not woozy or dizzy."

Shirley piped up. "Wilma-May, where did you get that mug?"

Wilma-May held up a *Zambra* coffee cup, a gold logo emblazoned on the side. She peered over the rim, mischief dawdling in her eyes. "I have no idea what you're talking about."

"You promised you wouldn't shoplift if we let you come on this trip," Gigi said.

"I didn't shoplift," Wilma-May said with a grin. "I wasn't shopping, I was eating. Somehow it fell into my purse. I think somebody in this group is trying to frame me."

I eyed her over the rim of my glasses. "I don't think anybody's trying to frame you. I think you had a little too much excitement last night."

Jackie raised a thickly penciled eyebrow and shimmied her shoulders. "There's no such thing as too much excitement."

"Amen," Wilma-May said.

Shirley shook her head.

I clapped my hands. "So, here's the agenda for today. It's Sunday. We have tickets for the Biltmore House and Gardens."

Smiley spoke through the *Oohs* and *ahs*. "Thank goodness they're not calling for rain until later today."

"Ein," Shirley added, "didn't Chris say you have a date with the police?"

"I'm checking in with Phillips this afternoon after the Biltmore House tour. Tonight, we go dancing. It's Halloween, time we had some fun. The bars downtown will be crawling with costumes and trick-or-treaters."

More *oohs* and *ahs* broke out.

"You've packed the day again," Chris groaned. "What happened to the Thomas Wolfe and Zelda Fitzgerald historic bus tour after the Biltmore House?"

"After I meet with Phillips."

Chris locked his eyes with mine. "Don't forget, we've got last-minute details to finalize."

I smacked the good side of my forehead. "The rings. I forgot." Looking at Chris, I asked, "Can you...?"

"Already got it handled."

Gladys gasped and pointed toward the mountains. Three striped hot-air balloons lifted over the city buildings below, floating westward. Everyone bounced to their feet, scurried onto the screened porch deck. Chris tagged close behind.

I stood to join them, but Smiley pulled me aside. "Ein, I don't mean to pry, but I can tell you're in some kind of trouble. I got something here if you need it." He unzipped his bag and removed a handgun.

"You're packing heat?"

"Dangerous times for politicians." He tapped it proudly. "I carry this G43 single-stack 9-millimeter semiautomatic. Just in case."

A lump tightened my throat.

"This bad-to-the-bone baby will put serious confidence in your hands and discourage the bad guys. Never had to use it so far, except for target practice, but I like knowing it's there if I need it."

"Thanks. I used to target shoot as a boy but learned to dislike firearms. I plan to solve whatever's coming without them. You know, take our guns, not our lives?"

"Hope you can, son." He slid the firearm back into his duffel bag and squeezed my shoulder. "But it's here with four rounds of ammunition if you can't."

"Thanks, Smiley."

He joined the others on the porch, and I started to follow him, but the newscast caught my attention again.

Asheville City Police are investigating the murder of a Buncombe County man hacked to death in the Rankin Street parking garage. The murder of 32-year-old Bucky Clement raises new questions about his father, Chet Clement, head of the Clement clan, and his lifelong ties to the United Survivalist Army."

The doorbell rang, followed by a familiar, agitated voice. As I crossed the Persian carpet, a loud "Fuck him!" quickened my pace.

The door flew open, slamming into me, throwing me backward onto the floor. Frank stood above me, waving a hatchet, Tonya beside him. Beefy, bear-sized hands squeezed my throat, his smelly, orange beard dangled in my face.

"Let go of me," I choked.

"Last time I saw you, Doc, you were on the floor," Frank snarled. "You son-of-a-bitch, where are my guns?"

Realizing my horizontal position only invited trouble, I kneed him in the groin, flinging him off me. I pulled myself up and met his face—feral with rage—just inches from mine.

"You killed Bucky," he shouted. "Hacked him to pieces."

"What the hell are you talking about?" I shouted, refusing to back down.

"The Real U.S.A. knows everything about you. Where you are. Who you're with. What you eat. Even when you shit. Now, I'm going to do to you what you done to Bucky." He raised the hatchet.

Tonya grabbed his tattooed arm. "No, Frank. He's not worth going back to prison." She nodded toward the screened porch where the others were screaming with laughter.

Frank lowered his arm, letting the hatchet dangle by his side. "You're right."

Tonya pulled back her leather jacket, flashing her pistol. "Let me blow the fucker's head off when nobody else is around."

As she spoke, I examined her more closely. Stringy blonde hair. Plump lips. Just like I remembered. But were they the same lips that howled at me from the Harley on I-26?

"Tell you what," I said. "Let's step outside and settle this in private. Peacefully. I don't want to alarm the others."

Frank sneered. Ain't nothing peaceful about this."

He brushed up against me and stuck his steely eyes in my face, spittle gathering in the corner of his mouth, foul breath almost choking me. His left eyebrow was pierced with two small, silver studs. "Like the way you peacefully cut up Bucky? Tell you what, pretty boy, this shit ain't gonna end peacefully."

Frank nodded for Tonya to follow. I joined them outside and closed the door.

Frank hooked his thumbs in the belt loops of his jeans. A sneer plastered across his freckled face. He examined me for a long moment before he spoke. "In bad times, you're the kind that raid folks like us, shoot us, and take our supplies."

"You got me wrong—"

"The ants work hard, save up food to last the long winter. Then along comes the grasshoppers, laughing and playing and mocking the ants for being so scared. When winter comes—oh hell yeah, and it comes—the grasshoppers ain't got shit, and they try to steal everything the ants worked for."

"You think I'm the grasshopper, and you're the piss ant?"

"I think you're a mutherfucker." Frank threw a fist at me. I caught his arm mid-swing and put a stronghold on him. He had underestimated me again. His eyes widened. I loosened my grip but kept my shoulders squared with his, refusing to back down even an inch.

"I warned you once already about sticking your nose where it don't belong." He met my gaze with narrowed eyes, swelling his shoulders and raising the hatchet. "Now I'm puttin' you on notice. You cross the line one more time—"

With the full force of his arm, he lifted the hatchet and swung the blade into the arts-and-crafts doorframe, burying it deep into the wood. "—and that's what I'm gonna do to your fuckin' skull, just like you done to Bucky."

Adrenaline surged like electricity through my body, but I was calm enough to know that if I showed an ounce of fear, one of us was going to die. And it wasn't going to be me.

I met his gaze without blinking. "Time to leave."

"Last warning. You go all raider on us, come for our shit? We shoot first, ask questions later."

His boots made heavy clomping sounds up the wide stone steps. Tonya, climbing in long strides behind him, looked back at me and snarled her puffy lips. "One more time, and you're dead meat, asshole."

With their exit and the *vroom, vroom* of the motorcycles in the driveway, I blew out a sigh of relief.

I glanced toward the porch where the others were absorbed in the air show. Their rowdy chatter must have drowned out the yelling. Working the handle back and forth, I pried the hatchet from the deep incision in the wood.

Just as I reached for the doorknob, another blood-curdling scream wailed through the woods.

Chapter Fifteen

I made my best effort at a relaxed façade on our tour of the Biltmore House and Gardens, even as a stampede of thoughts circled in my head like a school of sharks. One urgent question stayed in front, sharp as the hatchet blade: Who killed Bucky Clement?

Afterward, I dropped everyone back at the house and dialed Sergeant Phillips. I'd spent the morning nodding at sixteenth-century tapestries like they were personal friends. Surely, I'd banked enough goodwill with Chris to buy myself a time to justify attending to other matters.

Phillips answered on the fourth ring, and I suggested we meet for coffee to talk. She brushed me off with a polite apology and an "I'm slammed." It felt like dodging. Avoidance. "It's important," I said. "It won't take much of your time."

A long second. Then: "Okay, ten minutes, but only if we meet downtown—Tupelo Honey on College Street in front of Pritchard Park. I'm meeting Jim for lunch."

"You got it."

The trees shimmered in the afternoon sun as I slowed in front of the Asheville School for Boys. My alma mater spread regally across three hundred acres of rolling hills, broken by the ivy-covered stone buildings. Magenta and gold leaves blanketed the lawn like a rumpled quilt. As more leaves fluttered down to join the patchwork, a disquieting thought pierced my fond boyhood memories. In autumn, piles of dry fallen leaves could hide anything—even a body.

Farther down the road, I passed a cluster of storefronts and a pack of early trick-or-treaters making the rounds of local businesses. An adult chaperone, dressed as a genie—white harem pants and a red turban, blurred into something else in my mind.

Suddenly, the costumed children were replaced by pulse-pounding images of a black-turbaned Bucky: my shoe snagging it, a blood-drenched wig hanging from a bald skull, the corpse sprawled on the grimy garage floor. Empty eyes fixed on me. A plump, ghoulish mouth frozen in a leer beside scattered bits of brain.

Then unwelcome images of Frank elbowed his way into my consciousness—kicking the door. Accusing me. Splitting the doorframe. Pierced eyebrow. Rotten breath in my face. That threat: I'd pay for Bucky's murder.

Another haunting image followed fast, as if queued: Rudy Norris under a streetlamp, medals dangling from his dress blues. His desperate confession, delivered behind a cloud of cigarette smoke.

I can't seem to get past wanting to shoot somebody.

I pulled into a parking space in front of Tupelo Honey. The smell of homemade biscuits wafted from the storefront restaurant and yanked me from murder and menace long enough for my stomach to growl. I hadn't realized how hungry I was.

Inside, I thought I spied the back of Phillips's head. I glided across the room and leaned in—only to meet the startled face of a woman with the same silky auburn hair but none of the high cheekbones, full lips, or radiant, watchful eyes of Mary Phillips.

Red climbed into my neck and face. "I'm so sorry for the intrusion."

The hostess directed me to a chair by the window. I dropped into it, berating myself for the embarrassing habit I'd tried to break—mistaking strangers for people I knew. I ordered coffee and a ham biscuit and drummed the table for another fifteen minutes.

Phillips still hadn't shown.

I was about to ask for my food to go when a police cruiser pulled into a spot out front. Phillips hopped out, something cradled under her arm. She swung the door open, and the cool October air swept in, lifting wisps of her hair.

"Sorry," she said. "It's been a busy day."

I could've sworn the scent of cigarette smoke breezed in with her—maybe the lingering stink of the patrol car, maybe wildfire haze.

"No worries," I said. "Happy Halloween."

She scooted into the booth in front of me, ordered coffee, then slid a copy of my book on the table and pushed it toward me. "May I have the famous author's autograph?"

"Nope," I said. You missed your chance. You should've been at the signing."

Her dour policewoman's eyes stayed flat and unamused until I broke and chuckled.

I scribbled my name and best wishes on the title page and nudged the book back towards her.

"Why did you disappear on me?" I asked.

She answered with a question of her own. "Is that dried blood over your eye?"

I dabbed at the sore spot. "A souvenir from my stumble in the parking garage."

"Wiggins told me."

I cocked a skeptical eyebrow. "You didn't answer me. You knew we might be in danger, and still you left. After Chris told you that the heckler might've been the shooter, you roared off on your motorcycle?"

She paused, brushing back a strand of hair. "I chased your heckler all the way down Haywood, across to Prichard Park, back around to Wall Street. I called for backup. We scoured the area but didn't find a trace. Now, we know why. She took a left on Walnut Street and entered the Rankin Street Garage. If I'd known she was the suspect before Chris told me, I'd have saddled her—"

"You mean his—"

"*His* ass," she said. "Might've saved his life to boot." She flattened her fingers on the table. "After I lost track of who we now know was Bucky Clement, dispatch called me PDQ. Third murder at Mission Hospital."

"The senator," I said. "Plemmons."

"Right, since I'd worked the other two, I had to shoot over there."

"Serial killer." I shrugged. "I saw the report on WLOS news. In a hospital that's supposed to save lives."

"Why are you questioning *me*?" she asked.

"Just trying to get the facts. I want to make sure my family is safe."

"Fair." She nodded once. "But I knew you were safe as soon as Wiggins called. We've been on your case all day. Forensics is doing a rush job on the bullets fired at your car and the semiautomatic found in Clement's purse." She swirled her coffee with a spoon, took a quick sip. "We're getting to the bottom of it. You need to relax, leave it to us, and focus on your wedding."

"I'll relax when I know what the hell is happening," I said. "Not before. Remember that couple I told you about? Frank and Tonya?"

Her cup hit the table with a dull clonk, and she sighed. "Yes. Why?"

Although I sensed her irritation building, I wasn't about to give up. And she wasn't the type to let go, either.

"They paid me a visit at the house today. Frank, armed with a hatchet, and Tonya packing heat. They blamed me for killing Bucky and promised revenge."

"My guys are on it."

The casualness in her voice made something hot and reckless flare in me. I swallowed it down and kept digging. "Who do you think did the hack job on Bucky?"

"Not sure yet. But forensics confirmed the hatchet was the murder weapon—the matted hairs on it came from his wig."

"I did some digging, too."

Her eyebrows lifted. "Oh?"

"Bucky's family are big-time doomsday survivalists. They moved outside of Asheville to get away from big city life and prepare for the end of time."

"I have the battle scar to prove it," she said.

"I know," I said. "I also know about your hospitalization after the showdown with Bucky's older brother—Vernon."

She stiffened, likely surprised maybe that I'd poked around in her past. "Okay," she added, "I know more about survivalists than I let on. But I don't like you vetting *me*."

"I'm the suspicious type," I said.

She scoffed. "Maybe a little paranoid, too?" The edge was returning to her voice.

"Leave the psychology to me," I said, "if you want me to leave the sleuthing to you."

"The way I see it," she said, voice edging sharper, "Bucky decided to collect the five grand for heckling you instead of taking you out on the interstate."

"Maybe," I said. "Maybe not."

She narrowed her eyes. "What's that supposed to mean?"

"It means heckling doesn't equal attempted murder," I said. "How do you know he was gunning for me? There's more to this story. I want to know who bashed in his head—and why."

She twisted her paper napkin into a tight braid. "The Clements are a menace. Their farm is a training ground for survivalist guerrillas from all over the country. You preach against guns. Your public persona is a denouncement of everything they stand for. No wonder they went after you. They probably sent Bucky to do the dirty work."

"I preach against bullies and fear-based fanaticism," I said. "And gun violence—not against guns. Resilience is the best protection. You don't need a gun."

"Right now, Doctor, you're preaching to the choir," she said. "But they don't think like you. When Armageddon hits, all they worry about is people like you and me—zombies—coming for their supplies."

"And they'll be ready and waiting," I said, my fingers tapping the tabletop with caffeine-driven fingers.

Phillips froze with her cup halfway to her mouth and glanced out the window. Sunlight played on her face, her eyes pooling in the light. She flipped her hair over one shoulder, exposing the edge of the scar.

"Did Vernon Clement give you that?" I asked, pointing a tender finger toward her left cheek.

She winced, drew back on, and let her hair fall into place. For a long minute, she stared past me, then leaned forward over the table, squinting at my purple V-neck sweater.

"What?" I asked.

She reached out and gently plucked a ladybug off my shoulder. "These little guys are everywhere. They eat aphids. Nature's pest control."

She sprang to her feet, banging her knee under the table and sloshing coffee over the rim of my cup. "Sorry," she said, rattled—and I knew it was my questioning.

She leaned outside and blew the insect from her palm into the air. When she slid back into the booth, she looked like she was trying to regain control of our conversation. "Your ten minutes are just about up," she said.

I remembered what the bookseller said about her being a paradox.

"You were telling me about the scar," I said, blotting the spill with my napkin.

"No," she said. Then corrected herself. "You were asking." She hesitated. "You sure you want to hear it? It's grisly."

"I get paid to listen," I said. "Today's your lucky day. You get a freebie."

She exhaled. "There was a time I couldn't talk about it. But I've replayed it a million times." Her gaze flicked toward the door. "Jim'll be here any minute. He hates when I dwell on it."

She swallowed and began.

"I'll give you the cliff notes...I was a Buncombe County deputy. We got disturbance-of-the-peace complaints—machine gunfire, explosions— morning to night. I went to the farm back in a remote holler deep in the north Asheville mountains. I had a warrant for the owner who hadn't paid property taxes in years."

"Yeah," I said. "I know the story. What about the scar?"

"Hold on." Her jaw clenched. "When I stepped out of the cruiser and neared the cabin, somebody fired at me. I dove behind the patrol car. An angry voice yelled for me to get off his land. I yelled back that I had a warrant. He fired again. I called for backup."

Her eyes glassed for a second, then sharpened. "I'd already shot through the window twice. I thought he was dead. When back-up arrived, we approached the house, went inside, and discovered Vernon Clement on the kitchen floor...." She faltered.

I lifted my hand in a small, urging motion. "Keep going."

"When I reached down to check for a pulse," she said, "he lunged at me with a knife with a ten-inch blade. He slashed me, cheek to lips, with a ten-inch blade." Her fingers touched the air beside her face, not quite touching her skin. "I shot him between the eyes. Then I slumped to my knees. Blood everywhere, vision clouded. A blur of blasting sirens. the ER. Stitches, then plastic surgery. Vernon died. I survived…barely."

"That's pretty much how the newspaper described it," I said, taming the fury rising up in me, that wanted to stand up in my body and start swinging. The story tugged loose an old memory of Johnny and Mama that I didn't want today.

I wiped a drizzle of coffee from the corner of my mouth. My eyes followed the line down her cheek. Time had faded the ragged incision into the pale color of bone. "I'm sorry for what he did to you," I said, and meant it.

She looked away, caressing the scar with the back of her hand. "I lived. But I have to watch my back to this day. Old man Clement has threatened my life more than once—for trespassing and killing his son."

I watched her face, saw the same anger I felt rise up, but underneath I sensed hurt. "Old Man Clement, huh?"

"A mean son-of-a-bitch," she said. "Mark my words. He'll tie you to Bucky's death the same way Frank did—because you were first at the murder scene. Both of us might have to watch our backs from here on out."

I didn't want membership in this fraternity. But I was in it anyway— tied to Bucky's murder, the way Eldred had tied me to Big Jake's death. Doomsdayers ran on emotions, not reason. They shot first and asked questions later. And I was done living my life looking over my shoulder. I'd done enough of that as a kid—walking on eggshells around an unstable father, never knowing what would set him off any minute.

No siree. I didn't roll that way anymore.

I was in over my head—way, way over.

Phillips's eyes widened slightly. "Here's Jim."

Jim Warren strode in with an upright gait and rigid body posture that screamed military training. When he reached our table, I extended my hand into his sweaty palm, with a firm grip.

"Surprised to see you here, Ein," he said. "Joining us for lunch?" He hugged Phillips and slid into the booth beside her.

"No," I said. "Just tying up loose ends with the sergeant." I cocked my head. "Say, Jim, what branch of service were you in?"

Jim's fingers smoothed his pinstripe suit. "Why do you ask?"

Phillips made a face and shifted her body.

"A few reasons," I said, leaning forward over the table and lowering my voice. "Someone tried to kill me. Bucky Clement got hacked to death. Just trying to put two-and-two together."

Jim shrugged. "Wish I could help you out, buddy."

"What kind of guns do you keep around your farm?"

He squirmed, eyes batting glances between Phillips and me. "Why do I feel like I'm on the witness stand?"

"Ein, please," Phillips said. "He's just eager to get to the bottom of things."

I lifted my hand. "You said you lived off the land. I'm trying to figure out where self-sustainability ends, and radicalism begins."

Jim exchanged another quick look at Phillips—the same one as before. "We have enough guns and ammo to protect us from wild boar, coyotes, and bears," he said briskly, then turned to Phillips. "How's your day been?"

I could take a hint. Message received. Topic closed. I stood, feeling like a big city intruder who'd leaned too hard on the wrong porch rail. "I better head out."

We said goodbye. Outside, I walked back to my car, shaking my head. For me, the matter was nowhere near closed. There was no world in which I could simply let Bucky's murder go, let the cops handle it, and focus on my wedding.

My life was at stake. All of our lives.

And something didn't add up with Jim—the way he brushed me off about his service, his guardedness about guns, the furtive glances with Phillips. Not just now. Back at the station, too.

I had plenty of suspicions about Phillips as well. The abrupt departure after Bucky's murder. The reluctance to meet with me. The way she dodged and bristled when I pressed for answers.

Interrogation or eagerness? Maybe a little of both, but I told myself I was in protection mode.

Sure—she was a cop, and Jim an attorney, both pledged to uphold the law. But cops and lawyers could be criminals, too. When someone suffered the kind of trauma Phillips did, it could often cause an explosive, unpredictable temper. Phillips was capable of anything. Or there could be simple explanations for their actions.

That's when it hit me.

I wanted the facts straight, I had to face Bloody Bones—this time wearing the skin of Old Man Clement.

Chapter Sixteen

I wound up the mountain to our rental house on Clampton Street. The dashboard clock blinked 5:30 p.m. The windshield wipers made loud smacks, smearing away a light drizzle, their rhythm somehow distant, as if I was hearing them from the bottom of a well. My mind kept circling the same dark drain: Bucky Clement's murder.

Fog and clouds cloaked the car, shrouding it in a wet hush. Daddy used to say cloudy skies were Mother Nature's way of shielding us from evil. I had a more profane version, but it still comforted me. After the drought, I couldn't help feeling relief and gratitude for the rain.

Just before our driveway, a young dark-haired man stepped from the roadside and flagged me down, yanking my wandering mind back to the present. He motioned for me to roll down my window. After everything that had happened, my first instinct was suspicion of the stranger. I almost kept going.

The rain had drenched his long black hair into stringy ropes. He must have been standing out there for a while.

When I finally eased to a stop, he swabbed the soggy locks from his eyes, latched wet fingers over the window frame, and hunched his head inside. In a heavy French accent, he said, "Pardon, but you are renting the house next door, no?"

"I am." I offered my hand. "Ein Pope. Is there a problem?"

He hesitated, drawing air sharply between his teeth, then replied, "I was going to your house to speak with you. I live up there." He pointed toward the ridge. "I hate to be a—how you say?—party pooper, but if your friends could keep down the noise, we would appreciate it."

Only then did I hear it—bass thumping the ground through the wet air, a dull heartbeat under the rain. I combed my fingers through my hair. "I do apologize…Mr.…?"

"François Moreau." He shook my hand. "My wife is an artist. Her studio is just there." He pointed to an upstairs corner room of the house. "We moved here for the quiet, for her to work."

"I'm sorry for the disturbance," I said. "It's not like my friends to be disruptive. They're probably having a little reunion. I assure you, it won't happen again."

"*Merci.* I would appreciate that."

After we said our goodbyes, he waved me away. As I moved forward, I looked up at his house on the ridge. Behind sheer curtains, a human form lurked in the shadows—watching. It peered down at me, then slipped out of sight.

In my rearview mirror, François stood motionless in the middle of the road, soaked through, his eyes tracking me all the way to the end of the street.

When I parked the car, I craned my neck at François. He was still there— mannequin-still, holding that long, fixed stare. Strange. But whatever curiosity I had left about the Frenchman shrank beneath a heavier weight: guilt for being gone so long—away from Chris, away from the wedding— and dread at the thought of walking into an eager house full of enthusiastic partiers.

I grabbed the wooden banister and clacked down the stone steps in the drizzle. The timber handrail groaned and creaked against my weight. The vibration of pounding music vibrated under my feet. Lady Gaga's voice belted out *Bad Romance*.

Before opening the door, I tried to put on a party face. While Chris focused on wedding prep, I'd been digging my heels deeper into the survivalist mire, barely sparing the wedding a thought.

I scraped my feet on the doormat, edging the unlocked door open. The deafening burst of music hit like a physical force. I expected to see Smiley,

Gigi, and her sisterfriends throwing their arms around each other, toasting drinks, and letting loose on the living room dance floor. I scanned the main circular room, and my mouth fell open in shock.

Instead—the room was empty.

Booming music boomed off the walls, ricocheting through the house.

Caught in a bad romance....

My teeth rattled from the blast—and from something colder rising beneath my ribs.

The open door banged against the doorjamb behind me.

I whipped my head around.

No one.

I arched my eyes toward the driveway. Only one other vehicle sat in the circular drive: Smiley's government van with *Suwannee County* emblazoned on the side—one of the perks of being the mayor of Whitecross, Florida.

I moved through the house, poking my head into each bedroom. Ceiling speakers hung in every room, Gaga stalking me as I called out, "Chris? Gigi? Smiley? Shirley? Anybody?"

I clamped my hands over my ears to soften the blast and took long strides down the hallway, trying to locate the stereo system.

Rah rah ah-ah-ah....

Every room was empty.

"What the hell?"

I ran back into the great room and jerked open the console beneath the wide-screen television.

Nothing but wires.

Want your bad romance....

I rounded the computer desk, opened a closet door, and there it was.

I punched the "off" button. The mother monster fell silent, but my ears still rang from her spirited anthem.

Somebody has to be home.

The sudden funeral-parlor quiet started to creep me out. I threaded back through the house again, slower this time, to make sure I wasn't losing it.

For a long minute, I stood freeze-framed, thoughts slipping away like drops of mercury. Shaking. My legs weakened. Lightning stitched the windows. Shadows zigzagged across the walls. The only sounds were from around me and inside my own body:

Peals of thunder rattling the windows.

Hard-hitting rain making gullies down the glass.

The thud of my banging heartbeat.

The *tick-tock* of an old grandfather clock in the hallway.

Then, a sharp, flat *thwack* of something smacking the entranceway floor where I'd left the door ajar.

I jerked my head toward the sound, sucked in a lungful of air.

And that's when I heard voices.

Chapter Seventeen

"Whew, it's raining buckets out there," Smiley said, flicking the wet off his silver hair.

The sisterfriends shuffled through the door behind him, dodging the downpour, shopping bags swinging from their arms like Christmas ornaments. Above us in the circular drive, I heard Gigi call, "Thanks for the lift," and moments later, she scuttled down the wide stone steps, bursting through the door and shaking off the rain like a soaked mutt.

"Where've you been?" I asked.

"Grabbed an Uber and went downtown for a bite," Gigi said, curling her wet arms around my neck. "Everybody'd warned us about how hard it is to find a parking spot in this town."

"The neighbors complained while you were gone," I said, irritation bleeding through my words. "Could we all make sure the music's turned off when we leave?"

Gigi frowned. "What music?"

"We haven't had music on the entire time we've been here," she said. And as she spoke, it dawned on me—Gigi barely listened to music, and she wouldn't have known where the stereo was anyway. Plus, Reba McEntire was more her speed.

With a nervous laugh, I asked, "Is this a Halloween prank?"

Dead silence.

"And another thing," I added, pushing on. "I asked that you lock the door when you leave, but it was left wide open—again."

"We locked the door and double-checked," Chris said, sliding off his wet shoes with his good hand, eyeing me with a peculiar look. "I was the last one out."

The exchanged glances between him and Gigi told me they weren't joking, causing me to sputter, "I don't understand…I—"

A crash of thunder made the floor shudder again.

Had Frank and Tonya come back?

"You okay?" Chris asked gently, nursing his injured arm, stepping closer, and placing a comforting hand on my shoulder.

I shrugged out of his touch. "Of course I'm okay."

The shrill, harsh tone of my voice startled me. Everyone's eyes were on me now, watching. Chris's lips tightened into a firm line. I shook my head, baffled. "I don't know what the hell's going on."

I retreated down the hall into our bedroom and stretched out on the bed, staring at the ceiling.

Chris followed and clicked the door shut behind him. "Hey. I approved the rings. They're beautiful. The jeweler's polishing them."

"Thanks for taking care of that," I said, in a half-hearted attempt to sound grateful. "You're sure you locked the doors?"

"Positive."

He rounded the bed, stood in front of the sliding-glass doors. Two shades of red blazed the room—the drenched autumn leaves tumbling down the mountain outside and the flush of his ballooning neck muscles, as he struggled to rein in what he called his *Asian temper.*

"Then how did—"

His body went rigid. "What?"

"Nothing."

He glared at me, his voice razor-sharp. "Do you think this could be one of those *brownouts* you write about? Maybe you need to practice what you preach?"

The word landed hard. I'd coined *brownout* to describe memory lapses caused by burnout. As much as it stung to hear it flung back at me, I knew better than to push him when he was like this.

"Probably." I conceded. "Just give me time to sort it out. I'll be fine for the wedding. I promise."

"We were supposed to tour the historic district today," he said. "Remember? Since we got to Asheville, all I've seen is your back."

"I was with Phillips, discussing the Clement case."

"Now you're a detective?" He plopped into a stuffed chair across the room. "Are you even sure you even want to get married?"

I propped myself on one elbow. "Chris…I…."

My hesitation sealed it. Chris bristled, his mouth set in a grave line. Hurt, flashing in his eyes, said my stammering had stretched out too long. Enough for it to look like work—yet again—coming between us.

"Of course, I want to get married. Our lives are at stake here."

"So is our wedding, Ein."

"There's just something I have to do."

He shot to his feet. "That's what I thought—more work. And this time it's not even *your* work. Why don't you let the cops handle it?"

I sat up on the side of the bed. "I wish I could, but—"

"We always said we could read each other without words," he said, walking to the door and gripping the doorknob. He turned back to me. "I knew at your book signing. I saw it in your eyes. You've got cold feet, and this case is your excuse."

His face hardened like he had decided. "Now I understand the meaning of being *wedded to work*. I can't compete with your mistress anymore."

"We can work this out," I said, grimacing, too late to take back the unholy word that tumbled out of my mouth.

"We? *Work* it out?" He laughed sharply. "Everything is work for you. *I* don't have anything to work out."

He opened the door, stepped into the hallway, then paused, swinging it closed halfway behind him, stopping short and opening it wide again. "You know, for a psychologist, you're one fucked-up dude."

I didn't want to see on his face the hurt I heard in his voice, but I nevertheless rolled over on my back, hitched my hands behind my head, and stared at him. I felt the same pain I saw in his eyes. All I could muster was more stammering. "Chris…I…."

He stood there a moment longer, not saying anything. When he finally spoke, his voice was tinged with quiet anger. "Something's different about you. I'm worried about your mental health."

The door clicked shut behind him.

That's when the fury hit. The doomsayers didn't need guns to terrorize people. They worked slowly, quietly—sowing doubt, turning loved ones against one another. They knew we would do their dirty work for them and do ourselves in.

* * *

Adrenaline launched me off the bed and out the front door. I slammed it behind me and sloshed through the downpouring rain, shoes sliding in the muddy drive. I needed answers, and this French dude was my only lead. Maybe he could tell me if he saw any strange goings-on around the house.

When I knocked on his door, I didn't know what questions to ask or answers to expect.

No answer.

I knocked harder, my hand landing heavy against the wood this time. Security cameras under the eaves of the house scrutinized me. Footsteps moved closer, then a chain slid through a metal trough on the inside. The sluggish door moaned as it opened partway, snapping the chain taut.

I stepped back, hands raised, careful not to threaten the young blond woman, peering from the shadows, eyeing me up and down through the slit. Only the left half of her face caught the light—and it was striking.

"Sorry to bother you," I said. "I'm staying next door, just down the mountain. I think someone may have broken into our place."

"Broken in?" she said, a thick French accent sharpening her words. "These things do not happen here."

"I spoke to your husband earlier," I said. "I wondered if either of you saw anything unusual."

Her eyes flew open. "My husband?"

"Yes. He stopped me on the road earlier." I pointed down the hill. "Down there. Said his name was François, that he lived here, that you're an artist. Told me the music was too loud. My apologies."

"Artist?" she scoffed, sloughing off the label and staring a hole through me.

"My husband didn't tell you such things."

"Yes, he did," I pressed. "You were looking out of the window down at me. Don't you remember?"

"Mon Dieu! My husband is dead. Has been for quite some time now. There is no long-haired Frenchman named François who lives here. Why do you invent such things?"

"But he said—"

"You must leave. You upset me, bringing this to my doorstep."

"I don't mean to upset you, Ma'am." I braced my hand against my head. "I'm just…shaken, is all."

"I do not know you. Surely you must call the cops, yourself. I cannot help you. Once more, please go."

"I'm sorry to disturb you," I muttered. "Good night."

Shock clung as I bounced back down the steps. The door snapped shut behind me.

I wanted to tell the others—especially Chris—but I was stuck between a rock and a hard place. After the Mama incident, he already thought I was losing it. If I told them a dead man stopped me in the rain to complain about music, they swore they never played, they'd surely call for a straitjacket.

The feelings of being back in Asheville began to sour into the clabbered taste of fear. But I had to put on my game face. I promised everybody a fun night out at *Babette's Feast*, a popular downtown nightclub. The Halloween dance started at nine. Somehow again, I had to get a grip and pull myself together—so everybody else could still have a good time.

Chapter Eighteen

We drove two cars to *Babette's Feast*. The sisterfriends rode with me in Smiley's van, while Smiley took Gigi in the rented Toyota. Chris wasn't feeling well and said he'd lie down for a nap and meet up with us around 9:30. Time alone with the women gave me a chance to prepare them for what lay ahead.

I told them to expect some women would actually be men, some men would actually be women, some men would be men, and some women would be women.

Wilma-May struggled more than the rest. "I'm downright confused," she said. "I think I'll just keep my mouth shut."

That'll be the day, I thought. A silent Wilma-May comes with a statute of limitations.

Standing in line to pay the cover charge, the *boom-boom* of the pulsing music and the pumping vibrations rising from the dance floor energized us. I caught myself tapping my foot. The sisterfriends' animated chatter and wide-eyed excitement—this being their first gay bar—proved contagious, and for the first time all day, my spirits lifted.

Wilma-May struck up a conversation with a patron behind her. "Well, aren't you a pretty girl," she said to a masked Liza Minnelli lookalike in a slinky, sequined, black floor-length gown.

"Why, thank you, dahling," the tall raven-haired beauty replied—in a deep husky James Earl Jones baritone.

A white-haired Wilma-May shot me a toothless grin and mouthed, *Oops.*

We paid our cover charge to a bald man with pierced ears. "It's eighties night," he announced, stamping our hands for re-entrance. His muscles rippled beneath a purple T-shirt that read: *Babette's Feast, Where Your Hunger Is Satisfied.*

We shoved open the door. Gigi and Smiley clamped their hands over their ears until they adjusted to the loud electronic dance music. Lit, carved pumpkins circled the huge open space of the restored warehouse. A neon skeleton flashed orange, green, and yellow against brick walls. From the ceiling, a massive, mirrored jack-o'-lantern rotated, scattering strobe-lit yellow squares across the walls and wooden dance floor.

The sisterfriends gaped—grinning, tapping their feet to the beat, bouncing, soaking it all in—Trump masks, zombies, gremlins, bloodsuckers, and Beetlejuice costumes shimmered and shifted under the swirling lights.

The air was thick with weed, spilled beer, and perfumed sweat. The dance floor churned a boiling cauldron of hip action and flesh in sexually provocative moves. Shirtless men, locked belly to belly, swayed on the dance floor to the tune of *Careless Whisper.* Women pressed lips to women. Men embraced women, hands roaming necks and breasts.

From a barstool, beer in hand, I chugged, watching the sisterfriends. I expected Wilma-May to think she'd landed in Sodom and Gomorrah. Instead, she was dancing—arms flailing joyfully—while Jackie, slick with sweat, hooted and twerked in a low squatting stance.

Nearby, a whirling Shirley spun in tight circles, clutching her bun in place as tortoiseshell clips—that usually anchored it high on her head—sagged at the neck. But that didn't stop her from circling a jubilant Gladys, twirling, her movements like a spastic happy dance.

I scoured the masked faces and half-clad bodies for Chris. But there was no sign of him.

Across the dance floor where the crowd thinned, I spotted Rudy Norris— dressed in army camouflage fatigues, an M-4 slung over his shoulder. *If only it were a costume,* I thought. I moved in his direction, but a new song dropped. The crowd surged, the dance floor thickened, and he vanished in the crowd.

I climbed the stairs toward the upstairs bar for a little quiet and felt eyes on me. I sensed someone following me. I whipped around and caught sight of a yellow hockey mask—Jason Voorhees. Like dozens of others, he wore combat fatigues. He leveled his gaze at me, then made an abrupt turn and headed downstairs, melting into the crowd.

I continued my climb, reminding myself about Phillips's warning not to jump at every little rustle in the bush. Packed bodies hung over the railings, clutching bottles of beer and shouting down to the dance floor. I elbowed through limbs and thighs crowding the staircase. Unfamiliar searching hands squeezed my biceps. The fruity vapor of amyl nitrite poppers wafted over me.

A Diana Ross impersonator lowered a vial from her nose, flicked her hair, and declared me *hot*, then swiped a long red fingernail across my cheek, hissing the sound of steam rising off heat. I rebuffed the touch and retreated.

I trotted back downstairs to the club's entrance, wound my way outside, and scanned the parking lot, hoping for a sign of Chris. A cluster of Vegas showgirls in feathered headdresses, Pennywise the clown, and someone clad in a Hazmat suit passed a joint, chuckling among themselves.

Eyes traveled the length of my body again.

When I turned to go back inside, the Jason figure was watching me from the doorway. In a hurried expression, he took a final drag from his cigarette, ground it under the heel of his black combat boot, then disappeared back inside. I followed him, trying to tell if his camouflage matched Rudy's—but the glare of the strobe lights made it impossible to tell.

Phillip's comment about me being paranoid took center stage in my mind. I tried to ignore the chill that lifted the hair on my arms. I strolled back inside, took a seat at the bar, and ordered another beer. The masked man beside me nudged a joint in my direction. I took a hit and nodded thanks. My eyes roved the room. One masked face blurred into another, but the Jason masquerader and Rudy were nowhere to be seen. *Maybe "Jason" was just coming on to me,* I reasoned.

The sound system boomed: "Ladies and gentlemen—it's time for *RuPaul's Drag Race!*" The bar and dance floor emptied as the masked crowd gathered around a stage at the far end of the warehouse. A Joan Rivers impersonator clicked her nails against the mic, imploring, "Can we talk?"

Perfect time to hit the restroom without having to stand in line.

A little woozy from the weed, I stood, tossed a few singles, and braced against the bar for a second to get my bearings. My legs still stiff from the fall in the garage, I descended the wooden stairs to the bottom level and entered the empty restroom. Standing at the urinal, I heard "Joan Rivers" quip, "My cousin Doris is so dumb, if she saw a sign that said *Wet Floor*, she would—" A mix of cheers, laughter, and applause erupted from the upstairs crowd.

On my way back up the narrow stairwell, I gripped the railing, moving slowly to keep my balance. Halfway up, I heard heavy breathing. Movement wavered at the top of the stairs. Swiping away the haze in my eyes, I traced a figure at the top.

The menacing Jason stood there—blocking the stairwell.

I stopped. My hand tightened on the railing.

A terrible fright gripped me.

I backed down a step, then froze.

In his left hand, he raised something large and round above his head. He hurled it right at me.

It barreled down on me fast.

Something heavy and dark crashed into my face and chest.

I tumbled backward in a flash of numbing pain.

Blood spurted.

I lay crumpled, dazed.

The electronic bass drum beat inside my head like a percussive thunderbolt. The wattage from the strobe lights blinded me.

My eyes rolled back in their sockets.

And everything went black.

Chapter Nineteen

A kaleidoscope of faces whirled through my head.

Mama on a motorcycle, aiming a gun straight at me.

Phillips—grim, scar-faced—her police cap pulled low over her brow.

A witch's hooked nose, greasy strands of hair flopping into piercing eyes.

A raised hatchet. Military camouflage. A bandanna-wrapped head.

A menacing Jason hockey mask riddled with holes.

And Bloody Bones—eyeless, flesh dangling from his frame like drooping sleeves on a choir robe.

Somewhere down deep, I searched for the thread binding the nightmarish images together. But before I could figure that out, more urgent questions popped to the surface.

Where am I? Am I alive or dead? Am I grown—or still a boy?

Sweat-soaked and delirious, I turned and twisted. Each movement sent a dagger of pain slicing through me. My mind clawed its way toward consciousness, still halfway back in the jungle—seven years old, running for my life.

A hand cooled my forehead. A familiar voice, filled with worry, whispered in my ear.

"Ein, can you hear me? Ein?"

A man's voice—deep, gravelly.

The sharp hiss of a woman's sniffles, her murmured words swallowed by the man's mumbled reply. A familiar stroke gently brushing my arm. I recognized the man's pleasant smell.

I fought to open my eyes against the stabbing light.

"Ein, it's me, Chris."

My tongue felt swollen, useless.

"C-h-r-is," I slurred. The thick sound was all I could muster.

"He's coming to," another voice said. "Ein, it's Grandma, son."

The door clicked open. Rubber-soled shoes squeaked across the floor.

"How's the patient?" an unfamiliar voice asked. "Looks like the nosebleed's stopped, and the swelling's gone down some."

"He's coming around," Chris said.

I wanted to see his face so badly, but for now, the solid comfort of his hand holding mine would have to do. I exhaled. My body loosened, melted into the cradle of crisp, warm sheets.

Without warning, a crushing tightness seized my right arm, ballooning until I feared my skin would surely split open. "His blood pressure's 130/90," the stranger said. "It's come way down from before."

I felt something cool slide inside my ear.

"Temperature's down, too. That's a good sign. The doctor's making rounds now—she'll be in shortly. Here's the call button. Let me know if you need anything."

"Thank you," said Chris.

The door creaked shut. The squeak of rubber-soled shoes faded down the hallway.

Fluttering my eyelids open, I squinted at the pinprick dots in the white ceiling squares. My head throbbed with a savage headache. I blinked, rubbed my temples, and took in the room. From the hallway, a blade of bright light sliced through the crack beneath the door. Smells of floor wax, antiseptic, and a slight scent of disinfectant permeated the air. Chris stood on one side of the bed; Gigi sat in a chair on the other side.

"Where am I?" I asked.

"The hospital, son," Gigi said. Her face was drawn, her eyelids droopy. "You've been here for three days. We're already into November."

"Three days?" My voice cracked. "What happened?"

Chris released my hand and rubbed the scabby wound on his arm.

"I see you got the bandages off," I said, clutching my head against another jolt of pain shooting through me.

"A few days ago," he said in a solemn gaze. "You had too much to drink and fell down the stairs at *Babette's Feast*. It was a nasty tumble. No broken bones, but the doctors say you're lucky to be alive."

"I…didn't…fall." Memory came stampeding back. I tried to sit up, gasping at the stabbing pain spearing my ribs, and squinched my face. "Someone threw something at me…flung it into my chest…on purpose…they were wearing a Jason hockey mask. And I wasn't drunk. I took one hit off a joint, but somebody must've spiked my drink."

Chris flicked his eyes at Gigi. She bit her lower lip but said nothing.

"Spiked your drink?" he asked.

"Yeah. Maybe Rudy Norris—that vet who came to my reading…I saw him there…." I scrubbed deep sleep from my face, muttering. "Or Frank and Tonya. They threatened me again when they barged into the house."

"What house?" Gigi asked. "When?"

Both their brows furrowed.

"You don't believe me."

"No, no," Chris blurted. "We…your chest is swollen with huge purple bruises. You obviously hit something…or something hit you."

Gigi said nothing, limiting her reaction to a sympathetic tilt of her head.

"You know I'm not a liar," I said.

"I know that, son." The tone in her voice carried a heavy weight. "Sergeant Phillips investigated. She said there were a few scuff marks on the wall, but no evidence of an attack. And not a single witness—even though the place was packed."

"Phillips?"

"You were so out of it, you lost your balance and fell," Chris said. "You crashed into the banister, or something, on your way down. That's her conclusion."

"*Her* conclusion? Dammit, why doesn't anybody listen to *my* conclusion? I fell because this Jason Voorhees character tried to kill me."

"Oh, son…." Gigi put her face in her hands and wept. Between gasps, she said, "Jason Voorhees is a character…out of a movie. He's not real."

"I know that," I said, exhausted. "I meant someone wearing a Jason mask. Not *actually* Jason." I sighed, feeling like I had been away too long in some strange land. "So, you know I'm not lying—but you still don't believe me. You just think I'm nuts."

Sadness rose in Chris's sunken eyes. "I heard there were lots of costumes Halloween night," he said. "Maybe you did see a masked person at the top of the stairs looking down at you, but you were so wasted…."

He curled his palm around my hand, but I flinched and pulled it back. "I was drugged, Chris." I flicked my eyes back and forth between the two people I loved most. "You of all people know I never drink myself blind—enough to get totally blitzed."

His black eyes avoided mine, and he spoke in measured words. "Lately, you've been going nonstop. Hardly sleeping. Obsessed by this Bucky character."

I nodded. "I've been a little overwrought, but—"

"It's not just the spill at Babette's," he interrupted. "You've been jumpy, easily startle. Even the sound of a yelping fox set you off. You've been on edge ever since the car shooting. Ever since you stumbled over the body in the parking garage."

"Of course I'm on edge. Who wouldn't be? I'm not *just* a psychologist. I'm a human being with feelings."

"I'm not a psychologist," he said, "but maybe everything that's happened on this trip is getting to you—plus the pressure of the wedding."

Gigi dabbed her nose with a Kleenex and slid onto the side of my bed, searching my face. "Son, Chris told me you saw your mama on a motorcycle, shooting at you. Then, you thought you saw Ada Lea peeping at you in the woods."

"*Saw,*" I said. "Not *Thought.*"

"Son," she said tenderly, "your mama's been dead since you were little. And Chris and I double-checked the rental house before we left. I know for a fact the music wasn't blasting. And the door wasn't left unlocked."

They exchanged glances, Chris shaking his head in agreement.

Through pleading eyes, I looked at Gigi. I wanted to scream, "If you don't believe me, ask François, the neighbor, that French guy. He'll back me up." But he didn't exist either, according to his so-called wife.

Gigi and Chris swapped glances again. Chris spoke in a somber, measured tone. "Phillips talked with the woman next door. Said you banged on her door and told her François, her husband, had asked you to turn down the music. The woman verified there is no such person, that her husband has been dead for years."

"What?" I tried to raise myself off the bed, winced from the pain, and collapsed back into the pillows. "Can't you see? I'm being set up. They're trying to make me look deranged, to destroy my credibility."

"They? Who, son?" Gigi asked softly.

I faltered, then sighed. "Can't you two see?" I examined their faces. "Somebody's trying to make it look like I'm crazy. I'm being set up."

"When they first brought you into the hospital, you were mumbling something about Bloody Bones." Gigi put her palm against my forehead, eyeing me with a warm smile. "I remember when you were just a little thing, scared to death of that monster in the woods. I'd be snapping pole beans on the back porch, and you'd scramble up the steps, choking on your words, saying Bloody Bones was after you. I'd grab you up in my arms and hold you real tight and rock you until you fell asleep."

"Yeah, I remember." I tried to smile, but the bruised ribs and despair muzzled me.

"The hospital staff said you mentioned something about Jason and a mask. We finally realized you were talking about a movie. Hon, neither the sisterfriends, nor Smiley, nor I recollect a Jason costume that night."

"There were lots of costumes you didn't see, Gigi. There were hundreds of people there, and you guys didn't mingle like I did. I was searching for Chris, inside, outside, upstairs and down, hoping he...e" I turned toward him. "Hoping you would show up."

"I mentioned the mask to Sergeant Phillips. She checked it out," Gigi continued. "The manager stated emphatically there wasn't a Jason costume at the club that night."

My pulse raced. "What the...? You believe none of this happened?"

"You've banged your head in two hard falls since we've been in Asheville," Gigi said, "I wonder if—"

"What are you saying?" I interrupted.

"The MRI was clear, according to the doctors," Chris said. "Everything looks okay."

I didn't appreciate being treated like a whack job by the two people closest to me. Why wouldn't they listen to what I was telling them?

I inspected Chris's face. "What happened to our trust, our dedication to each other?"

Chris stood abruptly, the back of his legs toppling the metal chair backwards onto the floor with a loud clang. "I can't take this anymore." His deep, black eyes snapped a bluish color, and his golden skin flushed red as he pointed his finger at me. "After your total lack of interest in our wedding and your *work infidelity*—isn't that what you call it in your book, Dr. Pope? When work becomes more important than the people you love? And you have the nerve to flip this around and question *my* trust and dedication?"

Gigi rounded the bed, grabbed his shoulder. "Chris, don't. He needs our love and understanding."

"Maybe I'd like a little of that, too," Chris said.

I glared at them both, fuming myself. "You're talking about me like I'm not even in the same room." My eyes scanned Chris for answers. "What happened to us? We were never like this before."

Chris, top-heavy with anger, bent his head forward, taking a deep breath and speaking in a soft, controlled voice. "What happened is I let it go on, living in a fool's paradise, thinking one day things would change. Now I see that's never going to happen."

He smacked my car keys on the bedside table with his palm. "Your car's in the visitor's parking deck. First level. You'll see it as soon as you walk in."

Without another word, he turned and walked out of the room.

I slunk back against the pillows, staring at Gigi for an explanation—anything to help me make sense of this. "Gigi, please do me a favor. Check the frame outside by the front door. You'll see the cut Frank made in the wood. He very likely could be the attacker on the stairs, too."

"I'll do that, son." Wagging her head, Gigi looked heartbroken. "I promise." She sighed. Her hands went limp, falling into her lap with a heavy plop, as if to say *I give up*, hitting me like an ominous foreboding.

I'd never been so misunderstood, felt so alone. I couldn't decide which was worse—that the people I loved didn't believe in me or that, for some reason, Phillips had stacked the deck against me.

Combing fingers through my hair, I looked beyond the hospital window, far out into the darkness. The majestic mountains loomed, and the roads below curled far off into the distance, headlights winding like rope lights through the streets.

I couldn't say exactly what lay in waiting amid those twisted roads, but I knew something wicked was coming for me—not Bloody Bones. I knew it wasn't really Bloody Bones. But it was just as deadly—this time, more real.

The knot in my chest reminded me not to be afraid. If I could survive Bloody Bones—if I could survive Johnny Devillers—I could survive any-thing.

I was determined to find out who the attacker was, whether anybody else believed me or not. I planned to make whatever went down next happen *for* me, not *to* me.

Whatever I was searching for was looking for me, too. Once we found each other, it would complete the circle.

As soon as I got out of this place.

Chapter Twenty

After Gigi left, a nurse entered my hospital room, carrying a meal tray. Her bleached-blonde hair stuck to the sweat on her forehead. "Here's our dinner," she said, crossing the room in squeaky, rubber-soled shoes.

"Our?" I asked. "Are you eating with me?"

She giggled. "No, silly. It's *your* dinner." She slid the meal onto the rolling bedside table and wheeled it snug up against my chest.

"What all's wrong with me?" I asked.

"Bruised ribs, busted lip, bloody nose, and black eye." She brushed her hands down the front of her blue scrubs and primped her golden hair in the mirror above the sink.

"We're lucky, though. That fall could've done serious damage, a concussion, broken neck or ribs. The imaging shows nothing broken. The doctors said you should be discharged tomorrow."

"That's a relief." I noticed the security badge hanging backward around her neck. "By the way, what's your name?"

"Missy," she replied. "It's probably a good thing you're here."

My brow wrinkled. "How come?"

"With the riots going on."

"What riots?"

She blinked. "That's right, you've been out of it. The new legislation to ban assault rifles and military-style weapons. People marching in the streets with their AK-47s, claiming they're protecting their Second Amendment rights. There was a firebombing in Atlanta, ransacked neighborhoods outside

Charlotte. Three trash-can explosions overnight in Chicago, St. Louis, and San Antonio. A woman killed in Minneapolis, blocking ICE with her car."

I cocked my head. "Were they connected?"

"I don't know." She reached for her remote and pointed it at the TV. "Let's turn on CNN." The television anchored high in the corner flickered to life. Wolf Blitzer's commanding voice filled the room.

"Cities across the country are on high alert after a spate of coordinated attacks by a group calling itself the United Survivalist Army or U.S.A. Authorities are describing them as homegrown terrorist cells. Churches and public buildings have been graffitied with the slogan *Prepare to Survive or Die*. A backpack containing a homemade pressure-cooker bomb was discovered this morning at a New York City train station. After a knife attack at a Minnesota mall, the suspect reportedly shouted, 'Prepare to survive or die,' before being killed by police."

A somber Blitzer leveled his gaze straight into the camera.

"Ladies and gentlemen, these are not just isolated outbursts. They appear to be well-organized and carefully executed escalations across the country. These groups have long expressed a goal of overtaking the federal government. In fact, I'm just receiving a report that the FBI is aware of threats made to government buildings, including in Washington, D.C. Stay with us as we continue our coverage. We'll be right back."

A camera panned, showing footage of an enraged mob tearing through Baltimore stores with assault rifles and a man returning home from work, mowed down in the street by an angry mob, then set on fire. A rioter yelled, "People have to die so the rest of us can be free."

I shook my head. "Survivalists are a dangerous bunch."

Missy looked up from the foot of the bed, where she was folding a blanket. "There's nothing wrong with responsible preparation. The evening news never warned us about the housing collapse in 2008, did it? With all that's going on—water shortages, gas shortages, and forest fires—you never know what's coming next. Sometimes you have to take matters into your own hands." She smiled proudly. "My husband and me are storing water and nonperishable food good for twenty-five years in case of emergencies."

She drew closer, rolled the bed table to my chest. "Speaking of food, we haven't touched our meal."

The smell of the dark meat and instant mashed potatoes swimming in gravy, a carton of whole milk, and a slice of white bread turned my stomach. I rolled the table to the bedside.

"I'm not eating that."

"Don't we like country-style steak?"

"I love steak—real steak—but even a filet mignon wouldn't satisfy my appetite right now."

"Let me cut it up." She moved toward me, eyes darting toward the door. "That'll make it easier."

I swatted at her hand. "No, really. I'm not hungry."

"We need our strength." She persisted, wheeling the bed table back and pinning it tightly against my chest.

"We?" At first, I chuckled, then shooed her away again.

She giggled again. "*You* need *your* strength."

"Why are *we* being so insistent?" I mocked, pushing against the table, tightening against my ribs. "I'm not three. I'm quite capable of cutting up my meal."

She lifted the steak knife, reaching toward me. "We've been through a lot." She backhanded yellow tresses of hair that flopped in her eyes. "Let me help."

I grabbed her wrist, noting the strong resistance in her grip, and shoved it away, an uneasy feeling nagging at me.

Her eyes glared, face reddened. She looked at me with a beguiling smile, spoke with a razor-sharp edge. "Oh yeah," she said. "There are lots of stubborn patients like you."

Without another word, Missy turned away and stormed out. The soles of her shoes screeched through the doorway, and I heard the faint squeaks fade down the hallway.

Lying there listening to her retreat, I realized what was niggling at me: news about a serial killer targeting hospital patients. Knowing that the victims had been government officials was cold comfort. I vowed to be on high alert for the remainder of my stay.

The television was still blaring. A CNN correspondent in Philadelphia interviewed a bearded survivalist hoisting what looked like an AK-47. "Half the population pays no taxes and depends on aid from the federal government," he shouted. "And now they're telling us we can't carry guns! Hell no!"

The man raised his assault rifle in the air and fired a few rounds.

What's happening to our country?

I grabbed the remote and clicked off the TV, maneuvering my body deep into the stiff, scratchy sheets, trying to shake loose the disturbing images of the newscast and confrontation with "Nurse Ratched."

A hazy confusion clawed at my brain. The hospital room dissolved into mixed, foggy daydreams, replaced by rougher images from another time.

A tsunami of memory crashed over me.

* * *

One overcast summer day when I was seven, my best friend Alvin Dukes and I set out on a familiar adventure toward the banks of the Suwannee River. A thick stand of live oaks, laced with Spanish moss, separated my house from the water's edge.

Bloody Bones territory—though I didn't know then.

We began our trek without a care in the world. Slapping my arm around his shoulder, we trudged the beaten path arm-in-arm through the dark jungle. We plucked blackberries and popped them in our mouths. We caught June bugs in our small fists, tied string to their legs, and watched them buzz in circles like kites above our heads.

Even on the brightest day, the thick canopy shaded the forest floor. That particular day was cloudy, the jungle unusually dark.

Alvin dangled the string in front of him, wig-wagging his head, tracing the flight path of his airborne June bug. "My mama says the police were at your house. Told me she heard a ruckus. Says your mama and daddy were at it again."

Heat flooded my neck, and my face grew hot, shame turning me scarlet. "Cops had the wrong house," I lied, turning in circles to keep up with my high-flying June bug.

From the corner of my eye, I saw Alvin's forehead scrunch. I could tell he knew I was lying. Instead of pressing me, though, he went along with my story and changed the subject.

"My granny says Bloody Bones lives in here. Says he eats young'uns."

"I ain't afraid," I lied again, knowing Granny Dukes was never wrong.

"Granny says we shouldn't never come in here alone 'cause he roams the woods looking for fresh meat."

"Bloody Bones?" I shivered. "Yeah, Daddy says he's outside my bedroom window at night to get me to stay in bed. Says he looks like a skeleton, bloody meat hanging from his bones, sharp claws to slice you with. Says if I get out of bed, he'll eat me. Never said nothin' about him livin' in the woods, though."

"Granny says he does, and she'd know. Told me he only eats young'uns—he don't like grown-ups 'cause they don't taste tender. So, if you come in here with your mama or daddy, you're okay. But if you come in here with just you, you gonna get eat up."

Alvin's family lived in a tribe—a block of five houses that ran in a strip perpendicular to the sandy road where our house stood. Granny Dukes was the matriarch of the clan. All us kids ran to her when we got hurt playing. More times than I could count, when I played hide-and-seek barefoot in the grass, she put her snuff spit on my beestings. And it worked—took the sting out and kept swelling down. Word was, she could stop bleeding by citing a Bible verse. If Granny Dukes said Bloody Bones lived in the woods, it must be true.

"Ever seen him?" I asked.

"No, but sometimes you can hear him whisper if you get real still." He put his arm out in front of me like a gate. We paused. A grasshopper flitted across the worn trail. We listened to the wind hiss through the treetops, bending the creaking live oaks, crackling their limbs.

I swatted absentmindedly at a bumblebee buzzing my ear, fixated on the sound of a woodpecker's jackhammer drill.

Every now and then, a twig would snap, and Alvin would say, "Hear that? That's him."

His crooked eyes held wild, wide anticipation. People made fun of Alvin, called him "cockeyed," but I didn't care about his crossed eyes. He had a good heart, liked me, and that's all I cared about. Plus, we had fun scaring each other.

"Hear what?" I asked.

"Shh...that sound. Listen."

"All I hear is the wind in the trees," I lowered my voice to a whisper. "And my June bug buzzing."

"Yeah, but if you listen real hard underneath the swish in the trees, you can hear something else." His eyes skimmed me, a smile twitched on the edge of his mouth.

The wind picked up. A light breeze carried the faint scent of honeysuckle.

I cocked my head. "Oh, now I hear it."

Alvin blinked hard, his freckled face impaled with shock. "You do?"

"Yeah. I hear a low howling."

"You do?" His mouth hung open, his cowlick stood at attention, fingers fanned, ready to take flight.

The ground rumbled with thunder. "Hear that?" I asked. A bolt of lightning lit the treetops. From the shadows behind us came the crunching of leaves, a deep groan.

"We gotta get the hell out of here," I said.

"You said a bad word." Alvin jerked my faded T-shirt in the direction of the river.

"We can't go that-a-way." I pleaded. "Water draws lightning. We'll get struck dead for sure." I nodded toward the groaning sounds. "We gotta get back home."

"You crazy?" Alvin's trembling finger pointed toward the hollow moaning. "I ain't going t'word it."

"We got to."

"Then let's make a run for it."

"Heck no. If we run, we'll make too much noise," I said. "And he'll eat us for sure. We have to tiptoe, so he don't hear us."

We startled at the sounds of thrashing in the thick bushes, the rustling of something being dragged through the brush.

I froze.

My heart thumped out of my chest.

Alvin bit his bottom lip.

I shoved away terrifying thoughts of being gobbled alive by Bloody Bones. I knew this was our only chance of survival. I took a deep breath and stomped hard through the forest, toward the moaning and thrashing.

I put one slow foot carefully in front of the other. Alvin tagged behind, his hand on my back. We hunched our small bodies, as if our bent posture might effectively hide us from the clutches of the monster.

We tiptoed until we neared the rustling bushes. Alvin started a nervous whistle until I jabbed him in the ribs.

"Shut up," I hissed. "You wanna get eat up?"

We arrived at the place where the dreadful racket grew loudest, the bushes shaking in a convulsing rhythm.

A bald, scabby head rose from a clump of kudzu.

Large, bloodshot eyes darted back and forth.

A jittery hand lunged.

Broomstick legs tottered.

Alvin took off, hooting and hollering, leaping high off the ground as he ran. I tore behind him, but not before recognizing the familiar figure. I ran, glancing back over my shoulder, wondering why he was sprawled in the bushes.

I sprinted hard, hurtling over fallen logs and tangled brush, gasping against resistant tree branches snaring my hair and tearing at my cheeks. Hateful blackberry briars slashed my legs as if, once again, Daddy was beating me for doing something wrong.

Darkness hovered.

A slow drizzle started, growing quickly into a stinging rain, beating me hard with a relentless force. As lightning snapped overhead and thunder rattled under my feet, I ran faster, hitting the wet ground harder with each step.

We were running for our lives, running from our fears. Only difference was, I'd seen the boogeyman.

What had the neighborhood drunk—Johnny Devillers, my scabby-headed daddy—been doing splayed in the bushes, nursing a bottle of liquor?

I ran and ran until my eyes sharpened on the distant porch light bobbing in front of me, a flutter of questions jabbing my stomach.

What would I find at home?

Would everything be quiet and calm?

Or would all hell break loose?

Late into the evening on that muggy summer night, long after the rain had stopped, the sweltering heat lingered at the corners of the house. When I turned to face the open window, the rusty springs under my mattress squeaked, and a spear of moonlight shot across my pillow. The attic fan drew dead air out of the house, pulling a cool breeze through the screen. Most nights I had to ignore the sounds of scraping chairs, breaking glass, and shuffling feet, but that night was quiet.

That night, Bloody Bones slept in the woods.

Above Mama's lonely whimpers, I savored the coolness against my face, the sweet smell of honeysuckle, and the soothing calls of cicadas and whippoorwills.

My might had been tested. I had faced the bloody beast that inhabited the forest, the same monster that lived in my house. I had proof that Bloody Bones existed, from old marks and new wounds, the bruises on my face, the cuts on my legs. With my own two eyes, I had seen him for the creature he was.

Now it would be my duty to wear my strength and courage, bear my scars, and remain vigilant of danger lurking all around me.

Chapter Twenty-One

In the early hours of morning, I awoke to a creaking sound, sensed eyes upon me. A figure stood in the doorway of my hospital room, cradling a potted plant. The pointed toe of a black stiletto heel slowly eased the door open.

Strutting across the shiny floor, Phillips scrunched her nose and frowned at the pungent plate of dry food. She slid a pot of burnt-orange mums onto the bedside table as she spoke. "Your grandmother called me last night," she said. "Told me you'd come around. I thought I'd pop in for a visit."

I stared at her in silence.

She shrugged out of a navy-blue overcoat and flung it on the end of the bed, revealing a sleek red dress beneath. Dragging up a chair, she dropped beside me, concern tattooed on her face.

"I was worried about you," she said. "Glad you're feeling better." She rubbed her hands together and leaned her head sideways, expensive earrings dangling from her lobes. "I called your brother Bobby-Cy, like I promised. He asked me to keep him updated on how you're doing. His nervous voice showed how much he cares about you."

"Glad somebody does." I glared out the window. Ice-cold ran through my veins like saline dripping in my IV.

She blinked at my attitude. "What's wrong? Still feeling bad, huh?"

"I've never felt better." The sarcastic answer landed hard. My eyes didn't meet hers, and I wasted no time on pleasantries. "Sergeant Phillips—Mary Phillips, Motorcycle Mary—whoever you are these days—why did you tell my family there was no evidence of an attacker at *Babette's Feast* and that

François Moreau died years ago?"

"Because…." She hesitated at first. "Because it's the truth."

"I think you're lying."

She winced but looked at me dead-on, her voice controlled. "The day after your fall, my officers and I paid a visit to the bar. According to the owner, the staff judged the best Halloween costumes that night. Said they judged every outfit. He swears there wasn't a Jason costume in the house. Said he'd remember—*Friday the 13th* was one of his all-time favorites."

"Who was the owner you spoke to?"

"A Mr. Norris."

"Rudy Norris? The vet with PTSD who asked for help at my book launch?"

"That's him. I thought he looked familiar."

"You believe the story of an unstable man—possibly tied to Bucky Clement's murder—over me?"

"He's a shady character," she admitted, "but he's not connected to Bucky's death. Mr. Norris speculated you probably had too much to drink and wandered off. Said your 'posse,' as he put it—your grandmother and her friends—were searching for you after you staggered from the bar. He gave us permission to search the premises. We scoured the place but found nothing to indicate an assault. And, according to your doctor, the bruises on your chest resulted from the fall itself."

"Nothing you've said proves that I wasn't attacked."

"That's true." She gave me a quizzical look. "But nothing you say proves you were. Any witnesses?"

"No. Everybody was at the other end of the dance floor watching the Joan Rivers drag show. That's when I hit the restroom to skip a long line."

"I see."

"What about François Moreau?" I asked.

"I visited Moreau's home on Clampton Street. Had over an hour's conversation with his widow. She was nice enough to take time out from packing."

"Packing?"

"They're moving."

"What? Where?"

"She said somewhere quieter. I didn't ask where, and she didn't specify. But she said you frightened her—pounding on her door, claiming her dead husband stopped you in the road, complaining about loud music."

"Bullshit!" I tried to sit up, but my body wouldn't cooperate. When I rose, a shock wave of pain shot through me. My eyes scanned the room for my clothes and car keys. I wanted to hop out of bed and drive straight to Moreau's house to confront her again.

I lowered back into the pillows and asked, "Why do I get the feeling you're hiding something?"

"Hiding something?" She looked genuinely offended. "I'd be crazy to risk my career covering up something like that?"

"Oh no," I said coolly. "Let's get one thing straight." I wagged a finger at her. "Thanks to you, everyone thinks *I'm* the crazy one. But I know what happened. Somebody's trying to frame me."

"Why would you include me in that?" she asked. "I'm simply stating the facts. And for your information, I did some digging and located François Moreau's death certificate."

I groaned. "What about Bucky Clement? Are you even trying to find his killer? You don't even know for certain he was the motorcycle shooter. Did you analyze the photos Chris sent you?"

Her eyes shot up. "What photos?"

"The motorcycle license plate. Fuzzy, but readable. He said he would send them to you."

"I didn't receive any photos from Chris."

How convenient for her, I thought, *given the fact that several damning letters on the license plate matched hers.* But I kept that to myself. I didn't want to show my hand on that score.

"Look, here's what we *do* know," Phillips said, visibly frustrated, trying to remain calm. "Forensics did a blood spatter analysis of Bucky's blood. The cast-off patterns show he was bludgeoned four times. Ballistics matched the bullets in the semiautomatic in his purse and the bullet holes in your Land Rover. That confirms he was the shooter—and likely the prowler."

"But we still don't know who killed him," I said evenly, leveling my steel-eyed gaze at her. For all I know, *you* murdered him."

She jerked her head back. Her hand flew to the scar on her cheek as if I'd slapped her. "Now you *are* sounding unhinged."

"You had a motive."

She frowned, apparently mystified by the accusation. "What motive?"

"Retribution," I said, my eyes narrowing on her scar. "For what Vernon Clement—Bucky's brother, did to you."

The color drained from her face, turning it ashen. "That's absurd."

"Chris saw you chase after Bucky. You claim you ran straight down Haywood Street. I say maybe, just maybe, you turned at the corner of Haywood and Walnut, chased him into the garage. Next thing I know, you hop on your Harley, roar off into the sunset, and I trip over his body."

She allowed me a patronizing smile. "Can we be serious for a minute?"

"Sure," I said. Here's serious. Somebody has tried to kill me—not once but twice. Maybe three times if you count the Copperhead. After Bucky's death, you told me your officers had everything under control, to enjoy the wedding festivities and time with my family. Now, the wedding's canceled, I'm lying in a fucking hospital bed, and my family thinks I'm psychotic. Is that serious enough for you?"

"I'm truly sorry this hasn't worked out for you," she said. "But I've investigated high and low to confirm your story about the loud music, Moreau's complaining dead husband, your fall, and the Jason mask. I haven't found a shred of evidence. No one, including your family, Mrs. Moreau, your doctor—even the folks at *Babette's Feast*—can verify any of it."

"I know," I said quietly.

"I placed twenty-four-hour police surveillance at the hospital entrances. Patrols on every wing of this building. I'm working your case and the hospital killer case around the clock. We believe they may be connected." She stood and grabbed her coat. "In fact, I have a meeting with hospital administration. So, if you'll excuse me."

She slipped on her coat. "Hope you get out of here soon." She paused, absentmindedly caressing her scar with the back of her hand. "There's one more thing."

"What?"

"When your grandmother called last night, she said you mentioned a gash by your front door made by some dude named Frank. She checked it, said the wood was perfectly smooth. As a favor to her, I swung by and examined it myself. There was no cut in any of the wood around the door."

Phillips locked eyes with mine—hard, cold, accusatory. "You're making matters worse sending us on wild goose chases." She pulled the collar tight around her shoulders as if to muffle any further discussion of the matter, then turned, clicking the door shut behind her.

At first, I was floored. Then, I was steaming. Somebody was working hard to make me look insane. The irony wasn't lost on me how the tables had turned. Phillips's inaction had forced me into playing cop. She still had no explanation for why Bucky Clement tried to kill us in the car chase—if, in fact, it *was* him—or any clue about who else might be coming for me.

"These things take time," she'd said. "We're working on it."

But when you feel like a sitting duck, time is a luxury you don't have. Moving forward, if the police couldn't protect me—or uncover the truth of who was after me—I'd have to track them down myself.

Chapter Twenty-Two

No more delays. Itching to find out what was going on, I grabbed my cell phone and Googled Mrs. Moreau's phone number. Every muscle in my body ached. If I moved too fast—or sneezed—pain flared through my ribs, but my anger dulled the aches, making it easier to bear.

I punched in the number. After several rings, a woman answered in a thick French accent.

"*Bonjour.*"

"May I speak to Mrs. Moreau?" I asked.

"Please, may I ask who is calling?"

"Dr. Ein Pope."

A long pause. "Ah. You again, Dr. Pope? What can I do for you?"

"I need to talk to you."

She cleared her throat. "I thought I made it clear—"

"Mrs. Moreau, I've been hospitalized. Somebody tried to kill me."

A beat. Then: "I'm very sorry. But why do you keep bringing your problems to my doorstep?"

A man's voice murmured in the background, asking, "*Qu'est-ce que c'est?*" followed by Mrs. Moreau covering the receiver and launching into a muffled interchange with someone. My French was too rusty to follow more than the tension in a half-heard conversation.

"Hello?" I said.

"*Excusé moi.* One moment, Dr. Pope."

More muffled voices.

She came back on the phone. "Dr. Pope, I apologize for the interruption. We are in the process of packing, and I had to give instructions to my assistant."

"Moving?" I prompted.

"This is correct. I am quite busy now. If you will excuse me—*Ciao*."

A click on the other end, and the line went dead.

I lowered the phone, seething. Mrs. Moreau had painted me as unstable, planted doubt about my sanity, and now she was skipping town.

We'd see about that.

* * *

By noon, I sat on the side of the hospital bed, getting help dressing before discharge. Thankfully, shift change had brought me a nurse with firm boundaries and a calm presence. She carefully threaded my arms through the sleeves of a loose-fitting shirt.

A knock at the door.

A bobbing head peered through the crack in the door. Jim Warren stretched his head farther inside. "Hey, Ein. Mind if I come in?"

"Jim, what a surprise."

The nurse handed me my shoes, saying, "I'll come back in a few minutes."

I thanked her, and she slipped out.

"Mary told me she was stopping by," Jim said. "Thought I might catch her."

"She just took off. Said she had a meeting." I buttoned my shirt. "Come on in. Take a load off."

Jim rounded the bed, pulled up the empty chair beside me. "She's been burning the midnight oil with these two cases," he said. "I hardly see her anymore, unless I can catch her for lunch. I shot over here, hoping to grab a bite with her in the cafeteria."

"You're either a brave soul or a deeply committed fiancé if you're willing to chance hospital food."

We shared a chuckle, then his lips turned grim. "She told me about your accident. You look pretty banged up. You okay?"

"Oh yeah," I said. Unsinkable."

"Well, maybe my good news will cheer you up."

"Good news?"

"I looked into that Frank character you asked about. Name's Frank Mallory—goes by Red. Probably why I didn't connect it before. I've seen him around at some of our community sustainability meetings. And a few times at target practice."

"Target practice?"

"A shooting range over in Leicester."

Jim slid awkward fingers through his slick black hair, clearly gauging my reaction, concerned maybe I'd find a shooting range offensive. "Rough-looking guy. Mid-thirties. Freckled face. Scraggly red beard—real Jeremiah Johnson vibe."

"That's him."

"He's part of a group calling themselves *Gawkers*. Always carries a gun. Got a pretty long rap sheet, too—petty burglary, assault, public intoxication, and such. Never goes anywhere without a menacing-looking chick named Tonya Clausen. Big lips, nose ring. She's pretty much under his thumb 24-7, does whatever he says. They live in a doublewide off Leicester Highway, a few miles from us. Got a storage shed packed with emergency food and supplies."

I exhaled. "Frank Mallory and Tonya Clausen, huh? It's my estimation they…*she* might've carried out the assault on the interstate. Either that or the cowards got Bucky Clement to do their dirty work. They're furious over his murder, probably because they lost their puppet."

Jim nodded. "Red obsesses over the end of days and how we'll survive. At sustainability meetings, he makes some pretty peculiar claims. Says we need to take down the unprepared now to keep them from stealing our resources when the end comes. Tonya, right there by his side, parroting everything he says. Claims if SHTF lasts more than two years, we're all dead."

I cocked an eyebrow. "So, you know about SHTF?"

His eyes flickered—too quick, the face of someone who'd let out more than they had meant to. "I just know *of* it." His voice dropped to a whisper. "Stands for 'Shit Hits the Fan.' That's all I know."

Few people, except for insiders, knew about SHTF. It was survivalist code for the day when the apocalypse comes. Silence stretched between us as I studied him. "So," I said, "are your sustainability folks hardcore survivalists?"

"Oh, hell no." Jim flapped a dismissive hand. "There's a difference between sustainers and survivalists? What survivalists like Red call 'the end,' we sustainers call a power outage. A water shortage. A dangerous weather system. We believe in community—like one big family sticking together in time of need in a crisis. Like folks used to do on the farms back when I was a kid."

I nodded. "Yeah, I remember that, too."

But as he spoke, I sensed him backpedaling. Distancing himself from Frank and Tonya.

"Problem is," Jim continued. "When Red stands up to speak, he rambles on about how we'd better stop depending on government and start stockpiling guns for Armageddon. He's online with survivalist cells around the country. Sharing preparedness tips, survival gear, and spreading the word about prepping tactics."

"It's worse than that."

Jim cocked his head. "How so?"

"He's actively communicating with prepper cells around the country, all right, but Frank's not just sharing. He claims he and thousands are secretly planning an armed rebellion against the government of the United States, an attack on Washington, D.C."

"Doesn't surprise me. I'd steer clear of Red if I was you. You don't want to get on his bad side. But he's more a braggart than anything. Puffing up like a toad makes him look more important than he is. I wouldn't take him seriously. He's more bark than bite. Not smart enough to pull off something of that magnitude."

"I'm not convinced," I said.

Jim looked down at his buzzing phone. "Ah, a text from Mary. She's out of her meeting." He stood, offered his hand. "Glad I ran into you, Ein."

"Thanks for stopping by." I nodded and smiled.

It was impossible to ignore his burdened look as he reached for the doorknob. The weight in his slumped shoulders shrunk his normal upright posture. Worry etched deep lines across his face.

I slipped on my shoes, replaying his comment. *Target practice.* The description of his fifty-acre farm I'd pulled up online. It sounded like a prepper's paradise. And his knowledge of survivalist codes like SHTF was more than casual. He seemed to know a lot more about survivalists than the average person. And why would he drop by on a man he barely knows?

Maybe he was trying to distance himself from the rest of the survivalist pack. Maybe he was minimizing the danger of Frank's threat, because acknowledging it—even though he admitted Red attended community meetings—meant confronting something closer to home.

"You don't want to get on his bad side," Jim had said.

Too late.

Chapter Twenty-Three

Exiting through the hospital's automatic front doors, I drew in the fresh mountain air. On the walk to the parking garage, I called Mrs. Moreau again. The phone rang for a full minute.

No answer.

I hung up and spotted a text from Gigi. She and Smiley were on their way to pick me up and take me home while the sisterfriends browsed the galleries on the grounds of the Grove Park Inn. I texted back that I was doing great and would join them for dinner. She "yelled" at me.

Her shout came in all caps—*DO NOT GO ROAMING AROUND ASHEVILLE IN YOUR CONDITION. WAIT FOR US.*

I sent her a smiley face.

The mild breeze on my face made it easy to see why Asheville was famous for its breathing porches. And my heart ached at the memory of sharing that piece of history with Chris. A sudden gust sent dry leaves clattering along the pavement beneath a crisp blue sky. I welcomed the wind in my hair, the chirping robins in the trees, and the ravens hitchhiking on a seventy-degree updraft.

The RAV4 rental car was right where Chris said it would be—easy to find on the first floor in the visitors parking deck. I opened the sunroof and wheeled onto Biltmore Avenue. The pain had dulled, but coughing or twisting too quickly sent stabbing knives into my ribs.

Hunger pangs clawed at me—I hadn't eaten all day—but nothing would stop me from heading straight to Mrs. Moreau's house.

Her driveway was empty. I pulled in anyway, climbed the front steps, and rang the doorbell.

No answer.

From inside came a faint shuffle, then a low thud, followed by hurried footfalls. I pressed my ear to the door, listened hard for a long minute, then rang the doorbell again.

Still no answer.

I returned to the car. Backing out of the driveway, I saw movement in the upper corner of the house—the room François had indicated as his wife's studio. A figure parted the curtains, then quickly moved away from the window and out of sight.

I was curious, but not surprised, that nobody answered the door. I decided to let it go for now. Mrs. Moreau lived just down the street. She couldn't avoid me forever. My thoughts were set on *Babette's Feast*.

On my way to Babette's, I detoured for a barbecue pork sandwich at *Twelve Bones* located near the French Broad River. Funky eatery. No frills, and—according to *Good Morning America*—home to the best barbecue in the country. Barack and Michelle Obama never missed it when they came to Asheville. Neither did I.

After scarfing down the sandwich, I drove to *Babette's Feast*, hoping someone might be there in the early afternoon. The bar was located on the west side of town, in a rough stretch, lined with huge two-story warehouses and lots of industrial buildings. Squat breadbox houses dotted the street that snaked along the French Broad River. Next door to the club, a large industrial complex housed a gym called *Limbs, Legs, and Loins*.

My tires crunched on the gravel as I pulled into the parking lot. The dashboard clock inside the Toyota read 1:17. Climbing the steps to the club, I heard a low rumble of music. I paused on the landing at the double-door entrance. I heard movement inside. Scraping chairs and rattling glasses. I was entering the lion's den—but peril had become my sidekick lately.

Thanks to Johnny Devillers.

I took a deep breath and rapped on the red wooden door, its peephole barred with iron. After a few seconds of waiting, I pounded, this time with my fist. The door swung open. Rudy Norris, cigarette dangling from his lips, stood in the doorway eye-to-eye with me. Even in civilian clothes, his bushy eyebrows and emerald-green eyes were unmistakable. The memory of him decked out in head-to-toe camo flickered through my mind.

I extended my hand. "Ein Pope. We met at the Malaprops' book signing."

"I remember," he said, aiming his tattooed hand. "You wrote that book on guns and trauma." His limp handshake lacked the grip of a man accustomed to combat, much less shooting a gun. It felt more like a hand that had experienced manicured care.

"That's right." I tented my eyes from the sun with my palm and observed him. "You served overseas, asked a question about PTSD." If he hadn't told me that he'd served overseas, I wouldn't believe he was a decorated war hero.

"Good memory."

"I'm looking for the owner of the club," I said gingerly. Phillips had told me he owned the bar, but I didn't want to be presumptuous.

"That'd be me," said Rudy. One of his emerald-green eyes widened. The other, a lazy eye perhaps, tried to match the wider one, and his lips spread into a smile.

"Small world, huh?" I said.

His lanky stature met my height, and his arm muscles bulged and twisted like a curled wisteria vine, bursting through a dandruff-sprinkled purple tee shirt that read, *Babette's Feast: Where Your Hunger Is Satisfied.*

"Where'd you get that shiner?" he asked, swiping a nicotine-stained hand over his close-cropped hair. "You got some bruises and a mighty fine knot on your forehead, too. You been roughed up pretty bad. Been in a fight?"

"This?" My forefinger settled at my black eye. "A nasty fall."

He nodded in a "stuff happens" kind of way and changed the subject. "Hey man, I gotta tell you how much your book has done for me. I use that Grounding Technique deal all the time. Keeps me from losing my shit."

"That's good to hear," I said. "But my book isn't a substitute for therapy. Are you getting treatment for the PTSD?"

"Oh, yeah." With his hand scraping at his scruffy five o'clock shadow, he studied the floor before he spoke. "I go to group therapy once a week over at the Asheville V.A."

"Good deal," I replied. "I'm leading a PTSD group over there in a couple of days."

A flash of surprise flickered on his face. "What brings you to this neck of the woods? The bar ain't open till seven."

"I got these bruises and black eye from a spill on your stairs Halloween night."

He smacked his palms together. "No fucking way! You're the dude that fell?"

"Afraid so."

"Some lady cop came around asking questions, but she didn't say who it was." His face paled, raised a bushy eyebrow. "You ain't filing no lawsuit, are you?"

"Oh, hell no. Nothing like that," I said.

He looked relieved. "Whew, that's good. I was off Halloween, but I heard about the accident. They said when the police and medics came, the sirens drowned out the Joan Rivers drag performance. Miss Rivers was not pleased. They musta been coming for you."

My jaw tightened. You say you *weren't* here Halloween night? I could've sworn I saw you."

"Naw, I got dressed up and hung out in the bars downtown that night. I spend enough time here as it is. Ain't no fun being here when I'm off, too much like work."

"I understand." I didn't let my suspicion show. "I hope you don't mind me asking questions. I was pretty shit-faced that evening, and I'm retracing my steps, trying to put two-and-two together."

"That female cop was snooping around, asking questions. You know her?" he asked.

"Sergeant Phillips?"

"Tall, good-looking chick. Scar."

"Yeah, that's her. I know *of* her," I said. "I hear she's a ball buster."

"Nice piece of ass, though, huh?" He chuckled.

I bristled and said, "I don't want to get on her wrong side or involved in a lawsuit, either. Mind if I ask what you told her? Just so you and me have our stories straight?"

A sly, conspiratorial smirk spread over his face. "Nothing really. When cops come snooping, man, I watch my mouth." He took a long, hard drag off the cigarette. "I ain't seen nothing, ain't heard nothing. I made up a bunch of shit, told her I was here that night. She asked if I remembered a Jason mask. I went all ape shit waving my hands, pretending *Friday the 13th* was the best thing since wet pussy, and I ain't even seen the fucking flick. I told her I was all over this place that night and seen a lot of costumes, but a Jason costume didn't ring no bell."

I nodded.

I was certain I saw him that night. If he lied to Phillips, he could be lying to me, too. Why would he lie unless it was him wearing the Jason mask? Or unless he was protecting whoever it was.

"I think I throwed her off. I don't want to get involved in no shit, man." Snickering, he turned in a half circle, the cigarette dangling from his lips, and made a nervous wiggle of his palms in the air. "The last thing I need is to get sued." That last was directed at me, I could tell.

"Well, you don't have to worry about me because a lawsuit is the last thing I need, too."

"Come on in and look around if you want to, partner." From behind a cloud of cigarette smoke, he thumbed the air at the inside of the club, pushed the open door wider. "Come right in."

"Thank you."

He slapped his arm around my neck, welcoming me inside. "Buddy, you don't have to worry about me. I ain't no snitch. Besides, you saved my life with that book of yours. Make yourself at home. I'll be over yonder in the office if you need me."

Puzzled that nobody remembered what I clearly saw, I scratched my head. Taking in the full panorama of the huge open space for a minute, I observed Rudy through the glass window of his interior office, slamming a file cabinet, shuffling papers, and strewing mail into piles on a desk. I spied the bald man with two pierced earrings, the one who took our admission and stamped our hands on Halloween, washing glasses and wiping down the bar. I wanted to question him, see if his memory was any better than his boss's, but I decided that wasn't wise while we were within eyeshot of Rudy.

The sparkle and glitter of costumes, flashing strobes from the jack-o'-lantern mirror ball, and razzle-dazzle of booming electronic music from Halloween night had faded under the drab reality of daylight. The dismal brick walls were devoid of dancing laser skeletons.

My shoes stuck to the muck with each step on the grimy floor. The stench of stale cigarette smoke mixed with sour beer wafted from the dance floor.

I swung back in Rudy's direction, caught him sucking on a cigarette and staring sideways at me before disappearing into the darker recesses of the office. That image triggered a flashback of the night of Bucky's murder: Rudy leaning inside a dark doorway beneath a streetlight, smoking a cigarette, and blowing clouds of smoke.

Rudy was a pile of contradictions. I didn't know what to make of him. But one thing felt certain.

I was in the right place.

I was sure of what had happened that night. Proof was hiding somewhere inside this building.

It had to be.

Chapter Twenty-Four

My phone vibrated with a text from Gigi.

Where are you?

Babette's Feast, I replied.

Come on home.

Soon, I texted back.

I retraced my steps from the bar to the downstairs restroom, struck again by how cold and unwelcoming the place felt in broad daylight. I inspected the scuff marks alongside the stairwell wall where I'd been hit.

Nothing stood out.

In the restroom, I searched the trash cans, but they had already been emptied. I climbed the stairs to the upper bar, checked for objects about the size of whatever hit me, and examined stools and chairs.

Nothing quite fit with my memory.

Recognizing I'd come up empty-handed, a strange sense of displacement bubbled up inside me. I had been attacked, but all traces of it had been removed. Through one of the exterior windows, I noticed two squirrels sparring on the limb of a sprawling oak tree. Absently, my gaze traced the line of the tree trunk to the ground, where a large green dumpster sat in the alley. The plastic bags piled inside it showed it hadn't been emptied in a while.

I backtracked toward the entrance, deciding to check out the dumpster. Through the glass window of his office, I saw Rudy on the phone, tilted back in his swivel chair, boots propped on his desk. Slipping past him, I unlocked the door to the main entrance and wedged a brick in the jamb to prop it open, groaning as I bent.

Outside, I approached the dumpster and climbed over the rim, tried to ignore the stab in my ribs. I ransacked through the rubbish, gagging at the stench of rotting food commingled with stale cigarettes and alcohol. As I slogged through the much, bizarre images of a scene from *I Love Lucy* flashed in my mind. At an Italian vineyard, a barefoot Lucille Ball, a squeamish expression on her face, stomped around in a vat of grapes, pressing them into wine.

At first, I was squeamish, too—papers, receipts, soggy cardboard squishing underfoot. But once I got used to the mush, I was able to tolerate it. Determination settled in at the thought of information I might find.

I stooped, unearthed a rickety chair with a broken arm, shoved it aside, and poked underneath. I kicked away beer cans and liquor bottles in my way. Squatting, I plucked a heavy round object from beneath the trash.

I straightened, lifting the ball with me, circling it in my hands. The weight of the object shot a sharp pain through my chest. Upon closer examination, I realized it was a medicine ball used for workouts, twenty-five pounds maybe, with handles on each side.

Probably discarded by the exercise club next door, I reasoned. Just as I was about to toss the ball back into the mound of trash, a smear of what looked like blood on one side caught my eye.

Then it dawned on me.

The medicine ball was the same size and shape as the round object that rammed my face and chest. Heart pounding, I crouched and began to dig with a vengeance. My hands were smelly and filthy, ribs screaming, but I didn't care. If someone had discarded a Jason mask, I was determined to find it, even if the odds were against me.

The faster I worked, the more the hairs on my neck prickled. I felt eyes from far off drilling holes into the back of my neck. I stood and looked up. Through the swaying limbs of the oak tree, Rudy peered down at me from a warehouse window.

When our eyes met, he vanished from sight.

He probably thought I was crazy, but I didn't care. I was a shrink: people always think shrinks are a bit unusual. I hunched down again, blanching from the pain. After a long spell, I came to the bottom of the metal crate. Finding nothing, I stood erect, leaned against the inside of the container, and cradled my bruised ribs. With an unsoiled patch on the back of my dirty hand, I carefully wiped sweat from my brow.

At least I had the medicine ball—proof of something.

I swung one leg out over the rim of the dumpster, gasping from the pain seizing my chest, pausing for the spasm to pass. From that angle, something caught my eye—latex dangling from an interior hinge, barely visible in the corner of the container. Earlier, I'd dismissed it as trash. Now, I saw the mask from the inside—exactly how the wearer would've peeled it off before tossing it away.

A bone-chilling quiver shot through me.

I jerked the latex from its perch, turned it inside out.

A Jason mask!

I rubbed it between my fingers. Disturbingly lifelike, the soft, flexible foam latex looked and felt like real human skin. I sniffed it and, in spite of the other overpowering odors, including my own, it was clearly the smell of sweat.

I crunched it into a ball in my fist.

I'd found what I came for.

With considerable effort, I managed to heave the medicine ball over the top of the dumpster. It landed on the concrete below with a solid thud. Grimacing, I swung my body out of the dumpster, brushed off the grime, and marched back to my car.

Baffled.

If Phillips had searched "high and low" for evidence as she claimed, how had she missed the mask and the medicine ball? I was a psychologist, not a private detective, yet I'd just found both pieces of evidence in under an hour.

Clearly, she was hiding something. I slung the medicine ball, along with the mask on the passenger seat and went back inside the club. I trotted down to the restroom to wash my hands and clean off my loafers, absentmindedly whistling the tune to "She'll Be Coming 'Round the Mountain When She Comes."

I clambered back up to Rudy's office, humming the song, excited about my find. He sat hunched over a magazine, rapping a pencil against his desk. Without looking up when I entered the doorway to his office, he asked, "You know what that song means, don't you?"

It took me aback at first. "I guess it means the supply train led by horses into the Appalachian Mountains."

"Nope," he said, continuing to flip through the magazine. "It's about the destruction of the world. It means we're all gonna die."

I shrugged. "How do you figure that?"

Standing, he flung the rolled-up magazine aside. As it unfurled, I caught a glimpse of the cover—*Psychology Today*. I was a hundred percent certain it was the issue featuring one of my articles based on my new book. It struck me as an odd choice for the bar-owner vet.

"We sing it at church—*When the Chariot Comes*, an old slave spiritual from 1899. In 2012, they renamed it *Jesus' Chariot*."

"So, you're a religious man."

"Got to be," he said, his lazy eye drooping. "You got to have something to hold on to when you might blow up and start killing any minute."

"That's understandable," I said, shifting heavily on my feet at the build-up of tension in the room.

"It's about Jesus riding in on the chariot to bring the End of Days. *She* refers to the chariot Jesus'll be driving on his way down."

"I didn't know that."

As the two of us headed toward the entrance, Rudy burst into song, matching the same tune I'd been humming, but changing the lyrics.

"O King Jesus, he'll be driver when she comes, when she comes. O King Jesus, he'll be driver when she comes. She'll be loaded with bright Angels when she comes, when she comes. O she'll be loaded with bright Angels when she comes...."

The religious zeal in his voice was his way of coping with PTSD, but it made my skin crawl. As he sang, his lazy green eye caught mine, and it didn't take a bead off me. Here I was on a beautiful autumn afternoon, standing in a sleazy gay bar, covered in muck, serenaded by a war vet with PTSD, rejoicing about the imminent death of all humanity. The entire scene creeped me out.

At the doorway, I reached out my hand. "Thanks for letting me take a look around."

He didn't take it. His lazy green eye, competing with the normal one, lifted to meet my gaze again. He twisted his jaw, the barest hint that he was upset. Lighting an unfiltered cigarette, he held it between his teeth. Then, through a fake smile, he tilted his head and asked, "Why're you snooping through my garbage for?"

Thinly veiled anger behind a smile that earlier had shown admiration made me wince. "I thought you said make yourself at home."

He flinched as though I'd slugged him. "I meant inside. You said you wanted to look at the stairs, not rummage through my trash. You shoulda ask me."

"I'm sorry if I offended—"

"Find what you come for?" His bushy brows shot up, the lazy green eye held an unnerving glower.

"I think so." I stepped down from the threshold.

"Okay, then." He dragged hard on his cigarette and flicked it in a wide arc into the parking lot. It landed in a pool of stagnant rainwater, made a quick hiss as the embers quenched into a smoldering sizzle. The spiteful gleam in his gaze told me he was about to lose it. He muttered a terse "Goodbye" and slammed the door in my face.

On the way to my car, the churning in my stomach made it easy to ignore the fitful gust of wind, lifting tufts of my hair. Sliding under the steering wheel, I wondered why Rudy hadn't wanted me in the dumpster.

That led to another thought.

Why had nobody at the bar admitted seeing a Jason mask?

And why hadn't Phillips found evidence that was so easy to uncover?

Growing up, when Grandma Gigi got spooked about something, causing an unexplained chill to run through her, she'd say a cat was walking across her grave.

That same chill clung to me now.

Only this time, it wasn't a superstition, and it wasn't my imagination.

This time it was real—the irrefutable proof someone had attacked me lay in the seat beside me.

Now, I just had to figure out who wore it.

Chapter Twenty-Five

With a fresh lead, I pulled out my phone and Googled costume shops in Asheville. Only one popped up—on Lexington Avenue. I cranked the engine and headed to *Costumes Galore*, hoping to learn if the mask had been purchased there.

Lexington Avenue was a busy downtown street, buzzing with life. Funky boutiques and art galleries spilled onto the sidewalks, outdoor cafés hummed, and taverns glowed beneath string lights. Tourists browsed the streets shoulder to shoulder with locals sporting purple Mohawks, trendy tattoos, pierced noses, and carefully curated weirdness.

Inside the costume shop, a short line of customers snaked toward the checkout counter. A few customers were still returning Halloween rentals days late. As I stepped in, a putrid odor hit me.

I sniffed my clothes.

At first, I imagined it was my anger rising—then realized it was the dumpster stench clinging to me. The offensive odor made me self-conscious enough to keep a good distance from other customers as I took a few minutes to wander the aisles, checking out the paraphernalia.

At the front of the store, shelves of wigs, hats, and masks lined the walls. I rubbed the texture of a few masks—vinyl, silicone, foam—then smoothed my hand over a felt top hat and a velvet burlesque skirt.

The makeup counters overflowed with everything from eyelashes, cake makeup, and pasties to devil horns, fake blood, and Dracula fangs. The back half of the store showcased an extensive collection of rental costumes. The place was a one-stop shop for everything from beaded flapper dresses to gangster zoot suits and Disney princess gowns.

When the line dwindled out, I advanced to the checkout counter, set the mask down, and asked, "Do you sell anything like this?"

"Phew!" The clerk wrinkled her nose and waved the air in front of her face. "We sell plenty of masks, but that looks nicer than the ones we carry. There's not much demand for high-end stuff. You have to go online to find the really good ones." She studied the mask. "May I?"

"Of course."

"Whew, it stinks to high heaven."

"Sorry. I fished it out of a dumpster."

She giggled with the delight. "Trust me, you'd be shocked at what comes back in here on the masks and costumes. Occupational hazard." Flipping the mask back and forth between her beefy fingers, she said, "My little brother used to have a cheap version of this. Got it for his birthday."

"Do you stock anything like that?"

"No Jason masks. And nothing this nice. This one's latex—professional grade. Expensive, too."

"How expensive?"

"A wide range. The cheap ones go for about fifty bucks. A realistic latex mask runs up to three thousand. I'd put this one at the high end."

"Wow. Where would someone buy it?"

Her forefinger dug into her right cheek. "Plenty of places online. I bet you could find one on Amazon or eBay, specialty horror sites. I'd search 'latex Jason mask' if I were you."

I slipped off my glasses and chewed the arms of the frames. "What makes latex better than vinyl or silicone?"

"Comfort," she said. "If you're wearing it for a while, like on stage or at a costume party, latex breathes better. You don't sweat as much than, say, silicone or vinyl. Latex fits like skin—moves with your face. Looks real."

"Uh-huh." I nodded, appreciative of her knowledge. "Thanks for your help."

"My pleasure." She handed the mask back. "I'll never forget. My little brother used to scare the heck out of me. I'd be looking at him one minute, and before I knew it, he'd throw on the mask and sneak up on me."

I laughed. "Don't turn your back on him."

She cackled. "That's the thing about latex. You can flip it on and off in a matter of seconds." She gave me a once-over. "But you might want to scrub that one first."

As the bell jingled over the door, signaling another customer, something dinged in my head.

"Thanks again," I said, turning away.

"No problem." She pumped sanitizer onto her palms and rubbed them together before directing her attention to the new customer.

The same jubilation I'd felt finding the medicine ball pulsed through me again. I almost started to hum, *She'll Be Coming 'Round the Mountain*—then stopped. After Rudy's apocalyptic spin on the tune, it felt tainted with survivalist fervor.

But that didn't stop the elation I felt or suppress the grin on my face.

"Now we're getting somewhere." The words leapt from my lips as I stepped back onto breezy Lexington Avenue. I walked south, pumping my fist in the air.

A boutique owner, placing a Buddha statue in her window, shot me a smile. And the parking garage on Walnut Street beckoned me through a swirl of colorful autumn leaves.

The pieces were finally falling into place.

You can flip it on and off in a matter of seconds, the clerk had said.

That explained how the mask-wearer had gone unnoticed at *Babette's Feast* on Halloween night.

And the steep cost mattered. A high-quality mask like that wasn't cheap—and dumping such an expensive item in the trash made no sense.

Unless they were discarding evidence.

Plus, whoever wore it had money. And they hadn't worn it all night. They'd hastily slipped it on in seconds only when I was nearby.

Unlike the hundreds of revelers dressed to impress, the Jason mask hadn't been a costume at all.

It had been a weapon.

And it had been meant strictly for my benefit.

Chapter Twenty-Six

Eventually, the ferocious joy at the spoils of dumpster-diving began to fade. The costume shop discovery reignited my enthusiasm, but it didn't quiet my anger. The more I thought about how the ordeal had derailed my wedding plans—and fractured my relationship with Chris—the hotter my blood ran.

A towering wave of fury bubbled up in me, ricocheting from Frank to Rudy to François. The overpowering smell of the medicine ball and latex mask, curled on the passenger seat, grew unbearable. I rolled down the windows to air out the car. Even the hospital shower was no match for the rancid dumpster-diving smell. I needed a do-over.

I could risk the Starbucks drive-thru on Patton Avenue—grab a double-shot latte—then swing back to the rental house and make another stab at questioning Mrs. Moreau. The newfound evidence would finally convince Gigi—and hopefully Chris—I wasn't losing it and put them at ease.

I snaked the car up the mountain to the rental house, slurping java. I hit Clampton Street, glanced toward the Moreau house, and did a double-take. A man raked leaves in front of the house. He saw me, paused, and leaned on the rake, tracking my every move as the car edged into the driveway behind his vehicle.

He propped the rake against a tree and ambled toward me.

Anger seared the closer he got.

My impartial psychologist mind tamped it down—*maybe there's a reasonable explanation*—but the moment he slung his long black hair from his eyes and reached out his hand, my restraint snapped. I gripped it hard.

He twisted his jaw in pain, then said, *"Bonjour,* what is up?"

"You tell me." I wanted to call him a lying son-of-a-bitch and coldcock the smirk off his face. Instead, I dug my nails deep into my jeans.

"What is this supposed to mean?"

"Don't play innocent with me," I said. It took effort to keep the words steady. "You got me into a shitload of trouble."

His dark brows dipped, hunching in the middle. His accent thickened. *"Je ne comprends pas."*

"You understand me just fine, asshole," I snapped. "Remember when you stopped me right there and complained about the loud music?" I pointed to the road.

"Oui. Of course."

"Then why did your so-called wife tell me—and Officer Phillips—that you were dead?"

"Oh, *that?"* He smirked and swatted at a fleet of orbiting gnats, circling his sweat. "Is that all?"

"All?" I flung open the car door, jumped out, and lunged at him. "You prick! You got people doubting my sanity. You better do some quick explaining before I choke that fucking smirk off your goddamn face!"

When my hands lurched for him, he jerked back out of my reach, and the pain in my ribs triggered a guttural groan.

"Whoa, whoa." His eyes were wider, and he was more terrified than I intended for him to be. "Please—allow me to explain."

"Yeah, you better explain," I snarled.

The magnitude of the angry words, squeezing through my gritted teeth, were out of proportion. I'd just threatened bodily harm on a man for lying. But it wasn't just the lie. Phillips believing in me mattered—central to finding the truth, to keeping my family safe.

"It was not my intent to cause trouble for you," he stammered, his eyes roving the area around us, apparently to see if anybody was within earshot. "My wife thought maybe you were in some kind of trouble. Police prowling, asking questions. She figured the less she said, the better."

"She let us think you were dead. Phillips told me after digging, she found your death certificate."

"*Oui*, my father—François senior—he recently died. *Tres triste*. He lived with us, but you see, this confusion is better for you *and* for me, I think."

"Why are your lies better for me or you?" I folded my arms.

"If I am involved in some complaint, perhaps I would be called to testify. I cannot afford to get involved with the authorities."

"You're the second person today telling me he doesn't want to get involved with law enforcement. When I hear that, it usually means one thing—you're hiding something."

He dropped his head, stared at the ground, chipped the newly-raked grass with the toe of his boot, unearthing the fertile smell of soil.

"What are you hiding?" I pressed.

With a hung head, he muttered, "My green card, it has expired. The visa has been…held up…a matter of red tape."

"Your red tape is not my fucking problem!"

"Of course it is not," he said.

"What *is* my problem is that my grandma is worried sick. And that pisses me off. I'm trying to think of one good reason why I shouldn't turn you over to ICE."

"Please," he said quietly. "For my wife. If I am deported, she is all alone."

I highly doubted his red tape excuse, and the last thing I wanted was to aid and abet someone breaking immigration law. I took a deep breath. "Here's the deal. Your secret stays with me—on one condition."

"Thank you, sir."

"I said on one condition. You call two people and tell them the truth."

"I'm glad to do it,"

"Today. Not tomorrow or next week. Or I make one call and see that ICE has your ass in jail before midnight. Got it?"

"Of course, yes, of course," he said, wringing his hands.

I fumbled for my wallet, slipped out one of my cards, and jotted the cell numbers for Gigi and Phillips on the back. With a shaky right hand, François slid the card into the pocket of his T-shirt.

"Okay, I think we're done here."

"I will make those calls at once." He turned back toward his house.

"By the way, François, your wife says you're moving."

"This is correct."

"Not back to France?"

"No. Not far from here, though. Somewhere quieter—More private."

"Where there's no loud Lady Gaga music," I said, laughing, padding back to my car.

The car squeaked into the circular drive at the end of the street. I stuffed the mask in my coat pocket to show Gigi and breezed down the stone steps toward the rental house.

Pausing at the front door, I rubbed my hand over the doorframe. Smooth as a baby's butt.

Why had someone covered Frank's tracks? And how without anyone noticing?

Shivering at the thought of yet more unannounced visitors, I opened the door. The sound of chitchat and laughter rose above the spray of showers, slam of closet doors, and blast of blow dryers. Gigi and her sisterfriends must be dressing for dinner.

"Let's put some light on the subject." I snapped on a switch by the door. A ceiling fan and overhead light sprang on, shooting shiny fingers of light across the round open room.

Gigi sat in one of the overstuffed chairs, looking small and shrunken in the shadows. When the light came on, she put down her cell phone, sprang from the chair, and stormed toward me, scratching a rash on her arms. "Oh, thank heavens."

"Don't scratch," I reprimanded.

"Where in the hell have you been?" she asked, wagging her middle finger. "You've given me a stress rash!"

"Taking care of business. Slammed all day."

"Don't say *slammed* in front of me again," she snapped. "After what happened, my heart can't take it."

My grandmother was not one for subtleties. Her baby blues beaming, she threw both arms around my chest and squeezed me in a crushing hug.

"Ouch!" I cried, pulling back, trying not to roll my eyes at her hysterics. She fanned her palm in front of her face. "Pee-ew. What's that smell?"

"Dumpster diving. For evidence."

"You stink, son." She planted a kiss on my cheek, anyway, the faint scent of her lavender cutting through the funk. "Speaking of evidence, the Frenchman next door called before you walked in, apologized for upsetting me. Said he misunderstood Officer Phillips's question, something about translation. Told me you were right. He did complain to you about the music blasting."

"Mighty nice of him," I said.

Her eyes searched my face, her brow furrowed with concern. "Last time I saw you, you mumbled somebody tried to kill you. How're you holding up?"

"Right now, my caffeine-adrenaline cocktail is holding pretty good. You?"

"Relieved that you're out of the hospital. But look at you, you need a haircut before the wedding. You're not growing a ponytail just because we're in Asheville, are you?"

"Never mind that." I pulled out the mask, dangled it in front of her. "Check out what I found."

"What in the name of...?"

"Evidence."

"You found the mask you kept talking about in the hospital."

"In the dumpster behind Babette's. The folks at the costume store told me this kind of mask is easy to pull on and off in a flash. That explains why nobody else saw the Jason character." I stooped, playfully put my nose against hers. "So, you see, I'm not losing it."

"Well, I'll be." She looked relieved that her grandson was not headed to the loony bin. "So there really was a Jason mask?"

"A hundred percent. And there's something else. I found a medicine ball in the trash bin at Babette's."

"Medicine ball?"

"A twenty-five-pound weight the size and shape of a basketball with handles on each side," I said. "That's what the Jason impersonator hurled at me from the top of the stairs. I'm certain of it. I plan to send it for DNA testing."

"Well, son, for what it's worth," Gigi said, "I never thought you were crazy, only that you had too much on your mind."

"My theory is that Phillips missed the medicine ball because I was too out of it to give a description of the projectile, leaving her with little to go on…" Hesitation made me give voice to a sudden thought. "Maybe the mask and ball weren't in the dumpster when Phillips investigated. The attacker might've waited until after the search, figured he was home free, and tossed the ball and mask into the trash."

Her baby blues beamed at me again. "See how smart my grandson is."

She plunged into the vacant chair with a grunt, exhaled a sigh of relief, and settled back against the cushions. "I feel like a weight the size of that medicine ball thing has been lifted off me. Have you told Chris about this news?"

Her comment wiped the smile off my face. "I haven't heard from him. I keep getting his voicemail."

"He called to see how I was doing," she said. "He's back in Charlotte. Packing up. Plans on moving back to Seattle with his parents. Until he gets on again with American Airlines."

My heart sank. "He still thinks I consider my work to be more important than him, that I have cold feet about the wedding."

"Do you?"

"No. I'm sure about marrying him now more than ever."

"Then keep calling until you get him."

"I will." I stood. "First, a quick shower. Then I need to run a few errands and get back here in time for dinner."

"And I have to finish dressing. Please be careful, son." Gigi headed toward her bedroom, then tossed a verbal caveat over her shoulder, aiming her middle finger at me. "We're still on vacation."

"Don't worry about me. As soon as I take care of some business."

In the bedroom, I peeled off my putrid clothes. As the warm water splattered against my lathered body, the next steps surfaced. The shooting range where Jim said he'd run into Frank. And Frank's doublewide only a few miles away.

I toweled off, pulled on a fresh pair of jeans, and grabbed my laptop, plopping down on the bed.

The discovery of the medicine ball and mask had proved Sergeant Phillips was either unwilling or unable to properly investigate this case. If she couldn't—or wouldn't—do her job, I would.

Time for more amateur sleuthing.

Chapter Twenty-Seven

S itting on the bed, internet browser open on the laptop, I navigated to *whitepages.com* and typed in "Frank Mallory, Asheville." Two hits, but only one with a Leicester address: *2401 Lonesome Dove Road.*

There it was: a background check. I punched in my credit card, and the report opened in a new window. Voilà—Frank had received a dishonorable discharge from the Marines. As Jim mentioned, a long rap sheet and several brushes with the law for petty theft had led to a stretch in jail.

I clicked on ChatGPT, which stated that the government doesn't publicly reveal names on the no-fly list because it's treated as an operational security tool, but it did provide names of foreign terrorist organizations. ISIS, al-Qaeda, Hamas, and Boko Haram topped the list.

Then I followed a link to a rogue organization, called IDART, the International Center for the Defense Against Radicalization and Home-grown Terrorism. It stated the website's mission, to track activities of hate groups around the country, adding that al Qaeda's brand of radical homegrown extremists has increased since 9/11, identifying over five hundred survivalist cults nationwide, eight in North Carolina alone. The members numbered in the thousands, causing me to wonder how many national cells Frank had been in contact with.

I scoured the names of known radicals of white supremacist groups. Ku Klux Klan, Aryan Nations, and Blood Tribe popped up. Names tied to convictions included Dylann Roof (Charleston church shooter with neo-Nazi ideology). James Alex Fields (convicted Charlottesville attacker). Robert Bowers (convicted Pittsburgh synagogue shooter). Timothy McVeigh

(Oklahoma City bomber). Ronald Thompson (Raleigh mass murderer).

Another link headlined, "Extremist Militia Survivalist Groups."

After one click, the *Gawkers* (local chapter of The United Survivalist Army) was listed right there with the Oath Keepers, Three Percenters, The Base, and various other Neo-Nazi cells, along with names of suspected (not convicted) survival terrorists. There it was in black-and-white. I hovered the cursor over the name "Frank Mallory, A.K.A. 'Red'."

A full profile depicted Frank as a right-wing, radicalized loner, marginalized even by a small group of battle-hardened fighters. Unafraid to die and hell-bent on using weapons to fight the government. His anti-abortion rants accused Planned Parenthood of selling baby parts. He'd been arrested for physical assault on patients entering the facility.

IDART identified Frank as a member of the controversial United Survivalist Army with the subtitle, "The National Network for Survivalist Training." I didn't like the sound of that and clicked on the link. A quick skim of the group's website, and it was clear where the narrative was going. The U.S.A. prided itself on the "snake shake." An animated GIF depicted the disembodied arm of a doomsayer extending a handshake to an unbeliever. As the hands clasped, the survivalist's thumb morphed into the head of a sharp-fanged serpent. Its fangs sank deep into the hand of the unprepared. Blood drizzled down the unbeliever's arm.

Flashes of the Copperhead, coiled around my leg, me doing a St. Vitus dance.

Right there in the center of the page, a photograph showed Frank in a red sweatshirt, five words printed in bold: *Prepare to Survive or Die.* A caption under the picture read, "Are you prepared for what's coming? One day soon, in your lifetime, your going to see mass chaos beyond what most people are prepared for. If your not prepared, your our enemy and deserve to die."

I couldn't help but pause at the incorrect use of "your." A small detail in the scheme of horror that was the United Survivalist Army, but the grammarian in me cringed, nonetheless.

The local survivalist cell's website served as a national clearinghouse for hundreds of other groups from Pasadena to Peoria to Pittsburgh. I followed links to dozens of sites featuring podcasts, newsletters, and blogs. All in the same vein: "What To Do If Someone Steals All The Water You Stored?" and "Beside Food, What Should You Stockpile In Your Bug-Out Bag?"

The prepper cells also brazenly advocated attacks against unprepared zombies and those who spoke out against "Prepare to Survive or Die."

That was me—in spades, and my new book made me the bullseye.

I clicked on a YouTube video titled "Weapons You Need for SHTF."

Twenty-plus million views.

Several men huddled in a semicircle, brandishing firearms. The sounds of gunshots blasting in the background.

A bald, scruffy-bearded man scarred with pockmarks narrated. Fingering his overalls with one hand, he held a shotgun in the other. "If you're prepared for a scenario where the walking corpses of your family and neighbors are trying to eat you alive, you'll be prepared for the zombie squad. If you ain't, that's what I can help you with today. I'm standing at an outdoor firing range with fifty-yard lanes for pistols, shotguns, and rifles. This facility also contains a hundred-yard area for special bolt-action anti-sniper rifles."

I leaned in closer to the screen and squinted at a sign behind the narrator: *Buncombe County Shooting Range.*

"Oren, step to the side a minute so I can get a wide-angle shot of the range," the cameraman said.

The bearded narrator moved off camera for a few seconds, then stepped back in view. "Now let's get started," he continued. "After SHTF, every man oughta have three firearms in his arsenal: a rifle, a shotgun, and a pistol. I'm holding a Russian-made Saiga-12 shotgun. When modern civilization collapses, you can pack some heavy firepower, no jams, and they keep on trucking."

"Hold it up so I can get a close-up," ordered the cameraman.

Raising the shotgun, the narrator continued. "You can get them for any kind of kill, from animals to zombies. This thing will kill a man or a deer. It will protect you, and it will feed you. Watch this." The suspendered man aimed at a target and fired, hitting the bullseye. "Woo-hoo, this mean mutherfucker will scare the shit outa your daughter's boyfriend! Now Red's gonna talk about pistols."

Frank Mallory sauntered on camera in full military camouflage. He held a small handgun and looked directly in the camera. "If they come to take our guns, we'll give 'em our ammo first. Right, boys?" The men in the huddle raised their firearms in a unison rally cry. Frank aimed the gun into the camera.

"Hey man, not cool," the cameraman said. "You're trippin' me out."

"Sorry, man." Frank lowered the gun, shrugged it off, and continued. "For zombies, you need a 380 pistol with a six-shot magazine that'll hit the small brain area. This LCPZ Zombie Slayer is perfect for that. Now, if you need long range to hit a zombie the way you want to, this AK-74 Russian assault rifle with 45-round magazine will break his pelvis and bone structure down, and he can't get to you."

"Yup, that rifle is a great setup for dismemberment," the cameraman said. "Hold it up, Red, let us get a good look at it."

Frank craned his neck. "Who's got the fucking rifle?" He reached sideways off camera to one of the men in the huddle. When the camera swung to follow his reach, the man passing the rifle raised his elbow, turning his back to hide his face.

I couldn't believe my eyes.

I could've sworn it was Jim Warren.

Squinting, I clicked on the red dot, slid it backward to replay the video, and moved closer to the screen. Sure enough, it was a dead ringer for Jim Warren. Decked out in a T-shirt and jeans. When he raised his elbow, I saw what looked like a tattoo on his upper right arm, but I couldn't make out the image.

At least Jim was honest about one thing: he had seen Frank at target practice.

But this wasn't just target practice. It looked more like camaraderie. A fraternity of men with like minds and shared beliefs, whooping it up.

In all my years of studying and writing about survivalist cults, I'd never seen anything as blatantly violent and well-organized as what I watched unfold on my little screen. My chest felt as tight as a dormant grenade ready to detonate.

Taking a deep breath, I closed the laptop and leaned back against the headboard, squeezing my head between both palms. The survivalist yahoos were everywhere. And I was walking—eyes wide open—right into the thick of them.

Chapter Twenty-Eight

After a measured climb up the wide stone steps—bracing myself against the pain—I slid into my car and headed downtown to the police station. A realization struck me on the drive. In vindicating myself through François and Rudy's stories, I had also vindicated Phillips. At least when it came to her witness interviews. On that score, she deserved an apology.

Still, history hadn't proven her trustworthy when it came to handling evidence. I racked my brain for who could be trusted with the mask and medicine ball riding shotgun. To be on the safe side, I settled on the only potty-trained officer I knew in town: Wiggins.

Aside from responding on the day of the shooting, Wiggins hadn't been involved in my case. Hopefully, he'd still be willing to meet with me. My adrenaline spiked at the front door of the precinct station. I emptied my pockets and passed through the metal detector. The officer on duty raised an eyebrow at the mask and medicine ball but waved me forward without question.

I gathered my belongings on the other side and strolled down the corridor, taking the elevator to Wiggins's third-floor office.

The receptionist was a heavyset woman with enormous, round tortoise-shell glasses and a nervous tongue that darted in and out as she slumped over a computer, shuffling paperwork on her desk. She glanced up, eyebrows arched in a questioning look.

"May I help you?"

"I'm here to see Officer Wiggins."

"He's not in," she replied. "He's working a big case with Sergeant Phillips over at the hospital. I don't expect them back today. Can I take a message?"

I inquired about having the smudge on the medicine ball DNA tested. She assured me the ball would be safe in her care and promised to pass it along to Wiggins. But she cautioned that the department's backlog could take up to six months before the results came back from the state lab in Raleigh. She said a private DNA clinic across town could turn results around in a few days, but it wouldn't be cheap.

I thanked her and headed to the clinic.

My route took me through the impaled granite guts of Beaucatcher Mountain. The tunnel divided the historic, early–twentieth-century skyline of downtown Asheville on the west from the sleazy motels and fast-food joints on the east, where the clinic sat.

Normally, the dark, womb-like tunnel comforted me. This time—during the nineteen seconds it took to plunge from daylight on the downtown side into the lonely blackness and back into daylight on the other side—my heart nosedived.

Images swirled of Chris explaining how Beaucatcher Mountain got its name. An 1880s legend about a father teasing his daughter for strolling the mountainside with her beau. Over time, the joke morphed into the name "beau catcher." Smiling, Chris had squeezed my shoulder with both hands, insisting that we hike Beaucatcher Mountain before our wedding. I agreed.

We never did.

Now I brooded in what we therapists call *shouldy thinking*.

Humph, some psychologist you are—unable to practice what you preach. Trust isn't built on empty words—it's built on keeping promises, on showing up. After my screw-up, what would it take to redeem myself?

I burst out of the tunnel, harsh sunlight stabbing through the gray sky, snapping me back to the present. The DNA clinic was just another mile down Tunnel Road on the left. Inside, a staffer led me straight to a room and swabbed the inside of my cheek. After a few minutes of paperwork, she sealed the swab and the smudged medicine ball for processing. She informed me that the cost would run between four and six hundred dollars, and the package would be overnighted from Asheville to their testing lab.

Within two or three days, technicians would generate a DNA profile on the items. I asked if they could date the age of the smudge on the medicine ball. I wanted to head off any claim that I'd planted my own blood on the ball. She assured me they could. When the results were ready, I'd receive a lab-certified PDF copy by email, and the medicine ball would be available for pick up at my convenience. I held onto the Jason mask. Testing it would be pointless until a suspect had been identified.

One mission accomplished. On to the next.

I sat outside the clinic, twiddling a pen between my fingers, falling into my usual internet loops of news sites and social media. On my Facebook page, disgruntled survivalists had posted threats and anti-government rants aimed squarely at me. I fought the urge to respond and instead thought about the shooting-range video and Frank's address—outside the city limits just off Leicester Highway.

Time to check it out.

I plugged the address into my GPS and drove due west, cruising down I-240 to Patton Avenue before turning right onto Leicester Highway. Drab gas stations, strip malls, and pawnshops deepened the gloom of the gray day. Three more miles out, and the heavy traffic, asphalt, and concrete gave way to pastureland and fields of crops. A sign on my left announced the *Buncombe County Shooting Range*. Two miles later, the GPS showed a left turn onto the unpaved Lonesome Dove Road.

I nosed off the blacktop where sidewalks fell into crumbled ruin. I drove along its length for another quarter of a mile past a junkyard and a string of dirt driveways. A rusted, dust-covered backhoe stood in front of mounds of excavated dirt. Several dilapidated trailers with postage-stamp yards were littered with dirt-caked cars, rust-streaked tin mailboxes, and yappy, unvaccinated dogs running loose.

On the right, a leaning mailbox showcased *2401* in peeling black letters. I squeaked to a halt on the side of the road beneath the blaze-red canopy of a maple tree. The lonely double-wide trailer was plopped in the middle of nowhere, hard-edged and bleak against the soft sway of surrounding pine trees. Two motorcycles tilted drunkenly sideways near the trailer steps.

I killed the engine and rolled down the window. Metal ticked as the motor cooled. In the distance, a dog barked just below the gentle snapping of sheets on the clothesline. I surveyed the wreckage of two dismal lives. From the outside, the place could've housed any struggling, hardworking family. But the dangerous underbelly that lurked inside didn't qualify.

The drab afternoon edged into evening as the clouded sun sank behind the bend of creaking pines. The ridges, bursting with orange and yellow foliage, morphed into blackish blue. Tonya Clausen emerged from the narrow metal door, her stringy bleached-blonde hair, swollen lips, and huge eyes catching my eye as she descended the steps. She moved to the clothesline and started pulling laundry. In this domestic role, she looked innocent, almost harmless—even pretty.

Over Tonya's shoulder appeared Frank Mallory, the red beard and broad sloping shoulders, sucking on a cigarette and belching loudly. He swung onto the motorcycle and his thick, tattooed arms goosed the engine. He roared away in the opposite direction, a swirl of red dust trailing him.

Tonya gathered an armful of laundry and slunk toward the trailer. She put one foot on the first step and stopped. Snapping her head around, she stared steely-eyed at my car. Apparently recognizing my face, she dumped the armful of laundry on the porch, bolted inside, and reappeared seconds later with a shotgun.

Her lip curled. She glowered, raised the firearm, and pulled the trigger.

The gun jammed.

Time went into slow motion. I floored the gas and made a hard U-turn, slinging small rocks and red dirt. In the rearview mirror, I saw her raise the weapon and fire again—this time in the air. My last glimpse was of her standing on the porch, the shotgun resting on her hip.

I pressed on the gas. My tires stirred a red haze of dust that stole her away.

Chapter Twenty-Nine

Our dinner destination was located in Biltmore Village, the gateway to the famous Biltmore House Estate and Gardens. Originally designed as a "company town" for the estate workers in the late 1890s, Biltmore Village evoked the charm of a quaint European hamlet.

With its fan-shaped, tree-lined streets, old railroad depot, and compact English cottages lining historic brick sidewalks, the village was Gigi's favorite attraction in Asheville. She and her sisterfriends especially loved the Cathedral of All Souls, the crowned jewel of the planned community. They were eager to browse the former cottages now converted into upscale boutiques, art galleries, and fine restaurants—like the Corner Kitchen, where we had dinner reservations.

As we approached the restaurant, Shirley pressed down her hair bun and exclaimed, "This looks like something straight out of *Downton Abby!*"

"Wait till you get a load of the food," I said, holding the door open for the group.

Gigi had reserved the best seats in the house: a large, oblong dining table on the first floor. The window beside us framed a postcard view of Biltmore Village's Christmas lights, already strung through the trees lining the streets. One thing about Gigi—she had impeccable taste and insisted on the best when it came to dining. Her motto was simple: the quality of the meal is only as good as the placement of your table.

While we waited for the servers to prepare the table for us, I discreetly scrolled through my messages, hoping for one in particular.

Nothing from Chris.

Once we sat down, the lively dinner conversation flowed—carefully avoiding any mention of Chris's abrupt exit or conspicuous absence. The omission spoke volumes. Everyone knew. Gigi would've told them by now.

After polishing off a meal of scallion-and-bacon grilled mahi-mahi, I leaned back, rubbed my belly, and took a final sip of Chardonnay. "That was delicious! Excellent choice, Gigi."

"My filet mignon was outstanding, too," Smiley said, dabbing his mouth with a napkin.

"I like this place," Jackie said, downing a gulp of Burgundy.

"One of the best meals I've ever had," Wilma-May declared, smacking her lips. "But tell me something—what was that sign in the ladies' room about?

"What did it say?" I asked.

"Something about letting the yellow mellow and the brown go down."

"Wilma-May!" Shirley glared. "Where are your manners? I'm still eating, if you don't mind."

"It's classical Asheville," I said. "Water conservation. Especially with the drought."

Wilma-May rolled her eyes back and forth. "Huh?"

I gave it another try. "Save water?"

"Oh, I get it," she said, pleased by her light bulb moment. "Oops, I flushed."

Shirley quickly redirected the subject. "Girls, after dinner, what do you say we browse the shops?"

"Did you say *browse* or *carouse*?" Jackie asked. "I for one prefer to carouse after a good meal."

Shirley's lips tightened in a line, and her serious tone didn't go unrecognized. "You're worse than her," she said, pointing at Wilma-May.

"I'm just sayin'," Jackie responded, once again pushing her perfectly rounded hair into the shape of a helmet.

"I read in the tourist guide that the New Morning Gallery reopened after Hurricane Helene. Gladys chimed in. It's just around the corner and is supposed to have great stuff."

"No browsing for me," I said. "I've got some digging to do before heading to the Clement farm tomorrow."

"Digging?" Shirley asked.

"Research."

Gigi frowned. "No, he's digging all right—his own grave." Her eyes landed on me. "Are you brain-dead? I don't want you going out there."

"We've already had this conversation, Gigi."

Gladys piped up. "Chet Clement was my brother-in-law, as all of you know. We weren't blood kin, but Bucky *was* my nephew. When Chet was married to my sister—may she rest in peace—he was such a gentle soul. I don't know what made him and his two boys go off the deep end like they did—except maybe his second wife."

"Sounds like they were radicalized by the doomsayers," I said.

Gigi huffed. "Well, don't be surprised if you find me stowed away in the trunk of your car."

"The rental car doesn't have a trunk," I said. "You'll have to come up with something better than that."

"Don't give her any bright ideas," Smiley said, looping an arm around Gigi. "Now, honey, don't you go getting sassy. We've been married less than a year, and you're trying to make me a widower. I'm keeping my eye on you while you keep your eye on Ein."

Gigi flung the cloth napkin into her plate and turned to scold me. "You won't listen to reason. Never have, never will. You're so hard—" She stopped mid-sentence. Her face drained of color, eyes widening.

"What's wrong?" Smiley asked.

"Oh—nothing," Gigi said quickly. "Thought I saw somebody I recognized."

"You look like you saw a ghost," I said.

"Maybe I did."

"Who?" Gladys asked.

"Somebody I don't much care for." Gigi nodded toward a table at the far end of the restaurant. All eyes followed her gaze.

"I don't see anybody I know," Gladys said.

Jackie leaned forward. "It's that sergeant lady."

I craned my head. Phillips stood from her chair. Jim Warren held open her overcoat.

"Shit," I murmured. After what I saw Jim doing in the video, acting natural around him would be impossible. And I'd already called Phillips on my way back from Lonesome Dove Road and told her about the medicine ball and Jason mask. She was none too happy, accusing me of interfering with a murder investigation.

"They're leaving," Jackie whispered. "Let's pretend we don't see them."

"That's like ignoring an eight-hundred-pound gorilla," I said. "They have to walk past our table to exit."

"Be nice, everybody," Wilma-May said, sitting straight up in her chair, clamping her elbows on the table, and sliding her chin into the cradle of crossed hands. "The Lord said, 'Turn the other cheek.'"

I decided that the Lord was referring to a different part of my anatomy and turned my back. Facing Gigi, I let her throw the first greeting. The large window facing me reflected the couple as they neared our table. They stopped. Via the wavy reflection, I watched the surprised expression on Phillips's face, stopping short, when Gigi waved.

Hair cascading onto her shoulders, her eyes raced around the table before she spoke. "Hello, ladies," she said, then stared at the back of my head, adding, "and gentlemen."

I turned and stood. My voice was polite but tightly guarded. "Hello, Mary."

"Ein, you remember my fiancé Jim," she said coolly.

"Of course," I replied, forcing a smile as I shook his hand. "Good to see you again, Jim."

"Nice to see you upright," Jim said.

Phillips gestured around the table, acknowledging the women she'd already met. Gigi introduced Smiley and the others. Just then, the peal of the Westminster bells from All Souls Cathedral grandly declared the time.

"Man, it's getting late," I said. "I'd better get going."

Phillips shuffled her feet, nudged Jim in the side, and said, "We should go, too."

"Nice meeting all of you," Jim replied.

As they exited, Phillips gave the sluggish door an angry jerk. It moaned in protest before opening wide. A stern-looking Jim shot me a glare as he held the door for her. A blast of pungent, smoky wood-fire wafted inside. Jim scuttled down the steps, but Phillips lingered on the porch, fumbling in her overcoat, then raised a cell phone to her ear.

I felt the vibration and glanced down. *Mary Phillips.* I punched the *Accept* button.

"Can I have a word with you?" she asked.

"Sure."

"Out here."

"Excuse me," I said, rising. I'll be right back."

Outside, the night had turned sharp and cold.

Phillips crossed her arms and spoke in a stilted voice. "So, we're clear now where we stand. Right?"

"Meaning?"

"Like I said in the hospital, I'd appreciate it if you'd stop meddling and leave the investigation to Wiggins and me. I don't want another dead body on my hands. And I'll need you to turn over the evidence you found."

Her comments brought back the earlier phone conversation when I'd rubbed the mask between my fingers, the feel of latex further galvanizing my resolve. "Too late. The medicine ball is no longer in my hands. I sent it off for testing. And I'm holding on to the mask."

"What is wrong with you?" she snapped. "You're already in a shitload of legal trouble for interfering with a murder investigation. You could go to jail. And you're making it harder for us to do our jobs. Not to mention you're putting your life in danger."

"I've been in over my head for a while now."

"Ein, listen to reason. We're close to solving the serial murders at Mission."

Jim pulled in front of the restaurant and rolled down the window. Mary, are you coming?"

"Just a minute," she shouted.

She turned back to me and continued. "We've linked the hospital murders to a radical survivalist cell. The entire facility is on high alert. We're on the lookout for a blond woman impersonating a nurse—she's been roaming the halls for months, pretending to be on medical staff. Every patient she murdered was either a cop or government official."

"Sounds like you'd better watch *your* back," I said. "You're a cop."

The scar on her face tightened into an ugly grimace. "You stubborn ass."

"Yeah, well, it's genetic. By the way, what do you know about the United Survivalist Army?"

She stiffened. Then stormed toward Jim's car, muttering. "I should've thrown you in jail when I had the chance."

"Bring it on, Motorcycle Mary," I called after her.

She hopped into Jim's car and slammed the door. Hard. Watching them speed away, I stood there for a moment, licking my chapped lips.

She'd really hit the roof if she knew I planned to visit Chet Clement the next day.

Chapter Thirty

While the rest of the crew toured Biltmore Village, I headed back to the house, leaving Smiley and the women to return in his van. The sun had set more than an hour before. In the headlights, the birch trees stood bone pale against the dark.

As soon as my feet hit the porch of the rental house, I remembered I'd handed my only key to Smiley. I frisked the pockets of my sports jacket and jeans, just in case. Above my head, a set of wind chimes jangled an angry tune. A folded aluminum chair clattered against the side of the house. The temperature was dipping. Exasperated, I grabbed my cell phone and tried to call Gigi.

Straight to voicemail.

Dammit! Why do people always turn off their cell phones just when you need to reach them?

The climb back up the stone steps made me huddle against the strong, cold wind, whirling fallen leaves in circles, nearly blowing me sideways. It made sense to wait inside the car, hoping to get a call back from Gigi.

Cranking the engine, I flicked on the heater and angled close to the blasting air, savoring the warmth against my face. I slipped my laptop from the backseat and turned on the overhead light. Waiting for my computer to boot up, I spotted something rustling in the bushes. Stiffening in alarm, I turned off the heater, cracked the window, and listened in silence.

It was just the bending trees straining, leaves waving like palms of the dead. Whining wind slashed at the car, whipped leaves into shadows against the windows. By now, Tonya would've told Frank about my car idling outside their house. He could be coming for me. A few more moments of listening, and dead silence lingered in the air. The movement must have been caused by the howling wind. Satisfied with that conclusion, I slid the cell phone from my coat pocket, scanned my contacts, and dialed Chet Clement.

After several rings, an elderly, gruff voice answered.

"I'm looking to speak to Chet Clement," I said.

"Speaking," he growled in a suspicious tone.

I gave my name and explained who I was. Mr. Clement acknowledged he knew me by name, which didn't surprise me.

"I'm hoping I could pay you a visit tomorrow. I'd like to discuss a few things with you in person," I said.

"We ain't had no visitors in a coon's age," he snapped.

Despite Chet's reluctance, he agreed to meet in the morning. After clicking off the phone, the thought of Chet hosting drills for survivalists on his farm brought a twist of nausea, the trepidation clawing its way into my chest.

After half an hour spent checking emails, my eyes grew tired from the glare of the screen. I leaned my head back against the headrest, let my tired eyeballs retreat into their sockets, and gave them a gentle massage. When I opened them again, the bent trees around me creaked and whined in agitation, casting long shadows that danced like ghosts on the hood of the car.

Another flash of movement, this time coupled with the crackling leaves of footsteps outside the passenger side of the car. With my pulse thundering, I jerked my head around at what looked like a darkly cloaked figure skirting briskly around the hood. The form made fast, jerky movements like Frank Mallory and had the shape of his sloping shoulders, his height, and bulk. I flicked off the inside car light and snapped on the headlights.

Everything was black except directly in front of the headlights, where an upsweep of wind herded the leaves and sent them dancing in circles. Splintered moonbeams shimmied through swaying branches across the passenger seat and floor of the car. My thumping heartbeat dwarfed the howl of the wind and the crunching of tortured tree branches.

Suddenly, a distorted face smashed against the passenger-side window, fingers scratched on the glass. A closer inspection showed bits of debris and tree limbs clicking against the car.

The incessant clamor distracted me from serious research. I turned off the laptop and stretched my arms, letting my body sink into the seat.

Just as my muscles began to loosen, the car rocked. Something tugged on the handle from the passenger side.

A bear?

The car shook as something struggled against the locked door. A body pressed against the passenger-side window—this time unmistakably real. The whites of two wild eyes glowed in the darkness. The large pupils swooped back and forth, landing on me, then vanishing.

It wasn't a bear.

Human palms slid over glass and smacked hard against the window. Palms morphed into hammering fists, circling the car, powerful enough to break the glass. A flat face smashed against the window next to me. Hands flailed against glass and metal, desperate to get to me.

My adrenaline soared wildly, pumping its chemicals into my bloodstream. My heart slammed against my ribcage. I released the emergency brake with my foot, slung the car into drive, and floored the accelerator.

The vehicle lurched forward.

"Wait!" came the frantic call of a heavily-accented voice. "Are you okay?"

"François!"

I jammed hard on the brakes and shoved the car into park.

A dark-clad François ran up to the driver's side, yanking back his black hood, his tousled hair raked by the wind.

"What the fuck?" I snapped, lowering my window.

Flustered, he flapped his hand against his chest. *"Mon Dieu*, I feared you were dead. How do you call it, uh…carbon monoxide—I thought you must be poisoned. I was trying to reach you, was a second from breaking one of the windows."

"You can only die from carbon monoxide poisoning if you're in a closed area or the exhaust pipe is plugged. I'm fine. At least I *was* fine until you scared the crap out of me."

He pointed up at the ridge. "From her studio, my wife sees your car idling; you are slumped over the wheel. She insisted I come check."

"I was on my laptop, man. Got locked out of the house and had work to do."

"My god!" François bent at the waist, pressed his hands into the knees of his jeans to catch his breath. "I have never been so frightened in my life."

"Yeah, well, me either." With the back of my hand, I wiped my forehead, leaned it against the steering wheel. "My heart's still thumping ninety-to-nothing."

"Next time, please knock on our door," François said. "We have a spare key."

"What?" My eyebrows lifted. I gaped at him. "Why would you have a key to this house?"

"My wife and I own the rental company. I keep a key for emergencies, so if someone gets locked out on a weekend or holiday."

"You mean you've had a key to our house this whole time?" I asked.

"*Oui.* So?" He seemed surprised by my reaction. "I thought you knew. They did not tell you?"

"Who are *they*?"

"Mountaintop Getaways, my booking agency. The manager usually tells renters I'm the owner, live next door, and keep an eye on the place."

Or prowl around the place, turning on stereos.

My face flushed. I rubbed my temples, tried to keep my voice calm. "My grandma made the reservation. Maybe they told her."

"I am sure." He took his wallet from his back pocket and plucked out a business card, flipping it back and forth between his fingers. "I should have given you this the other day. If you need anything, anytime, please. I will run and get you the key."

As he headed off in a trot, I called to him, "Hey, François, I appreciate your lending me a hand, buddy. I have another question for you. Trying to sound curious instead of accusatory, I asked, "Have you been inside the house since we arrived?"

He approached the car again. "Of course not. Why you ask?"

"Just a few unexplained things since we've been here."

He came a step closer. Something broke in his voice as he asked, "What things?"

I waved my hand. "The day you heard the loud music, there was nobody in the house. Just made me wonder."

"I come into the house only if there is a problem—plumbing, electrical. The day I met you in the rain, I was headed to knock on your door. I would not have let myself in. So no, I have not set foot on this property since the time you have been here—until tonight."

"I see."

The Frenchman held a long, defensive stare before dropping his voice. "Be right back with a key." He jogged off into the dark, my headlights lighting his path along the driveway.

François Moreau had a key to the house we'd been sleeping in, and his wife had to know that. I licked my parched lips, thought about the prowler outside on our first night, the unlocked door, the sound system on full blast.

He had mentioned carbon monoxide poisoning.

I stepped out of the car to inspect my tailpipe and make sure it wasn't obstructed. Mud and leaves clogged it.

I glanced up the ridge. A single light from the upstairs window glowed in the dark. A white veiled curtain, shimmering in the wind, silhouetted the figure of a woman.

Then she vanished.

A wild shiver speared through me.

My stomach rolled, making a slow climb into my throat.

Chapter Thirty-One

That night, I didn't sleep. Memories of Chris held my rest hostage, no matter how hard I tried to push them away. I imagined his drowsy head on my shoulder, his playful cleverness looping through my mind like a film reel. I stared at the empty space beside me, picturing the deep amber valley between his shoulder blades where I loved to lay my head, breathing in the sweet, familiar scent of his skin.

Chris wasn't just handsome—he was irresistible. Irreplaceable.

And now he was gone.

My life had unraveled since coming to Asheville. I lay awake, my thoughts spinning, searching for a way to stitch it back together. Gigi's advice—to keep calling Chris until I reached him—felt like my best option. I tried to show some restraint, forcing myself to wait an hour between calls.

In the darkened bedroom, even the dim glow of my phone stung my eyes. I imagined Chris's phone chiming beside a table set for two, ringing beneath a blaring television, waking the body next to him in bed—until his patience wore thin, he checked the caller ID, saw my name, and hit *Decline*.

When reason finally clawed its way back, I reminded myself it had only been two days since he left. It was unlikely he'd already moved on. I tried replacing that image with one of him alone, quietly packing his things, but that didn't help either.

Exhaustion won.

I left a voicemail asking him to email me his photos from the I-26 attack instead of sending them to Phillips. I hoped it sounded like a plausible excuse for all the calls.

I must have drifted off around four a.m.

When the alarm went off at six, dragging myself out of bed felt impossible. Then I remembered my scheduled visit with Chet Clement. Adrenaline surged. My heart rate spiked. My leaden legs finally obeyed.

From everything I'd heard, Old Man Clement was the most dangerous of them all. According to the police, his son Bucky—firing from a motorcycle— had nearly killed me. I knew I was putting my life at risk, but I needed answers. If Bucky was responsible, I had to know why.

I stripped and stepped into the shower. As I lathered up, I noticed my chest wasn't as sore as it had been the day before. Peppermint shampoo and warm water—spattering my face, beading on bruised skin—revived me. All that was left was coffee. Lots of it.

After toweling off, I pulled on my jeans. Aside from the tux I'd packed for the wedding, denim was all I'd brought. In Asheville, casual was the norm. The understated look would also keep me from appearing, as Gigi would say, "uppity" for my meeting with Chet Clement.

Before leaving, I stuck a note on the coffee maker reminding everyone I was heading to the Clement farm. After a stop at Starbucks for a tall double-shot latte, I pressed the gas and cruised alongside the French Broad River before exiting onto Highway 21. Old houses and small cabins dotted North Asheville, tucked among mountain ranges, rolling farmland, and remote hollers deep in the blue folds of Buncombe County.

I took the last sip of coffee and slid the empty cup into the holder. My hands were clenched so tightly around the steering wheel my knuckles were white.

So that's what white-knuckling-it feels like.

My subscription to *Survival Today*—the flagship survivalist magazine— had familiarized me with the American Preppers Network mindset, articles like "Building Your Survival Pantry" and "Preparing for Collapse." Accord- ing to them, the war between the prepared and the unprepared had already begun—at least in their minds.

They preached that time was running out, that they'd been warning people for years. If the United Survivalist Army ever took control of the country, survivalists would finally have a national platform, and America would devolve into a nation of bullies and fearmongers—armies of Johnny Devillers and Frank Mallorys slinging AK-47s while shopping at Walmart or grabbing dinner at Pizza Hut.

Fifteen minutes later, after more twists, exits, and turns, the road narrowed to a single lane. I guided the car along the curving blacktop as it carved a crooked path through the Blue Ridge Mountains. Cresting another ridge, granite outcroppings burst through the mountainsides, closing in around me.

Another mile and the terrain opened. The RAV4 zigzagged through rolling green hills that stretched as far as I could see. Hay bales—some painted with jack-o'-lantern faces—dotted the fields. Alpacas, horses, and cows grazed in open pastures. In the distance, an entire mountainside burned. The red inferno glowed against the sky, smoke stinging my nose and tightening my stomach.

Another cataclysmic sign survivalists would cite as proof the end was near.

The car reached the southern edge of the Clement farm. My GPS flashed: *Entering Unverified Territory*. I eased off the gas, crawling alongside a split-rail fence marking the long boundary of the property and guiding me toward the entrance.

The land rolled across multiple ridges before dipping into a deep valley where the farmhouse sat. A dilapidated cabin with a rusted metal roof, a massive red barn, and several outhouses clustered around the main house. Beyond them, a ridge rose sharply, crowning the scene with an imposing backdrop.

I turned onto the private drive. An archway framed an open gate, a handmade *Clement Farm* sign dangled from its center, creaking in the breeze. Gravel crunched beneath my tires as I followed the winding drive toward the house. Farther up, a store-bought red sign warned: *NO TRESPASSING. VIOLATORS WILL BE SHOT ON SITE.*

I pulled up in a cloud of dust. Lowering my sunglasses, I studied the clapboard house, its peeling white paint shedding like snakeskin. Rusted cars lay tipped on their sides in the yard. A dust-covered Dodge pickup sat in the circular drive, two shotguns mounted in racks behind the front seat. An old sofa—draped with what might once have been a bedspread—sagged on the porch.

Chet Clement stood braced against a porch post, a wad of chew bulging his lower lip, a pistol holstered at his hip. His thumbs hooked into his bib overalls. His expression was blank, carved from stone. Deep wrinkles lined his face. Half of his left ear was missing. Tired eyes gleamed behind thick glasses beneath bone-colored hair.

As a greeting, he spat tobacco juice off the porch, where it splattered into a dark mound near the steps.

The hostility didn't surprise me. Bucky Clement had been gunning for me. I was here because I needed answers.

I stepped out and introduced myself. When I reached out my hand, he leaned forward and shook it. "Chet Clement. Welcome to Clement Farm." He studied me, then nodded toward a large, wide-hipped woman behind the screen door. "That's my wife."

She stared at me, her long dinosaur neck jutting forward, swaying as if scenting danger. Simply dressed, an apron tied at her waist, her mousy brown hair—streaked with gray—was pulled into a loose bun.

"Pleasure to meet you, Mr. and Mrs. Clement." The low buzz of wasps in the eaves filled the hard stares and long silence before the old man spoke.

"Call me Chet." He limped down the steps, jerking a thumb toward the door. "You can call her Lilly."

My gaze drifted across the land. "Quite a spread you've got here, Chet."

He hooked his thumbs into his suspenders. "Place is fallin' down some, but it's been in my family over a hundred years." He spat again. "Aim to keep it thataway."

"I'll put something on the stove," Lilly muttered, disappearing inside.

"We ain't here to socialize, woman," he called after her. She didn't hear—or ignored him.

"Ah, hell. She'll do it anyway." He motioned for me to follow. "C'mon. I'll show you around a spell."

We passed an herb garden beside the house. Laundry snapped on a clothesline in the backyard, the grass beneath it trampled flat, I assumed by United Survivalist Army's marching boots. Between the flapping sheets, human-shaped paper targets peeked out—bullseyes riddled with bullet holes.

The long walk from the farmhouse to the barn had me wondering what this sightseeing tour was really about. The smell of tobacco drifted off him as I struggled to keep up with the short, bow-legged man, whose quick limp carried him forward faster than seemed possible.

I threw him a guarded glance now and then, listening as he launched into a tirade. "I reckon we live in a time when folks don't know how to take care of themselves. They want the gov'mint to do everything, and believe you me, it does—runs our lives, taxes honest, hardworking folks like me to death, then turns around and hands it all to the freeloaders—the bloodsuckers."

Using my hand as a visor against the sun, I surveyed the property. In the distance, a calf bawled, and the faint ding-a-ling of a cowbell echoed from one of the lower pastures. Smoke from forest fires hovered over the mountains, drifting toward the farm as if on its own mission.

I'd studied survivalists, but seeing it up close was a different matter—intriguing and unnerving at once. After reading about the local cell, I wasn't sure what Clement was capable of, so I kept a close eye on him. I pointed to camouflage netting stretched over several storage units and a large yellow bulldozer. I already knew the answer, but I asked anyway to stay engaged. "What's the netting for?"

He squatted, pinched dirt between his fingers, then stood and flicked it off his hands. "What you see here is a self-sufficient farm. Good, rich soil—a merciful place. We grow our own vegetables, raise our livestock—pigs, cows, and over yonder, a chicken coop. All you need is a source of fresh water." He nodded toward a small lake. "That pond over yonder by the clump of mountain laurel is stocked with a right smart of mountain trout."

Chet's finger turned forty-five degrees toward a thick forest. "That wooded gorge over yonder is full of wild boar, bear, and deer. It'll provide food…if it don't get burned up." He squinted at me over thick wire-rimmed glasses. "Only other thing you need is a healthy dose of paranoia."

"Paranoia?" I asked, my unease growing with each step. It was becoming clear he hadn't brought me out here just to show off a farm.

"Paranoia. Mistrust." He gestured to the strung-up camouflage netting and the thick woods beyond. "They give me cover. When gov'mint drones fly overhead, they can't see what I got. My boy Vernon burrowed a cave into that mountain. After hollowing it out, we lined it with iron shipping containers sealed with foam for food and ten-by-ten oil drums holding fifteen hundred gallons of fuel. When SHTF comes, we're ready. We'll bow-hunt a right smart instead of shooting—quieter. Folks won't know we're here."

"Looks like you've thought of everything," I said, aware of the pistol holster tapping his hip.

"Yup. The end of days ain't long off. Plain and simple." He sniffed the air. "You can smell the firestorms from here, and Hurricane Helene kilt all them people in Asheville—might've near took us out, too. That's just the start. It won't be long now. Wars and rumors of wars… and I even got me a bomb shelter with ninety-degree turns in the tunnel."

I could've sworn something like suspicion smoldered behind his glasses as his eyes traveled the length of my body. "Radiation goes in a straight line. When—*not if*—but when the nukes come, them ninety-degree turns'll keep it from reaching us."

We cut through a grove of kudzu-strangled trees, the light dimming under a mesh of leaves. The deeper we went, the more the land changed—first a clear dirt trail, then tangled roots and briars, then an open field of waist-high weeds.

As I swished through the growth, a sick certainty settled in: Chet was taking me as far from the house as possible.

I should've turned and run like hell, but Johnny Devillers taught me the one thing not to do was run.

I knew I was taking a risk. I also knew it was worth it—if I could get information to stop the constant threats against me.

"Do you mind me asking how you make a living?"

"I own a small moving company—Two Preppers and a Truck. Part-time work, mostly helping folks relocate to secluded, undisclosed places where they don't want to be found. We do confidentiality contracts. Probably like what you do in therapy."

"Come to think of it, I might've seen your ad in *Survival Today*."

"Gets a lot of calls. 'Post-Collapse Real Estate: Move and Hide Now, Before the Digital Infrastructure Collapses.'" He shook his head. "Shame we gotta hide out in our own country nowadays."

He was as hardcore as any survivalist I'd met—maybe more, in his own way. Realizing how far we were from the main house, I slowed. "How much farther, Chet?"

He stopped and squared up to me. "Let's just say I don't want my wife to hear or see none of this." His eyes flicked toward the house, then back to me.

The razor edge in his voice raised the hair on my arms. His palm slid over the pistol grip.

"See what?" I asked. My mouth went dry.

With lightning speed, the old man drew.

One arm snapped around my neck in a chokehold. The other jammed the barrel to my temple.

I swallowed—loud enough to hear it.

"Mr. Clement, I came here in peace. What're you doing?"

"Name's Chet."

Then the air shifted—thick with the cloying stench of rot, something dead in the weeds nearby. Flies lifted in squadrons, humming over their feast.

I knew that smell.

I'd smelled it when I stumbled over Bucky. I'd smelled it when I found our cat bloated on the swampy banks of the Suwannee. I'd smelled it the night my little sister burned in the house fire our drunken daddy caused.

Death is death. Animal or human, the odor is the same—an awful certainty you never forget. Your eyes water. Your nostrils burn. It lodges in you. And no matter how hard you try, the moment you remember it, your brain resurrects the stink, and you feel the finality all over again.

Now it was back—unmistakable—as his trembling hand drove the pistol harder into my skull, demanding I call him Chet.

"Chet," I repeated, blinking fast, wondering maybe what I smelled wasn't the body in the weeds, but death coming for me.

A twitch in his cheek tightened into something close to a scowl. "I've showed you all my secrets. Now I reckon I gotta kill you—unless you tell me yorn." He spat a stream of tobacco juice at my feet.

My body went rigid. My heart hammered up into my throat.

"What would you like to know?" I croaked.

"You lied a right smart, accusing my boy of shooting at you," Chet growled. "I read all about it in the papers. Now you best tell me why you made up that story—right quick—before I blow your fucking head off."

Chapter Thirty-Two

"I didn't lie. I swear."

The gun ground harder into my skull as the old man's hand twitched.

"Didn't lie, my hind foot. Shit, you lied through your teeth." His eyes darted from the porch to my face. Sweat bled through his khaki shirt, and the air reeked of perspiration and Skoal-foul breath. "It weren't possible for Bucky to do what the papers claimed." The hammer clicked as he cocked the pistol. "Why'd you finger-point him?"

I flinched and licked the sweat as it slid off my forehead onto my cracked lips. "With all due respect, sir—"

He pressed the barrel deeper into my temple. "Name's Chet."

"Chet—over a year ago, I saw a photograph of Bucky. When I found him dead in the parking garage, it clicked where I'd seen him before. The Bucky Clement at my book signing looked like the same man in that photo—and the same one who pulled up beside me on a Harley and fired into my car."

Chet shot me a sideways look, like I'd lost my mind. "Motorcycle? That boy never straddled one in his life. I'da bought him one just to watch him try. And it'd take a skilled marksman to pull off what the papers said. Much as I tried, my Bucky couldn't shoot worth a damn."

"If your son didn't shoot at us," I said carefully, "then I want to know who did."

The pressure eased. He loosened his arm from my neck and lowered the gun to his side. I exhaled.

"I reckon we best head back toward the house." He turned and pushed through the weeds. I followed, rubbing my throat where he'd choked me.

"The whole notion of Bucky on a motorcycle, firing a gun like that—it's plumb crazy," he said, limping harder as he holstered the pistol. "If you truly believe my boy tried to kill you, you're crazier than a goddamned bedbug."

"Then how do you explain the bullets in the semiautomatic found in Bucky's purse matching the ones pulled from my Land Rover?"

He stopped and angled his head at me. "You believe that shit? Bucky wouldn't know what to do with a semiautomatic—or any gun, for that matter. He spat into the weeds. The law's crooked as a snake. Everything you say he did—the motorcycle, the shootin'—that's police work. That goddamned policewoman framed my boy and probably killed him, too. Same as she killed Vernon, my oldest."

"You mean Sergeant Phillips?"

"I mean Motorcycle Mary." He wiped sweat from beneath his pincushion nose. "You know her? You got city-slicker ways about you, same as her. You both talk like southern Yankees. If you're friends with her, I'll kill you right here."

"I—I don't know her," I stammered. "I just know *of* her. I met her."

"I wish Bucky was the shot they claim," Chet said. "But he never touched a gun. Took him target shootin' since he was knee-high, but he feared 'em. Hated the noise. Couldn't even get him to hold one, much less aim it."

I nodded. I understood that kind of fear.

"And a motorcycle?" he added. "Forget it. That boy didn't have a daredevil bone in his body."

As his version settled in, I felt something ugly shift in my gut. I'd taken Phillips's word at face value. If Chet was right, Bucky Clement couldn't have been the shooter. Which meant the gun in Bucky's purse had been planted. Phillips could've lied. She could've framed him.

Chet kept talking. "Bucky liked dolls when he was little. When my niece asked him to style her hair for prom, he was all over it. Always gentle. Liked dressin' like a girl. Never understood it—but I never judged him." His voice dipped. "They say he was dressed up the night he took a hatchet to the head. That true?"

"Yes, sir."

The tenderness in his voice caught me off guard.

"Now Vernon," he said, his jaw tightening. "Vernon was different. He knew guns. And Motorcycle Mary took them both from me. Took everything."

For a moment, I felt the weight of his loss. Then the Johnny Devillers part of me hardened. I wasn't here for sympathy.

"But why would she kill Bucky?" I asked.

"Revenge." Veins bulged in his neck as his arm sliced the air. "For the scar. Vernon gave her that scar—marked her for life. She calls us crackpots? She broke into my house while I was gone and shot my oldest between the eyes for the thrill of it. She loves killing. She's aiming for Chief of Police, and she'll do whatever it takes." He glared at me, his voice cold. "If I find out you hurt my boy, I'm coming for you. So now you got two folks to watch."

A chill crawled up my spine.

I thought of Phillips gently lifting a ladybug from my sweater and setting it free. I couldn't reconcile that woman with this story. Still, Chet's accusation echoed what the Malaprop's bookseller had said.

She'd just as soon shoot you as look at you.

As we headed back, I wiped sweat from my lip and asked, "The papers said neighbors complained about gunfire at all hours—that Phillips came out here for disturbance calls."

"I got a right to shoot on my own land." He wiped his mouth and pointed to a granite outcrop forming a flat ledge. "Let's sit a spell."

We settled there, overlooking the valley boxed in by jagged ridges. My gaze drifted to the yard behind the house—the human-shaped targets, the trampled weeds, the heavy boot prints.

After a moment, I said, "Word is this place is a military training site for the United Survivalist Army."

Chet snapped his head toward me. "I served in Vietnam. I earned my right to bear arms. I got a license, and I ain't broke no law. Folks complain about gun noise 'cause they want our guns taken away."

"Fair enough. I'm just trying to understand."

"Then understand this: I mind my own business and the Good Book."

His voice roughened. "Bible says there's a time for everything—even killin'. They'll have to kill me before they take my guns."

"In other words," I said, "mind my own business."

"Damn straight." His voice cracked. "The law took my boys. Me and Lil got nobody. What we do here ain't nobody else's concern."

Stripping it all down, my mind raced. Could Phillips have killed Bucky out of revenge? Had she planted the gun? And if so, how did she get it? And if that wasn't Bucky's face grinning from the Harley as bullets tore into my car—whose was it?

Then Lilly's voice rang from the porch. "Coffee's on. What's takin' y'all so long? Something wrong?"

"No," Chet called back. "Everything's fine."

She squinted toward the gate. "Then why's there a police car idling out there?"

Chet's face twisted as he stared at me. "You bring the law with you?"

"No, sir. I came alone."

He cupped his hand and yelled back, "Damned if I know. Get back inside."

Then, to me—low and sharp—"Boy, you playing me?"

"No, sir."

"I don't believe you," he said. "I trust you about as much as a goddamned Copperhead."

A flash of the Copperhead slithered up my leg.

He turned toward the house. I lagged a few steps behind, wondering if Phillips had tracked me—wondering what she might already be planning.

Chapter Thirty-Three

Loose boards creaked under our feet as Chet and I crossed the front porch. The midday sun flared off my car's windshield, blinding us both. Chet shaded his eyes and squinted toward the farm entrance. "I don't see no cop car." He stomped into the house.

I scanned the drive and the stretch of blacktop beyond it. "I don't see anything, either."

Was Phillips having me followed? She'd been furious that I'd come out here alone—*concerned for my safety*, she'd said. Now I wondered if it wasn't concern at all, but fear I might figure something out she was hiding.

The screen door shrieked open as Chet kicked it open, an M4 rifle in his hands.

"If one of them motherfuckers steps foot on my land, I'll blow their fuckin' heads off." He aimed toward the road, then lowered the barrel. "Ain't no law enforcement." He let the rifle sag at his hip and took a long breath.

Inside, Lilly banged pots and scraped pans. The smell of home cooking drifted down the hall. We stepped into the dim interior. Lilly met us halfway, wiping her hands on her apron.

"Won't you come on in, Doctor?"

"He's gotta be going, Lil."

"I'd be pleased to stay a while," I said, curious now—drawn toward the underbelly of this family.

Chet's mouth tightened, but Lilly led me into the living room. Chet dropped into a worn La-Z-Boy, kicked off his boots, and propped socked feet on an embroidered footstool. Lilly guided me to a tattered maroon couch, a cream-colored homemade coverlet draped over the back.

Pressed-tin ceiling tiles—painted pale blue—hovered low overhead. Sheer curtains twitched in a restless November breeze, letting in cool air, but the room resisted daylight.

The house—no, the whole farm—felt suspended on life support. Empty. Mourning. Not just two sons, but a way of life that had slipped beyond their grasp.

Time had marched on without them.

"What's the grub today?" Chet asked, avoiding my eyes.

"You'll see," Lilly said, shuffling back to the kitchen.

My attention drifted to a side table crowded with family photos. One stopped me cold—a man flanked by two women.

"Isn't that Eleanor Roosevelt?"

Chet leaned forward and pointed. "Yup. That's my grandpappy in the middle. On the other side's Mrs. Roosevelt's companion. Don't know her name. Grandpappy was her personal pilot—flew 'em wherever they needed."

He sifted through the frames and lifted one. "This here's worth something."

A woman cradled a banjo. She wore a rhinestone-trimmed denim blouse with fringe down the sleeves, cowgirl boots planted wide.

"Who's that?"

"The love of my life," he said. "Hillbilly Lilly. That's what they called her. She played with the Skillet Lickers. Toured the South. Live radio, too."

"So, Lilly's a musician."

"We met at a station in Tampa. I worked the transmitter. When she came to play, I adjusted her mic, looked into them brown eyes—love at first sight."

"Come and git it," Lilly called from the back of the house.

As we walked into the kitchen, a myriad of sounds welcomed us. Clanging pots. Clinking plates. And the soft scurrying of Lilly's feet.

"Fried chicken raised right here, creamed corn, stewed squash from the garden, biscuits, sweet tea—coffee later," she announced proudly. "Cooked it all on the wood stove."

We sat. Chet tucked his napkin into his collar. Lilly planted her elbows on the table, bowed her head, and blessed the food. We ate in silence at the white enamel table, outlined in black with silver-colored metal legs. Chet tore the chicken away from the bone with a vengeance, like a man starved, grease glistening on his fingers.

After a long spell, Lilly broke the silence. "Ya'll been talkin' 'bout Bucky."

Chet looked up, startled. "How'd you know that?"

"I seen the red in your eyes."

He glanced across the table at me. "Can't get nothin' past that woman."

"This calls for tears," she said quietly. "But I ain't got none left."

My throat felt the clutch of my grief. Barely able to swallow, I took a long swig of tea to get the food down.

"Got a Little League game to referee this afternoon," Chet said.

"Don't change the subject." Lilly reached into her apron pocket and pulled out a folded sheet of yellowed paper. She spoke in a grim voice. "I found a letter in my safe-keepings box that Bucky wrote as a boy—first time visiting the beach to see his Uncle Howard."

"Don't," Chet said, staring at his plate, drumming his fingers.

"I have to. Whilst the doctor's here." Hurt inflected in her voice. "It's the only way I know how to get you to open up."

"I told him everything he needs to know." Chet's eyes shot daggers at me. "You see what you done, coming here opening wounds?"

"You shut up," Lilly said. "Doctor's welcome in my home. You and me deal with hurt in different ways. And this time you ain't steamrolling over my heart."

Through steely eyes, her long neck swaying, she turned to me. "Doctor, Bucky wouldn't hurt nobody. He was a kind soul."

Her fist hit the table so hard a fork jackknifed and landed with a clang.

"Mind yourself, Lil."

"I'm tired of you and me pretendin'," she said, voice edged like broken glass. "I want us to mourn him—together. Feel something—you and me—instead of you hidin' out in the pasture snifflin' behind my back."

Chet squirmed.

Some people get self-conscious in the middle of an intimate conversation between strangers, but not me. I stayed still. Listening was my work. I met Lilly's hard stare and saw a heart locked tight with pain.

"Would you like me to read it?" I asked.

She nodded. "I'd be obliged."

Chet shot me a furious look. "Damn you to hell! This has got too far." He scooted the chair out behind him and stood. "Comin' in my house, messin' in my business."

"Set back down," Lilly demanded, palm raised. "And hush."

A defeated Chet plopped back into the chair, stared at the table, and pushed his plate aside, letting out a long sigh.

She placed the letter in my hands. The ink was faded, the child's smudged handwriting uneven. I read aloud, doing my best to keep an even tone.

* * *

Saturday Morning, June

Dear Daddy and Mama Lil:

I miss you very much. I have been to the ocean two times already and I found three pretty rocks. Two are purple and one is white, green, and black. We had a picnic today. A crab pinched my big toe today. I went swimming and I pulled up a weed that was pink and black. I was scared of it. Have the chickens mated yet? I hope so because I want some biddies when I come home. Having a wonderful time. Are the baby ducks okay? A airplane, I mean a jet just came over the house now. It jarred the house and scared me. Uncle Howard is watching the baseball game now. It is a home run. Them jets scare me all the time. We are going to the beach again Friday. Aunt Judy got a sunburn so she walks like a starched shirt.

Here are some kisses

X O X O X O

Your son, Bucky

* * *

A single tear slid from Lilly's eye, circled through the wrinkles in her face, and trickled onto the top of her apron. Chet broke, folding over the table, sobbing into the cradle of his arms. Lilly bit her bottom lip, rubbed his back, then mouthed at me, *Thank you*.

I nodded.

"Pantry's full," she said softly, caressing his hand. "We'll get by."

Chet raised his head and removed his glasses, wiping his eyes with the heel of his hand. "Doctor, you best be going."

I stood. "Thank you for the delicious meal."

She managed a sad smile. "Thank you, Doctor."

I shuffled behind Chet, mumbling as he limped to the front door.

On the porch, he muttered, "You made my life worse coming here, stickin' your nose where it don't belong."

"I didn't mean to pry."

"I'm tellin' you what I told that damn Rudy. If you come back, I'll kill you for trespassin'."

The screen door slapped shut behind us.

"Rudy?" I asked.

Chet slumped onto the porch sofa. "Rudy Norris. Bad influence. Bullied my boy somethin' awful."

"The owner of Babette's Feast?"

"Owner, shit. He runs it but don't own it. Owner's a bald-headed man name of John Babette—muscular guy, wears two earrings. Rudy's a drifter, never owned nothin' in his life—manages places. That queer bar. That rental company—Mountaintop Getaways."

"Mountaintop Getaways?"

"You deaf? Rudy's one crazy motherfucker. Told me it give him pleasure seein' the blood of the unprepared spilled. Now, how fucked up is that? Goin' around braggin' to folks he served in Iraq."

My stomach tightened. If Rudy managed François' rental company, he had access to our house keys, too. I glanced at my watch and edged one foot onto the steps. "I gotta be going. Appreciate the information."

I headed for my car, but before I climbed in, Chet called out.

"Wait." He limped to the edge of the porch. "I ain't the type to go again' my people, but there's a few bad apples. Rudy's one. Another troublemaker givin' us a bad name is nicknamed Red somethin' or another."

"Frank Mallory?"

"That's him. Big ole red-headed fucker. If you want to find Bucky's killer, go to Smoky Mountain Tavern, a hole in the wall, down by the French Broad River. I 'spect you'll find everythin' you need to know."

I nodded. "Thank you, sir."

"Name's Chet." His eyes narrowed. "I got a feelin' me and you ain't finished yet. Don't come back here no more lest you got news of Bucky's killer."

"Okay, Chet." I slipped behind the wheel, my mind full of more questions than answers.

As I drove away, my mind churned with images of Frank, then Rudy. As manager of Mountaintop Getaways, he had access to keys for all the rental properties. He claimed he wasn't at Babette's Feast the night I was attacked. He was such a liar I couldn't take anything he said at face value.

I wondered if he drove a Harley.

I cranked the engine and spun my wheels, crunching gravel down the driveway. The rearview mirror showed the old man, slumped on the porch sofa, spitting tobacco juice, Lilly's steady hand on his shoulder—until a twist in the road erased them from sight.

Chapter Thirty-Four

On my drive back into town from Clement farm, I had plenty of windshield time to replay the haunting image of Chet Clement kicking open his screen door, with an M4 in his hands. He meant business. But what nagged at me more was the way he'd said *Smoky Mountain Tavern*—like it wasn't a suggestion so much as a warning.

My next step was to check out the beer joint but not without a handgun. Arming myself would raise the stakes—raise the odds of getting killed or killing someone else. As someone who abhorred violence, it meant crossing a line I'd spent my whole life avoiding. But sidestepping hadn't worked.

My daddy taught me how to rope steer and shoot every kind of gun on the planet. "Start 'em young," he'd say. When I was nine, he strapped an AK-47 around my neck, proudly dubbing me his "biddy boy soldier." He lined up cans in the backyard with the care of a surgeon and made me shoot them one by one. The assault rifle was nearly as big as me, and I hated the crack it made—the violence of the sound. I preferred the hum of my computer, the quiet click of the keys.

When I refused to target-shoot and instead holed up in my room with my computer, Daddy shipped me to gun camp. Every summer, I spent a week practicing combat with boys my age. Real military weapons were shoved into my arms, and I was made to shoot at human-shaped targets that popped up from behind barrels.

Until my shoulder ached and my ears rang. But I knew if I failed, Daddy would beat me, so I gave it everything I had.

And they pinned medals on me for top marksmanship.

As I got older, I understood what I'd been unable to name as a child: Daddy hated me from the day I was born—he resented the attention Mama gave me, resented the way her love shifted to me. In turn, I learned to hate the guns and violence my father worshipped.

And I learned not to become like him.

But I'd avoided it as long as I could. I was left with no other choice. It was time to arm myself. Not out of pride but out of survival.

It was still early. The tavern wouldn't start jumping until nightfall. So, I swung by *Asheville Guns & Gear* on Sweeten Creek Road. The tires juddered over last winter's potholes as the city slid past my windows.

A tattoo parlor. A vacant car dealership. A couple of stoplights and bridges. Then, Mission Hospital, where young residents in blue scrubs and white lab coats streamed across Biltmore Avenue toward a parking deck. My tires bumped over railroad tracks. An old woman stood with a shopping bag, patiently waiting for a bus, cell phone glued to her ear. A trolley packed with tourists went by me in a whoosh, fingers pointing at sights I no longer knew how to see.

Watching strangers safely go about their lives was comforting and disorienting at the same time. How could other lives keep rolling along while mine felt freeze-framed—one I'd do anything to fast-forward through? Of course, I only saw people from the outside. I didn't know what burdens they carried, what fears prowled the corners of their minds. When I considered that, I felt less alone. Common wounds. Different shapes. Same ache.

I swung left off Biltmore Avenue onto Sweeten Creek. The gun store lay ahead—squat, dilapidated, empty-looking. I nosed into the barren parking lot, took a breath, and stepped inside.

The dimly-lit shop was crowded with rifles, semiautomatics, and handguns—rows upon rows, metal and polymer and intention. The sheer number of choices was overwhelming.

A leather-jacketed man with a beer gut, drooling tobacco juice, appeared from the back of the store, the sound of a flushing toilet behind him. Zipping his pants, he swung sleepy eyes toward me. "What can I do for you?"

"I'd like to purchase a handgun."

"Got a permit?"

"No," I said, hoping this was the sort of place that wasn't bothered by technicalities.

"It ain't gonna happen today, then." His face was half-hidden by pork chop sideburns. He swiped his hand over his slicked-back ducktail. "Gotta get one from the Buncombe County Sheriff's Office, and my computer's down. Won't get repaired until tomorrow. Else I could get electronic approval in a split second."

Shit. "I can't wait until tomorrow," I said. "I need that gun today. I beg you, sir—if there's any way you could—?"

I knew the jail time I risked if I carried illegally. And after Phillips checked me out on her computer and learned I was arrested for Big Jake's murder, the risk of being denied was too great. But the risk of *not* protecting myself was even greater.

The man examined me with an arched brow and a shit-eating grin. "Oh, I get it. You in some kind of trouble?"

"No trouble," I said, shaking my head. "Trouble's after me, though."

"Then use your fucking fists." He shot me a thorny look, lifted an empty Dole's pineapple can from below the counter, and spat into it. "That's why god gave you hands—for fightin'. I don't get why everybody nowadays thinks they need a gun to settle their differences."

"It's a little more complicated than that, sir."

"Complicated, shit!" He wiped his mouth. "Sounds like you're yellow. Hidin' behind a gun. You need to man up, son."

I cringed at the term "man up," my mind searing white-hot with Daddy's rules.

"Don't be such a pussy. I'm gonna make a man outa you, yet."

Stomping feet. Closet door squeaking. Clothes hangers shrieking against a metal rod. Clothes smashed against the wall. A leather belt yanked from the racks. The painful swing of leather against my back. Angry welts rising on my tender skin. Me scrambling, him jerking me back. My face slammed against the wall.

Mama saw me gushing blood and screamed for him to stop. She swept me behind her like an angry wildcat, hammering him in the nape of the neck with a fire poker. He grabbed her by the throat of her nightgown and accused her of loving me more than him.

He fisted her in the jaw, and she fell to her knees wailing, the fire poker clanging as her face landed against the cold, wooden floor. His knuckles had robbed her of her Angelina Jolie good looks, put dark circles around her eyes, and deep lines in her cheeks. His signature punch made her look older than her years. Already, she'd begun to walk with a cane.

My last memory of Mama was standing side-by-side in front of the smoldering ruins after Daddy had set our house on fire in a drunken rage. She was screaming for my little sister, begging the fireman to let her back inside.

I watched Mama's bare feet as she struggled against the fireman's strong arms, saw the black boots of his unit running toward the house.

I didn't know yet that my sister wouldn't make it out alive.

But I knew our lives would never be the same.

"Hey, mister—are you on something?" the gun seller asked.

"On something?" I blinked hard, bracing my hands on the counter.

"Your eyes look glassy, like you're somewhere else."

"Just high on life," I said—a sarcastic cover for how my heart ached.

"Well, I got a business to run," he snorted. "You're gonna have to beg, borrow, or steal from somebody if you want a gun—but it ain't gonna be from me."

Beg, borrow, or steal.

A lightbulb went on.

I just begged. I wouldn't steal.

But borrow?

"Yeah," I said, backing away. "Thanks for your help."

As I pushed through the door, the man shouted after me, "Use your fuckin' fists!"

I drove back over railroad tracks and potholes, past Mission Hospital and McCormick Field—past people living their lives I could only understand from the outside—back to Clampton Road. I climbed the curving street to the house on the ridge and screeched to a halt in front of the rental.

I looked up at François's house. Two bodies moved erratically in an upper window where a sheer curtain wavered in the wind.

I skipped down the stone steps, flew into Gigi and Smiley's bedroom, and rummaged through their closet. Smiley's duffel bag sat on the floor. I unzipped the bag and slid the handgun from its holster.

I lifted it out.

My fingers glided over the semiautomatic. The weight of the powerful weapon gave me a strange, shameful comfort—solid as certainty. I plundered through the duffel again until I found the ammunition.

Standing, I drew a breath and loaded the magazine. The vague smoky scent unearthed a boyhood memory—firecrackers after a Fourth of July explosion.

Except this wasn't a day to celebrate.

It was a day to mourn.

I recoiled at the thought of betraying my Buddhist beliefs, using the force of a firearm for protection. I'd spent my life trying to be nothing like my old man. And yet here I was, loading a gun, preparing to defend myself the way he taught me.

Mixed emotions dogging me like shadows, I shuffled back into the great room. The sun slipped behind the western mountains, and darkness began to cloak the house. The temperature outside dropped into the forties. I pushed the thermostat to seventy, kicked off my boots, and propped my socked feet on the coffee table.

Then I glanced down—thanks to Smiley—and stroked my new best friend, the G43 single-stack 9mm semiautomatic lying beside me on the couch.

Chapter Thirty-Five

It was around 7:00 p.m. by the time I pulled into the gravel parking lot of the Smoky Mountain Tavern. I angled into a tight spot between a jeep and two double-parked motorcycles. Above the squat cement building choked in kudzu, a crescent moon hung low and watchful. From inside my car, I heard muffled music and saw shadowy figures behind a large glass window—hands and bottles raised high, bodies swaying. A red neon sign with several burned-out letters pressed against the inside glass blinked weakly, several letters burned out: *S oky Mou tain T vern.*

I stepped out, stretched my legs, and had an absurd thought that today wasn't a good day to die. Still, the risk was worth it. Chet had said a handful of troublemakers made all the survivalists look bad—proof of a fracture in their ranks. The low rumble of voices rose and fell in a strange incantation, layered over the constant whine of insects in the bushes. A handmade cardboard sign taped to the door read *"FDGB Tonite."*

I pulled my leather jacket tight, felt the reassuring jab of Smiley's gun against my chest, and pushed through the squeaky wooden door.

Inside, I stuffed my hands in the pockets of my jeans, out of place amid a sea of military camouflage. I squeezed just past the threshold, boxed in by hunched shoulders. The stench was thick with spilled beer, the prickly sweat of damp body heat, and sour-smelling clothes.

In the background, a whiney guitar and Lainey Wilson's voice pumped, *If I smell like smoke, it's only 'cause I've been through hell*—nearly drowned out by beer-guzzling patrons, mostly men. Naked light bulbs dangled from the low ceiling, casting weak yellow beams over the dark, drab room.

I'd arrived at the tail end of a rally. Spectators with raised rifles faced a hooded man, dressed head-to-toe in black with two eyeholes cut into the fabric. I'd read that doomsday survivalists wore black at night so they could move unseen and infiltrate secure places, complete deadly missions.

A chill lifted the hairs on my arm. The memory of Daddy taking me to a Ku Klux Klan rally washed over me—and I shoved it back down.

From a small stage draped in a Confederate flag, the hooded man, speaking with a heavy accent, raised both hands.

"Prepare to survive—or die," He roared.

Arms shot up across the room.

"Prepare to survive—or die!" The crowd echoed the rally cry.

I swallowed the geyser of bile that shot halfway up my throat.

"We are a band of brothers and sisters," the man continued. "We do what is best for our members and their families in the struggle for survival."

Beer bottles and rifles rose in a united toast.

"Unless we act to protect our Second Amendment rights, the end will come sooner than you think. The federal government, they are changing laws to take what is ours and giving it to the blood suckers."

"Damn right!" yelled the vaguely familiar bald man beside me. Over his military camo, he wore a red T-shirt stamped *FDGB* in large white letters—the same letters pasted from the entrance door. A wad of chew bulged his bottom lip. He turned to me. "Where you from?"

"Here," I said, staking my claim to Asheville with more confidence than I felt.

"Ain't seen you before." He studied me, wiped his scruffy beard with the back of his hand.

I nodded, willing myself not to look self-conscious. I'd worn jeans, open denim shirt, leather jacket—close enough to fit in. But even the cowboy boots didn't quite cut it.

Then, it clicked—the bald head, scruffy beard, the okra-fried drawl. "I thought you looked familiar," I said. "I've seen your YouTube videos—the ones you narrate from the shooting range. I'm a big fan."

His face broke into a grin. He reached out and shook my hand. "Name's

Oren. Oren Ralls."

"Ein," I said, meeting his grip.

From the stage, the man in black pressed on. "The zombies are bringing America down without firing a shot. They infiltrate our government. They feed off handouts and want us to do the same. When civilization collapses, they'll ravage everything we've saved. Are you goin' to let that happen?"

"Hell, no!" The YouTube narrator beamed at me, taking me into his confidence.

With Oren Ralls apparent acceptance, my fears of being outed as a "zombie" eased. I started to relax a bit as I listened to the man in black.

"Their ears are deaf to our clarion call."

Boos and catcalls erupted. Guns lifted. Two-handed salutes flashed through the crowd.

"My fellow *Gawkers*, the ship is sinking. It's time to grab the deaf and blind zombies by the head and shake them until they wake up. If they do not listen, you know what to do next."

Cheers and wolf whistles filled the room.

"We must preserve our homeland no matter what it takes. The United Survivalist Army has united our people. At the appointed time and place—known only to true believers—we will celebrate our victory with FDGB. Spread the word! The moment is almost upon us."

Then, with a flourish: "And now, the man you really came to see—Military leader. True patriot—give it up for Oren Ralls."

Oren took the stage, raised his arms, declaring, "Prepare to survive—or die."

The crowd mirrored him—louder this time, "Prepare to survive—or die."

I scanned the assembly of survivalists from around the nation—former cops, firefighters, and radical military vets—angry with the United States government for betraying them—ready for war against their own country.

Oren accepted an iPad from the hooded man. The scruffy-bearded Ralls looked out over raised fists and began a roll call, his tone booming and reverent.

"Sam Weatherford, Live Oak, Florida."

"Here, Sir!"

"James Heath, Little Rock, Arkansas."

"Here, Sir!"

"Blake Lopez, Austin, Texas."

"Present, Sir!"

Listening to the head count—states scattered across the country—I thought of Chet's words about a few bad apples. Standing there, it felt like the whole barrel was rotten. But he was right about one thing—I'd find everything I needed to know here. Just by entering the room, I'd learned more than I expected.

I knew survivalists were intensely dedicated to their cause. Now I saw with my own eyes how far doomsayers would go. Just as they'd done for their country when they served, they were prepared to sacrifice their lives for their new army.

I milled through the yellowed light, thick clouds of cigarette smoke, and the glow of Carling Black Label and Budweiser signs, while Oren continued the roll call.

Drunken eyes followed me.

"Here, sir!" Near the back, a man in an FDGB T-shirt emblazoned with a coiled snake raised his fist, then swiped a hand over his slicked-back mullet.

The snake shake.

A toilet flushed, and a leather-jacketed man with a beer gut walked out of the bathroom to join the man with the mullet. He lit a cigarette, elbowed his friend, and, from behind a cloud of smoke, thumbed the air in my direction.

I nodded toward the gun-shop salesman with pork chop sideburns and ducktail.

He cocked his head, confused maybe, then exchanged a nod of recognition, not warmth.

When the roll call ended, my gaze roved the room. I wondered what FDGB meant and who was underneath the black hood. I crossed the grimy floor, felt my shoes stick to the muck of cigarette butts and sloshed beer.

Under the soft twang of Hank Williams crooning "Your Cheatin' Heart," I slid onto an empty barstool and ordered a Coors. I downed it fast.

Out of the corner of my eye, I noticed two figures near the entrance. Through the smoky haze, I made out a tall, broad-shouldered man with a smaller figure beside him. When they stepped further into the light, I saw Frank and another man—both in combat boots and military garb—shouldering assault rifles.

When Frank spotted me, he smirked and elbowed the man, who abruptly turned and disappeared into the crowd. Frank mingled through the smoke-filled room, going from table to table, swaying and glad-handing other patrons.

He sidled up beside me, smacked down a wad of bills, and ordered a Guinness, waving to his buddies while he waited. When the bartender slid the beer down the slick counter, Frank scooped it up with one hand, adjusted his rifle with the other. He guzzled the beer, slammed the empty bottle on the counter, and ordered another one.

"Where's your sidekick?" I asked, refusing to pretend we hadn't noticed each other.

"Well, if it ain't the grasshopper." He swept his eyes toward me and, through slurred speech, said, "Jail. She struck two men in the face with brass knuckles. Broke 'em up pretty bad. They said she can't come back in here."

"Somebody else is broken up pretty damn bad, too," I said.

"Yeah? Who's that?"

"The Clement family. I just paid old man Clement a visit."

Frank straightened; his body swelled. "What'd I tell you about sticking your nose where it don't belong?"

"I imagine you know a man by the name of Rudy Norris."

"Hell yeah, I know Rudy. What business is that of yours?"

"Chet Clement told me Rudy liked to bully his son, Bucky. Just wondered if Rudy had any beef enough to want to kill him."

"You askin' the wrong person, Grasshopper."

Nursing my beer, I looked up at the big man. "Where were you the night Bucky was killed?"

Frank lowered his head into my face. "You accusin' me, Grasshopper?"

"Nope, just asking. Did you and Tonya attack us when we drove into Asheville?" Then, I stirred the pot with what couldn't be true after talking with Chet. "Or maybe you got Bucky Clement to do your dirty work, then got rid of him so he couldn't snitch on you."

Red-faced, Frank smirked, then his lips flatlined. "Why don't you get the fuck out of my seat and go chirp at somebody else?"

I'd had about enough of his crap. After a long swig of beer, I stood up and inspected the back of the barstool. "Damnedest thing…I don't see Piss Ant stamped on it." I tilted my beer in the direction of the empty seat behind him. "There's another one right there."

A glower fixed on his freckled face. "I want the one you're in."

He broadened his shoulders and steel-eyed me.

I used an expression from the Johnny Devillers playbook. "Want in one hand and shit in the other." Then, I turned my back on Frank and spoke over my shoulder, "See which one fills up first."

"I'm gonna fuck you up this time!"

He jerked the back of my jacket, pulling the stool down and sending me sliding on my back across the floor. My skin stung from skating over the layers of grit.

Pulling myself upright, I felt for my gun. Before I could land on it, Frank hit me with an uppercut. The blow came fast and hard, threw me against the bar.

I swung at him and missed. He answered with a hard fist to the side of my head. My ears rang, but I managed to stay on my feet. One thing Johnny drilled in my head before punching me was, "No matter how hard they strike, stay on your god-damned feet!"

A swelling crowd in battle dress gathered around us. I felt the circle of heavy, besotted eyes descend on me. "Beat the shit out of the city slicker, Red," yelled one man.

I gave him a stiff right jab to his jaw.

His strength surprised me, his adrenaline surging maybe because his *Gawker* buddies were watching. As if he hadn't felt the punch, Frank's head protruded forward, charging at me. He planted his shoulder into my chest, lifting me up by my butt cheeks, and spearing me hard onto the concrete floor. I had to get up, but he had knocked the air out of me.

Stay on your god-damned feet!

Standing and wheezing hard, I wiped the hair out of my eyes, reached for the gun again. This time I found it in the left inside pocket of my leather jacket and pulled it out. "Okay, goddammit," I said. "You don't know what big-time fucked up is. You come one step closer, and I'll blow your piss-ant brains out."

Seeing the gun, Frank backed off, throwing up his callused palms and scarred knuckles in a surrender sign. He examined me for a long minute, then smirked. "I bet you don't even know how to use that thing."

I kept my eyes fixed on Red, waiting for him to make a move on a weapon of his own. "Try me, Piss Ant."

"Whoa, Frank. Looks like you've met your match." A voice broke the tension from outside the crowd.

The onlookers parted an opening for Oren Ralls, an obvious sign of respect. He stepped inside the circle, "Hey dude, you're all right." He threw an arm around my shoulder. "Not many people have the balls to take on Red the way you just done."

Then he growled at Frank. "Leave him be. He's with me." Oren's tone mirrored bad blood between him and Frank. From the snickers in the room, I sensed the other men didn't like him much, either.

The gun shop owner appeared and slung an arm over my shoulder. "Hey, I thought I knowed you. You the one I told to use your fists. Where'd you get that damn Glock? I didn't sell it to you."

"A friend," I said, wiping a smear of blood from my mouth.

Seeing me shielded by his comrades, Frank's face twitched. "This beer's going straight through me. I gotta take a piss."

After he disappeared into the crowd, the men surrounding me continued to jabber about how I stood up to Red. I vaguely heard one of them mention David and Goliath. But my attention drew to the other side of the room at a pair of gaping, beady eyes on me.

The familiar figure cut me periodic glances, stepping behind support posts to dodge my gaze. The hairs on my arms started to lift as I nonchalantly ambled in his direction. The closer I got, the farther away he moved, clearly trying to hide. He pulled his red hat, emblazoned with *GAWKERS*, low over his elongated face.

A dark, shaggy-haired man weaved through the thinning crowd, joined the man in the red hat, and they left together. I knew my status, after standing up to Frank, wouldn't last long. As I headed straight for the door, a hand snagged my arm. "Hey buddy. FDGB. Catch you at the tunnel," Oren said. "I expect you in combat gear this time, locked and loaded."

I nodded, feigned that I understood, and looked through the window. Outside, the shaggy-haired man stared back at me.

It was François.

The man in the red hat glanced back over his shoulder.

His sneer was a dead giveaway—Eldred Nunn.

François and Eldred hopped into a car and peeled out of the lot.

I quick-stepped to my car, wiping a small patch of blood from my face, putting the pieces together.

By now, Eldred had told the Real U.S.A. everything about me.

The Real U.S.A. knows everything about you. Frank had said. *Where you are. Who you're with. What you eat. Even when you shit.*

That meant Oren's "buddy talk" was nothing but a setup. His parting words pulsed in my head like the sign *S oky Mou tain T vern* flashing back at me from inside the window.

FDGB

Tunnel.

Combat gear.

Locked and loaded.

Chapter Thirty-Six

The next morning, I woke to find the red digits of my bedside clock blinking *5:30*. I yawned, replaying the night at the tavern, turning over the friendship between Frank and François, and wondering what they were up to. I sat on the side of the bed and ran my fingers through disheveled hair. My thoughts turned to the tunnel and FDGB. I hadn't seen the letters mentioned anywhere on the websites I'd combed through.

Before anyone else stirred, I slid on my glasses, grabbed my laptop, and Googled FDGB, stunned at the number of hits—T-shirts and drinking mugs inscribed with FDGB, extremist references, and slang definitions.

Wikipedia said it was a German organization, part of the National Front, formed shortly after World War II with compulsory membership. Its leaders were members of the ruling Socialist Unity Party of Germany. Another search claimed it meant *Fall Down Go Boom*—slang for mayhem.

Mayhem and *Socialism* rang in my head.

The site defined FDGB as "an abbreviation for a very severe kind of crash that will leave a smoking crater wherever the victim lands."

"Holy shit!"

Was the U.S.A planning to blow up Beaucatcher Tunnel?

The thought caused a cold breath to brush along the back of my neck, followed by a loud, hard exhale. The exhale was mine, but the cold breath? Where did that come from? My body knew before my mind caught up. Psychologists call it intuition; I call it survival.

I looked up from the computer. Beyond the sliding glass doors, morning fog hugged the valley below, spreading like a rumpled blanket over the city.

The rising sun shot spears of light through the mist. *Beautiful illusion,* I thought. The Asheville mountains had a way of doing that—making you forget what weighed on your mind.

Running did that for me, too—calmed my body, cleared my head. The pressure of trying to figure everything together lifted like steam rising off a sunbaked street after a summer rain.

I laced up my Nikes, stretched my hamstrings against the stone stairs, and jogged downhill, curling around the mountain before turning onto Town Mountain Road.

The early-morning run summoned images of *Look Homeward Angel*—Thomas Wolfe walking this same road. I ignored the sting of the cold as I tore down the steep grade in long strides—easy down, hard up. I reached College Street, crushed fallen leaves underfoot, and turned past City Centre onto the empty downtown streets.

After the run, I showered, dressed, and headed east to the Veterans Administration Medical Center to speak with the PTSD group. As I drove onto the hospital grounds, dark clouds rolled in, shrouding everything in foreboding, and I thought of Chet.

He'd said it wasn't Bucky Clement I needed to focus on—it was Rudy Norris or Frank, a.k.a. Red. After seeing Frank with François, I added the Frenchman to the list. Even Chet could be a suspect. One thing I'd learned about survivalists, was they were either close-mouthed—or lying to throw you off. For all I knew, my encounter with Chet had been a setup.

The old mustard-colored buildings loomed—stark, drab, sharp-edged against the snow-heavy clouds tumbling over the mountains.

After parking, I shouldered my backpack, my ears stinging from wind gusts. The metal fasteners on the American flag clanged an urgent call against the flagpole. I climbed the steps to the hospital entrance, my pace keeping time with the sound.

By the time I neared the main entrance, the sky had darkened to coal black, stampeding over patients—on crutches, in wheelchairs, or supported by family—hurrying through the automatic sliding doors, their breath white from cold.

Inside, sharp medicinal smells—embedded in walls and floors—filled my nostrils. Shoulder-to-shoulder patients jammed the waiting rooms, some slack-jawed, lifeless eyes gaping at televisions mounted on the walls.

My phone vibrated against my hip. I stiffened when I saw Chris's name and tried to punch *Accept,* but the call went straight to voicemail. Before I could call back, Dr. Mitchell Ford—the rotund, baby-faced head of the medical staff—approached me, hand extended.

"Welcome, Dr. Pope. The group's been looking forward to your visit." He removed the stethoscope that hung around his neck and tucked it into his lab coat pocket.

"My pleasure," I said. "So have I."

"This way," he said, moving his hand forward.

The grayish-haired, blue-eyed man led me through several winding corridors to another wing. We entered a large therapy room, buzzing with low-rumbled conversations. Men and women of every ethnicity sat in metal folding chairs—young Iraq and Afghanistan vets, some amputees, others bandaged. Older men with beards and long hair wrapped in bandanas, likely Vietnam-era. A ceiling fan carried the aroma of stale cigarette smoke and pores thick with alcohol.

My eyes scanned the room of troubled faces, searching for Rudy. As latecomers slipped into seats, Dr. Ford worked the room, trading easy banter with the vets. The softened looks on their hardened faces told me they trusted him.

Just as I was about to give up, my gaze landed on a scruffy-haired man with bushy eyebrows. He turned toward me. No lazy green eye. Not Rudy.

Dr. Ford ambled over. "Ready to go?" he asked.

"One quick question," I said under my breath, steering him aside. "Is there a patient named Rudy Norris in this group?"

He rubbed his chin. "Don't recognize the name. Why?"

"He told me he attends weekly PTSD group therapy here."

"I run the only groups like this in the hospital," he replied. "Never heard of him. And the only absentee today is a woman."

"Maybe it was another group."

"Tell you what. I'll check the system after I introduce you—if you don't mind my stepping out."

"That'd be great."

After the introduction, I took the only empty chair in the circle. I asked the eight men and three women to share their names and brief descriptions about their challenge with post-war trauma. I'd worked with vets for years and never tired of hearing their stories—the courage, the pain, the sacrifice. It reminded me of why I did this work.

Once everyone had spoken, I talked about the path to resilience. The group was all ears. Minutes later, Dr. Ford slipped back in and settled into a chair in the back of the room. After a few guided exercises, I distributed handouts.

When the hour ended, the vets lined up to shake my hand. Several, eyes wet, pulled me into bear hugs, thanking me for the session. Moments like that grounded me.

After the last patient had trickled out the door, a smiling Dr. Ford shuffled from the back of the room and shook my hand. "Thank you for your time today," he said. "That was powerful."

"It's an honor. Thank you for having me." I rifled through my backpack and handed him several journal articles on trauma. "You might find these useful resources."

He flipped through them, nodding. Then his brow furrowed. "By the way—there's no patient named Rudy Norris in our system."

The flat statement stopped me cold. "And…there's no other VA hospital close by?"

"No. This facility serves a hundred-mile radius. If he attended weekly groups, he'd be here. I didn't find him anywhere in the national VA system, either. Could he be using an alias?"

"I don't think so."

Goosebumps popped up on my arms. Chet's assessment had been spot-on. *He tells folks he served in Iraq, but I don't believe it for a minute.*

I shouldered my backpack, said goodbye, and headed outside, eager to hear Chris's message. Quick-stepping to the car, I jerked the phone from my coat pocket. I hunched my shoulders against the wind—cold, bitter, and unforgiving—shoveling snow down the back of my neck. I raised the collar, pulled the coat tighter.

Several messages popped up on my phone. Sliding behind the steering wheel, I pressed play on the message from Chris.

"Ein… you need to call me back. Right away."

I pressed *call back*. Chris answered. I had the photos enlarged, but never got around to sending them to Phillips. After I got your message, I opened them and…. "It was Phillips all along."

"How do you know?"

"The license plate—MOTOR-M-6279. "I did a search of public records in North Carolina. When I typed in the plate number, the system showed me—registered to Mary Elaine Phillips. Asheville, North Carolina, along with vehicle make, model and year—even the tag expiration date."

It sounded damning—and explained the inconsistencies in how she'd been handling the case—but something still didn't add up.

"You need to take this to the police," he said.

"Which police?" I shot back. "She's one of them—a member of the family in blue. She'd discredit me, convince them I'm crazy. And then she'd know I'm on to her."

"What're you going to do?"

"Dig deeper. I'm looking into several people. Now, I need to throw Phillips in the pot along with Rudy and the rest."

"Who's Rudy? What do you mean 'all the rest'?"

"Things turned more complicated since you left."

"How's that possible?"

"I'm playing my cards close to the chest, waiting with my new sidekick."

His voice dropped. "Oh, I see. Someone new? That was fast."

"No, no, I mean…it's a handgun."

"Handgun?" Alarm in his voice.

"The only good thing Johnny taught me was to shoot."

"I'm coming up to Asheville!"

The line clicked, then went dead.

"No, dammit, Chris!"

I tossed the phone into the passenger seat. I didn't want him walking into danger. I kicked myself for telling him about the gun.

I was on a collision course with the survivalists. Now, Chris was headed right into the thick of it. I had to get Gigi, Smiley, and the sisterfriends packed up.

I had a feeling this wasn't going to end well.

Chapter Thirty-Seven

I floor-boarded the car back to the rental house. Snowcaps loomed on the distant mountains. Under bright blue skies, the snow was melting, and the roads had mostly cleared. Typical Asheville weather—snow one minute, sunshine the next. My tires spun on the occasional patch of slush and ice.

My mind spun, too, replaying everything that had happened since we arrived. Rudy was a fraud, flashing military medals for attention. Phillips and Jim were an unsolved puzzle. Frank and François were pals. And a suspendered survivalist named Oren had befriended me, expecting I'd show up at the tunnel for FDGB, whatever the hell that meant.

As I entered Beaucatcher Tunnel heading west, the elegant arch stonework, beveling the dark mouth of the passageway, caught my eye. I zipped through the guts of the mountain and exited on the other side. My cell phone beeped.

I pulled into an empty parking lot. An email from the DNA clinic. My pulse jumped as I opened the PDF. The report confirmed the dried blood on the medicine ball matched my DNA and dated it to the night of the attack.

"Yes!" I shouted, pumping my fist.

I gunned the engine and screeched back onto the blacktop, my rear tires skittering over ice. I scaled Town Mountain Road, forcing myself to keep the speedometer under forty, wary of skidding off the mountainside. When I turned onto Clampton Street, my eyes swept the house for signs of anything wrong.

A note from Gigi was taped to the front door, saying they'd gone to tour the caverns at Linville Gorge—about two hours away. The limestone caves were a popular destination for visitors wanting a peek of the Blue Ridge's subterranean underbelly.

Beside her note, another sheet of paper flapped in the breeze. In block letters, it read: *Your Going Down.*

Relief washed over me knowing Gigi and her posse had left town for a spell.

What stood out, beyond the threat, was the misspelling. My mind jumped to Frank's website where he used *your* for *you're.* Then again, the error could've come from someone whose first language wasn't English.

I grabbed the note, unlocked the door, and stepped inside. I flopped down in the great room and called Gigi to check in, careful not to worry her with mention of the license plate or the note.

"I'm getting to the bottom of everything that happened," I told her. "You all enjoy yourselves."

"We're staying two nights at the Linville Inn," she said. "Almost there now. François said it can easily take a couple of days to see everything."

A finger of unease traced my spine. "When did you talk with François?"

"This morning. He waved, and we chatted for a bit."

"Gigi—listen to me. Don't tell anyone where you're going or what you're doing. Anyone."

"Ein—"

"The blood on the medicine ball matched my DNA." I trampled over her words, unwilling to hear another lecture about paranoia.

A pause. "Okay, son. I love you. Please be careful."

"*You* be careful," I replied. "And I love you, too."

I opened up my browser and typed "RUDY NORRIS/ASHEVILLE." After an exhaustive search, nothing.

"Did you mean: *Rex* Norris?" my search engine suggested.

I changed the entry to "REX NORRIS/ASHEVILLE."

Bingo.

Rex Jamey Norris's Facebook page popped up. The profile photo showed the same scowling face—bushy eyebrows, lazy green eye, and all. He hadn't locked down his account. The "about" section listed his employment at Mountaintop Getaways and Babette's Feast.

Whitepages.com put him in an apartment on Clingman Avenue in the River Arts District along the French Broad River. Public records showed a divorce, a criminal history, but no military service—nothing suggesting PTSD. His rap sheet included petty theft, domestic violence, drunken disorderly conduct, and several other brushes with the law.

A delightful human being, all in all.

On IDART—the same site I'd used for Frank Mallory—I found him again: *Rex Jamey Norris, a.k.a. Rudy Norris.* He'd served time for defacing an African-American church and flagged as dangerous, tied to multiple anti-government fringe groups.

The site linked to the United Survivalist Army webpage—the one Chet had said Rudy designed. In the photograph, Rudy wore the same red FDGB T-shirt with the coiled snake emblem I'd seen on guys at the Smoky Mountain Tavern

Except his shirt spelled it out: *Fall Down Go Boom.*

What the hell?

There was only one solution. It was Saturday. Babette's Feast stayed open until three or four in the morning. Maybe, with Rudy working, I could gain access to his apartment. A risky proposition—but if he was the shooter, the answers would be there.

Sometime around 10:00 p.m., I dozed off, my head falling limp against the back of the sofa. A sudden glare through the window jolted me awake. The crunch of gravel and the swoop of the beams told me it was a car in the circular drive.

The headlights went out.

Footsteps on the porch.

I grabbed the handgun.

The doorknob turned.

The door creaked open.

A large figure filled the doorway.

Raising the gun, I rubbed my eyes.

"Who's there?" I called into the shadows.

No answer.

Had Gigi and the sisterfriends come back early? Or were François and Frank joining forces against me?

The image neither moved nor spoke.

I stood, audibly cocked the gun, and shouted, "You better say something before I blow your fucking head off!"

"Ein—Jesus!"

"Chris?" I gave a tentative answer to the familiar voice.

"It's me."

Dropping my hand, I let out a whoosh. The pistol tumbled onto the sofa, and I moved toward him through the unlit room. Even in the dark, I felt him.

"You shouldn't be here," I said. "You know the danger."

"I wasn't staying away," he said. "Knowing I might never see you again. So, I caught a flight from Charlotte."

Our bodies collided gently in the dark. We folded into each other, entwining and molding together as we always did. The heat from his skin made me shudder.

"I'm glad you're here," I whispered, "but you shouldn't have come."

"Remember our pledge?" he asked. "Together through thick and thin, till death do us part?"

"Those are marriage vows. I thought you wanted to call off the wedding?" I said.

Chris didn't say anything, answering instead with a gentle kiss on my lips. For a moment, we just held each other in the stillness.

I moved to the wall switch, flicked on the overhead lights, and slid the dimmer to low.

"I couldn't let you go through this alone." Chris's dark eyes held a deep sadness.

"I appreciate that, but I don't want you in the line of fire just as things are starting to come to a head."

As we moved to the couch, Chris's eyes zeroed in on the handgun. "I don't like the looks of this, Ein. Why don't we just get the hell out of Dodge?"

"I'm not a runner, you know that. If I ran, I'd never be able to live with myself." I picked up the firearm, slid it onto the end table where it was out of sight, and took a seat on the cushy sofa.

"I'm too close to find who tried to kill us."

I told him about the note, the misspelling of *your* for *you're*, Frank and François, FDGB.

"Last night I went to a local survivalist hangout and had a run-in with Frank."

"Wa-wa-wait, *why* were you at a survivalist hangout?" Chris asked.

"The point is, I saw Frank hanging out there with François. Apparently, they're best buds, and their coalition is planning something called Fall Down Go Boom."

"Is that where you got the scratch?" Chris swiped at the cut on my cheek.

"Doomsday radicals. My new book exposes them. Anybody who opposes them is fair game. But I did meet one or two at the bar. They admired me for taking on Frank only because they don't like him."

"How does Phillips figure into all of this?" Chris held up his phone. "The bike's registered to her."

"I'm not so sure she does. She despises the survivalists, so she says. She was scarred by one of them. Besides, she's an educated woman. She would know how to correctly spell *you're*."

"If we know she's the shooter, why keep digging, chasing more trouble?"

"I've stumbled into something bigger than Phillips, even if she is part of it—which I'm not sure of." I inhaled and rested my feet on the coffee table. "I don't trust her, but I need to check out this Rudy character."

"You mentioned him on the phone. Who is he?"

"The so-called vet who asked about his PTSD at the book signing."

"Oh, yeah. He shot out the door to track down the woman…uh…the man in black."

"He's not who he says. He's a compulsive liar, impersonating other people: a soldier, bar owner…who knows what else? Maybe even a blonde on a motorcycle shooting at us."

"I'm sorry." He sidled up close to me, sadness lingering in his eyes. "When you needed me, I bolted."

I slung my arm around him and squeezed. "It's the other way around. I'm the one who should apologize. I put everything else before you and the wedding."

"What matters most is we're a team." He made a lopsided grin, his head gently falling onto my shoulder.

"You must be wiped. Why don't you go to bed?"

He raised himself up, yawned, and stretched his arms. "You're right. I'm pooped. You coming, too?"

"I'll be up for a while, seeing if I can dig up anything else on this Rudy guy."

It was another half-truth.

I was about to take my biggest risk yet.

Breaking into Rudy Norris's apartment.

He would have every right to shoot me.

I didn't know if I could pull it off—but I was determined to try.

Chapter Thirty-Eight

fter Chris fell asleep, I closed the computer and pushed away from the desk. I left him a note and headed to the River Arts District. The Internet confirmed Chet's claim: Rudy managed—but didn't own—Mountaintop Getaways. François had told me *he* owned the rental company. That meant Rudy and François had to know each other—unless, once again, I was being lied to. Frank claimed he knew Rudy, and I'd seen Frank and François hanging out at the bar.

Regular Three Musketeers, these *Gawker* guys.

Situated on the lower south slope of downtown Asheville, the River Arts District had once been a graveyard of brick and stone—abandoned buildings that had seen better days. More recently, it had reinvented itself as a scrappy arts community buzzing with character. To get there, I zipped down Coxe Avenue through the South Slope, past Twin Leaf Brewery, hung a right on Hilliard, then a left on Clingman Avenue.

With my handgun riding shotgun, I passed former factories, warehouses, and a train depot converted into studios for working artists. The historic 1930s buildings housed painters, glassblowers, metalworkers, and potters. At this hour, the showrooms and galleries were dark, the streets deserted, with virtually no foot traffic.

Renovations along the French Broad River sat shoulder-to-shoulder with a trucking and grading company, a stone quarry, and a railway yard. A smattering of run-down houses, rusted *Asheville Citizen-Times* boxes, and dilapidated apartments dotted the mountainside surrounding the area. Rudy's place was one of several lofts located in an old hillside warehouse, three levels high.

I pulled underneath a streetlight in front of his address and killed the engine. Stepping out, I took a quick survey of the neighborhood. Insects hummed in the bushes. Elevated train tracks stretched beyond the apartment complex. Vagabond kudzu seemed to outpopulate the people, lacing the buildings, snaking telephone poles, and smothering clumps of trees—morphing its prey into eerie images of dinosaurs, monsters, and cartoon characters.

The ground vibrated as I climbed the stairs. A train horn blared, trundling along the tracks. A musty smell wafted from the corners of the stairwell. A dog barked inside one of the units. The base of a stereo thudded from another. On the top floor, I found the door bearing Rudy's apartment number.

I pressed my ear to the hollow-core, heard nothing but the fading of the rumbling train.

I knocked.

Waited.

Knocked again.

I tried the handle.

Locked. Of course.

I would have to resort to more intrusive tactics.

Unless….

Surely nobody still leaves a key under the mat.

I rolled back the doormat. *Nobody but Rudy, that is.*

I plucked up the key, inserted it in the lock, and turned. The door creaked open, my heart thudding in sync with the *clack-clack* of the train hurtling over the tracks. Inside the doorway, a beam of moonlight shot across the loft's hardwood floors.

What're you doing? Close the door, you idiot.

I might not be cut out for breaking and entering.

I shut the door, and I flipped the light switch. Bare bulbs, each dangling from a single wire, cast a paltry glow across the large open living space. Dimness suited me just fine. I tiptoed through the spill of light, grimacing at the smell—soured beer and stale cigarettes.

A poster of the Snake Shake hung above a worn leather armchair angled toward a tattered sofa. My eyes landed on the Holy Bible on the coffee table beside a stack of *Survival Today* magazines.

The contradiction pulled a nervous grin on my face.

I flipped through back issues of "The Top 5 Guns Everybody Should Own to Survive SHTF," and "Are You Prepared to Survive Armageddon?"—accompanied by a picture of a man posing in a Hazmat suit. Another issue advertised for United Country Realty: *"Strategic Relocation Realty: Confidential Real Estate Services for Preppers. Your Secret is Safe with Us.*

A copy of my book lay next to the stack of magazines, the cover torn off and *BULLSHIT* scrawled across the title page in thick, red Sharpie.

Lovely.

I continued to search and came upon a notebook. Flipping through it, I realized it was a journal. The handwriting—and misspellings—were unmistakably Rudy's. One passage caught my eye.

I dream about the day the apocoalipse hits. When the Chariot Comes and we are redy. The U.S.A. will take back all that was taken from us and rain supreme. We pulled off the Alabama pipeline explosion. One down, two to go. Next stop attacking Fort Bragg then opening a can of whoop ass on Washington, D.C. and blowing the zombies of the government to hell. It will be great joy seeing their blood spilt until Jesus takes us back up into Heaven.

My skin crawled beneath my black leather jacket.

I closed the journal and moved on, passing a cramped galley kitchen into the bedroom. I headed straight for the closet and folded back the warped louvered doors. Several slats were broken, others missing altogether. Police and military uniforms—likely fake or stolen—hung beside an assortment of women's outfits. On a high shelf, blond wigs perched on featureless Styrofoam heads, silently taking stock of me.

Were any of those from Halloween at Babette's? Didn't Rudy say he wasn't there that night?

A gnarl tightened my chest. Intruding in someone's personal space was creepy. I removed my glasses, wiped my hands over my face, and made myself breathe.

Rudy smoked weed, loved to party, and worked in a bar where alcohol and drugs flowed freely. He impersonated police officers, soldiers, and god knows who else. A nurse, maybe?

Something sinister was at work here. Aside from his impersonations, cross-dressing, wacko religion, and membership in a twisted doomsday cell, I hadn't found anything to indicate he was a murderer. No motorcycle gear. No smoking gun.

Empty-handed, except for the threatening note and the mask from the club—evidence that might or might not hold his DNA.

A chilly breeze quivered the sheer curtains from a nearby half-opened window, brushing them against a queen-size bed.

That's when I saw it.

A small arsenal of weapons on the floor at the foot of the bed—knives, handguns, an AK-47, an M-4, boxes of ammo—I'd somehow missed in my hurry to reach the closet.

I shivered.

Peeling my eyes away, my gaze traced the yellow-stained water pipes, snaking along the wall by the bed, crossing the vaulted ceiling, and dropping at the end of the room next to a cluttered desk.

I made a beeline for the shiny new computer towering amid stacked papers, zigzagging like a mountain range. The computer-geek in me preferred digging through Rudy's digital files more than the mess strewn across his desk. Flipping open the screen, I hoped he was as careless with computer access as he was with his apartment.

After trying some of the obvious password options—"survivalist," "U.S.A.," "livefreeordie"—I grew discouraged. On a whim, I rifled through papers and yanked open Rudy's desk drawers. It was probably a lost cause. Who would leave a password just lying around?

Apparently, the same kind of person who would leave a key under his doormat.

Jackpot!

A neon-yellow sticky note, inside the top desk drawer, stared up at me, covered in a long string of letters, number and symbols in Rudy's handwriting. I typed in the password and shook my head. Paranoid enough to stockpile weapons. Yet, careless enough to leave a house key under the mat. Savvy enough to create an air-tight password, but forgetful enough to leave it where anyone could find it.

I'd seen his type in my office many times. Able to intently concentrate on their interests, yet oblivious to the world around them. This combination of hyperfocus and careless mistakes was a hallmark of attention deficit disorder.

I pushed aside my tendency to diagnose strangers and dug into Rudy's computer. At times like this, I was glad I'd chosen computers over target practice as a boy.

His computer used a Virtual Private Network routed through old Swiss military bunker servers deep in the Alps to mask its activity. User data was protected by nearly impenetrable physical barriers, reinforced by Switzerland's famously strict privacy laws.

A dozen alarm bells went off in my head. Sure, there were plenty of legitimate reasons to use such a service, but it was tailor-made for hiding nefarious behavior.

Nefarious behavior like hacking.

Following the digital trail, I identified intrusions to two targets: the Pentagon and Fort Bragg, North Carolina.

Rudy had discovered computer security holes and hacked into the Pentagon's databases, accessing classified information and disrupting both incoming and outgoing transmissions. Piecing together digital tracks and emails, I saw he'd also breached Fort Bragg's computer systems, installing malware designed to take over the network.

Holy shit.

The discovery stole my breath, but I couldn't afford to freeze. I had to figure out the endgame. If I knew what the Real U.S.A. planned to do once they controlled Fort Bragg's computers, maybe I could stop them.

The clomp-clomp of fast-ascending footfalls thundered on the outside stairs. I dashed to the door, clicked it shut, and listened.

The footsteps drew closer. A key slid in the lock—Rudy.

I dove into the closet.

The front door clicked open.

Footsteps smacked against the hardwood floor. I reached inside my jacket for my handgun—and realized I'd left it in the car.

My insides shuddered.

I'm a lousy burglar.

Rudy hadn't noticed anything yet. Through cracked wooden slats, I watched him peel off his tank top and jeans. In nothing but Jockey underwear, he paraded to his music system and played "Green-Eyed Lady" by Sugarloaf. It felt like a million years since I'd heard that song.

The music burst through the surround-sound system, echoing through the loft. Rudy admired himself in the wall mirror above the stereo, dancing in lazy circles, crooning as if *he* were the green-eyed lady.

I kept him in sight through the broken slats as he flexed his muscles. There had to be a way out. I scanned the nearly black space for something— anything—I could use as a weapon. All I saw were vague shapes of hanging clothes.

Watching him preen, I felt second-hand embarrassment, oddly sorry to witness such a private moment. He pranced toward the closet. I shrank into a squat in a far corner, shirt hems draping my head. He flung the folded doors open and tugged the string snapping on the light bulb above my head. I felt certain I'd been exposed, but he wasn't looking my way.

He grabbed a red, full-length sequined gown and a blonde wig from one of the headstands. He backhanded a piece of lint from the dress, raised the outfit above his head, and slithered into it, adjusting the wig and sliding into a pair of red heels.

When he sauntered back into the living area, I edged toward the closet door, hands trembling, and squinted through the broken slats. What had I gotten myself into? This survivalist nutcase had an arsenal at his feet. If he discovered me, I was finished.

Dancing and posing in front of the dark-spotted mirror, he mimed the lyrics, palms up, lips pursed, hips swaying beneath the red gown. With his free hand, he lit a joint, drawing in with a swift sucking sound.

At that moment, my cell phone rang.

Loudly.

Shit—I swore it was on vibrate.

I wrestled it from my jacket.

Chris.

He must have woken up and panicked when he realized I was gone. Frantically, I flipped the ringer to silent and shoved the phone into my pocket.

Too late.

"What the fuck?" Rudy's body jerked toward the closet, the joint dangling from his lips.

He blew a thick smoke cloud that drifted in my direction, his eyes following it. I shrank back to avoid the light, though it was pointless. He knew exactly where the sound had come from.

I was royally fucked.

Terror clutched my throat as he charged the closet, flung open the doors, and snarled through a haze of cannabis smoke, "It's you! What the fuck are you doing in my closet?"

His growl was as menacing as the lazy green eye glued to me. He inched closer, blew smoke in my face, then flicked the joint to the floor, crushing it underfoot. He stabbed a forefinger at me, his face flushed red, and he barked, "First work, now my house. I'm gonna knock some of that pretty off you once and for all!"

He spun and raced toward the weapon cache on his desk.

That was my opening. I took it.

I flailed a path through uniforms, gowns, and jeans, wire hangers tangling in a nest on the floor, and sprinted for the door. Behind me, Rudy tripped over the sequined gown, crashing spread-eagled onto the floor. He yanked it over his head and lunged for a weapon.

My heart beating wildly, I scrambled down the stairs two and three at a time. On the second level, I fumbled for my car keys. They slipped from my grip and plunked—two floors below—into a clump of bushes.

Crap!

Feet clomped on the steps behind me—but no gunshots. Small mercy.

When I hit ground level, my eyes backtracked upward. Rudy, now in a sweatshirt and sweatpants, glowered from the railing above before charging after me—again.

The sound of pounding feet down the steps.

I glanced at my car, then up and down the street.

Nowhere to go.

Paralyzed, I wiped sweat from my brow, tore off my leather jacket, and slung it into the bushes.

I was doomed.

Just run, dammit.

Anywhere.

Just run like hell!

Chapter Thirty-Nine

My eyes fell on the narrow crest of earth running alongside the apartment building. I clambered up the slope and onto the train tracks. Glancing back, I saw Rudy in hot pursuit. He waved a weapon in the air—a handgun, maybe, or a knife.

Running for my life, I jerked my phone from my jeans.

But who could I call?

Several bullets whizzed past my hip. Tiny, brilliant sparks flashed as a spray of rounds ricocheted off a metal rail in front of me.

I had to act fast.

Wiggins?

Breathing hard, I speed-dialed the officer.

No answer.

Who else can I call?

There *was* one other person—but I'd be taking a huge risk. It might put me in even worse danger.

Rudy was gaining on me. Desperation grabbed hold. I hedged my bets, putting my money on Rudy as the killer. Considering the gun pointed at me at that very moment, it was a reasonable assumption. The only choice was to take a leap of faith.

I punched speed-dial again.

When Phillips answered, her rage didn't let me get a word in edgewise. "What the fuck are you doing calling me this time of night?"

"Listen to me," I said.

"No, you listen to me. You threatened me at the restaurant with 'Bring it on.' Are you fucking kidding me?"

"I'm in trouble."

"You sound like some jerk in a B-grade detective movie! You can't blame me anymore for people thinking you're nuts. You're doing a damn good job of it on your own!"

"Listen to me. I need your help." I pleaded between gasps, my feet pounding the tracks.

"Please!"

"Hell no! And what's with the heavy breathing? This is lunacy! You need help, alright—a different kind of help."

She kept berating me.

My lungs burned.

I could barely draw air. I slowed to a jog.

Gasping, I finally managed to get the words out. "Shut up for a second and listen to me."

"No, you listen to me for a change. You're the worst son of a—"

I hung up.

Ahead, a trestle carried the tracks across the French Broad River. If I could make it to the other side before another train came, maybe I'd lose Rudy. I pushed harder, sprinting as fast as my legs would carry me.

It wasn't fast enough.

Rudy was right behind me.

The fast crunch of his feet closed the gap.

Sweat-soaked hair flopped into my face, sticking to my eyes and mouth. A strange thought flashed in that moment of near-certain death: *I should've listened to Gigi and gotten a haircut.*

I spat hair from my lips and slapped it from my eyes.

I made it onto the century-old railroad trestle. Yellow concrete abutments, submerged in the river below, lifted the expansion bridge high into the air. Iron girder overhangs loomed above. The tracks stretched a good quarter-mile before reaching land on the far side. I ran, bouncing and stumbling over the ties.

I glanced back. Rudy had made it onto the trestle.

Fear slowed me down. Anger made him fast.

He was gaining.

Below us, rushing river water crashed over rock beds and boulders.

My lungs screamed.

Midway across the trestle, more bullets zipped past me, pinging off the metal overhangs, throwing me off balance.

I tripped and slammed hard onto the railroad ties, the impact knocking the breath out of my body.

My ribs!

I rolled off the timber and the steel rail onto a narrow strip of gravel—perilously close to plunging into the icy French Broad.

I lifted my head and snagged my phone to dial 9-1-1.

It slipped from my slick fingers, plunging with a loud splat into the water below.

I hauled myself up and kept going, hobbling now.

A far-off whistle announced an oncoming train.

Fuck!

My heart jackhammered my ribs.

There was no way I could reach the far side before the train hit the trestle.

Nowhere to go.

No time to stop.

No choice but to keep moving.

Maybe I could still make it.

The warning horn sounded far away, but I knew the rumbling locomotive would need nearly a mile to stop.

I had no more than sixty seconds to do something—anything.

Danger barreled toward me from both directions: the train ahead, Rudy behind.

So, this is what it's like to see death coming.

My eyes searched the river below, wind whipping my back. I was at least ninety feet above the water. If I didn't splatter on the rocks, the impact of the water alone would kill me.

The fast-approaching horn blared again—and I felt the sudden grip of my arm from behind.

Rudy!

He squared himself, his lazy green eye holding me with malice. He aimed his right hand, the gun glinting in the moonlight.

"You zombie motherfucker!" he screamed above the roar of the barreling train.

Breathing hard, I jerked free and fisted his hand down, fear strangling my voice.

"I know about your plans."

I grabbed his wrist, wrestling for his weapon.

"You stuck your nose where it don't belong too many times," he snarled.

The gun went off, a shot fired into the air.

The gun shop owner's voice reverberated—*Use your fucking fists.*

I shrieked and fisted Rudy square in the face. He staggered back, startled, the gun flying from his grip, skidding across the tracks.

Blood drizzled from his nose.

The thundering locomotive's headlight cast both of us in its glare. Rudy rose, lunging an arm around my neck in a headlock.

He bent me forward and began punching my face.

Again. And again.

Summoning every ounce of strength, I snapped my head back and broke free. Numb from the blows, his vermilion-smeared knuckles told me I was bleeding. He drew back and drove his fist into my stomach.

I moaned in pain, the sound echoing over the water. With everything I had, I buried my fist into his jaw. He fell backward, skidding on the tracks. Raging, he shoved himself upright, planted his fist into my gut, forcing a deep groan from my insides. An uppercut to my chin threw me sideways, staggering, then collapsing onto the rails.

The end was moments away. Time slowed.

It seemed to take forever.

Blood gushed from my nose, gurgled into my mouth, saturated my shirt.

Shafts of pain lanced through me, and I felt my life force draining. My body was shutting down. If death was inevitable, I prayed Rudy would knock me unconscious before the train mangled and dismembered me.

I struggled to crawl off the ties, but Rudy dragged me back and stood over me. The screaming horn bore down, sucking the breath from my lungs. His lazy green eye hovered above me, triumphant beneath a bushy brow. The barreling train's headlights backlit his twisted smirk.

To finish me off, he raised a jagged stone and thrust it toward my head.

I rolled off the tracks onto the narrow gravel path, ignoring the steel spikes stabbing into my back.

Strength was fading. I dragged myself upright and flattened my back against an iron girder. With hitching breath, I wound my fingers tightly around the metal overhang and clung for life.

My chest heaved.

The engineer blasted the horn again and hit the brakes.

But it was too late.

The train erupted with a horrendous screech of metal.

Sparks flashed from the tracks.

Rudy stood and laughed in triumph, his back to the train, strangely oblivious to its approach. He gave no reaction to the ear-splitting noise—drunk on victory or stoned out of his gourd.

The train roared. Horn screamed.

Rudy's uncomprehending eyes.

A gruesome howl—half glee, half confusion.

With a thunderous boom, the locomotive took him with it, the steel behemoth pancaking his body, smearing him from view.

He was gone.

Stunned and weak-kneed, I kept my back rigid against the iron overhang, gripping the girders behind me. I shut my eyes against the gale force of the Norfolk Southern boxcars blasting inches from my battered body.

The pressure from the wind threatened to pull me onto the tracks.

Perspiration dripped from my forehead, burning beneath closed eyelids. Finger sweat loosened my grip.

My knees buckled, lurching my body forward.

The wind from the spinning train still tried to yank me underneath its wheels before an adrenaline jolt slammed me back against the iron girders.

Eyes shut, I imagined myself already dead.

The train finally ground to a halt far down the line, leaving an eerie silence, broken only by traffic hissing across the I-240 overpass above me, a faint car horn in the background, and the river rushing below.

My nostrils couldn't detect it yet.

But I knew the familiar cloying smell of death would soon fill the air.

City lights speared through the darkness and swung warped shadows around me. The thought of Rudy's bloody remains—his armless and legless torso splattered across the tracks into pink bits of bone and brain strewn about—made me puke.

My consciousness dimmed.

Darkness clouded the edges of my vision.

I slid down the girder, the cold iron girder soothing my back.

Top-heavy with exhaustion, my knees gave out, and I slunk onto the gravel. My head lurched forward, banging the steel rail.

The horrifying moments replayed in my mind—Rudy's right arm raised above me, first the gun and then the stone. His snarl as he aimed at my head.

And then the realization hit, crashing through me like another freight train.

"Oh, my god. No!"

Rudy had grasped the stone in his right hand.

He wasn't left-handed.

My body went limp.

And blackness descended.

Chapter Forty

Sore and bruised, I woke with a cold compress on my head, surrounded by Chris, Phillips, and Wiggins.

"Where am I?" I lifted myself from the pillows, my hands digging not into gravel but…a stiff mattress.

"You're back at the rental house, you stubborn ass!" Chris said, tracing the line of my bare shoulder with a finger. The irritation in his voice didn't go unnoticed. "You almost got mowed down by a locomotive. Are you trying to kill yourself?"

"Oh, hell no!" I put a hand over my eyes and flopped backward. I vaguely remembered the sirens and the paramedics hovering over me. "My head's killing me, and I'm sore all over."

"You're swollen and bruised," Chris said. "Nothing broken. They released you from the ER. You owe Phillips a thank-you for getting you home safely."

"It's a miracle you survived that train," Phillips said.

"Thanks for the ride home," I said with a sigh.

She reached for the coat draped over the bedpost. "Here's your Glock. And your leather jacket." She slid the handgun into the inside pocket and slung the coat over the corner post.

"Thanks. What about my car?" I asked. "I dropped the keys in the bushes outside Rudy's apartment."

"I drove the Toyota home with my extra key," Chris replied. We'll look for the other set when you're feeling better."

"When you called," Phillips said. "I thought your heavy breathing was another attempt at being dramatic." She shrugged. "After I hung up and cooled off, I realized you might be in real trouble and had your call traced. I hope you've finally learned your lesson, Einstein."

"Screw you, Phillips." I shut my eyes and shook my head. "You're the last person I want lecturing me right now."

She tilted her head. "Listen, asshole, I'm tired of babysitting you—spending my valuable time tailing you so you don't get your head blown off."

"*Babysitting?* So that *was* you lurking outside the gate at Clement Farm? I don't need your protection."

"Yes, I see you're doing just fine on your own," she said in a sarcastic tone.

"I know more about this case than you."

She grimaced. "Leave the case to those of us who know what we're doing. You'll save us—and yourself—a helluva lot of pain and hassle." She swiveled her eyes at Wiggins. "We already knew Rudy was our man, didn't we?"

Wiggins nodded. "We were about to close in on him before you showed up. We found the handgun he chased you with lying on the side of the railroad tracks."

Phillips folded her arms. "Case closed."

"I suggest you have the semiautomatic tested before you start celebrating," I said. "Rudy's not your man. Case reopened."

Phillips chuckled. "Yeah, and the Pope's not Catholic."

"You go down your road," I said. "I'll go down mine."

"Rudy was a radical survivalist," she continued. "A cross-dresser with blonde wigs. An arsenal of weapons. We think he killed Bucky over a personal dispute tied to the prepper cell and came after you because of your anti-survivalist platform."

"That certainly would be the obvious conclusion," I said.

Phillips shot Wiggins a smug grin and shook her head.

"Except…" I paused. I hate to break the bad news, but Rudy was right-handed. The shooter on the bike was left-handed. Like you."

Phillips squirmed, her face flushing red, then referenced Wiggins for a reaction.

Wiggins shifted his weight, clearly reluctant to contradict a fellow officer.

"Being left-handed doesn't convict someone of murder."

"Correct," I said. "But being right-handed effectively excludes a suspect who fired at a car full of people with his left hand. Besides, where's Rudy's bike?" I hiked my eyes from Wiggins back to Phillips. "And bike paraphernalia?"

"That's not relevant." Phillips grabbed the end of the bed and leaned against it, as if she needed the support. "He could've borrowed or rented a bike."

She was floundering, and we both knew it. "Or stolen one that just happened to have the same license plate number as yours?" I locked eyes with her, cornering her with a hard glint.

Chris slapped me on the arm. "You said you weren't going to give that away."

"But now it's time," I said.

Phillips sighed, crossed her arms, and pretended to be weary. "Time for what?"

"Time to put the facts on the table." I sat up straighter. "Or, as Gigi would say, 'It's time for truth-telling.'"

Chris jumped in. "I took some snapshots of the shooter's motorcycle as it passed us on I-26 and had them enlarged in Gainesville. The license plate number matches yours."

"You've been investigating *me*?" Phillips rebuked. Instinctively, her hand went to her holster. "For what?"

I was quick to point it out. "What's with the hand action on your gun?"

Wiggins eyed Phillips with suspicion and took a slight sidestep, his gaze fixed on her holster.

"I don't know what's going on here," Phillips said, "but you've got your facts wrong. There's no way the tag on that bike belongs to me."

"No," I said evenly. "You've got *your* facts wrong. "You're trying to pin the murders on a dead man—Rudy Norris—when it was you all along." I addressed Wiggins. "So, Officer, what're you going to do? You've got a suspect standing right beside you."

Wiggins frowned, took another small step back from Phillips. "I don't see any reason to—"

"No reason to arrest Motorcycle Mary?" I said. "Let's review the facts. First, she drives a Harley with a license tag matching Chris's photo of our attacker's bike. That alone is pretty convincing. Don't you think?"

Wiggins didn't flinch.

"Second, she's a cop," I continued, "trained to pull off maneuvers most bikers couldn't—manipulating a bike's controls with one hand while firing with the left. What else?" I tapped my temple, pausing for effect. "Let's see, she's left-handed. Imagine that. Not to mention she's had full access to Mission Hospital. She even said herself the two cases were probably related."

"What about motive?" Wiggins asked, clearly grasping for doubt. "Can I see the photo? Sorry, Sarge."

"Humph," Phillips said. "Nothing to be sorry about."

Chris slipped out his phone, found the image, and handed it over.

Wiggins's eyes widened. "That sure looks like your tag." He passed the phone to Phillips.

She squinted at the image, genuine surprise registering across her face. "That's my number, no question—but anyone can order fake plates online. And yes, it's a Harley, but that's not my bike."

"What do you mean?" I asked, my voice cracking.

"I own a Sportster 1200. This is a badass custom Harley Bagger—twenty-five grand, at least. I couldn't afford it, much less handle it comfortably."

Chris and I exchanged looks. "Then, how do you explain the tag?" Chris asked. We didn't know the slightest thing about motorcycles.

"I don't know, but I promise you I'm no Jolene Van Vugt."

"Who?" I asked.

"Jolene Van Vugt—the top stuntwoman in the country—performs death-defying tricks on motorbikes—wheelies, flips, and burnouts. She travels with Extreme Motor Cross. I'm a big fan, but I couldn't maneuver a bike like that, especially one-handed."

All I had left was sarcasm. "So now you're pinning the murders on poor, innocent Jolene, who doesn't live within spitting distance of Asheville and can't defend herself."

Phillips shot me a dismissive look and handed the phone back to Chris just as it buzzed.

He glanced at the text. "At least there's some good news."

"What's that?" I asked.

"Gigi's texting me from Linville Gorge. She's been trying to reach you—texts, emails, voicemails—wants to know why she hasn't heard back."

"Tell her my phone is at the bottom of the French Broad River." The edge to my voice didn't conceal my irritation. "Is something wrong?"

"No, actually the opposite." Chris smiled. "They're having a blast exploring the caverns."

"Don't tell her about my latest brush with death on the railroad tracks."

"I won't." He eyed his phone again. "She says François is on his way down to personally show them around."

"What?" Alarm shot through me, bolting me upright, groaning. "I told her not to—why would François do that?"

"Guess he's a pretty stand-up guy," Chris offered.

Wiggins turned his head toward Phillips. "Isn't that the French guy we questioned?"

Phillips nodded. "Yeah. When we started looking into Rudy Norris, François popped up. They were associates, but the more we dug, the more the evidence pointed to Rudy, so we focused on him."

"That makes sense," I said. "So did I. But François owns Mountaintop Getaways. Rudy worked for him. And Frank and François hang out together." I swallowed. "If François is involved, then Gigi and her sisterfrends are in danger."

The room went dead quiet.

All four of us looked at each other. We knew squat about François.

"Holy crap!" Phillips blurted.

"We've got to get down there," Wiggins snapped.

"I'll run a computer search while you drive," Phillips said.

Wiggins shot a panicked look at me. "Do you know where they're staying?"

"The Linville Inn."

"I'll text Gigi to stay put," Chris said, his fingers already flying across the keypad.

"That county's out of our jurisdiction," Wiggins said, "but we'll alert local law enforcement." He turned to Chris. "You can ride along—just stay out of the way."

"No problem," Chris replied absently.

Phillips and Wiggins tore out of the bedroom. Chris tossed me his phone, tagging behind them.

I was marooned—and hated it.

In pajamas and bare feet, I hobbled onto the floor to follow them, clutching the stabbing pain in my side. I was in no shape to help, but staying put felt worse.

I lumbered into the living room and peered out the window at the house on the ridge. Several men were loading furniture into a moving van.

A shadowy figure appeared in an upstairs window, parting a gauzy curtain, watching the activity below.

I rubbed my sore shoulders and braced against the pain in my chest. The noise of Phillips, Wiggins, and Chris scuttling out the door faded away.

My gaze stayed on the dark figure in the window.

The medicine ball. The hatchet. The attacks. If—and how—they fit together.

It was clear that François was tied to the United Survivalist Army. I even wondered if he was the hooded man with the accent at the tavern. I thought of all the times I passed his sprawling house, glimpsed a shadowy figure peering down from the upstairs window, then vanish.

I wondered if someone inside that room was a lookout for the survivalists—watching me all along.

I slipped gingerly into a pair of sweatpants and my leather jacket.

It was time to find out what was going on in that upper room.

Chapter Forty-One

A moving van was backed up in the Moreau driveway, four black plastic trash bags stacked at the curb. The lettering on the side of the van read: *Two Preppers and a Truck,* Chet Clement's moving company. Blinking against the unwelcome sunlight, I shaded my eyes with my hand, thought I recognized one of the movers.

A stout, suspendered man with a quick limp, like Chet's, eased into the side door of the house. But I wasn't about to embarrass myself with my bad habit of mistaking folks.

"Where are they headed?" I called out to a husky, bald man rolling a desk up the ramp into the truck.

"Somewhere out in the boonies," he said. I'm not allowed to say. "You'll have to ask Amélie."

"Who?"

"The lady of the house."

"Is she here?"

"Upstairs." He gestured his chin toward the second floor.

I continued up the winding driveway to the open side door the movers were using to load furniture onto the truck. Out of the corner of my eye, something inside the open garage gave me pause—a Harley with the Harley Bagger insignia. The same model Phillips had identified from Chris's photograph. No license plate.

Huh.

I stuck my head inside the open door. "Anybody home?"

No answer.

Scanning the backside of the house, my eyes landed on a steel basement door. A young man carrying a floor lamp brushed past me through the doorjamb.

"Excuse me," I said. "Do you know where I can find Amélie?"

"Somewhere inside." He pointed and continued toward the truck.

"Hello?" My voice echoed in the stripped-down room as I slid through the side door. The den was nearly empty—just a few boxes and a lone floor lamp. The sparse look of the open space reflected François: elusive and inscrutable.

I edged past the staircase into a small dining room. A table and two chairs were the only furniture remaining. On the table sat a Tiffany-style lamp. Beside it, a framed photo showed a blond woman performing a backflip on a Harley. A gold motorcycle-shaped trophy in the shape of a motorcycle gleamed beneath lamplight.

I lifted the trophy, leaving a clean circle in the dust. The inscription read: *First Place, Backflip Competition—Amélie Moreau, April 1, 2016.*

Freshly dried blood clung to the trophy's base.

Footsteps creaked on the stairs. I set the trophy back, aligning it precisely with the dust ring.

A perky young woman in bib overalls bounced into the room, carrying a box, her swishing red ponytail smacking her face.

"Are you Amélie?" I asked.

"No way," she said cheerfully. "I'm helping Mrs. Moreau pack."

"Would you tell her a neighbor would like a word with her?"

She eyed me like I was trouble. "Our bad if the moving van disturbed you."

"Not at all. I just have a question."

"She's napping," the redhead said. The lie landed flat. "Could you come back in an hour?"

"Sure. If you'd let her know Ein Pope stopped by, I'd appreciate it."

She studied my face. "Looks like you've been in some kind of trouble."

"Oh, this?" I touched my bruises, suddenly remembering the black eye and swollen cheekbones. "Wrong argument. Wrong person."

A twist in her chin made it clear she was trying to figure me out. As I turned to leave, she grabbed a stack of photographs from a shelf and began wrapping them.

"May I?" I asked, reaching for one.

"No." She plucked it back with a protective hand, gave me a suspicious head-to-toe scan, and squatted over the cardboard box.

"Sorry, I didn't mean to be pushy."

She tilted her head, then hesitated. "I guess it's okay—but don't let Mrs. Moreau know."

"Deal."

She handed it to me and said, "That's her, back when she toured with the Motocross Circus. One of the first women ever to perform professionally. They called her the female 'Eve Knievel'."

The photo showed a stunning young woman with long, golden hair performing a back stand on a motorcycle.

"Remarkable," I said, thinking of Phillips's comment about how nearly impossible it would be to ride one-handed at highway speed while firing a gun.

You'd have to be a daredevil to do that.

The redhead's voice fell. "Too bad what happened ruined everything."

"What happened?"

"The accident." She pulled off her hair band and twisted her red ponytail into a bun, pinning it on top of her head. "Sorry—my hair's driving me crazy."

"What accident?" I asked.

She froze mid-wad of a newspaper and gazed up with skeptical eyes. When I didn't say anything, she stammered, "You're a neighbor...I just assumed...I shouldn't be talking out of turn."

"I didn't mean to pry," I said gently, "just concerned."

She smiled. "That's kind of you. After the fire, I started assisting Mrs. Moreau. They're fed up with city life—moving deeper into the hills. More privacy."

"Fire?"

She placed a final wrapped frame into the box and stood. "The explosion." She looked sideways at me, then checked over her shoulder to make sure no one was listening. "At Madison Square Garden." She lowered her voice. "Mrs. Moreau was the star performer in the Motocross Circus—the only woman in an all-male club. You didn't know that?"

"No, I didn't."

"Something went wrong during the motorcycle backflip." She craned her neck to check the stairs. "The bike exploded midair just as she was coming out of the flip. Broke a few bones and charred her face pretty bad."

I bristled, held my ribs. "I'm so sorry."

"They didn't think she'd live. My name's Nancy," she said, extending her hand. "The woman is tough as nails, but now a recluse."

I met her reach. "Name's Ein Pope. I rent next door."

"I probably shouldn't be telling you this," she said. "If you talk to her, please play dumb."

"Scout's honor." I raised three fingers.

A shrill cry rang out from upstairs.

"*Est-ce que c'est tu, François?*" Then a desperate howl. "*François?*"

"She heard you. I'd better check on her," Nancy said.

I could tell by the way Nancy fidgeted she was nervous. "Of course. Please tell her I'll call on her later. And thank you."

Nancy hurried up the steps.

On my way out, a framed picture on a bookshelf caught my eye. From a distance, it looked like a drawing of curving lines. Up close, it was unmistakable—a handshake. I lifted the frame for closer inspection. The thumb of one hand was a viper, its fangs biting into the hand of the other, blood dripping over the sides. The same image I'd seen on the internet, on the survivalist's T-shirts, and in Rudy's apartment.

The snake shake.

I fumbled through the books on the shelves, not yet packed. I removed a volume titled *La Fin du Monde* and pawed through the pages. Like Nancy, I made periodic scans over my shoulder. I examined the spine of another book, *When Paris Went Dark,* and one called *Radical Relocation: Finding a*

Safe Landing Place (English Translation) by Arnaud Montague.

Toward the end of the shelf, one title caught my eye. *Si Vis Pacem, Para Bellum.* I recognized the Latin phrase meaning *If You Want Peace, Prepare for War.*

I flipped the book over and saw it was written in French, not Latin. Using my rusty French, I translate the back cover blurb.

Before the end comes, you must realize that raiders and marauders will be out there, willing to kill you and take everything you've worked for, everything you stockpiled to keep your family alive. How far are you willing to go to ensure your family's safety? If you are willing to take it as far as it needs to go, then read this book.

I shivered.

From upstairs, a scream pierced through the half-empty house. I cocked my head and slid the Montague book back in place. Another agonizing wail rode on a gust of wind that swept down the stairs through the open side door, this time carrying my name.

"Dr. Einstein Pope!"

My pulse quickened.

I couldn't tell if it was a wail of fear or rage. But the shrillness jerked my eyes toward the staircase.

I'd found several damning clues in this house, and I wasn't about to stop now.

What was behind that steel basement door?

* * *

I snuck outside and circled to the back of the house. Craning my head and seeing no one, I opened the door and stepped into a vast room, housing ceiling-to-floor electronic equipment. I locked the door behind me.

What the hell?

A massive flat screen on the wall near the door displayed a live view of the entryway outside the basement. I prayed it was only a feed—and that I hadn't been recorded walking in. The same wall housed four clocks marked

Mountain, Pacific, Central, and Eastern time zones.

I strolled across the green carpet, carefully running my hand over the beige, suede-like fabric panels—soundproofing, I guessed.

My eyes surveyed the large room, landing on a tier of curved computer terminals, rows of screens, fax machines, laptops, and printers hooked up to six huge CLEO flat-screen monitors—two in front and two each on the right and left walls.

My heart kicked hard, excitement and alarm colliding. The tomblike silence pressed against my ears. Anyone could stumble on me at any second. I kept my eyes posted on the surveillance screen at the outside entry.

I approached a terminal and hunched over the keyboard. It was a long shot to hope I'd luck out twice, but I had to try. Five frustrating minutes later, it was clear the system was locked down like Fort Knox—no password, no clues, nothing.

Not wanting to linger and risk getting caught, I turned to leave.

What I saw nearly toppled me over.

A floor-to-ceiling whiteboard spanned the entire wall beside the door. Every inch was covered—papers and newspaper clippings taped alongside handwritten notes in dry-erase marker. Three maps shared space with blueprints of the Alabama pipeline, the one that supplied gas to a large portion of the eastern seaboard.

I'd been so mesmerized by the high-tech setup, I'd missed the low-tech gold mine right in front of my face. I double checked the lock again and flicked my eyes to the video feed. Secure. The monitor showed nothing but trees swaying in the wind.

Then I went to work.

A mural on one section of the room was drawn like a family tree. At the top, *THE REAL U.S.A.,* carved in thick black letters on a scrap of oak that read…. *When the Shit Hits the Fan, Prepare to Survive—or Die.* Below sprawled a multitude of logos and tribes: *Proud Boys. The Watchtower. Prepper Nation. DeathWatch. Mortifagos. The Gawkers.*

A photograph of Senator Clarence Plemmons, plastered over a dartboard, hung below. Someone had drawn devil horns on his head and a Hitler mustache across his lips. Next to the dartboard was a crude sketch—Wayne Herman grinning, going to town doggy-style on a crying Clarence Plemmons. And beside that, an image of Ronald Thompson, the Raleigh mass shooter, posed Christ-like, an angel's crown painted above his head.

On the far left of the whiteboard, neatly printed, were the words: *Fort Bragg Team.* Underneath was a grainy, black-and-white photo of Eldred Nunn. Three more photos hung in a horizontal line beneath his, as if to show Eldred was the team leader.

I recognized the scruffy-bearded man in the first photo from YouTube and the prepper rally at the Smoky Mountain Tavern. The label under confirmed it: *Oren Ralls.* The other two faces were strangers: David Atwood—shaggy-haired, pockmarked—and Rick Towers, sporting a mustache and mullet.

A nervous chuckle slipped out when I realized the first three letters of their last names spelled RAT.

An email printout taped under their pictures read, *Background checks on Oren Ralls, David Atwood, and Rick Towers complete. Cleared for takeoff.*

Next to the photos was a sheet of paper with monogrammed letterhead *A.M.* Goosebumps rose on my arms as I read the note in perfect cursive.

To everything there is a season, and a time to every purpose under the heaven: a time to kill, and a time to heal; a time to break down, and a time to build up.

I moved on to a row of newspaper clippings, carefully trimmed and taped in place. One from *The Charlotte Observer* described the Raleigh anti-gun rally where fifty-eight people were killed and nearly four hundred injured. The gunman's name—Ronald Thompson—was underlined in red with a scribbled note:

See you in Heaven, Ron.

Another clipping showed Republican senators whose family members had perished in the Raleigh shooting. The article reported the tragedy reignited debate over gun laws. Someone had slashed the senators' faces with thick red Xs.

The third clipping almost stopped my heart from beating.

It was from the Arts section of *The Mountain Xpress*—an announcement for my recent reading at Malaprop's. A red bullseye had been drawn over my face in felt-tip marker, with one word printed beside it in all caps: NEUTRALIZE.

Breathing deeply until the room stopped spinning, I steadied and moved on to the three blown-up maps taking up the right half of the board. The first—smaller map—was Beaucatcher Tunnel and its surrounding streets. Sketches on the map showed the location for a stage and lighting equipment. FDGB was written across the tunnel's archway.

Fall Down Go Boom. I shuddered.

The other two maps were larger. And far more ominous.

Fort Bragg.

The Pentagon.

On the Fort Bragg map, someone had circled various points around the military campus and written *security checkpoint* next to each circle. Arrows leading to each checkpoint tracked paths of entry.

Swallowing hard, I remembered what I'd found on Rudy's computer—evidence of a cyberattack designed to take over Fort Bragg's computer systems. At the time, I was unsure of the endgame.

Now it stared me square in the face.

A breach of electronic security measures in order to penetrate the physical perimeter of the largest military installation in the world. With shaking hands, I faced the Pentagon map. Fear gripped me of the possibilities the doomsayers might have in store for this target.

I thought of January 6, 2021—a date that will live in infamy. I was witnessing a replica of the attack on the Capitol. My stomach tightened as possibilities unspooled—each worse than the last—to attack, disrupt, vandalize, riot, loot, assault, bomb, and kill the zombies running the American government and their followers.

If this mob pulls this off, the destruction will be bigger and more deadly than the attack on the Capitol.

Muffled voices outside the door interrupted my snooping.

I stiffened.

The security feed showed movers milling around near the basement entry, smoking cigarettes and shooting the breeze.

I'd been down here too long.

Once they had finished their break, I crept back upstairs and slipped back into the house through the side door.

Just inside the door, a foyer led to a large open kitchen off the dining room. Dishes, pots, pans, and flatware waited on the counters to be packed and shipped to their new home. My eyes fell on a set of double doors, just beyond the kitchen, leading maybe to a walk-in pantry.

A silver padlock secured the door—but the key had been left in the lock. Curiosity crushed whatever manners or concerns I had left about being rude or intrusive. I was well beyond that point. Seeing no one around, I turned the key, slid the lock off its hinge, and pulled the doors open.

Ceiling-to-floor shelves held an enormous cache of supplies. The weapons alone were staggering. AR-15s, AR-10s, a Colt M4 Carbine, and several AK-47 assault rifles were stored—alongside handguns, explosives, and boxes of ammunition.

To my right were piles of Army fatigues, night-vision goggles, radios, and walkie-talkies. Stacks of gold bullion bars jammed inside the remaining shelves. Running my fingers across the shiny gold bars made my breath stagger. I remembered a line I'd read in *Survivalist Today*:

After SHTF, paper money and credit cards will be chicken feed. Only gold bullion will have currency value.

On the left shelves: Hunting knives. A police officer uniform. Blue nurse scrubs. Two blonde wigs. Several latex masks. And under the bottom shelf—a black plastic bag with an oblong shape protruding from it.

I glanced over my shoulder. No one.

I bent down, reached inside the bag, and slid out a license plate. To my eye, it looked like a real North Carolina tag. The red letters and numbers shot a pulse-pounding shiver through me.

MOTOR-M-6279.

Chapter Forty-Two

I carefully put the incriminating license plate back into its bag, tucked it under the shelf, and replaced the lock on its hinge. For a split-second, I considered making my presence known—but something in me said not yet.

Nightfall lengthened dark shadows across the empty floors. Movement echoed from upstairs, and a voice sang along with Miley Cyrus to "Flowers."

My eyes traveled back to the photograph of Amélie Moreau's mid-backflip. I stepped closer, lifted the frame. There she was, frozen in glory from her Motocross Circus days, staring straight at me. I tried to imagine someone so beautiful committing such a brutal act—firing at a car full of people. But the image that rose wasn't Amélie. It was Mama. I'd bet my life on it.

Hard thumping on the upper floor sounded like someone dancing to the music. I edged back to the staircase. "Nancy? Mrs. Moreau?"

Feeling like the prowler I was, I placed a foot on the first step and hesitated—considering whether to go up or get out and call the police. I crept slowly up the steps, the music growing louder and more frenetic.

"Hello? It's Ein Pope from next door."

"I can buy myself flowers, write my name in the sand," the voice crooned along between gasps of breath.

At the top of the stairs, my beating heart kept time with the music.

"Talk to myself for hours, say things you don't understand."

I paused next to the wooden banister, searched around me. Below, the young man I'd seen earlier grunted, heaving a large box through the side door. The hallway ahead was dark. Music blasted from a room at the far end—the same room where, day in and day out, that shadowy figure had watched me come and go.

"I can take myself dancing, and I can hold my own hand."

I tiptoed over a maroon-and-blue Asian carpet runner stretching the length of the hallway. Through a crack in the half-open door, I peeked inside. The room was empty—except for a single figure.

"Yeah, I can love me better than you can."

The sight nearly took my breath away.

A perfectly toned body, muscles straining through black tights, spun on a bare right foot. Yellow hair fanned wildly in circles around her head like a golden halo. Her arms flung outward in flawless form as she belted every lyric to the song.

"Can love me better, I can love me better, baby."

Noticing something, I stooped, narrowing my eyes into slits. As she spun, the left side of her face showcased a classic beauty—high cheekbones, perfectly sculpted nose, and plush lips. Her right side came into view.

A monster.

A raw creviced cheekbone. No ear. A hollowed eye socket drawn into a snarl for a lip.

I clamped a hand over my mouth to keep from gasping. Despite knowing I could be discovered any second, I was too stunned to move.

When I glimpsed the left side of her face, the room seemed to swell with joy—music ricocheting off the walls, her body flying free, the abandon of her spinning form. But when the right side circled around, the room shrunk with fury—a survivor's rage, the kind that said she'd been snared in a trap, turned into a scrapper and would never allow it again.

I'd learned long ago that beauty and brutality are two sides of the same coin. My training taught me when push comes to shove, the scrapper always wins.

My heart ached for her because I was a scrapper, too.

Watching the contradiction spun a far-off memory.

At age nine, Daddy let me pick out my first puppy from a litter of six. I picked the runt of the litter. His littermates growled at him, nosed him from their mama's nipples as though he was an outsider. I wanted to name him Pistol. Daddy told me I couldn't have him.

"The runt is nature's way of weeding out the weak," he said.

But I was drawn to Pistol. He needed somebody, and I guess I did, too. So, I insisted on him, and the dog breeder took my side.

"Some runts turn out to be submissive when they're bullied by their siblings and can't get their share of mother's milk," the breeder said, "but others learn to protect themselves and become scrappers. Even though they might not look like it, they can kick some major ass."

Only then did Daddy let me take Pistol home.

The ruined lip on the right side of Amélie Moreau's face looked nothing like the Angelina Jolie lips that I'd distinctly remembered from the rider who fired at us on I-26. On the surface, it couldn't have been her.

A smile so perfect must have been painted on. Hmm.

Everything else fit: Amélie's motorcycle skills, the cache in the downstairs closet, the communication hub behind the steel door, the spare key to my rental house—even the swap of *your* for *you're* pointed to a flawed translation from French to English.

Somebody in this house was the shooter.

A hand suddenly clamped down hard on my shoulder.

"What do you think you're doing?"

I spun around to find Nancy, shoving stray red hairs behind her ears, her hands trembling. "Are you some kind of pervert?"

"Heavens no," I said, straightening from the squat. "You told me Mrs. Moreau was sleeping, but I heard the music. I was waiting for her to finish her workout."

She sized up my swollen face and black eye again. "Listen, Mister, I saw you snooping in the downstairs closet. I don't know what you're up to or what kind of trouble you're mixed up in, but you're scaring me. You can't just barge in here—you're gonna get me fired."

The music cut off. Heavy breathing and a sigh of relief drifted from the room.

Footsteps grew closer.

Slinging a towel over her shoulder, Amélie stepped into the hallway, saw me, and screamed, *"Mon Dieu!"* She threw up her hands, slung the towel over her disfigurement.

"What is this?" She turned on Nancy, venom in her voice.

"I—I'm sorry, Mrs. Moreau." Nancy quavered. "This is Dr. Pope."

"You idiot!" Amélie snarled. "I told you I did not want to be disturbed—especially by this man." The towel against the disfigured side of her face, she turned on Nancy. "What do I pay you for?"

I extended my hand. "I've been trying to reach you before you moved. I'm sorry for the intrusion. This isn't Nancy's fault. I was overly persistent."

Shock pinched the good side of Amélie's face. She ignored my hand. The towel loosened enough to show her right cheek, drooping into a half lip and toothy snarl. Her glare traveled the length of my body, leaving little question of what she thought of me. She spoke in a heavy French accent. "I know who you are. You are not a neighbor. You rent from me. I heard your unwelcome voice in my house earlier."

"If I could just have a minute—"

"I have nothing to say to you. Leave my house."

"I want to apologize."

"For what?"

"For intruding—and for the loud music interfering with your art—"

"What bullshit," she sneered. "François tells everyone I am an artist. *Les gens...*" she stammered. "The people assume I hide away with my paintings. He tells the lie because he does not have to explain *this*." She jabbed a free finger at her face. "I am no artist. I can barely draw—what you call—stick figures."

I faltered. "I'm sorry for alarming you the night I was locked out of the rental house—"

"I have no idea what you are talking about."

"Then why did François...?" I trailed off.

"It is not your loud music that disturbs me, Dr. Einstein. It is your loud mouth."

I stiffened. "Beg pardon?"

The fury in her tone was palpable. "I have seen the title of your book on Amazon, *Take Our Guns, Not Our Lives,* and read the garbage you have written about preppers, most of it outright lies, anything to make a buck."

"I'm afraid you have the wrong impression—"

She skidded over my reply, rage simmering just below the surface, and launched into a diatribe. "The Russians, the Chinese, they have broken into the Pentagon's security system, stolen CIA secrets. In Washington and surrounding areas, the entire electrical grid failed once already. Global warming has created violent weather and killed citizens across this country.

Those are facts, Dr. Einstein, not my *impression.* We merely prepare for these threats, yet you warn the masses we are dangerous fanatics. You are a psychologist. People listen, they believe you. And they do nothing. They sit on their haunches, look at their navels, go to their inner "resilient zone," as you call it, and think *that* will save them from SHTF. Sir, you will have the blood of millions on your hands. Now, please leave my home."

"The blood of millions?" My lips formed an incredulous half smile. "Ma'am, that's so extreme."

"I'll show you out," Nancy said.

"Wait." I raised a palm. "I'll go—but first I want to talk with Mrs. Moreau about a few things."

Nancy blurted, "He went inside the downstairs closet."

I shrugged. "She's right. I snooped. Now that the cat's out of the bag, I'd like to talk with you about the basement and closet's contents. From the looks of it, you're planning to start a caliphate in your new location."

Amélie drew in a sharp breath. "How dare you!" Her hand morphed into a fist. That basement is off-limits—even to me—and that closet is locked. François will go mad when he finds you broke in."

"The key was in the lock," I said.

"What's this?" she asked.

Nancy's eyes volleyed between Amélie and me. "Mr. Moreau opened the closet before he left, took something out, and must've forgotten to lock it."

Amélie exploded. "Idiot! How many times must I tell him?"

Shifting her feet, Nancy said, "I should've checked. I'll put the key away."

"You will do nothing of the kind!" Amélie barked. "Stay here!" Storming downstairs, she yelled over her shoulder, "I will go."

"What's in there?" Nancy whispered, dumbly scanning my face. Fear competed for tears in her pleading eyes. "What's a caliphate?"

"None of your god-damned business!" Amélie shouted from the bottom of the stairs. Then, suddenly calm, as if she'd flipped a switch, she called back, "Nancy, be a dear. Pour Dr. Einstein and me a glass of wine."

Nancy shot me a baffled glance.

Amélie was up to something.

I was certain about that.

I was also certain I could use her sudden hospitality to my advantage.

A glass—or two—of wine was the perfect opportunity I needed to pry the truth out of her.

Chapter Forty-Three

I stood in the dining room while Nancy headed to the kitchen for wine. Mrs. Moreau sat on the opposite side of the table, keeping her head turned to the right so I could see only her left profile.

"I am sorry for the mess, Dr. Einstein," she said, swiping a finger across the table's dusty surface and nodding at the bits of receipts, paper, and bits of litter scattered over the floor.

"No worries, Mrs. Moreau. Dust and litter are the side effects of moving, like shedding old skin."

"How poetic," she said. "Come sit, please." She scooted a chair back and patted the seat. "You may call me Amélie."

Her sudden warmth made me suspicious. I wondered what she was up to but played along, forcing myself to focus on her beauty without lingering on her tragic disfigurement. Pity would only make me vulnerable to whatever was yet to occur between us.

Sliding into the chair, I did a double-take at the trophy standing nearby. The caked blood had been wiped clean from its base.

Nancy placed two wine glasses and a bottle in front of us. "Thank you," I said.

"French Chardonnay," Amélie said. "I hope this is…okay? My mother's favorite—and all that is yet unpacked."

I glimpsed the label. "*Oui*. Bougogne La Monatine—my favorite," I said lightheartedly, observing her with a skeptical eye.

"Ah," she smiled, "*C'est bon*. You have very good taste."

Nancy poured the wine and set the bottle down. "Will there be anything else? If not—and if it's okay—it's time for me to go."

Amélie took a sip of wine, smacked her half lip. "This is fine, Nancy. Enjoy your evening. I will see you in the morning." As the young woman turned to leave, Amélie added, "And Nancy, my apologies for losing my temper. This move has upended my equanimity. I hope you can forgive me, yes?"

"No worries, Mrs. Moreau. Don't give it another thought." Nancy grabbed her jacket and the rest of her belongings. Her eagerness to leave made me wonder what type of employer Amélie was. "See you in the morning, Mrs. Moreau. Goodbye, Dr. Einstein."

I waved. "Pleasure to meet you, Nancy."

On her way out, the young redhead dodged some of the movers hauling furniture from upstairs and squeezed through the side door. As she left, it occurred to me that Amélie might want me alone.

To silence me.

Permanently.

I stayed vigilant.

"Pardon me," Amélie said, standing. "I must make myself presentable." She fiddled with the right side of her face, keeping only the left side visible. "I will return shortly." She headed upstairs.

In her absence, I scanned the room and noticed an open box in the corner I hadn't seen before. I crossed over and peered inside—guessing that Nancy had left the box half-packed when she caught me observing Amélie dancing.

I sifted through the old black-and-white photographs: a younger François and Amélie arm-in-arm standing beneath the Eiffel Tower. A faded image of a young ballerina mid-performance. I pawed through old, yellowed letters and faded pictures, but one photograph in living color jumped out at me.

Mama.

And Gigi.

Why was this among the Moreaus' belongings? And who was the woman in the middle?

I plucked the picture from the box, flipped it over, and read the note scrawled on the back.

Here you go, François. It's the only closeup of Ein's mama I could dig up. When

I was back in Whitecross, I rifled through Mama's picture album. My mama and Ein's mama was friends back in the day. The lady in the middle is my mama, on the right is Gigi Pope, and on the left is Ein's mama—Ada Lea Pope. I showed it to Red. He says it's easy as shit to blow up Ada Lea's picture and custom make a latex mask from it. Let me know if it don't work and I can steal a better one next time I'm home when Mama ain't looking. Hope when Amélie puts it on, it scares the living hell out of that sona bitch. Eldred.

A hot scar seared through me, knifing deep into my stomach. I tightened my eyelids to stop the moisture from swelling behind them. That explained Mama's face on the motorcycle. In the woods.

Ain't it so, boy, ain't it so.

The heavy tread of footsteps on the stairs straightened me. I quick-stepped back to the table, pushed my glasses back up my nose.

"My mother used to say presentation is the mark of a true woman," Amélie said as she approached the table. She slid both palms down her denim jeans, tugging the oversized black leather jacket tight. The hard clomp of combat boots, reaching all the way up her shins, seemed to ground her with confidence.

Seating herself across from me, she continued. "My mother was elegant. Radiant—a ballerina in Paris—worked undercover during the war." Tilting her head to one side, she fingered the silver cross at her throat. "I always wanted to be just like her…an impossible task. I was always, how you say, black sheep."

She turned toward me, offering a full-frontal view of her face—beautifully sculpted on the left. A half-mask concealed the charred right side, an inserted glass eye filled the vacant socket, and blond hair swept over the missing ear. She dabbed the left corner of her naturally plump lip with a white linen napkin from her lap, careful not to disturb her recently applied gash of Rita Hayworth red.

The stuntwoman lifted a cigarette from a pack of Winstons, tapped it on the table before lighting it with the lighter in her left hand, and exhaled a cloud of smoke. "They will not have these where I am going," she declared.

"Cigarettes?"

"Store-bought ones. We will roll our own." She shrugged. "*Très triste.* After SHTF, there will be no lighters. Only matches—and few of those."

"And where's that?" I asked.

"How you say, uh…'in the boonies?'" She took another long drag on the cigarette. "I must apologize, Dr. Einstein. You and I do not see things the same way, but there is no excuse for the manner in which I spoke to you." She raised the wine glass to her lips with a trembling hand. "It is the stress of living with a man determined to keep me hidden."

Her sudden turnabout in transparency, along with her nervous apology, was probably another attempt to cover her diatribe upstairs and plead innocence to what I'd already discovered.

"Your husband?"

She nodded. "François has kept me prisoner because of my disfigurement. He will not be seen in public with me and insists on telling—how you say…*tout le monde*…um…the whole world—that I am an artist who prefers isolation to do my work. Now, he will move me farther into the hills. More isolation."

What looked like real tears welled in her eyes. "I do not want to take advantage of your counseling skills, but…I have no one to confide in. You see, François…." She faltered, dabbed her tears with the napkin from her lap.

"Take your time." I heard my psychologist voice emerge, feeling myself snapping into the familiar role, but refusing to be manipulated, I held empathy at bay.

"François is a dangerous man. He has committed heinous crimes. They are now catching up to him. He is moving us to a place where we cannot be found."

My heart thumped wildly in anticipation of what she was about to say. But she could be playing me. Calm spread across my psychologist game face. "What kind of crimes?"

"Bear with me," she replied, her shaky hand lifting the glass to her lips. She took a few gulps of wine and set the glass clicking against the table.

My cell phone rang. I arched my brows at her. "Do you mind?"

"Please."

It was Chris calling on Gigi's cell phone.

"Ein, we're here and just found out that François escorted the ladies through the caves."

I groaned.

"You know how Jackie is. She started flirting with him, saying she loved his accent, and off they went together. He came back alone, saying she got lost in the caves. There's been no sign of her since."

A catch lodged in my throat, my mouth going dry. I pushed back from the table, crossed the open room, and lowered my voice. "I just learned François took something from his stockpile here—probably a sidearm. His wife claims he's dangerous. Keep your eye on him. What about Gigi? Is she okay?"

"Yeah, the rest of the sisterfriends are fine."

"You okay?" I asked.

"Don't worry about me. I'm more worried about Jackie. The rescue squad is searching the caverns. They say they've only got a few more hours before the temperature drops. I'll keep you posted."

"Okay. I've got the phone on me." I hung up, slipped it into my pocket, and returned to the table.

"Is everything okay?" Amélie asked.

My hand waved away concern with an upbeat tone. "Oh, yeah. Every-thing's fine." I dropped back into the seat to finish playing Amélie's little game.

Boots echoing on the hardwood floor. The bald-headed mover poked his head around the corner, "Mrs. Moreau, it's getting late. We're calling it a day. We'll finish up tomorrow."

"Thank you, Ralph." Amélie flashed a thumbs-up and turned back to me.

The alcohol lubricated the conversation, heightening the false intimacy. She lifted the framed photograph from the table and gave it a wistful gaze. "I had so much freedom then. Oh, how I loved flying through the air on my bike." A troubled expression replaced her fading smile. "Now, I have no liberty. One day, I wake up and realize the awful bargain I have struck with

CHAPTER FORTY-THREE

François."

"You mean the sacrifice of your freedom?" I asked.

"*Oui*. Precisely." Her posture stiffened.

"Why are you telling me this, Amélie?"

"I want to be free of his diabolical ways—free to live a normal life." She tapped ashes onto the floor. "If François finds out I told you, he will kill us both. I have tried to leave, but he threatened to kill me if I did."

I nodded toward the closet. "What about that stash?"

"François's. The wigs, masks, nurse uniforms, weapons—all of it—his. Everything. He forces me to guard them." Her shoulders sagged. "I am stuck in purgatory."

I must have reacted, because she raised her hand. "Do not misunderstand. I believe in preparing. Albert Einstein—the man you were obviously named after—said that if the bees disappear, we have only four years left on earth. Scientists say their numbers are dropping at an alarming rate every year."

She pressed the napkin to her lip. "Preparation is essential, yes. But I do not want to be a guard *or* a prisoner. I want my life back. I am tired of carrying François's burdens, his atrocities, and deceit."

Amélie flung her hands into the air. "*Mon Dieu*, if you knew what he has done—what he plans to do."

My heart splintered.

Gigi.

"What he plans to do?" I asked. "Did you know that he's escorting my grandma and her friends through the caverns at Linville Gorge?"

Amélie clicked her tongue. "He told me only that he had to stop someone from something. He did not say who, or what. But mark my words—the only reason François would drive that far is to…how you say…do in your friends. He knows the caves. He will make it look like an accident."

Alarm in my belly, I stared at her and asked, "What are you saying?"

"By now, they are probably all dead." She poured herself another glass. "More wine, Dr. Einstein?"

"No, thank you." I rubbed my temples.

In a matter-of-fact tone, she added, "My husband wants you dead, too."

I bristled. "What?"

"He has been after you since the day you drove into Asheville."

"You're saying it was François who fired at us on the interstate?"

"Eldred told him that the famous Dr. Einstein Pope's grandmother wanted to rent our house for a wedding. François leapt at the chance. The powermonger he is enjoys—watching, toying, waiting. The difference with you is he was waiting for the right moment to neutralize you."

Why was she telling me this? To make François the target, maybe, and take the heat off her?

"In your absence," she continued, "he entered your rental house and blasted the stereo. When that failed, he—how you say—lost his shit. I watched from my window as he stuffed your exhaust pipe with mud and leaves, hoping carbon monoxide would finish you. When it did not, he attacked your car with his fists and pretended concern for your safety."

"All he did was draw attention to himself."

"A desperate man is not rational. He is afraid of you—afraid you will uncover his plans. This is why he invented the story about his visa being delayed." Her mouth twisted. "Nonsense. He was simply…simply how you say, gaslighting you for sport. He even forced me to tell you he was dead."

"You mean he was there when I called?"

"Beside me. He gestured for me to lie. Just as he lied to the police about the loud music. And to you about his green card." She leveled her eyes at me and her face half-grimaced. "He does not have a green card. He is here illegally. I have dual citizenship. France and the United States."

"And his relationship to Rudy?"

"Ah, Rudy. His puppet. François told the poor boy to wear the mask on Halloween. Said it was a fitting night to neutralize your meddling ass so you can't ruin his plans."

I wasn't sure I trusted Amélie's story, but it seemed to add up. "What about the ax cut that Frank Mallory put in the doorframe?"

She threw her head back and laughed. "Frank's a carpenter. François made him fix it."

"And the motorcycle in the garage?"

"My husbands. I have not been on one since the accident. I cannot bear it."

"He rides, too?"

"Of course." She tilted her head. "More of a daredevil than I ever was. We met performing with Motocross Circus. His act was much more treacherous than mine."

She brushed a lock of golden hair from her good side. "I live with his foolishness, how you Americans say, twenty-four-seven." Suddenly, she looked around. "Where is Nancy? I need an ashtray." Looking over her shoulder, she called out, "Nancy…Nancy, where are you?"

"You told her she could leave." I reminded her.

A shiver surged through me. Something about her—maybe the alcohol—was off.

"Yes. Of course I did." She continued smoking, the cigarette ash lengthening.

My phone buzzed again. I peeked down.

A text message from Phillips.

Still no Jackie. Now the rest of the women are missing.

I texted back, *You think Chris herded them to safety?*

No sign of him, either.

François?

Gone.

My stomach did a free fall.

I glanced at Amélie. Her besotted eyes, thick and weighted, kept falling shut. Dangling embers from the cigarette landed on her chest, burning a pin-sized hole in her blouse.

I forced a smile through my panic.

"Something wrong?" Alcohol slurred her speech through half-lips.

Through a parting cloud of smoke, her ragged glass eye descended

Her real eye locked onto mine and shot daggers through me.

"You look scared, Dr. Einstein. I am scared, too. We are in the same boat."

Chapter Forty-Four

I fanned away the choking cigarette smoke, eyeballing Amélie with hardened scrutiny as she continued tugging at my heartstrings.

"They were supposed to keep the fuel tank low to prevent an explosion when I did the backflip. Before my jump, they told me everything was a go—but the tank was full. If they had prepared properly, this never would have happened."

Her forefinger stabbed the air near her face, spittle gathering at the corners of her mouth. "I noticed it when I settled onto the bike in front of thousands of spectators at Madison Square Garden. The needle was on full. But how could I ever show my face again if I—how you say—chickened out? And look where *that* got me. I cannot show my face anywhere anyway. After that day, I promised myself I would never be caught unprepared again."

My skeptical mind tried to resist the compassion in me. It reminded me the Moreaus could be working together, using my family as leverage. But after hearing her trash François and the story of disfigurement, I fell for it—hook, line, and sinker.

Amélie lithely hoisted herself up from the chair, murmuring to herself as she moved toward the kitchen, swishing her silver necklace. "I must find an ashtray."

"I'll be through here in a second," I said to the drape of golden hair down her back, keeping one eye on her, not forgetting the cache of weapons was accessible from the kitchen.

I texted Phillips. *Any word from Chris and the others?*

An instant reply. *Afraid not. We spoke with the manager of the Linville Inn.*

She heard a struggle in one of the rooms. Assumed it was personal and didn't intervene.

Did you check their rooms?

Yes. All belongings still there. Signs of a struggle in Gigi's and Smiley's room. Blood in Chris's room.

That jolted me. *How much blood?*

Lots. Sorry to tell you, but I've never seen anybody survive that much blood.

Frantic. I punched speed dial.

Phillips answered.

"What are you saying about Chris?" I asked.

"From what we can tell, François kidnapped Chris along with Smiley, your grandmother, and the other women. Ein...there was a lot of blood in Chris's room. Wiggins doesn't think Chris made it."

My heart sank. "Could some of the blood belong to François?" Even as I asked, I knew I was grasping at straws.

"It's possible," she said, "but not likely. The room was trashed. There was a struggle."

"Chris wouldn't go easily. Neither would Gigi or Smiley." My voice rose with the tempo of my heart. "If I hadn't taken Smiley's gun, he could protect them—"

"Don't go there," Phillips cut in. "You couldn't have known. Local law enforcement is on it. But there's something else. François had help. He couldn't have done this alone."

I mumbled. "Frank or Eldred."

"Or Amélie," Phillips warned, breathless now, uncharacteristically nervous. "Listen to me, Ein. She's just as dangerous as François—maybe more. Stay away from her."

"Why? She's pathetic."

"She's a former nurse. She frequents Mission Hospital, targets police and government officials. Our evidence puts her as our number one suspect in the hospital stabbings. Security cameras caught her leaving the garage on a motorcycle minutes after Clarence Plemmons was killed. Rudy Norris was there too—likely her accomplice."

"Okay." My sight was trained on Amélie now even more.

"One more thing. She was having an affair with Vernon Clement. She plotted revenge on me for killing her lover."

"Got it."

"Wait—there's more." Phillips hesitated, exhaled a long sigh. "I could get into a shitload of trouble for telling you this. It's classified. If this gets out, I'm done—"

"What?"

"You're not to mention this to a soul."

"Roger!"

There's an FDGB rally tonight. As many as five thousand doomsdayers—survivalists from around the country are descending on Asheville at midnight near—the Beaucatcher Tunnel."

"Tonight?" My mind zoomed back to the basement map, the stage drawn just outside the tunnel.

"The Asheville Police Department isn't taking any chances after the Raleigh massacre. National Guard. FBI. Marines—all are on full tactical alert, taking unprecedented steps from ground to air. I need to get back asap!"

"Don't leave my family until you know they're okay," I said, my voice rising.

"Dr. Einstein, is everything alright?" A voice traveled from across the room.

"Everything's fine," I said. "Just another minute."

"I've been ordered back, Ein," Phillips said. "I don't have a choice. It's in local hands now."

I pushed back urgent tears. "My family is more important than anything."

"This is critical. The FBI has spotters in elevated positions on rooftops—snipers with pinpoint accuracy. Bomb-sniffing dogs are surveying the grounds as we speak. And Ein? Leave that house—at once. Amélie Moreau is a deranged fanatic with a killer's instinct—especially if you're anti-gun."

"Got it."

We ended the call.

In the kitchen, Amélie was holding a sharp knife, slicing cheese with her left hand. I fought the urge to flinch—again—that she was left-handed.

She caught my eyes on her and smiled. "François uses this knife for gutting fish. It's all I could find. I hope you do not mind."

I focused on the blade, my suspicions shifting. "Mrs. Moreau, how do I know it wasn't you who tried to kill me the night I was on my computer in the car?"

Her body froze, her smiling profile held perfectly still, and she let out a nervous chuckle. "What kind of question is this? You know it was my husband. You spoke with him."

"I understand you're a nurse."

"That is correct."

"Ever work at Mission Hospital?"

"No." She paused the knife midair. "Why do you ask me these questions?"

There was something about the way she maneuvered the gutting knife that left me shaken. Maybe she was as skilled with knives as she was with motorcycles. "Does the name Sergeant Mary Phillips of the Asheville City Police ring a bell?"

"Ah—Motorcycle Mary," she muttered. "Word on the street is she likes being a cop because she gets to kill without paying the price."

"She killed your lover, Vernon Clement."

Amélie let out an audible gasp, then masked it in a razor-sharp voice. "How do you know about my personal life? It was a dalliance. Nothing more."

It didn't escape me that I was interrogating a fanatic with a knife—dangerous territory. But questions were my weapon.

"A dalliance? Or did you plan to kill two birds with one stone—me, and revenge on Phillips? You wore a mask made from my mother's photograph. Eldred supplied it. You attacked us on the interstate and tried to frame Phillips with a counterfeit license plate."

"You have a wild imagination," she scoffed. There is no such license plate."

I stepped to the closet, noting she'd left the key in the lock. I opened a door, rifled inside a black plastic bag, and waved the metal tag. "You mean this license plate? Sergeant Phillips's number?"

She whipped in my direction. The half-mask slid down enough to show her charred, droopy flesh. The toothy snarl and sagging glass eye stalked me as I inched toward the door.

"I have no knowledge of that tag," she snapped. "My husband planted it to frame me."

"Halloween night at Babette's Feast—you spiked my beer with Rohypnol and slammed me with a medicine ball."

Even from where I stood, I could see her hands tremble.

"Preposterous! You are gravely mistaken, Dr. Einstein."

"And you hacked Bucky to death when he threatened to expose the hospital murders. You planted a semiautomatic in his purse—the same one used on us—when we were coming around the mountain.

"Poor Bucky," she mocked, giving off an eerie laugh before catching herself. "Ahem, he was *my husband's* monkey—a miserable little puppet."

"Bucky was *your* monkey. François is *your* monkey. You thought I'd be *your* monkey, too. But you failed."

"What do you mean?"

The memory popped up. François nervously fingered the card I gave him with his right hand before sliding it into his shirt pocket. "François is right-handed. The shooter was left-handed—like you."

Her body made a violent jerk. Snarling, she plunged the knife into the cutting board. Her helpless mood switched to savage and unhinged.

She rushed toward me, screaming and punctuating each word with her fist. "*They* told me everything would be fine. Just like you—telling people to sit back and do nothing. I did nothing. Look where it got me!"

My anger had made me say too much. My belly quaking beneath my shirt, I made a quick stride across the room and stopped by the door. "Thank you for the wine, Mrs. Moreau."

She lunged, yanking my arm, forcing her weapon of horror upon me as she lifted her mask. "Look at me!" I averted my eyes at first, trying to conceal my repulsion. Then, I stared back at the one-eyed creature's half-nose and distorted lip and reached for the doorknob.

She drew a revolver from her leather jacket and pressed it into my back. "I did not want this. I told François to scare you off, but you think you are bulletproof. Now, I have a date with FDGB, and you are coming. Fall Down Go Boom. They do not like you, Dr. Einstein."

The barrel dug into my spine as she shoved me forward.

"Come," she said. "They are eager to meet you."

So that's why she kept me here until midnight.

I wilted, realizing too late—I really was her monkey after all.

Chapter Forty-Five

"Faster!" Amélie shouted, shoving me to my car, poking my ribs with the gun. Surprised by her strength, I didn't try anything. The daredevil had a hunger for danger—and killing—and she likely was waiting for an excuse to add me to her list of trophies.

A chilly November wind kicked up from the north, lifting wisps of her long blonde hair. We slipped onto the cold leather seats, and I started the engine. The dashboard clock glowed11:45.

"Go!" she barked. "FDGB starts at midnight. I don't want to miss a word of his speech."

"Who?" I asked, playing dumb.

With a contemptuous laugh, she threw her head back against the headrest and snarled through her half lip. "Why, Dr. Einstein, your name betrays you. You think you know everything. You'll just have to wait and see. Only those *in the know, know*—and you are not in the know. You are a mere sheep in wolf's clothing—a pussy, I believe you Americans call it."

My body jolted. Johnny Devillers had called me that my entire life. The insult hardened my resolve to escape once we hit the crowd. As I drove down Clampton toward Town Mountain Road, Chris circled in my head like a school of sharks.

"Everything you told me is a fucking lie."

"Not everything. Only the part about François dominating me." She made a contemptuous grunt in the back of her throat. "The opposite is true. I give the orders. He follows."

"What did you tell him to do to my family?"

"Go left," she said, waving the handgun. "I spoke with François when I went upstairs to change. He said they are being well taken care of."

"What does that mean?

"You'll see."

Images flashed through my mind—Chris, Gigi, the others, beaten, brutalized—dead perhaps at the hands of this madwoman. I mopped a trickle of sweat from my brow and drove in silence to the intersection of College Street.

"Another left," she ordered.

The light was green, but an Asheville city cop motioned for me to stop. Hordes of people, crossing the road in front of us, clogged the sidewalks and streets. Bumper-to-bumper license plates from Maryland, Virginia, and Tennessee—even as far as Nevada—slowed to a crawl.

All headed in one direction: Beaucatcher Tunnel.

I rolled down my window, hoping to catch the officer's attention, but Amélie pressed the gun into my side and huffed, "Do you have a death wish?"

I winced.

I calculated I might absorb one shot—two maybe—and still take her down. But she was strong—a scrapper—and I wasn't going to underestimate her. I needed to stay alive long enough to save the others. My timing had to be rational, not emotional.

I raised the window and leaned forward, staring at the scores of people. "What in the name of...?" Hundreds of devotees streamed into the city, carrying fold-up chairs. If I hadn't known better, I'd have thought it a Taylor Swift concert—except for the black-hooded robes and black hoodies, FDGB hats, American and Confederate flags. Preppers cradled guns in one arm, children in the other, placards raised high: *GUNS DON'T KILL PEOPLE, GUN CONTROL DOES!*

A busload of gun-rights supporters blared horns. One passenger shouted, "I don't need a thirty-round magazine to hunt deer—I need it to kill government tyranny!" A pickup with a rifle mounted behind the driver's head inched past, its bumper sticker said: *Don't KILL Open Carry.* Police helicopters whirled low overhead. Cops swarmed the streets.

The officer waved us through.

"*Aller à gauche.*" Amélie jabbed the pistol into my ribs, keeping it below the windshield. "Go left."

I swung left onto College Street. My heart slammed wildly inside my chest at the sheer volume of firearms—Remington 870 shotguns. Assault rifles slung over shoulders and leaning against hips. Handguns waved in the cool night air. I searched the blue uniforms, wondering if Phillips had made it back.

"How can the cops allow all this?" I realized too late I was speaking aloud.

"Open carry is perfectly legal in this state. Surely you must know this. I have a concealed carry permit. Do you, *Dr. Einstein?*" She belittled my name like a taunt.

The irony tightened my grip on the wheel. The concealed gun in my jacket would land me in jail—while the murderous hag pressing a revolver was protected under the law. I couldn't run. I couldn't shoot. I needed her to lead me to my family.

My only choice was to comply and bide my time.

If only I knew her plan.

Beaucatcher Tunnel loomed ahead, its massive stone mouth gaping open. Mobile floodlights bathed a field and stage to the left of the entrance. Searchlights roamed the sky. Black-hooded figures snaked from the field into the streets, blocking traffic, and waving handmade placards:

I Pay Taxes, I Vote, And I Shoot

The Second Protects the First.

Amélie directed me into a parking lot. Tires squealed to a stop. When she circled around to my door, I considered running—until spotting the sea of sweatshirts, emblazoned with FDGB, masked men wearing ICE hats, and camouflage jackets stamped *National Firearm Association* and *United Survivalist Army*.

She ordered me out, prodding me with the gun. Daggers of moonlight jutted across my path as I stumbled past sneers of shadowy faces.

"You'll never get away with this," I said.

Glowering from the other end of her handgun, she nudged me forward.

"I wouldn't doubt me, if I were you, Dr. Einstein."

We reached the bottom of the stairs beside the stage. Organizers and apparent admirers of the stuntwoman smiled and nodded at her. A scowling Oren Ralls briefly appeared in my vision—and then I saw David Atwood, a shaggy, pockmarked man in combat fatigues, one of the RAT leaders from the pictures in the basement.

"Amélie, what's up?" he said.

"Here is the one I told you about, *le principal*," she said proudly, as if she had been on a game hunt.

Atwood nodded. "As soon as the keynote speaker leaves, you take the stage," he said, extending his palm in the direction of the steps. "Eldred said to make an example out of Einstein."

The crowd buzzed with euphoria. A WLOS-TV Eyewitness News van broadcast live below the searchlights. A podium and microphone were positioned centerstage, flanked by an American flag curling lazily in the breeze.

Onlookers in civilian clothes—probably unsuspecting locals, lookiloos, and curiosity seekers—stood on the sidelines. Helmet shields obscured the faces of five thousand former U.S. soldiers, maybe, assembled under a black United Survivalist Army flag. Lined up in military formation, organized by branch, they marched in place, rifles held at port arms.

The militiamen, trained to shoot to kill, had a tactical advantage over the cops. The uniformed police officers and plainclothesmen led leashed K-9s through the crowd, visibly outmatched.

I craned my neck, looking for Phillips.

Nothing.

A hooded figure, shrouded in black, took the stage and worked the assembly. He looked out into the packed audience, waving and reaching down to shake hands with the crowd below. He approached the microphone, both hands in the air. The folds of his black robe dangled like flesh from the arms of Bloody Bones.

So, this was the evil waiting for me.

His voice boomed like hammer blows. "Comrades! When SHTF comes, the zombies who strip you of your guns will stagger the empty streets to steal what you saved. They will descend, locked and loaded, ready to shoot you, plunder your supplies, and steal your life savings. We must protect ourselves now from the unprepared bloodsuckers—thieves of our freedoms. Hail Victory!"

Seated preppers jumped to their feet with thundering applause, returning his zeal with vigorous rally cries: "Prepare to survive!" and "Give us our guns or die!" Placards waved in the breeze. Lights glowed from lifted cell phones.

Wailing sirens echoed from inside the tunnel. Blue lights flashed, and a caravan of black, bulletproof Cadillacs emerged from the opening. A detail of black-suited, quickstepping men encircled someone, ushering him toward the stage.

The black-hooded man spoke into the microphone. "Ladies and gentlemen, please give it up for the president of the National Firearm Association, Wayne Herman."

Deafening screams and cheers rose from the crowd.

The man's knitted brows and clenched jaw made him look angry. The NFA president was decked out in a black suit and red tie. A red baseball cap with *FDGB* in large white letters hung low over his brow. He cleared his throat and pointed his finger, speaking with fiery authority.

"Comrades! The gun control movement is gaining steam. Overreaching congressmen are stripping law-abiding citizens of the power to defend themselves. Our freedom is at stake. It's time for us to take up arms. It's time for the zombies to fall down, go boom!"

Applause and cheers.

"Hardworking people like you who founded this great country have become the victims of political correctness. Politicians are stripping you of your fundamental rights. You shouldn't have to beg for what you are guaranteed under the Constitution."

Amid a volley of reverberating jeers, firearms pumped in the midnight air.

"Gun control regulation is an attack on the freedom and liberties that our founders intended us to have. When you start taking away freedoms and privileges, where does the tyranny end? It's time for a new U.S.A. The United Survivalist Army!"

"Hell yeah!" David Atwood whipped out a Mexican flag and wiped his boots on it, then flung it into the crowd. Rick Towers, third on the RAT command, caught the flag with one hand and used a cigarette lighter to set it on fire. The police rushed to extinguish the flames, pushing back the circling crowd that had gathered around the burning flag.

An undaunted Herman continued. "The United Survivalist Army—the *real* U.S.A.—aims to rid the zombies who would steal your resources. FDGB will cleanse our great country and restore your Second Amendment rights so you can protect yourself instead of hiding in fear. We will clean them out."

As Herman paused and backed away from the microphone, the crowd exploded with chants of "Clean them out! Clean them out!"

He leaned back in and punctuated his speech with closing remarks. "Stand Back! Stay Ready! Stay Loaded!"

The chants swelled. A security team hurried Herman off stage and into the waiting black cars. With sirens blaring, they raced back through the tunnel.

Above chants of "Clean them out," Amélie chose her moment. She shoved me up the steps, herding me onto the stage at gunpoint—straight into the glare of lights and the roar of a bloodthirsty crowd.

Chapter Forty-Six

As we reached the microphone, Amélie gave me one final shove. A military command rippled through the United Survivalist Army formations, as if my mere presence threatened them. In unison, soldiers closed their bolts, set safeties on their rifles in the rearmost position, and assumed port arms.

"Prepare to survive—or die!" Amélie greeted the crowd, then pointed at me. "Do you know this man? He appears on TV and writes propaganda. He wants to take your guns and expose our preparations for SHTF. The enemy's name is Dr. Einstein Pope."

I glanced down at frantic hands, clawing at my ankles, eager to drag me into their savage grasp. I kicked them away, stomped on fingers, while Amélie let out a raucous laugh.

"The wolves are hungry," she growled, jamming the revolver into my chest—a reminder I was seconds from death.

Amid boos and jeers, a man rushed the stage and slammed a placard against my head, knocking my glasses crooked. Before I could recover, he tackled me. We scrambled up, and I landed a stiff uppercut to his chin, toppling him off the stage into the crowd.

I straightened my glasses and swiped a trickle of blood from my forehead, still caged—Amélie's aimed gun trained on me, agitators chanting, "String him up! String him up!"

Why hadn't the cops intervened?

An officer stared blankly, as if hypnotized by the chants. Maybe the police were watching and waiting to not further agitate the mob. Or maybe they were in on it.

On the far side of the stage, two men mounted the stairs, trotting Chris and Gigi ahead of them like circus animals.

Thank god—they're alive!

"Chris!" I cried, "Gigi!" I felt a burst of energy. "Don't worry—I'm here."

Amélie dragged the gun slowly across my heart, where it paused, reminding me I was still her caged monkey.

Chris looked exhausted, the skin around his eyes sagging and purplish, his shirt soaked with blood. A haggard Gigi—battered with disheveled red hair and puffy eyes—looked more pissed than scared.

One man shoved Chris, sending him stumbling at the hooded man's feet. "Delivering the goods, sir, as promised." Suddenly, it hit me. Frank Mallory pressed Chris against the floor with the butt of his gun, grinning up into the hooded man's face.

"You son-of-a-bitch!" I muttered.

White-hot fury tightened my frame, as Amélie jammed the gun deeper into my back.

The black-robed man stood over Gigi and Chris with an AR-15 braced against his shoulder. Having used one as a boy, I knew it could spit forty-five rounds per minute.

"Son, you okay?" Gigi yelled.

"Don't worry about me. Just stay calm," I said.

Frank's sidekick vanished then reappeared, shoving Smiley forward with a firearm. He pushed a weary, unsteady Wilma-May forward. She threw both hands in the air, collapsed on her knees, and howled, "Dear merciful Father!"

The other trembling sisterfriends straggled onstage behind her, gasping, shrieking, and clutching one another. I finally got a good look at Frank's sidekick. The sight of Eldred Nunn made my hands curl into enraged fists.

Why weren't the Asheville cops intervening?

The black-robed man removed his hood.

François.

He snapped his heels together and raised his hands in the two-handed

United Survivalist Army salute, then joined Amélie and me by the micro-phone, lifting her arm. "Thank you for your service, Amélie Moreau—our master strategic planner."

She turned and addressed the assembly. "My mother used to say, 'All birds have two wings, a left and a right. But maybe it's the bird itself that needs killing, not just one of its wings.'"

The crowd roared.

Gigi directed her ire at Eldred. "Speaking of Mama's, Eldred Nunn," she cried. "When yours finds out about this, it's gonna break her heart."

"Shut the old woman up." Amélie nodded to her husband. François drilled the butt of his gun into Gig's back, flattening her to the floor.

I almost lost it but held down my Johnny Devillers rage.

François took the mic. "Comrades, the government is stripping your Second Amendment rights. The United Survivalist Army is headed to Fort Bragg!"

He extended his arm in a wide arc. "What do we do with despicable people, useless eaters destroying the planet?"

"String them up! String them up!" The mob cried.

Chaos exploded. The rowdy assembly devolved into an angry mob.

Still, the survivalist soldiers and the Asheville cops held back.

A rock struck Smiley upside the head, knocking him unconscious. A pickup plowed into the flock of onlookers, and a riot ensued. Asheville cops in full riot gear—toting semiautomatics, clasping shields against their chests—descended on the rioters.

"Disperse," one officer shouted. "Back it up. Everybody!" another ordered.

Commands unheeded.

The crowd hurled rocks and insults at the police. Raised fists were coupled with shrieks of "Prepare to survive—or die!" Cops slammed rioters to the ground, released pepper spray, and clubbed others with batons. Civilian survivalists fought back, hammering cops with their placards.

Gunshots inside the tunnel blew out several ceiling lights. Angry rioters smashed car and storefront windows, spraying Asheville streets with splintered wood and shards of glass. Looters set buildings on fire. Plumes of smoke billowed into the starry sky, leaving sparks and ash floating to the ground.

Then a gun discharged within the crowd, and the survivalist soldiers charged into immediate defense mode. The click of safety releases cut through the night air as trained military fingers hovered over their triggers, assault rifles leveled at the men and women in blue.

A string of commands rose up from the columns of soldiers: "Ready! Aim! Fire!"

"Get down," Amélie ordered. We squatted behind the podium. The pointed gun at my heart never wavered for a second.

Trembling, I broke out in a cold sweat. I wiped my arm across my face, fighting my sliding glasses. I found a small crack in the wooden podium and squinted through the splintered peephole at slivers of action.

Gun-toting civilians joined the survivalist army as they opened fire on the Asheville police. Amid the fusillades of organized fire, officers dropped to the ground for cover. Some cops fled the rapid succession of shots—only to be picked off. Outnumbered and defenseless, the remaining officers huddled behind squad cars.

My body quivered at the realization I was witnessing an attempt to overthrow the government—a full-scale war playing out on Asheville soil. Gigi tried to get to where Smiley lay motionless. I yelled for her and the others to stay down.

Red tracers took out the police snipers stationed atop Beaucatcher Tunnel's stone arch and nearby rooftops. A police helicopter roared overhead, its spotlight slicing the darkness, a loudspeaker ordering a cease-fire. Near the tunnel entrance, a U.S.A. soldier stood, hoisted an RPG to his shoulder, and fired the missile—the helicopter exploding in a fireball.

The violence was so surreal, so horrifying, I wondered if I'd slipped into another Bloody Bones nightmare. I wanted it to be a bad dream, but with a sliver of clarity, I knew it was real to the bone—there was no waking up.

The explosion created a lull.

Convinced they'd won, survivalists' cheers broke the stillness.

Rifles waved high in the air.

François took the microphone, heavy accent booming as he congratulated the soldiers. "Men, this is a good step—but only a first step. We have more work to do. We set out for Fort Bragg now, then on to D.C., where the United States government will meet its Waterloo!"

The crowd burst into deep, full-throated revelry, cat whistles punctuating their cheers.

Below the rejoicing, I heard a faraway rumble.

A chopper in the distance.

The ground beginning to vibrate.

A fleet of rotary-winged aircraft thundering closer.

Overhead, a squadron of black Apache choppers whirled into view, their bulbous noses adorned with mounted sensors. I'd read Simmons Army Airfield at Fort Bragg operated a fleet of two dozen, heavily-armed Apache helicopters.

Now I understood why the outnumbered Asheville cops had hesitated— they were buying time, knowing reinforcements were coming.

Chills sizzled through me at the sheer size and speed of the badass attack choppers—bigger and deadlier than anything the police piloted. The mechanical *whop-whop-whop* grew deafening. As the copters closed in, pulsating vibrations juddered my bones.

Two Apaches swooped low, disgorging platoons of Fort Bragg soldiers who scattered across the field. Hurricane winds from the whipping copter blades cut into the gathering, churning up dust. I shielded my eyes from the glaring searchlights, blazing beacons onto the ground.

Behind them, other choppers hovered higher, firing heavy tracer rounds— fast, furious, unforgiving—red streaks ripping across the night sky. The first missile wiped out an entire survivalist column in a single fireball.

Amélie ground the gun harder into my back.

Another missile obliterated a second formation. A third, then a fourth, followed in rapid succession. Civilians fled in chaos. Beyond the stage, shrouded in a cloud of haze, more choppers hovered midair, unloading soldiers with backpacks in full combat gear.

Rick Towers, one of the three leaders of the RAT Brigade, climbed on the stage with an M4. He flipped the setting to automatic and squeezed the trigger, rattling off several rounds at the government foot soldiers.

A *rat-a-tat-tat* from the tunnel entrance. I ducked and peered around the podium. A Fort Bragg soldier had leveled perfect aim at the broad-shouldered man. A final burst of staccato gunfire riddled Towers' body, sending him slumping backward into a lifeless heap.

In the distance, tear gas hissed through the air. Amid blood-curdling screams, spectators—coughing and gagging—stampeded onto College Street, where the air was clearer.

Gasping, a hooded survivalist clutched her chest and made a mad dash before collapsing. Trampled by the frantic crowd, she clung to her screaming child. A Buncombe County EMS unit surged forward, checking the cloaked bodies lying motionless on the ground.

Automatic weapon fire crackled in a sequence of rapid shots followed by single rounds. Fort Bragg soldiers exchanged gunfire with the United Survivalists Army.

A crouched Amélie glared at me. "You make one wrong move, and I will kill you," she snorted. "Nothing would give me more pleasure!"

Out of nowhere, Oren Ralls appeared behind us. "I got you covered, Amélie," he said, wiping his sweat-matted hair. "Why don't I just kill the traitor and get it over with?"

I cringed at the eagerness in his voice.

"No," she replied, her ragged glass eye fixated on me. "I will do it myself. Don't rob me of the pleasure."

The automatic fire suddenly ceased. I hoped it meant the Fort Bragg soldiers had contained the survivalist army. I peeked again through the podium pinhole into the siege. Onlookers were dispersing. Puffs of smoke drifted low over bloodied, black-clad bodies, strewn across the nearly empty field. The sharp tang of gunpowder burned my nostrils.

The calm was shattered as a SWAT team swarmed the stage from the rear of the stairwell. They poured up the steps in balaclava ski masks, body armor, and ballistic shields amid bursts of crackling gunfire.

The lead officer, wielding an M4, aimed at Oren Ralls and blew a bullet through his jaw. The shaggy-haired man tumbled headfirst off the stage. The officer removed his mask and called out to me. "Ein, it's me, Brother Boy!"

Bobby-Cy?

A second officer spun and aimed at Frank. "Drop your weapon. Now!"

I recognized Phillips's voice right away. Frank smirked at the woman barking orders. Ignoring her command, he hooked Gigi's neck in the crook of his elbow, pressed his gun to her head, and dragged her backward, using her as a human shield.

Phillips raised her M4 and racked off a warning round. As she shoved in a fresh magazine, her eyes roved the stage, searching for anyone else in danger.

I couldn't wait any longer.

The hostage distraction gave me a split second—just enough.

I knocked the pistol from Amélie's grip. It clattered across the stage. I kicked it over the edge and shoved her down hard, slamming her head against the stage. She rose to her knees, her ragged eye locked on me, and I head-butted her square in the face, knocking her out cold.

François sprayed shotgun rounds, wounding a now-unmasked Wiggins in the leg near the front edge of the stage. As Phillips shouldered Wiggins to safety, she pivoted and aimed back at François. He crouched behind the far side of the podium. I pulled the Glock from my inside pocket and shot him in the shoulder.

The shotgun slid from his grip and clambered to the floor. He braced a hand against the podium. I fisted him twice in the chin—right hook, then left—just like Johnny'd taught me. François went down hard, blood spurting from his nose. He staggered up, drew a sidearm, and aimed at me. From my left, Bobby-Cy fired, driving a bullet straight into the back of his head, exploding the top of his skull in a spray of red.

I grabbed the shotgun and yelled at Frank. "Let my grandma go, asshole!"

"Come and get her, Grasshopper!"

An arm hooked my neck from behind, and I felt the cold thrust of a pistol against my jugular. The stench of armpit sweat hit as I craned my head—Eldred Nunn.

I elbowed him in the gut. He doubled over, and I kneed him in the face. When he straightened, Bobby-Cy pumped a bullet into his chest. Eldred dropped like dead weight, a vermillion spray squirting my jacket.

Panic splayed across Frank's face, his gun trembling against Gigi's temple. Her life on the line, I couldn't risk another second. I leveled the shotgun, planted my feet, and sighted. My blood-soaked finger slipped on the trigger. I smeared it down my jeans. Johnny Devillers's face loomed in my mind. With razor-sharp precision, I pulled the trigger, blasting a massive hole through the side of Frank's head. The impact pitched his body backward in a grotesque wobble.

Gigi slipped free from beneath his tattooed arm and crawled on hands and knees to check on Smiley as he came to.

With most of his head gone, Frank's body violently twitched and jerked until it toppled off the stage. His fingers fluttered in the grass below before stiffening.

I sucked in a lungful of air to squelch the uprush of nausea at the thought of killing another soul.

Don't be such a pussy. Daddy's voice raced through my head. *I'm gonna make a man outa you.*

"Hope you're satisfied, Johnny Devillers," I mumbled bitterly, feeling anything but.

Bobby-Cy and Phillips, ramming fresh magazines into their M4 Carbines, hauled Gigi and Smiley upright and to safety. I sprinted over, shouldered Chris, and covered the sisterfriends as they scattered off the stage and out of the line of fire.

Back on stage, I gazed across the near-empty field. A moving van idled, red letters emblazoned on its side: *Two Preppers and a Truck.* Fort Bragg soldiers and police were subduing the fleeing crowd, their jagged shadows bending like large ghosts against the Beaucatcher Tunnel stonework.

A cold shaft of steel buried itself in my belly.

The blade knew exactly where to go.

Halting. Turning. Twisting.

Slicing a passageway in just the right places.

Until it was satisfied, I was finished.

I hadn't given another thought to Amélie until—a memory flashed: *François uses this for gutting fish*—she had suddenly stirred and lifted herself up.

The knife slid slowly free, and a deep burning consumed me.

A formless, guttural sound escaped my lips.

My legs buckled.

My hands found the floor.

A glass eye reflected the blood-dripping knife dangling from her left hand. Her good eye traced the blade's ragged edges.

I dimly felt the vibration of heavy boots limping across the stage and faintly heard a familiar voice calling my name.

Then a cry from behind me: "This one's for killing my boy, Bucky!"

A gun blast.

A scream, then a dull thud.

A knife clattering amid murmured voices.

A flurry of scrambling footsteps.

Sirens wailing in the distance.

On the verge of losing consciousness, my cheek slumped against the cold floor, my glasses sideways on my face.

Funny, the things you think about to take your mind off dying.

A memory of Chet resurfaced like a fading beacon—saying he had a feeling we weren't finished yet. Now, with Amélie gone, our business was finally done.

My vision blurred.

Then, I was gone, too.

Chapter Forty-Seven

"Good morning, sweet pea. How're we doing?" The stout blond nurse laid a hand over my forehead, then straightened the rumpled sheets beneath my chin. "Doll, we've got to stop meeting like this."

When I looked up, recognition hit like a shock. *Dear god—the co-dependent nurse.* I lolled my head around on the pillow and moaned, "I must be in hell."

"Now, now. We're not in hell yet," she said, "but we came pretty close."

I looked around the room, recognized the familiar window, its glass fogged from the cold pressing against indoor warmth. Beyond it, ragged mountain ranges loomed.

"Here we are, together again," she said. "For a while, it was touch and go. They didn't think we were going to make it."

I lifted my right hand, following the IV line from a vein, across the crisp white sheets, to a metal stand. "How long have *we* been here?" I asked.

"Close to a week. That mean French lady tried to give us an appendectomy—just barely missed our vital organs. Thank heavens we're going to be fine. We're coming off some heavy-duty drugs, though."

"We feel like a tractor-trailer made a U-turn inside us." I lifted the sheets, eyed the layer of bandages covering my belly, then I looked up at her. "By the way, I forgot *our* name?"

"Dr. Einstein Pope," she answered.

I blanched. "No, not *my*-our-name." I pointed at her. "*Your*-our-name."

She slapped a palm against her chest. "Oh, you mean *my* own name?"

"Yes, for godsakes," I said, exasperation slipping through.

"Missy Lockhart."

"Missy, have I—not you—had visitors?"

"Good heavens, yes, a gracious plenty. The same three people show up every day. A sad old man with a limp comes and sits by your bed in the mornings. Usually later in the day, a hunky Asian man drops by with an older woman named… she snapped her finger…Gloria, no…Gigi. She cries a lot. "

"That's my grandma."

"Yesterday, Gigi brought a man in a sheriff's uniform. I had to tell him to stop punching you so hard—then he broke down crying. I didn't mean to hurt his feelings."

"You didn't." I smiled. "That was just a love pat from Brother Boy."

One day, a whole flock of weird, cackling women flounced into the room, flapping around your bed. One of them had a mighty strange way of trying to cheer you up. She bent over and kept shaking her booty in your face."

I cracked another faint smile. "That would be Jackie."

"Another one prayed over you, telling the others not to get too close, that they would crowd out the Holy Ghost."

"Wilma-May."

"What about the mopey one?"

"Gladys."

"And the one with the big ole bun on her head kept popping nerve pills?"

"Shirley."

"You've got a mighty impressive posse of women swooning over you. You're quite the celebrity, too. You and that lady cop are on CNN, FOX, *Good Morning America*, *The View*—all over the talk shows."

Missy fluffed several pillows behind me and propped me up to almost sitting. Still dazed, I surveyed the room from my elevated perspective. Flowers lined every surface of the tables and counters. Open-faced cards stood between bundles of lilies of the valley and roses.

"I'll go get lunch." As she turned to leave, the door cracked open. Mary Phillips stood in the gap.

"Back *despite* popular demand," I teased through a warm-hearted smile, grateful that she'd had my back all along. "If it isn't the infamous Sergeant 'Motorcycle Mary' Phillips, live and in the flesh. I hear you're dominating the airwaves."

"Not as much as you," she said, pleased. "But the media *is* beating down my door." She crossed the room at a brisk pace, cradling a newspaper, her gun slapping against her hip. She plastered a kiss on my forehead. "Greetings, asshole. They didn't think you were going to make it. I'm disappointed."

"Up yours, Phillips." I eased myself against the pillows, grimacing.

"You wish." She flipped her hair over her shoulder, checking out the get-well cards and flowers. "You've got a crapload of admirers. They must be bat-shit crazy."

She tossed the newspaper against my sheets. "Good news."

The New York Times. I took note of the dateline—Wednesday, November 11—and read the headline above the fold.

UNITED SURVIVALIST ARMY DEFEATED IN ASHEVILLE RIOT.

I savored the long first sentence. "On the heels of the Raleigh massacre, where nearly sixty citizens perished, a civil war in Asheville, NC, ended in Fort Bragg soldiers defeating the United Survivalist Army."

I glanced at Phillips. "So much for 'Whatever happens in Ashvegas stays in Ashvegas.'"

"There's more," Phillips said. "Your new book jumped to number five on the bestseller list, no doubt propelled by the national publicity."

I sighed and stared at the paper. "What matters more is the country can heal from its temporary insanity." I looked at her. "One thing still bugs me, though. I saw footage of Jim mingling with the United Survivalists Army at a shooting range."

"Like I said on the phone. It was top security. Jim and I were undercover for three months. He infiltrated a bunch at the Buncombe County Shooting Range. He tipped off the Secret Service and FBI about FDGB. That's why APD and the Army were ready."

"No wonder you two acted so strange." I gazed at her with admiration. "All that time I thought you and Jim were preppers, then you came in and saved the day."

She lowered her head, spoke softly, "I've gotta be honest. I feel a little hypocritical taking credit. You cracked the case, not me."

I shrugged. "Look at it this way. If you hadn't made so many mistakes, I wouldn't have corrected them. You led me to the killer." I raised one arm. "All I did was take the opposite rabbit hole you headed down."

"Asshole."

"Since we're truth-telling," I said. "I feel like a hypocrite, too. After preaching against guns, I killed a human being, became like the man I tried so hard to be unlike. Makes me feel less of a man."

"Hey, stop that." She cupped my hands. "I know that feeling. Sometimes we do things we don't want to do. Your father *killed* innocent people. You *saved* them. Big difference. You're nothing like him."

I adjusted my glasses and peered at her sideways. "I went down a few dead-end streets, myself. I accused you when you had my back. For that, I'm sorry."

Her lips slightly parted. "No hard feelings."

"Here we go," Missy sang in a high-pitched voice, bouncing into the room with a tray.

"What is it?" I asked, looking at the plate. "All the food here looks the same."

"Hamburger steak," she said, holding out a steak knife. "Do we need help cutting it up?"

My flattened palm shot out instinctively, despite the tubes. "No, we don't! Get that knife out of our face." I eyed Phillips and said, "I'm gonna need speech therapy when I get out of here."

When I drew my arm back, a flash caught the light. Yellow sparkles glinted from my finger. "It's the Mokume wedding ring Chris and I designed," I gushed. "Missy, how did this get on my finger?"

"That hot Asian man slipped it on while you were in hell. Said he wanted you to have it now, because he didn't think you'd make it to the wedding."

I held it up to the light, admiring the handcrafted layers of molten gold, patterned over a black background.

"What a beautiful design," Phillips said. "Looks like natural wood grain."

"Japanese metalworking—originally to decorate samurai swords."

We locked eyes. "You got a ring and a bestseller," she said, "and I got promoted to lieutenant."

I raised my hand for a high-five, my abdomen burning in protest.

"Prepare to thrive—or die!" I said.

Phillips laughed and slapped my palm. "Prepare to thrive—or die!"

Epilogue

There's an old saying, "The depth of your struggle determines the height of your success." I'm not sure I believe that. Where did the doomsayers' struggles get them? I find a bitter irony in the fact that Vernon, Bucky, Rudy, Eldred, François, and Amélie—all of them priding on being prepared—were the ones who perished.

Maybe they prepared for the wrong things. They feared demons on the outside instead of the demons on the inside—the real source of their terror. Like the little old lady searching for her glasses when they're on her nose the entire time, the preppers looked *through* themselves, instead of *within* themselves, for answers.

With Chris, Gigi, Smiley, and the sisterfriends in tow, I returned to Whitecross to recover for the winter.

Months passed.

November rolled into December. January ushered in a new year. My book didn't make it past number five on the bestseller's list—an inconsequential detail, compared to the importance of healing, mine and that of my loved ones.

Eventually, I stopped replaying the prepper stories in my head. My nightmares faded. Sleepless nights gave way to peaceful rest. My body, too, began to mend.

That spring, friends and family reconvened in Asheville for my wedding to Chris. We wanted to be married in a place like no other—a place rich in history and architecture, preserved from bygone days, surrounded by natural beauty, outdoor adventure, and food worth writing home about.

Gigi insisted I get a proper haircut before the wedding, so I booked an appointment at the Middy on French Broad Street. Jamie clipped my shoulder-length Samson hair into a shorter style—"more hip," according to Jackie.

The winter cold finally loosened its grip, and late May draped the mountains and valleys in blooming rhododendrons, dogwoods, azaleas, and mountain laurel. We were married at Cloud 9 Farm, nestled in the rolling hills outside Asheville.

Chris and I stood beneath a handcrafted mountain laurel arch. My brother, crooked-smiling Bobby-Cy Abbott, was my best man. The sisterfriends formed a circle around us. Gigi beamed as matron of honor. Shirley stood beside her, trying to keep her tilting bun erect, elbowing Jackie from pushing up her "weapons of mass destruction," as Jackie called her girls.

Wilma-May winked and whispered, "What a beautiful day for a wedding."

"Yes, it is," I agreed. "And you look fetching in that apricot gown."

"You look pretty hot yourself with that new haircut." She put her hand over her mouth and spoke softly through it with a mischievous glint. "This is one of them dresses I shoplifted years ago. I've got a whole closet full. When I got sober, I went back and paid for all of them."

"Glad to know some things have a statute of limitations," I said, raising an eyebrow as the contradiction dawned on me. Her dress was identical to the others. If she'd stolen it years ago, how could it match?

I smiled to myself. *I guess some things don't.*

At the tail-end of the ceremony, standing arm-in-arm with Chris, I spotted a hawk perched on a distant limb. It spread its majestic wings and soared overhead, screeching, "Keeaaar, Keeaaar." The wedding guests looked up as the bird swooped low, as if blessing our vows, before shooting back across the Carolina blue sky and over the mountaintops.

"Mama made it to the wedding after all," I murmured. "She said she'd come back and check on me. I knew she would."

Happy tears crowded my eyes—Chris squeezing my hand, Gigi winking, my brother fisting my arm, and Mama soaring overhead.

I dusted off a spot in my heart and placed the memory there, where it

lives on like a bullet lodged in bone.
  Ain't it so, boy? Ain't it so?

Acknowledgments

It is a thrill for me to see the second installment of the Einstein Brad Pope series morph into a book. I have so many people to thank for supporting me over the years. My literary agent, Dean Krystek, managing director at Wordlink Literary Inc., for his enduring support in representing me. For all of the friends who read early versions of the work and offered honest and direct feedback: Debra Dees, Sarah Elizabeth Malinak, Julie Smith, Andrea Karin Nelson, Sheila Sobel, Linda Scott, Elena Hartwell, Wiley Cash, Lee Child, K.J. Howe, Bruce Robert Coffin, Steve Berry, James L'Etoile, Peter James, Linda Sands, R. G. Belsky, Susan Crawford, and Rick Reed. And to my fans who kept asking me when the sequel would be available, here it is. I hope you enjoy it. To Jared Block, who shared some of his personal experiences that wove their way into the novel. And last but not least, to my husband, Jamey McCullers, for your unyielding support and patience as "I heal by day and kill by night."

Finally, I want to thank the editors at Level Best Books, Shawn Simmons, and Deb Well, for your knowledge and creativity that brought the book from a rough stone to a shining gem. Thank you.

About the Author

Bryan E. Robinson is an author, psychotherapist, journalist, and Professor Emeritus at the University of North Carolina at Charlotte. He maintains a private clinical practice and writes murder mysteries. His tagline is, "I heal by day and kill by night." His first novel, *Way DEAD Upon the Suwannee River* (2024) has been adapted as a stage musical comedy under the name of *Limestone Gumption: The Stage Musical. She'll Be KILLING 'Round the Mountain* is the second novel in the series.

In addition to his fiction, Robinson has authored forty nonfiction books, including his latest, *Chained to the Desk in a Hybrid World: A Guide to Work-Life Balance* (2023) and *Daily Writing Resilience: 365 Meditations & Inspirations for Writers* (2018). His books have been translated into fifteen languages, and he has written for over one hundred professional journals and popular magazines.

He has won two awards for writing and has lectured across the United States and throughout the world. His work has been featured on every major television network, and he is a monthly contributor to *Forbes.com*. He resides in the Blue Ridge Mountains with his spouse, three dogs, and occasional bears at night. You can visit his website at www.bryanrobinsonphd.com

AUTHOR WEBSITE:
  bryanrobinsonphd.com

SOCIAL MEDIA HANDLES:
  Email: bryanrobinsonphd@gmail.com
  Website: www.bryanrobinsonphd.com
  Twitter: https://twitter.com/BRTherapist
  Facebook: https://www.facebook.com/RobinsonBryanE
  Amazon: http://www.amazon.com/Bryan-Robinson/e/B00DPT3UJ6

Also by Bryan E. Robinson

Way DEAD Upon the Suwannee River